Praise for

HENNA HOUSE

"Eve is a natural storyteller."

—*Kirkus Reviews*

"I was enchanted by this book. It is a meticulously researched coming-of-age story . . . The prose style is clean, elegant, and descriptive . . . the events flow with vivid detail of everyday family life, multilayered threads, complex relationships, ritual and mysticism . . . *Henna House* pays a special tribute to Jewish history. Highly recommended."

—Historical Novel Society

"A welcome glimpse into this historical moment and little-known culture."

—*Booklist*

"Eve opens a window on a community, little known in the Western world, whose rituals and traditions were maintained for over two thousand years. Her appealing portrait of young men and women moving from an ancient life into modernity will captivate readers who enjoy historical fiction."

—*Library Journal*

"A captivating and evocative novel, at once intensely intimate and sweeping in scope. Nomi Eve is a wonderful writer—compassionate, intelligent, assured—and her deeply felt, richly imagined book will stay with me for a long time."

—Molly Antopol, author of *The UnAmericans*

"This was a book I had to read twice: the first time to rush through quickly to find out what would ultimately happen to the characters, and the second time to slowly savor the descriptions of these marvelous, exotic people and locales. Nomi Eve captivated me."

—Maggie Anton, author of the Rashi's Daughters and Rav Hisda's Daughter series

"Nomi Eve's novel is a heady mix of henna, history, and the power of words written on skin, sand, and paper. An engrossing, surprising, compelling read."

—Indira Ganesan, author of *As Sweet as Honey*

HENNA HOUSE

A NOVEL

❧

NOMI EVE

SCRIBNER

New York   London   Toronto   Sydney   New Delhi

SCRIBNER
An Imprint of Simon & Schuster, Inc.
1230 Avenue of the Americas
New York, NY 10020

First Scribner trade paperback edition August 2015

SCRIBNER and design are registered trademarks of The Gale Group, Inc.,
used under license by Simon & Schuster, Inc., the publisher of this work.

For information about special discounts for bulk purchases,
please contact Simon & Schuster Special Sales at 1-866-506-1949
or business@simonandschuster.com.

The Simon & Schuster Speakers Bureau can bring authors to your live event.
For more information or to book an event, contact the Simon & Schuster Speakers Bureau
at 1-866-248-3049 or visit our website at www.simonspeakers.com.

Interior design by Erich Hobbing

Manufactured in the United States of America

5   7   9   10   8   6

Library of Congress Control Number: 2013497612

ISBN 978-1-4767-4027-0
ISBN 978-1-4767-4028-7 (pbk)
ISBN 978-1-4767-4030-0 (ebook)

For Ahoova,
in whose kitchen I first savored *malawach* and *jachnun*
and other forms of essential nourishment.

My beloved is unto me as a bundle of myrrh,
that lieth betwixt my breasts.
My beloved is unto me as a cluster of henna flowers
in the vineyards of Ein Gedi.

—SONG OF SONGS, 1:13–14

Contents

Prologue

I loved Asaf before I loved Hani. I think of him looking out at me from deep within his cold armor. His eyes beseech me. Rescue me, they say. Melt my prison, breathe on my fate, and release me with the heat of your forgiveness.

Auntie Aminah used to say that there were people who died as they lived, and others who did "quite the opposite." She was referring to the lazy woman who died dancing, or the man with the energy of fire who lay on his deathbed like a snuffed-out ember. According to my aunt, such mismatched deaths left an imbalance for the angels to tinker with in the World to Come. Asaf's death was like that. He was a boy on a thundering horse, a child of the hot northern dunes—yet he died a cold, still death, trapped like a bug in frozen amber. But Hani died as she lived, inscribed with henna. Her killer took a knife and used it to trace her intricate henna tattoos, carving through the skin on the soles of her feet, her shins, her palms, the backs of her hands, her forearms; slicing her into an elaborate, bloody decoration. She was tied up and left that way and must have bled to death. If such barbarity had happened in Qaraah, or in Sana'a or in Aden, we would have assumed that it was the family of one of the brides. When a marriage went wrong, or a first baby was born dead, the henna dyer was often blamed, as if the henna dyer's art were more than art, as if it could really ward off or conjure evil. When I learned of Asaf's and Hani's deaths, I held my hands up to my face. I hadn't worn henna for many years, but the old markings seemed to appear on my skin—my own ghostly lacery. The henna elements on my palms became letters, the letters spelled their names. And there it was. Their stories inscribed on my skin, their smiles and sorrows my own tattoos.

Now I spend my days surrounded by my children and grandchildren.

In their laughter, I discern codes and secrets. Sometimes I decipher what I hear. Sometimes, I am stumped. Life itself has become a puzzle to be translated, a curse or a blessing written in the language of henna.

It was my husband who suggested that I write this story. He said, "This story will submit to you, and to you alone." His words made me wonder: Do stories submit to authors? Or do authors submit to the tales that tangle up their guts? I confessed to him that if I were to write about Hani and Asaf, I would have to write a love story, "For I never stopped loving them," I said shamefacedly to the man who had rescued me from their manifold betrayals.

He wasn't cowed. "Love them," my husband urged, "write them, and write yourself."

I tried to begin, but my story came out in a voice I didn't recognize. I tried again, and I failed again because my chapters were all told from a faulty perspective. Then I failed a third time. I finally realized that I was going about it all wrong. I didn't need characters but ingredients. I didn't need settings or scenes, I needed age-old herbal recipes passed down from mother to daughter, aunt to niece. I didn't need plot or point of view, but symbols so old they were once swirling in the dust of creation. I didn't need pen or paper, I needed stylus and skin. I am a woman of henna so I needed to rely upon the traditions and tools of my craft.

I began yet again, but writing in henna presented its own challenges. You see, the master henna dyers in my family always started elaborate applications in different places. Aunt Rahel always began with the palm of her subject's right hand because of the psalm: "If I forget thee O Jerusalem, then let my right hand forget its cunning." She liked to say that henna was prayer in color, and prayer was henna in words. My cousin Nogema favored the tips of the fingers. My cousin Edna always started by inscribing elaborate elements on the tops of her subjects' feet, because her designs depended most of all on symmetry and balance. And my cousin Hani, whose story I had set out to tell? She never began in the same place. She was the first to admit that her haphazard approach wasn't scientific and sometimes resulted in aesthetic disasters. But more often than not, Hani's designs were the most beautiful of all. When I was well practiced in the henna craft, I preferred to start with the underside of the forearm. My subject would stand before me with her arm raised, her hand on my shoulder. That way I could decorate the bottom of her bicep without smearing the top of the arm.

So you see, we all had our own tricks; the only thing you could say about all of our techniques is that in the end, the first line blended into the last like blood running through veins.

As for my story? Where should I begin? Should I ask my reader to extend an open palm so that I can inscribe my words in the warm gully of a branching life line, and our fates may mingle? Or should I ask her to recline on jasmine-scented pillows and let me begin with the tender soles of the feet, so that my story accompanies her wherever she goes, pressed into the earth, like footprints for posterity? Or should I demand my reader reveal her bosom, so that I may write these words upon her heart?

I have done a great deal of thinking about this matter. About where to begin a story that ends with blood and sacrifice. At last I have come to believe that my story begins on the day the Confiscator came to my father's shop for the first time. This man, the monster of my childhood, the ghost who haunts my dreams, casts the same shadow as all the other predators who have hounded my people since the dawn of time. Different men, they are all descendants of the same ancient darkness.

I was just five years old when the Confiscator came. We lived in Qaraah, a day's ride from the ancient city of Sana'a in the Kingdom of North Yemen. The year was 1923. Yes, this is where my story must begin. Many years have passed since I last sharpened my stylus, but I feel the old elements ready at my fingertips. Palm, soul, heart. If my hand is steady, the last line will blend into the first, and ends will embrace beginnings.

What was it that Aunt Rahel used to say to the girls and women whose limbs she would adorn with intricate and beautiful henna designs that marked the skin and pierced the heart? Whether they were there for a henna of solace or a henna of celebration, she treated them all with the utmost tenderness. She would beg them to relax, whisper soothing secrets in their ears, and comfort them with a blessing, a calming word. And then she would begin to draw . . .

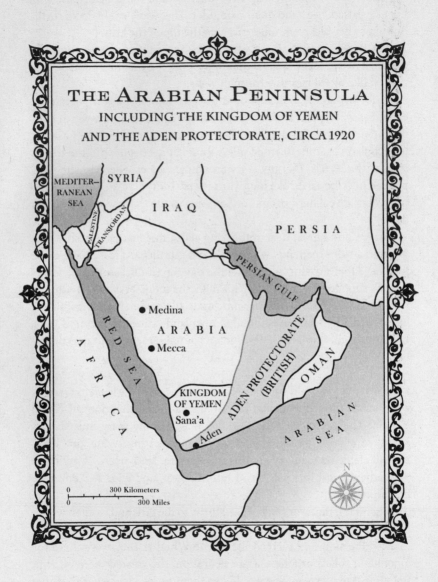

THE ARABIAN PENINSULA
INCLUDING THE KINGDOM OF YEMEN
AND THE ADEN PROTECTORATE, CIRCA 1920

MEDITER–
RANEAN
SEA

SYRIA

IRAQ

PERSIA

PALESTINE

TRANSJORDAN

PERSIAN GULF

● Medina

ARABIA

● Mecca

RED SEA

AFRICA

ADEN PROTECTORATE
(BRITISH)

OMAN

KINGDOM
OF YEMEN

Sana'a

● Aden

ARABIAN
SEA

0   300 Kilometers
0   300 Miles

N

Part One

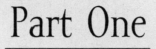

Chapter 1

"What is wrong with the girl's eyes?"

"Nothing, she sees fine." My father cleared his throat and looked down at his work—a single broad piece of leather lay over his bench—the flap to an ordinary market bag.

"But they are too big for her face."

"If you say so, sir."

The Confiscator moved closer, coming in front of my father's bench. I'd ducked behind my father, peeking out from behind his supply shelves. The stranger was tall, thick-shouldered, and had a face so long it seemed to drip down to his belly. He absentmindedly touched the hilt of the *jambia* sheathed on a belt around his waist. The curved ritual scimitar was exquisite—the blade a gleaming threat of forged iron, the hilt a mellow yellow Eritrean ivory, overlain with two jeweled serpents wrapped around the handle, a band of rubies at the thumb point, and an embossed hawk's head on the lip of the hilt, representing both mightiness and honor. He wore an expensive maroon silk djellaba with a black turban, and his beard was carefully tended.

"Eyes like that see either too much of the world or too little of it. And the color—greenish gold? Pretty and ugly at the same time. What is her name?"

My father opened his mouth and then shut it again without speaking.

"What was that? Her name, sir. Surely the imp has a name."

"Adela . . ." Almost a whisper.

"I have no daughters, only sons."

"Sons are a blessing."

"Indeed, they are."

My father coughed, a wet and phlegmy cough. He took out his handkerchief, blew his nose, and studiously avoided the man's gaze.

7

"Your health, sir?"

"My health is fine." My father coughed again.

"Eh . . . fine?"

And again, big grating hacks racked my father's body. The Confiscator's eyes narrowed; he stepped back until he was halfway out of the stall and screwed up his face in distaste—no, he wouldn't catch this plague, not if he could help it. And yet my father's obvious weakness clearly gave the Confiscator pleasure. A smile played on the corner of his mouth. He tipped his head forward to get a better earful of the miserable sound. And still he stared at me—looking at me, seeing me live a different life. For that was his job, to pluck children out by the roots from the soil of their birth and replant them in a different garden.

I stared back at the wealthy stranger. I wasn't afraid of him *yet*. I was really afraid only of my mother. No one's wrath or whims—not even the Confiscator's—could scare me by comparison. Even then, at only five years old, I saw him perfectly for what he was: a thief, an evildoer, and a descendant of Amalake. I wanted to spit at him, but I knew I would be punished for it in this life and in the World to Come.

"But I am not here to discuss your daughter A—del—a's un—for—tu—nate eyes." He drawled on my name and the word *unfortunate*, stretching them out. "No. I am here to order a pair of *bashmag* sandals for my wife. She sent me to your stall because her friends say you make shoes that do not hurt before they are worn in. She must have three pairs. She insists that you, and only you, make the shoes she will wear to her sister's wedding. And clearly I have been put here on earth for the sole purpose of seeing to her pleasure." He waved a beringed hand. His nails were long, manicured. "Here are her foot measurements. I will be back in two weeks to collect them. And"—the Confiscator nodded in the direction of my hiding place behind the shelves—"make sure the girl is here when I come to pick them up. Yes? You understand me? Good, good. It is good that we men understand each other."

My father didn't ask why the Confiscator wanted me to be there, and he didn't ask what would happen to either or both of us if I were elsewhere on the appointed morning. Instead, he asked the Confiscator a few questions about color, texture, and adornment and then recorded the order in his big ledger.

When the stranger left, I came out from behind the supply shelves. My father placed a hand on my head and patted me softly. He didn't say,

"That man is of no importance" because it would have been a lie, and my father was not a liar. Instead he murmured a snippet of scripture, referring to the miracle of sight and the clarity of spiritual vision. Then he picked me up and put me on his workbench and kissed my nose, before giving me scraps to play with as he began to ply the leather—making it supple with the caress of his tools.

I knew that the Confiscator was a bad man. I knew that my father hated and feared him. But it was only later that I understood that he was a bringer of nightmares, a kidnapper. History, religion, and politics had conspired to make him such. What did a little girl know of such subjects? But my father was wise—nothing like his ignorant and innocent daughter—and that is why a tear came to his eye as he tucked an errant lock of hair into my *gargush* when we left the shop that afternoon. He knew what I was to learn in the coming years—that his lungs were weak and his health fragile, and that as a consequence I was in danger of being stolen away from my faith and family.

History, politics, religion. I dip my stylus in the dark mists of time. The Confiscator worked for Imam Yahye. Imam Yahye wrested power from the Turks, and had become ruler of the Kingdom of North Yemen in 1918, the year of my birth. My family and all the Yemenite Jews dreaded the Imam's many decrees. The day the Confiscator first came to my father's stall, I couldn't have told you a lick about politics, but I could have reported how often my father and brothers came home stinking like shit, death, and piss because they had been conscripted to carry dung, cart off sewage, and haul animal carcasses. The Imam's Dung Carriers Decree relegated Jews to the jobs of refuse and carrion collectors. The Donkey Decree forbade the Jews of the North from riding horses. Instead, my father, brothers, and our friends could ride only donkeys, and they couldn't even ride our donkey, Pishtish, like hearty men; instead they were forced to ride sidesaddle, which limited their ability to travel. There was also the House Decree, which forbade us from building our houses as tall as the houses of our Muslim neighbors. And the Walkers Decree, which forbade us from walking on the same side of the street as a Muslim.

But the worst by far of all the Imam's decrees was the one that brought a tear to my father's eye the day the Confiscator paid us a visit: the Orphans Decree. It called for any orphaned Jewish child to be confiscated, converted, and quickly adopted by a Muslim family if a father died. This meant that Jewish children were ripped out of the arms of newly widowed mothers. That's why the Confiscator had lingered in my father's stall—because of my father's cough. The Confiscator had a quota to fill. Perhaps he had heard that the shoemaker was sickly. Perhaps he had had his eye on me for a long time already.

That night my parents fought. My father banged his fist on the breadboard and growled, "You must engage Adela—the bastard came to my stall sniffing around for children to put in his pocket. It is your duty as her mother to find her a husband."

I was the youngest of nine, the only girl, and my mother's last and least-favored child. I was a bitter afterthought—a thorn in the side of my mother's old age. She would have neglected to betroth me at all, leaving my fate to the whims of chance, but my father, who loved me well, intervened. That night, he reminded her that it was her duty to find me a husband in order to protect me from confiscation. The Jews of the Kingdom engaged their children as toddlers and married them off the moment they reached maturity. Once a child was married, he or she couldn't be confiscated. This is how it came to pass that my parents were arguing about my marital status when I hadn't even lost all of my milk teeth.

"If you don't, I will," my father threatened, "and for a man to make inquiries of this sort is unseemly. But I will do what I must if you refuse to do your duty."

"My duty?" My mother arched her back, stuck out her slackened breasts, and made a crude gesture toward her own sex. "If I had refused to do my duty, we wouldn't have a daughter or eight sons for that matter. Mmph. Don't speak to me of duty. Now take your dirty hand off my breadboard. Leave me in peace."

"But Suli, she is already five years old."

I was a spinster by our standards. A girl three doors up was engaged when she was two. The goat-cheese maker's daughter was engaged while still in the womb. I was like Methuselah, older than time and still unattached.

My mother wiped her nose with the back of her hand. "Leave me in peace if you expect dinner." As Father stalked out, she muttered after him, "What a bother, what a ridiculous bother."

The next time the Confiscator came to my father's stall, he didn't mention my eyes, and for most of the exchange he ignored me completely. But even though he didn't glance in my direction, I felt his gaze upon me. Not his "this-lifetime" eyes, as Auntie Aminah called them, but his "next-lifetime" eyes—the hooded eyes of the soul that can see into the heart of a small girl. And that is when I learned to fear him. When he saw right through me, making me feel simultaneously naked and invisible.

I crouched in the back of the shop. I was suddenly so afraid that he would take out his jambia and kill my father with a nick to the jugular or a swift downward blade to the heart, that I was almost sick when he finally said my name, "A-del-a, A-del-a, don't hide, little one. Come out and show your face." I emerged clammy and pale as a ghost. He knelt down so that the folds of his djellaba pooled around his feet. Then he pointed to a beautiful pair of shoes on the shelf, maroon with little embossed florets around the ankles. I had helped my father with the florets. He was teaching me how to press and stamp and glue leather. He didn't mind that I helped him, even though it was unusual for a girl to assist her father in his stall. My mother never cared where I was, as long as I wasn't bothering her. "My Adela works better than any boy," my father would brag, but my brothers would hear and torment me for the compliment—with pinches and slaps, and knuckle punches in places where the bruises wouldn't show.

The Confiscator smiled. "My, aren't they little masterpieces? Maybe when you are older your father will make you a pair like this. Perhaps even for your own wedding? No?"

My father produced one of the pairs of shoes he had made for the Confiscator's wife. The Confiscator reached out, grasped both shoes, and dangled them by the heels. In front of my eyes, the shoes grew tails, ears, and whiskers, turning into rats that the Confiscator could feed to the snakes on his knife.

"Ahh, the shoes are lovely. You are indeed a master of your trade."

"Thank you, sir, thank you for your compliments."

"But I suspect this will only whet my wife's appetite for such luxuries, and I will be forced to visit you again and again, rather than listen to her berate me for denying her her due."

On the way out the Confiscator turned, pointing a beringed finger at my father at the exact moment that my father let out a big phlegmy cough.

"I will be back, Mr. Damari," he croaked, "you can be sure of it. My wife, precious little frog, how can I help but spoil her? You understand how it is with pretty girls. Who are we weak men to resist their wiles?" I buried my face in my father's legs—though at the last minute I pried myself loose and glared at the Confiscator, a fatal mistake which turned me into a pillar of salt, like Lot's wife. "*Sha, sha,*" said my father as he ran his hands through my hair. I was cold but sweaty, my gargush askew. "Sha, sha, little rabbit, all will be well, sha, sha," he murmured.

Despite my father's pleas, my mother had no interest in "doing her duty" and finding me a groom to protect me from the Imam. She knew my father was just blustering when he said that he would take up the task of betrothing me. It wasn't a man's job. He wouldn't have known how to begin. No, my father would just have continued to occasionally bother my mother about it, but she would have continued to ignore him, and me for that matter, as she had done since I was born. But then my father's cough worsened and worsened, and he took to his bed. The Angel of Death hovered over our house. He lay ill for three Sabbaths. At the start of the fourth week of my father's illness, my mother sent me to the market for green onions and turnips for stew. I was making my way home when I saw the Confiscator gesturing to me. He was standing by one of the spice seller's stalls. I almost turned and ran, but his jambia pulled me forward, the jeweled serpents on his scimitar twisting around each other, tugging me closer, closer. I was in their thrall. They were alive, their emerald eyes looking deep into my heart, as the hawk on the hilt opened its beak to murmur into my ears, a wild bird-whisper that came to me in a language I knew but didn't know. The air was heavy with the midday exhalations of the market—cardamom, pepper, saffron, curry, and a curdled whiff of clarified butter from the cheesemaker's stall, an undernote of fly-buzzed slops and fermenting rinds from behind the fruit sellers' stalls. Somewhere a dog was crying, horrible howls as if he were being beaten. The Confiscator bent down to speak with me and smiled genially—clearly this was a man used to speaking with children.

"Your father is ill? Eh? That cough sounded like bad business. You'll tell him I asked after his health. Won't you? Won't you . . . A—del—a?"

I took a step back, and then another. But before I could get away, he reached out and touched my face, to the right of my right eye, and then winked at me. In my heart, I heard him speak without words: *We are one and the same, you and I. We are not strangers, are we? No, of course not* . . . Where his fingers grazed my forehead, I felt a burning pain. He turned on his heels, his djellaba swishing after him.

How did I get home? I don't remember. I burst through the door, my heart crazy with extra beats.

"What is it, Daughter? What happened?"

My gargush had slipped back over my braid. I panted, holding on to the doorpost. My legs would barely hold me up.

Coughing, my father struggled up from his pallet.

"Daughter, what is it? What happened?"

"The Con—fis—ca—tor," I stretched out his name like he had stretched out mine, breaking it. "What?" My mother came in from the back room. "What did you say?" I repeated myself. Her face blanched. She grabbed me by the elbow and made me sit down on her lap. I don't remember ever sitting down on her lap, either before or after that morning. She patted my head, and whispered, "Sha, sha, little girl" into my ear as I sobbed with the aftermath of my terror. But she quickly grew tired of comforting me, tipped me off her lap, snorted, and said, "Stop mewling and see to your chores."

That night I didn't sleep. A hot wind had descended on the mountains. It was an uncommonly warm spring, when the rains were few, and the sun seemed to be coming closer day by day, as if intent on collecting some debt from the dust and sand. That whole season men climbed up to their roofs and slept in the lightest of garments. Women too shrugged off their modesty and joined their men on the roofs, desperate for a cooling breeze. That night, on the roof with my parents, I lay hour after hour staring at the stars—the stars that seemed to rearrange themselves into constellations that frightened and rebuked me. Serpents and hawks and other angry animals were all perched on twinkling knife blades, hanging in the firmament above me precariously, threatening to fall. All night long I heard my father's rasping breath, punctuated by coughs that racked his body. I thought about the Confiscator. I wondered not *if* he would take me but *when*. My fear was a red-hot fire behind my face, stoked all night long by the waves of coughing that made my father groan and wheeze. My fear was justified. My father seemed deathly ill, worse than ever before, and the Confiscator had looked straight into my heart. He even knew my name. *A-del-a* he had said, breaking my name into jagged little pieces.

The night lasted forever. My father coughed. My mother tended him—reserving her pity for the small hours in between midnight and dawn, when she dabbed his burning brow with a wet cloth and murmured comforting words that she would never utter by daylight.

In the morning the heat broke, and the knife that hung above me in the sky sheathed its blade. My father had willed the worst of his sickness away. I don't know how he did this, but by morning prayers his fever had passed. The color returned to his cheeks and the strength to his legs. There was still sallowness to his skin, and he still coughed that horrible cough, but the immediate danger had clearly dissipated. Left behind was a stink—a foul odor of inevitability that made us all anxious and jumpy. In the coming weeks, whenever I went to the market I looked over my shoulder and cocked my ear for the maroon billowing *swish swish* of the Confiscator's djellaba. When I came home, my head was always filled with the ghost of my father's cough, a groaning cautionary lament that scraped the walls of our house even when his lungs were clear. My mother finally began looking for a suitable groom for me. "If only you could marry Binyamin Bashari," she said over and over again—to me, to Auntie Aminah, to my sisters-in-law, to anyone who would listen. She let it be known that if she'd had her choice, she would already have engaged me to Binyamin Bashari, son of our neighbor two doors up. Binyamin's father made blades for jambias. Jews were not permitted to wear jambia, but we were the masters at making them. Working with one's hands was considered beneath the Muslim men in the Kingdom of Yemen, so the work was left to us Jews. Accordingly, the men of our community became jambia makers, metalsmiths, wicker workers, jewelers, potters, tailors, carpenters, tanners, and rope braiders. Mr. Bashari had learned the craft of jambia from his father when he was just a boy. His father had learned it from his father, who had learned it from his father, who had learned it from his father, who had learned it from his father, and so on, back to the generations who came to Yemen in the retinue of Bilquis, whom others called Sheba the Queen.

Binyamin Bashari was my playmate, a sturdy, good-tempered boy with deep-set brown eyes and a wolf-muzzle jaw that made him look fierce, even when he was laughing. His mother was one of my mother's only friends, but Binyamin had been betrothed to a distant cousin from Sana'a since the day of his Brit Milah, when he was circumcised and engaged almost simultaneously, at the tender age of eight days. Disappointed, my mother had to look beyond the Bashari house, and cast her net widely over the eligible boys of Qaraah.

Alas, her early attempts were all for naught. A recitation of the boys she tried to engage me to reads like a liturgy of misfortune. It was my sister-in-law Sultana who gave me the most comprehensive accounting of my ill-fated fiancés. Sultana, no stranger to misfortune herself, didn't spare me any details. Both of Sultana's parents had died the year after she married my second-eldest brother, Elihoo. After eleven years of marriage, poor, sad, orphaned Sultana had only one living baby, a scrawny little thing named Moshe. Before Moshe, she had lost six babies all in their first year of life. And then one more died in her womb—a little girl so tiny and perfect that her beautiful little body fit into the palm of the midwife's hand. After their last baby died, my brother Elihoo almost took another wife, but at the last minute he canceled the engagement. Elihoo was a brute, but he loved Sultana and pledged himself to her and to her alone, whether they had living children or not.

According to Sultana, my first possible fiancé died of the pox just one week after my mother broached the subject with his mother. The second potential groom fell from the upper platform in the granary where his father worked, and broke his back, dying in agony after the passage of two Sabbaths. The third boy's mother and father agreed to an engagement, but two days before the ceremony, the boy choked on a cashew nut, turned blue, and died at Torah school. The fourth went to sleep one night and never woke up. The fifth boy did not die in an accident or succumb to an illness, but was murdered by a crazy rope braider who lived in the bowels of the market. His headless body was found behind a bush near the bigger well around the corner from the Square of the Just, and his head was found in the madman's lair, along with the heads of three other victims.

After the last and most gruesome incident, my mother threw up her hands.

"There is no one for Adela to marry," she complained to my father, chopping nuts for baklava. "She's a bad-luck charm. An opposite amulet. What mother would want her for her son?"

At this my father slapped her, knocking loose one of her teeth.

She raked her nails across his face, drawing blood where there was no beard.

"We should send her to Aden," my father growled, "smuggle her with a caravan. Such things happen, you know. Children make it out of the Kingdom, I have heard talk of it . . ."

My mother widened her eyes and made a grotesque grimace, as if she had bitten into an apricot with a worm for a pit. "To Aden? Never. Better she be a Muslim than fall into the hands of your brother's wife, that Indian witch."

Even though I was just a little girl, I knew she was referring to my Aunt Rahel—a Jewess born in Alibag, India. Rahel had come to Yemen as a child, and married my Uncle Barhun in Aden. I had never met Aunt Rahel, but, for reasons I could not fathom, she was the witch in all of my mother's cautionary tales, the villainous harpy who would snatch me at midnight should I dare to dream of a fate other than the one Elohim had written for me in the Book of Life.

My father lifted a hand to slap my mother again. She raised the little bone-handled knife, and waved it in his face. He retreated. He knew, after all, that what my mother had said was true. None of the mothers of the Jewish boys of Qaraah wanted me for their sons. Why would they? Who could blame them? Perhaps the Confiscator was correct and my eyes were too big for my face. Perhaps I was doomed to live a life of misfortune. Some of my first memories are of playing with other little girls who had all been engaged since before they could toddle. They always made fun of me. "Adela," they cackled, "you will be orphaned and adopted, maybe they will call you Mustafina, you will pray to Mohammed, or you will be an old maid for sure." I kicked sand in their faces, and ran away to hide in Auntie Aminah's lap. Aminah was my mother's only sister. She was older than my already old mother by eight years. She had wrinkly skin, gray wiry hair, and, most impressive, a crippling hump on her left shoulder that made it hard for her to walk quickly, or even to breathe. She had never married because of her infirmities, but I had always liked her much better than I did my own mother. She would sit under the old frankincense tree behind her house, embroidering or darning. We had a frankincense tree too. Hers was up a little path, behind an old stone wall and some mint bushes. "Sha, sha, Adelish," she would say, "don't cry." But I couldn't help it, and my tears would mingle with the sweet scent of the resin from the tree, giving my sorrow a mellow tincture, though it didn't feel anything but bitter to my heart.

Sometimes I would hear my mother lamenting the conundrum of my groomlessness to her friend Mrs. Bashari, Binyamin's mother. "Maybe if we raise the price," she said, referring to my dowry. "Perhaps we should throw in the bone-and-pearl *sundug* case." My mother and her friends all spoke about me like chattel, and in time I even came to see myself as a calf to be sold at market, or as one of the ugly flat-nosed monkeys in the cage of the Somali curiosity trader. The poor creatures would poke their slick pink tongues out of the bars, and make crude gestures to passersby. Sometimes a wealthy man would buy one of those monkeys and lead it away with a collar and leash around its neck. The monkey would hop by its new owner's side, dodging the crush of the market throng, screeching and howling in coy terror at this new variety of imprisonment.

Chapter 2

The summer I turned seven, the Confiscator grew industrious. Until then, he had been either lazy or compassionate, and had made it a habit to pluck a Jewish orphan only every few months or so, but that season, he reaped a bountiful harvest. It began with poor little Devira Ladani. The story of her confiscation was told to me by my sister-in-law Masudah, who was married to my brother Dov. Like all Jewish women in Qaraah, Masudah collected stories of confiscation and worried over them, like amber beads until they were smooth as silk. Mr. Ladani was a maker of decorative cabinets. She told me that Mr. Ladani had begun to feel faint during the recitation of his morning prayers. Supposedly he swayed midway through the Ve'ahavta, the prayer that begins with the words "And you *shall* love G-d," which the sages interpreted to mean that all living beings will love God at some point in their future, no matter the paucity of their faith in the present. I don't know if Mr. Ladani had yet reached the point in his life that he loved God, or whether he merely liked Him, or only tolerated Him, but Masudah told me that Mr. Ladani swayed and nearly fainted upon hearing those words. The baker, who was standing next to him in the synagogue, steadied him, and made modest inquiries about the state of his health. Mr. Ladani insisted he was fine. After prayers, he went to work, for he was that sort of man—one who never missed a day of work as long as he could still sit at his bench.

He was finishing an order when he began to feel cold and then hot and then cold again and then very, very hot. He shivered, even though it was midsummer. He put down his file, wiped his blazing forehead with a corner of his apron. He picked up the file and tried to continue sharpening. It didn't take but another moment before he collapsed in his stall. When they took him home, he no longer knew his own name and his fever had risen so high that he went into convulsions. He was dead by midnight, and in the morning his wife was stricken too. She died at dawn the next day. How their only child, Devira Ladani, wasn't afflicted by the fever was considered a mystery and a miracle.

What to do with the child was a conundrum. No one wanted the poor girl—after all, how could anyone be sure she didn't carry the plague in the damp crannies of her bunched-up fists? But still, one couldn't leave a child alone in a house, and so she was ultimately taken in by the wife of Rabbi Tabib, who was as notorious for his controversial writings as he was praised for his compassion and civic good works. Mrs. Tabib was a good friend of Auntie Aminah. She told my aunt that Devira was the sort of girl who didn't make a peep or bother a soul and was always absentmindedly playing with a spool of thread or looking down at people's feet. Devira was at the Tabibs' for only one week before the Imam's men came for her. It shouldn't have been a surprise, but it was. A horrible surprise—the fierce staccato knock on the door, the way the Imam's men swaggered into poor Mrs. Tabib's house, sneering at her, ordering her around, and giving no explanation at all for the confiscation of the orphan, who had been nothing but quiet and sad and shy since her parents' death, and now screamed like a hysterical kid goat stuck by its neck in a fence. She even spat on the man who grabbed her wrists, and tried to kick his shins when he pulled her toward him with all the grubby tenderness of a lion fondling his next meal.

Mrs. Tabib ran after the Imam's men. She screamed and shook her fists as they disappeared down the Alley of Angels. "She was fierce herself," my aunt said with admiration. "She yelled to poor little Devira that she would come for her, that she would fight for her, that she would ransom her back." But none of this would happen. The Imam's men took the girl to Sana'a. The next day Rabbi Tabib himself went to Sana'a and met with the Imam's cousin-by-marriage, minister of Jewish affairs. The minister explained that little Devira had already been converted and adopted by a pious Muslim couple, and would be raised in accordance with the tenants of Islam. "And if you try to get her back, you will hang for your impudence, but why would you risk your life for her? She is not your relative anyway; we are doing you a favor by taking her off your hands."

After Devira Ladani, the confiscations grew more numerous. A month-old babe was wrested out of his mother's arms. The boy's father had dropped dead at his market stall. The child was given to a large Muslim family of coffee traders who renamed him Jibril after the archangel. Next to be taken was a four-year-old little deaf girl whose father was killed in a gruesome accident at the new iron forge. And then, in early spring, a six-year-old girl was confiscated. Her parents had both been killed when a horse-drawn carriage overturned in the late-day bustle at the Sana'an gate to Qaraah.

Fall in the Kingdom meant that we Jews were engrossed in preparations for the celebration of the New Year. It was also a traditional time for diplomacy. I was too young for politics, but had I not been, I would have known that the Imam was entertaining a high dignitary from the Aden Protectorate at a banquet in honor of territorial negotiations. The festivities lasted three days but resulted only in further stagnation and hostility. Supposedly the Imam served the British emissary baklava from the best bakery in all of Sana'a. When the emissary bit the pastry, he hit a whole almond and one of his front teeth cracked in half. There were no dentists in Sana'a, and the British emissary's howls of agony could be heard over the Imam's compound wall. Ever after, that night was referred to as the Night of the Broken Tooth, but it also signified a break in pleasant relations. After that there were no more banquets and no more amicable negotiations. The Imam raised an army and enlisted the help of the desert tribesmen—who had rifles that they had bought from the Italians in Eritrea—to force the Brits into the ocean. And while he wouldn't be successful in kicking the Brits out of Yemen, the Imam established temporary dominion over the emirates of Dhala and Beidha, and then sent his men further south to Audhali territory.

But I knew nothing of political machinations. My life was very small; it mostly consisted of helping my mother sweep and scrub, going to the market, carrying a little jug of water from the well, and pounding dough with the heel of my hand. I was being raised to be a wife and mother by a joyless woman who took no pleasure in the simple distractions life could have afforded her. Chief among those for women in our community were henna gatherings. My sisters-in-law, aunties, or neighbors would adorn one another while telling tales, singing songs, and sharing gossip, but my mother always refused to participate. Whenever she saw an elaborately decorated woman, she muttered cruel epithets under her breath. She had very few friends, and went about her daily duties with a sour expression on her face. If she caught me smiling, or humming to myself as I helped with housework, she would rebuke me. Sometimes in the market I would buy nuts from a pretty lady who always had exquisite henna tattoos on her hands and forearms. When she handed me my change, the coins would sit in the middle of her decorations. I would reach for the money tentatively, half-afraid of the forbidden markings, half hoping that they would magically rub off on my own skin.

Autumn passed quickly. Midwinter was soon upon us, and then early spring. But the spring was gusty, illness abounded, and I went about my chores with an old kerchief tied around my face by my mother, who believed it would protect me from ill winds. I hated that kerchief, for it chafed my neck and made me sweat under my gargush. I often untied it, letting it trail over my shoulders when I was out of sight of our house. One day I was in the market, shopping for persimmons for my mother's Sabbath jelly. I had my basket of fruit, and was walking along distractedly when I tripped on one of the corners of the kerchief and fell. My basket tipped, scattering the orange fruit in the dirt. I hoisted myself half up, and reached a hand in the hard-packed market earth to grab one plump fruit. Just as my fingers curled around it, there in front of me were the fancy maroon shoes with embossed flowers that my father had made. And above them, the daintiest ankles I had ever seen, swathed in gold pants under a dress of rich magenta brocade with an overlay mantle of brown silk.

"What good fortune!" A voice boomed from somewhere on top of me. "It is the little Jewess splayed at our feet. The very one I picked out for you. Remember I told you about her, the shoemaker's daughter."

I froze. I knew it was the Confiscator. My heart almost jumped out of my chest.

"Oh, Mamoon," purred the Confiscator's wife in a high silvery ribbon voice, a voice as fancy, impractical, and ornate as the shoes she wore, "you have such exquisite taste. When will she be mine?"

The dirt under me smelled sour of garbage. I tasted blood from my lip, which had banged into my teeth. I sucked in my breath, and kept staring at those shoes, which I myself had helped to make.

"The father is not long for this world. He will die, and then we will bring her home, just as I promised. She can be your pet, your daughter, or your servant. Whatever you wish."

The bangles on her ankles tinkled like bells, and when she moved her hands, at least ten bracelets slid up and down her wrists.

"Don't be a fool," she said, "the little capuchin would eat her alive, and the dogs would never share their scraps. She will be my daughter; I will call her Judi, or maybe Ruaa. What do you think? Will either name suit her?"

She spoke about me as if I weren't there. And then I realized that I wasn't. I had turned into someone else, a girl with a different fate. I thought about surrendering, becoming one with the dirt. Disappearing. But then fire blazed inside my whole body.

She bent down. I peeked up and saw that she was pretty—her wide face was shaped like a heart, with a pointy chin, green eyes slanting upward, full lips half-open, her tongue licking sharp little teeth. The bangles on her wrists tinkled along with the ones on her ankles. She picked up a persimmon from near my right knee, almost grazing me with her fingertips.

"Here, my darling, let me help you gather your fruit." Her nails were perfectly manicured with square tips, the persimmon a plump little sun in her palm.

I scrambled backward and then to my feet. I bunched the miserable kerchief up in my fist, turned, and fled, my arms pumping, chest heaving. Spit coming out of my mouth, snot running down my nose. Crying and running at the same time. Were those footsteps coming after me? Could it be? Didn't he know my father wasn't dead yet? Didn't he know that he had no right? Wouldn't someone tell him? Tell the Confiscator that I hadn't yet become an orphan? *Thud thud thud!* Yes, someone was following me, but it seemed that the market crowd parted for me, and then enveloped me. I didn't dare take the road, so I went through the yards, and when I got to Auntie Aminah's, three doors away from our own, I kept running, through her back garden, past the frankincense tree, down the path that led to the escarpment. And still those footsteps behind me. *Thud thud thud.*

"Adela!"

"Adela, it's me!" I turned, my whole body taut with dread and anticipation. But it wasn't the Confiscator. It was my friend Binyamin

Bashari. He had been in the market delivering his father's lunch when he saw me trip and watched the Confiscator and his wife bend over me. Now Binyamin threaded his brown hand in my own, and we ran together. Down the path, our footsteps making a mini-symphony with the buzzing of cicadas and the far-off call of a crow. The path led through a grove of citrons, down to an old culvert that marked the spot where a river had once flowed. The air was tangy, aromatic, and thick. We kept running until we reached a place where the culvert met the mountain and henna bushes grew along the lip of the escarpment. We ran for the safety of their cover, and when we pushed ourselves beneath them, we saw an opening in the mountain. We had to bend down and duck to get in, but inside was a space tall enough for us to stand. I sank down and held myself, rocking back and forth in the cool darkness of the cave.

For several moments neither of us spoke. Then Binyamin told me that after I fell, the Confiscator and his wife had turned to vultures. They grew wings and talons and beaks. He told me that he heard the Confiscator's wife caw, "When you are mine, little darling, I will comb your hair with a tortoiseshell brush" and then she turned back into a woman again, a woman whose laughter was high and shiny and pure as hate.

When Binyamin finished speaking, he flung a clumsy arm around me. I leaned into him. I knew that I might be safe for now, but even there, in the belly of the earth, I heard the tinkling of the bangles on the Confiscator's wife's ankles, and the reverberations of her awful words filled my head.

After that day, that flight, I took possession of that blessed little cave. Throughout that spring and early summer, I felt truly safe there. I knew the Confiscator would never find me in my earthen sanctuary. But it wasn't only the Confiscator that I hid from. I also hid from my mother, whose cruelty toward me often took the form of verbal rebukes, but also manifested itself in beatings that left my behind black-and-blue. I hid from my older brothers, and I hid from the future and whatever miseries it would hold. I grew to love that cave. I brought candles and set them into the stone crevices of the walls, and began stealing knickknacks from home—a little copper pot and tray, an indigo wood-husk pillow that smelled like Auntie Aminah's house, a small reed mat that I wove myself. Eventually I began picking up stones and twigs, and using the embroidery skills I had learned from Auntie Aminah, I made them into idols. I constructed a small altar and set my idols upon it. I was an uncommonly pagan child for a Jewish girl and imbued my stones with the names of goddesses I had heard mumbled by the fortune-tellers in the corner market stalls. I revered my idols like the tribeswomen of old. I knew what my mother would say if she discovered them; she would say, "If Elohim saw them, he would throw you in a pit and cover you with spiders." I didn't know much about theology. I couldn't read, and could murmur only the shortest of psalms, but I did suspect even then that my mother's threats were nonsense. I was of the naive opinion that Elohim was as much God of Little Girls as God of Men, so He would surely approve of my stitchery and compliment my cave-keeping. I kissed my idols, petted them, held them tenderly, and left them offerings of honey, sesame, herbs, or wheat. Whenever I left I prayed to Elohim to watch over them in my absence. I never stayed in my cave for long because I didn't want to be caught, though each of the women who were supposed to watch over me—my sisters-in-law, my aunties, and my own mother—always assumed that I was with one of the others.

A month or so after I tripped in the market, Binyamin appeared at the door of my cave. Even though he was my friend, I glared at him, "This is my place now. Swear you won't follow me again." He bit his lip. His wolf-muzzle face looked ugly to me. I noticed a fresh scab running through one eyebrow. His lips were puffy, as if he had been bitten by a bee. I knew that this meant that one of his older brothers had probably beaten him. He was always getting beaten. I was grateful that I was a girl, and that my mother hit me only on my behind and my brothers took care not to leave scars when they tormented me.

"I promise," he said with a crooked smile, brushing his hair out of his eyes. And that's all he said. My friend Binyamin Bashari didn't have many words, and those he had, he doled out carefully, as precious as the ruby chips his father mounted in the hilts of jambias.

But he broke this promise many times. Years later, Binyamin Bashari told me that he often followed me to my cave, and that he would sit underneath the bushiest henna plant and listen as I sang to my idols, and that sometimes in my absence he would go into the cave himself, and leave his own offerings to my goddesses with ancient names.

Chapter 3

The sun hung low over the graveyard and I ran out of my cave without bidding farewell to my idols. It was the summer of 1926. I had recently turned eight. I raced past the old grove of citrons. I was running because I hadn't finished my chores for dinner. I knew that my mother would grab me by the scruff of my neck, berate me, and then beat me for my torn leggings, my messy hair. I had to avoid her. I crossed my auntie's garden. Instead of going home by the road, I crept through the yards in between my auntie's and our own. The house just next to ours was that of our neighbor, a blind man who lived with his spinster daughter. She was a mistress dyer, and the back of their house was always filled with colorful troughs of dye skeins of wool and pieces of drying cloth that people brought for her to dip. She specialized in dyeing the red and black *lahfeh* scarves that married Jewish women wore over their *gargushim* for modesty. Drying lahfeh were pinned to lines on the periphery of the yard. Some were complete—and had red and white roundels winking out at me, like eyes on a face. Muslim women would buy lahfeh too, and tie them around their swelling bellies when they were bearing, thus borrowing the stranger magic of their Jewish sisters.

I ran in between the troughs, and crept through the crack in the wall that led into our yard. I heard cacophony from the kitchen—my brothers all talking at once, followed by my father's guttural sputtering, and his cough, always his cough. His coughing was worse when he was excited. What was he saying? He sounded so happy, but at the same time, concerned. I pulled a washbasin under the window, climbed up, and peeked in. What I saw was that the room was crowded. My father and brothers were clustered around a stranger. The stranger's arm was in a linen sling. He looked like an older clay version of my father left too long in the sun, drooped and withered from exposure. His skin was an ashen sickly gray. My brothers were all leaning into one another, arms flung over one another's shoulders. My mother was beside my father, holding a large wooden spoon. She was trying to quiet everyone down, yelling my brothers' names while jabbing the spoon in the air for emphasis. My father was speaking, "Oh my," he sputtered. "Tell me everything. Don't leave out a single detail."

The sickly looking man took a deep breath. He wiped his brow with his good hand, then he began, "We were in the middle of our annual western journey. We were traveling by boat from Bombay to Oman. Once on land, we hired camels and were crossing the southern edge of the Rub' al Khali. We reached a place called the Oasis of Screams. We stopped in the oasis to water our camels, and spent two nights enjoying the hospitality of the Bedouin who made their camp there. On the third night catastrophe struck. We were beset upon by a pair of criminals. I heard my camels moaning, woke up, went to see what the trouble was. When the thieves saw me, one drew a knife and slashed me deeply in the arm, you see, right here, just below the shoulder. The thieves made off with the bulk of my merchandise, and left me bleeding to death in a fetid puddle of sand where the terrified camels had pissed out their fear at the goings-on."

The man stopped talking. My father said, "And then what? Who tended your injuries?" But before the stranger could answer, I heard footsteps and jumped off the basin. I crawled under a nearby rosebush. Thorns stabbed my back, but I ignored the pain. If my mother found me eavesdropping, she would beat me with that wooden spoon. But the footsteps were not my mother's; they belonged to a boy who looked about my age. He was crouching down and staring at me under the bush, motioning for me to come out. Slowly, I obliged. Soon we stood face-to-face. I had never seen him before. I assumed that he belonged with the man in the house, but they didn't look anything alike. He was wearing a red cap, a wrinkled and patched brown suit. His gently sloping eyes were a startling eggshell blue. He had a pleasant upturned nose, high cheeks, and very pretty lips, soft and round like a girl's. His twisted earlocks hung all the way down to his chin. His front teeth were missing, though one was in the process of growing in. I too was missing my front teeth, and at the sight of his, I felt my tongue explore the empty spaces in my mouth. I was scratched up and tousled from my run home, my fall on the escarpment, and my tenure under the rosebush. My headdress had come askew, and the point was tilting toward my right ear, the tassels thrown over my neck. He crooked his hand, and motioned for me to get up. I righted my headdress and followed him around to the front of our house, where a donkey cart was tied to the hitching post. The donkey was out of the harness, eating from the trough my father used to feed Pishtish, our donkey, and Pishtish was tied to the other side of the trough, reluctantly sharing his dinner with the interloper. The boy climbed onto the cart and dug under some blankets. He pulled something out, scrambled back down, and reached for my hand. He opened my fingers, for they were clenched in a fist, and put something on my palm. It was a crude little amulet, a round wooden disk affixed to a square leather backing. I had seen one like this before. My brother Ephrim wore one around his neck for a while, before he was wed. I knew that in between the wooden disk and the leather backing would be a tiny piece of parchment writ with either an angel's name, or one of the many names of God. I wondered which name was inscribed on this little amulet—whether it was a name I knew, or one of the more mysterious names that were never pronounced when girls were listening. We heard a noise from the front of the house. The boy looked me straight in the eye and then nodded down at the amulet. I slid it into my pocket.

My mother burst out the front door. I instinctively crouched down and curled up into a little ball, the better to ward off her blows. Masudah said that she watched out the kitchen window and saw the boy step in between me and my mother, and that because he was there, my mother turned away. But my meanest sister-in-law, Yerushalmit, who was always out to get me and always saw trouble where others saw goodness, said that this was a lie and that the boy ran into the house and abandoned me to my mother's wrath. She added that my mother beat me, but with little enthusiasm, before ordering my sister-in-law Masudah to take me home, clean me up, and not to dare bring me back until the next morning.

That night I learned that the strange boy was my cousin Asaf, whose name meant *gatherer*. He was the youngest son of my father's brother— Uncle Zecharia, the man whose arm was in a sling. I had never met either of them before, but I had heard many stories about Uncle Zecharia. I knew that he was a spice merchant and a procurer of rare unguents and perfume ingredients. Once I overheard someone say that a precious vial of agarwood attar had been sent to a bride by my uncle Zecharia, whose relation to the bride was also unclear to me. Another time I overheard my mother call my uncle by a name that both shocked and amused me, for it was the same as a word that I knew—from eavesdropping on my brothers—that referred to a man's flaccid penis. Not long after, I heard my father brag to a friend that his brother was once the guest of an African prince in Djibouti. Another time, I heard him say that his brother had been involved in an ugly brawl with Chinese merchants in the Port of Mocha. My father had two living brothers: Uncle Barhun, who lived in Aden, and was married to my Aunt Rahel, the witch in my mother's stories, and Uncle Zecharia, the eldest, who had never before come to Qaraah. I never thought Uncle Zecharia's colorful travels would lead to our doorstep. But here he was.

After the attack, Asaf and my uncle had made their way through the Naquum Mountains. They came to us seeking refuge. My uncle was weak and in need of a place to rest and heal. Their cart was laden with their entire store of worldly goods, which, thanks to the thieves, had been reduced considerably. But among my uncle's meager possessions remained a true prize, a small deerskin Torah that he had somehow acquired from an Iraqi cedar-essence merchant. The Torah was in tatters, and should have been buried long ago. But Uncle Zecharia was the sort of man who saw wholeness where others saw deficiency, and was in the habit of reading the weekly portion from this sad little Torah, even though it would not have passed holy muster. The Torah had been buried under rags in the cart in order to protect it from the elements and criminal eyes. Now it was brought into my father's house and stored in a place of honor: the big wooden chest on the top floor of the house, in the men's salon. The chest had been part of my mother's dowry, and was decorated with bone and iron inlay. It was the only chest in the house that had a lock on it. It is hard to say what flustered my mother more, having to host her wounded brother-in-law or the deerskin Torah, for she venerated holy books, and saw it as a grave and fraught responsibility to be given charge of such a treasure, albeit a *pasul* one, fouled by its own poor condition.

But the deerskin Torah was not the center of attention, and only my mother paid it much heed. Uncle Zecharia was garrulous that first night.

He explained how even before the attack he had been growing tired of his itinerant life, and had been contemplating coming to Qaraah. Asaf, like me, was his father's youngest child, the child of his mother's old age. Three older children in the family were all married and settled in homes along his father's route—a daughter in Bombay, a son in Jerusalem, another son in Egypt, in a suburb of Alexandria. Asaf's mother had died giving birth to him, and he had spent his babyhood in the saddle in front of his father.

My sister-in-law Masudah had a pleasant heart-shaped face and big round cheeks that were always red like apples. Masudah had four living children and had buried another four. In Masudah's house, I was put on a pallet with her daughter, two-year-old curly-headed Remelia. Masudah kissed me when tucking me into bed, and then laughed and said, "By morning you will be engaged, little one."

I sat up, wide-eyed, "What do you mean?"

"Didn't you see? Your mother sunk her claws into that boy the moment he walked into the house. I wouldn't be surprised if you are already betrothed; after all, your uncle doesn't know about the bad luck you bring." My face must have fallen. "Silly girl"—Masudah kissed my nose—"your mother is wise enough to act quickly. She knows she must put forth a proposal before your uncle recovers and hears what they say on the streets of Qaraah."

Little Remelia shoved her pudgy hand into mine and fell asleep curled against me. I was awake for a long time. In my other hand, I held the amulet Asaf had given me. I wondered again which of Elohim's many names or which angel's name was written on the parchment. I wondered if he had made the amulet himself, or if it had been given to him. And if it had been given to him, by whom? When I finally fell asleep, I dreamed that he had been on the escarpment with me, and that together we found the amulet peeking out of the sand.

Masudah was right. My mother put forth a proposal that very night. First, she convinced my uncle that he was still dying, even though his arm was almost completely healed. She paid the tea seller to pretend he was a doctor and to come and pronounce my uncle's wound so infected as to lead to sure putrefaction. The tea seller was a hunched-over little man who could tell the weight of tea leaves to the half gram without a scale. He examined Uncle Zecharia's arm and then told him that he had only days to live. He told my uncle that though the flesh had healed over, the bone was dead inside the arm. He pressed so hard on the red angry scar that my uncle screamed and cursed and even whimpered. When the tea seller was gone, my mother came to Uncle Zecharia's side and delicately broached the matter of an engagement. Uncle Zecharia was a cautious man, and was in his right mind enough to lift up his head and say, "Sister-in-law, don't talk marriage to a dying man."

"Well, if you are dying, all the more reason to protect the boy from the Imam."

Uncle Zecharia, not having been back north in over a decade, did not know about the severity or heartlessness with which the Orphans Decree was enforced. My mother explained everything to Uncle Zecharia, though she neglected to tell him that I had an unfortunate habit of losing grooms. No, my mother judiciously kept this information to herself.

Uncle Zecharia nursed his wounded arm, and listened to her impassioned oratory. And then there was the banging on the door.

"Oh, what is that? Is someone there?" My mother ran to the door and made a great show of speaking to someone outside. Her voice rose in angry tones and in the end she slammed the door and walked back inside with a huff.

Masudah later explained, "Your mother very convincingly pretended that it was the Confiscator himself, come to collect the boy before your uncle was even dead in his grave. But really, it was the lampmaker's wife, speaking in a gruff voice and banging on the door with her clenched fists. With that, your Uncle Zecharia almost begged your mother to fetch the scribe that very night to write up the engagement contract. By the time you woke the next morning, you were already a bride, and Asaf was your groom. They made a solemn bargain over a cup of arak and signed the contract in a week's time."

It didn't take long for Uncle Zecharia to realize that he'd been tricked. When he went out to the market, our neighbors greeted him with downcast eyes and words of comfort. He quickly realized that he had unwittingly engaged his precious son to a girl who had the strange power of killing her grooms. He bellowed into our house, demanding that the engagement be broken. But my mother stood her ground and swore that if he dared break the engagement, she would make an amulet that would shrivel his manhood and make worms come out of his ears. I don't know whether my Uncle Zecharia was superstitious, or whether he believed my mother could harm him if he tore up our engagement contract, but he did back down—though not before calling me to his side and inspecting me, or at least, that is what Masudah called it, an inspection, though it didn't feel like what a farmer does to an ewe, or like what a woman at market does as she sniffs the navels of melons for sweetness. He was sitting on the jasmine-scented pillows in front of the hearth. He patted the spot next to him. I remember feeling unsure of what to do. I never sat with the men, my uncle was a stranger to me, and I rarely even ascended to this floor of the house, where the men reigned supreme, chewing khat and smoking their hookahs. My mother was in the doorway, chaperoning this interview. I stood in front of him for a moment, rocking back and forth on the balls of my feet. I think I would have opened my mouth and bleated like a lamb had he asked me to. But all he did was look at me. His gaze touched my heart and filled me with warmth. Until that moment I hadn't known that grown-ups could feel the same way that I did. There was wonder and hope and fear in his eyes, yet there was love in them too, and then finally, a gleam of recognition, as if we already knew each other, as if we were good friends.

Sana'a was within kissing distance of the southern lands of the Sauds. It sat on the narrowest point of a mountain plateau, almost eight thousand feet above sea level at the joining hands of two major ancient trade routes, one of them linking the fertile upland plains, the other Marib and the Red Sea. Our town, Qaraah, was ten miles south of Sana'a, high up on the peak of a lesser mountain. Behind our town was a gently sloping plateau formed by the joining of two mountain shoulders. The trip from Qaraah to Sana'a would have taken half a morning by donkey cart if there weren't mountains in the way, but because of the precipitous elevation, the trip took an entire day of riding.

"The light in Sana'a casts a buttery sheen," Auntie Aminah was fond of saying. She had spent several years there as a girl. "The houses are honey colored, the streets—when not defiled by refuse—glow sesame brown." My only visit to Sana'a was years away, so when I was just a little girl, I had to content myself with my aunt's comparisons. She pointed out the many ways in which Qaraah was not at all like Sana'a. We were a tiny new town while Sana'a was a sprawling metropolis, ancient seat of Ethiopian viceroys, Egyptian sultans, and Ottoman viceroys. Our salt market could boast only a handful of merchants, whereas in Sana'a there wasn't just one market, but also a cloth market, grain market, silk market, raisins market, cattle market, thread market, coffee-husk market, caps market, carpet market, brassware market, silverware market, and firewood market—home to hundreds of merchants hawking everything from khat leaves and elephant-tusk ivory to coriander seeds, potash, turmeric, silk thread from China, and kaleidoscope bolts of the finest Indian linens. Our houses were a paltry three or four stories high, compared to the eight- or nine-story towers in which people lived in Sana'a. But it wasn't just that Qaraah was small. I myself came to see the difference in the light. The sun hit the rocks around Qaraah at an angle that painted a ruby-red haze over everything. Houses were redder; food was redder; thoughts, arguments, dreams, laughter, marriages, births, and deaths were redder, a fact that made people think of blood more than they would if they lived elsewhere. As for me? My memories of my childhood are tinted by the color of that crimson sun.

I was eight years old at my official engagement ceremony in the autumn of 1926. My groom was a tender nine. It was a joyous and long-awaited day for my family, for it signified my protection from Confiscation. That is, if my father should live long enough for Asaf and me to reach maturity and wrap ourselves in the armor of matrimony. That day was filled with hope, Auntie Aminah told me. Hope for all of our futures. My father's health was precarious, but everyone knew that the Confiscator was mercurial and that sometimes an engagement document was enough to keep him at bay.

Heavy rain fell throughout that season. Auntie Aminah said that during a break in the storms, a hot wind bearing silty flecks of mud came in through our windows and coated everything with a layer of ashen dirt. She also said that the rain was sweet because the mountains were so close to heaven. I am sure that it tasted bitter and left everyone gargling with cistern water, but my auntie always embroidered her stories with as much skill as she embroidered my leggings, dresses, and head coverings. For the occasion I wore nothing more than my ordinary everyday *antari muwadda* dress of dark blue cotton. The whole front of the dress was embroidered with red triangles, white chain stitches, and cowrie shells called David's Tears, which were to protect us from sorrow and the evil eye. On my head, I wore a fancy triangle gargush my mother borrowed for the occasion. It was made of black velvet and framed my forehead with a straight row of silver beads that dangled over my eyebrows. The top was embroidered with red triangles and florets in rows that reached all the way up to a little tip, giving the hood its distinctive triangular shape. There were also twelve horizontal rows of triangles in the back of the hood, and silver-thread cords over the brow and down my neck. Two silver chains hung from either side of the hood, and the ends of the chains were silver bell tassels that touched my shoulders. Whenever I moved, the beads on my forehead tinkled, and the tiny bells on the tassels did too, making a pleasant noise that sounded like running water. The back of the gargush was decorated with a heavy triple-hanging row of Maria Theresa thalers—Habsburg Empire–era silver coins that had made their way east through the ports of Genoa, Trieste, and Marseille to Egyptian and Red Sea ports. When I was a child, the Arabian Peninsula was awash in them. I didn't know anything about the global trading currents that brought those coins to Yemen, but I did know that their tinkling helped me avoid the evil eye, and that demons scattered at the sound. Like all Jewish girls in the environs of Sana'a, I always wore a simpler version of this tight, heavy headdress from morning till sunset, both in and out of the house. My ordinary gargush didn't have the Maria Theresa thalers, but it did have the silver bells and tassels that tinkled whenever I moved.

I am told that I cried at the ceremony for no good reason, and that my groom ripped his pants on a nail on a bench. My brother Hassan said that we both looked like babies and that to prove it, in the middle of the ceremony, Asaf pissed his pants, though I am sure this is mean-spirited embellishment, for Asaf was surely old enough to hold his water. The ceremony was held upstairs in the men's parlor of our house. Parched treats were served, and the men—our fathers—cemented the deal over the signing of documents and the blessing and sharing of a ritual cup of wine. There was little celebration, though. According to Sultana, my mother had seen fit to put a holy-name amulet in the secret sleeve pocket of my dress, and to fasten a triangle amulet ring around Asaf's neck. The neck ring was fashioned with nine nails from different households, as was the custom. Inside the hanging pouch were the traditional magical elements that boys wore to pass through the dangerous crossings of their lives. There were a vial of mercury, baby teeth, dried rue, durra, and sesame. My brothers had all worn this amulet at their circumcisions and engagement ceremonies, and my mother kept it in the locked chest along with her other precious possessions. There was no music at the ceremony. None of the *tabl* drum or *shinshilla* cymbals of wedding festivities, no mothers clapping their hands over their mouths to say *kulululu*. My mother even refused to have my hands dipped in henna for the event, and so I was presented to my groom without the customary bright red palms of fertility and good fortune.

After my engagement, I was prohibited from seeing much of my groom. This was in accordance with tradition. A boy and girl promised to each other from the same family were not supposed to develop affinities for each other, lest they mistakenly grow up thinking of each other as brother and sister. "This would lead to the abomination of incest," Auntie Aminah explained. "Even if you are cousins, you can still be brother and sister in your souls. So you must not see him, or get to know him. There will be enough time for that after the wedding." Uncle Zecharia moved almost a mile away from us, into a house far from where most of the Jewish families lived in Qaraah. He and Asaf lived close to a little mosque and two doors from an old one-eyed caravanner from Najran, with whom Uncle Zecharia became friendly. On family occasions, Asaf was sequestered with my father, brothers, and Uncle Zecharia, while I was kept in the bosom of the ladies of the house.

My only real friend from those days was Binyamin Bashari, with whom I was still allowed to interact. We played the games of wild children—chasing lizards, squashing spiders, building forts out of sticks and stones, fashioning catapults out of straw, twine, and cast-off pieces of leather from my father's workshop. Some of my earliest memories are of Binyamin shimmying up onto the subroof of our house to get a ball of gutta-percha that had gotten stuck up there during our exploits. I was very impressed that he could climb so high.

Binyamin had been learning to play a long wooden flute, called a *khallool*. Sometimes he brought his khallool to the frankincense tree behind my auntie's house, and we would sit in the great big saddle of the tree and he would improvise reedy tunes as crickets chirped along to his tentative melodies. Occasionally Binyamin would bring me disappointing news of my husband-to-be. "He is no good at Torah school," Binyamin once told me. "He knows nothing of scripture, and refuses to learn the weekly portion."

"Why do you roll your eyes at my husband? Are you such a scholar that you can call him dumb?"

He shrugged and picked at a scab on his knuckles. "He isn't your husband yet."

"He will be."

"He acts as if he is better than us Qaraah boys. He doesn't talk to anyone, and keeps mightily to himself."

"Well, maybe he *is* better than you Qaraah boys."

"Is that what you think?" The half smile Binyamin usually wore turned into a scowl. And after that we never spoke of Asaf again, which made me glad because I knew that if the subject were to arise, I would once again speak words that would cut my friend, little ceremonial slashes to his soul, not to cause a mortal wound, just to draw blood and to relieve myself of a nameless burden.

But I was never sure that Binyamin really disliked Asaf. Once I saw Binyamin and Asaf leaving Torah school together. They were following the teacher, a tall, emaciated scholar from Taiz, who was everyone's favorite, even though he espoused the teachings of a messianist whose philosophies were controversial in Qaraah. Asaf was on the teacher's right, Binyamin on his left, and they were walking in the direction of the little well. Another time, I saw them walking together toward Binyamin's father's jambia stall. And a third time, I saw them sitting together on the low wall outside of the ritual bath, on a Sabbath afternoon. This time, they saw me too. But both pretended that they hadn't. I passed, angry with both of them, but mostly angry with Binyamin. My anger quickly turned to shame, for I was embarrassed that I cared.

Once or twice I caught Asaf's eye on the street beside the buckle and nail seller's stall. Once, I passed right next to him as he was going into the Torah school. Usually I saw him in the market. Uncle Zecharia began to spend his days in my father's leather stall. My father embossed his belts with a distinctive triangle and diamond design along the edges. Each belt maker had his own design, a signature on the animal skin. Asaf would attend school with the other boys of Qaraah in the morning, but in the afternoon, he would join his father at my father's stall, stamping the triangles and diamonds into the belts. My father also made decorative bags that he sold to the wealthier and more discerning matrons of Qaraah, as well as leather phylactery cases for the prayer boxes that men in our community affixed to their foreheads and forearms. Sometimes Asaf cut the straps for the prayer boxes, or helped my father with other tasks, like cutting the soles for the shoes he made for children. I don't think that Asaf ever knew that I had been my father's helper long before him. When Asaf or his father was in my father's stall, we both pretended that I didn't know a thing about leathercraft, though when they weren't there, I assisted him just as before.

When I went marketing with my sisters-in-law or my mother, we would visit the stall to greet my father, or to bring him a flask of hot sweet tea or a pot of egg and meat stew for a midday meal when he was too busy to come home for lunch. Uncle Zecharia was not good with his hands, and really "helped" my father only by keeping him company. Uncle Zecharia would try to romance customers into making purchases, but was not a very good salesman when it came to leather, a deficiency he blamed on himself. "I am a merchant of spice and scent," I heard him say more than once, "and have no talent for peddling dead flesh. Who can blame me after a lifetime spent inhaling the fruity delicacies this world has to offer?" When we visited the stall, Uncle Zecharia would always make a point to address me personally, saying things like, "Little Adela, what a lovely little collar, did you do the embroidery yourself?" He always complimented me on one thing or another, and I usually hid my face in my scarf and blushed. But Asaf wouldn't act anything like his father. He would keep his head bowed at his task, or look right past me and pretend I wasn't there. After all of these occasions on which Asaf ignored me, I began to feel as if his kindness in the garden on the day of his arrival had been a sham, and that the amulet that I kept under my pillow was a token from a different boy, one who had perhaps continued on his travels, not this cousin who had settled into our lives and was promised to me as my husband.

Chapter 4

I was engaged to Asaf in early autumn, but it wasn't until late winter of that year that we began to defy tradition and became friends. I was lonely most of the time those days. I was no longer supposed to play with Binyamin. We were getting too old to be alone together, my mother said. His mother agreed, and they both did what they could to keep us apart. I spent more and more time in my cave. I was on my way there when I heard the thundering of hooves. I turned with a start, feeling my heart in my throat. A boy on a chestnut horse was almost upon me. I ducked behind a bush. He sped down around the side of the cemetery, and then came back again. This time he slowed down when he got close to a tamarind tree, slid off the horse, and tethered the animal. Then he walked over to where I was crouching. I sucked in my breath. My fiancé.

I remember that a chill was in the air. It was the sort of day when the sun shines so brightly as to make one forget that the heat of summer is still months away. Asaf cocked his head to one side. He squinted and then turned his eyes into laughing stars.

"Come out, cousin. What are you doing here? All alone out here— you should go home. You know I can see you? Come out so we can talk."

I emerged from behind the bush. He seemed taller, lankier. I wondered when he had grown so much, or if I was just imagining that he had gotten so much taller since we had stood side by side, protected by the old magic of mercury, durra, and rue. I noticed a dimple in his chin, a smudge of dirt below his right eye.

I pointed to the horse. "Where did you get that mount?"

"What mount?"

"The horse tethered to the tree, stupid."

"Don't call me stupid."

"I'm sorry. But I would expect you to call me stupid if I tied a horse to a tree and then pretended it wasn't there."

He shrugged, kicked at a stone.

"The horse isn't mine."

"Of course it isn't. Where would you get a horse? And anyway, you aren't allowed to ride it."

"She belongs to Sheik Ibn Messer. A cousin of the Imam."

I looked at my cousin, my husband-to-be. His missing front teeth had grown in, as had mine. His complexion was a toasted sesame brown. His long hair fell in a tousled fringe out of the sides of a brown turban that had replaced his red cap. His earlocks were tucked into his turban. I think that is the moment I realized that Asaf was pretty, as pretty as a girl, but with boyish grit and swagger. The crumpled brown suit he had arrived in had been replaced by a man's dark blue *guftan* coat trimmed with cord. The cording had a gap on the front hem—not by accident, but because all of our men had their guftans made this way, with an imperfection, so that every time one looked at it, one was reminded of the destruction of the Temple in Jerusalem. Under the guftan he wore a white shirt with blue embroidery. The blue stitches on his shirt matched his eyes, which in turn matched the sky.

"Sheik Ibn Messer?" I was skeptical. "He lets you ride his horse?"

I knew who the sheik was. His summer compound was not far from my cave, though it was beyond the view of the escarpment.

Asaf stuck out his chest and squared his shoulders, holding himself in a stance worthy of such illustrious association. Asaf's last word, *Imam,* hung in the air, traveling up like a puff of smoke. I must have scrunched up my face, or otherwise showed Asaf that his explanation was lacking.

"Ibn Messer is a great man and a mischief maker," he explained. "He likes to let Jews ride his horses. He and Imam Yahye hate each other. They fight the way dragonflies fight, by buzzing each other's wings."

He bragged, "I am a better rider than most men. Ibn Messer holds races. Awards prizes. He said I could be a jockey if I weren't a Jew. Said I keep my seat better than most. And that the way I handle his horses, he is sure I could win."

Now I understood. The Jews of the Kingdom may have known next to nothing about the goings-on in the outside world, but we were experts in the political machinations of the Zaidi Muslims who ruled over us. Even I, a little girl, was old enough to know that there were several "little sheiks" in the mountain valleys surrounding Sana'a. And that every so often one rose up like a "cocky rooster," as my father would say, "to peck at the ground around the Imam's feet." All throughout the Kingdom there were tangled allegiances and loyalties. Imam Yahye, while autocratic, did not wield absolute power. And the farther one got from Sana'a, the weaker the yoke of his authority. But politics didn't interest me at all at the moment. I opened my mouth to say something benign and inconsequential like, "How far have you ridden?" but instead I heard myself say, "You aren't a man, you are just a boy."

Asaf seemed taken aback, as if he didn't know what conversation we were having—one about horses or one about us, about our future together when I would be less a girl than a woman, and he more a man than a boy. He was quiet for a moment, but then he shrugged and smiled. His eyes grew wide and his face opened up, like a present. He looked down the escarpment toward the horse. She had nosed around and found a mouthful of scrubby grass to chew on. "Do you want to meet her?"

"What is her name?"

"Jamiya. Come with me." He led me to the tree. "Put your hand on her flank, that's right, isn't she soft?" I breathed in deep. The rich animal smell filled my nose—a combination of wet earth and burnt caramel. She made contented little whinnying sounds as Asaf scratched between her ears. Jamiya flicked her tail, widened her nostrils. We stood there like that for what seemed like a very long time. Eventually Asaf mounted the horse and rode away. I watched him make a wide turn and disappear over the dunes to the right of the cemetery. From the back, with his earlocks tucked away, he could have been a Muslim boy. Later that night, as I lay on my pallet, I kept thinking about Asaf and Jamiya. I fell asleep dreaming of a princess who married a horse and spent eternity riding her husband through the fields of heaven.

A few weeks later Asaf and his father came to our house for an evening meal. It wasn't a Sabbath or festival day, but an ordinary midweek night. Uncle Zecharia usually paid a widow to cook for him and Asaf, but she was visiting her daughter who was in childbed, so my father had invited them to share our table.

During the meal, I didn't look at Asaf and he didn't look at me. He was seated in between my uncle and my father. Four of my brothers were there too. My mother and I served the men and then sat at the far end of the table to eat our portions of stew. When I got up to bring a new dish or to take one away, I pretended that I hadn't seen Asaf on the horse and he pretended that he hadn't seen me alone on the escarpment.

After the meal, I was sent up to the men's salon to bring them a tray of sweets. My brothers were reclining on pillows, chewing khat, and smoking hookahs. My father and uncle hadn't come up yet to join them. Asaf was sitting next to my brother Mordechai, who was speaking to my brother Dov. As I approached, Mordechai began telling a crude story. In our tradition, something was called "holy" when it belonged to the whole community—like a Torah or a synagogue building, a ritual bath or spice box used to mark the passage between Sabbath and weekday. This is why a loose woman was also called "holy," because she was shared by many. I knelt to put the tray on the little table and I heard Mordechai say, "Avihu's sister sure is holy. She lay with her own brother-in-law, with the neighbor, and with the neighbor's neighbor before being caught by her own husband, who turned her out and sent her back to her parents, pregnant with a bastard with four fathers, who knows, maybe more." Dov let out a great big self-satisfied guffaw. "Holy, holy, holy," he said through a big wad of khat, "she must be so holy that the angels themselves mistake her for one of their own." As I turned to go, he launched into a crude joke about a farmer who violated his goat, a baker who violated his fresh loaves, and a fisherman who sank his hook into the mermaid bounty of the deep blue sea.

My cheeks grew red. I was used to my brothers' boorish behavior, but it seemed to me as if they were telling these stories for my benefit, that is, to embarrass me in front of my groom. As I passed by Asaf he turned his head and caught my eye for the smallest little pebble of a second. In that second I thought his expression said, "Don't listen to them." And, "If I were older, and already married to you, I would protect you from your miserable brothers." Did Asaf's little glance really say all of these things? I don't know, but it was enough that I believed it so.

The next time Asaf met me on the escarpment he wasn't on Jamiya, but had come by foot. We stood without speaking for what seemed like a very long time. Asaf looked up at the sky. I followed his gaze and spied a pair of sooty falcons circling over the ruins of Yehezkiel the Goat's forge.

"Well . . ." Asaf kicked a stone, bit his bottom lip, and then ran his fingers through his right forelock, twisting it into a tighter curl.

"Well what?"

"Hmmm."

I looked back up into the sky. The falcons were flying away. Asaf shifted back and forth on his feet and narrowed his eyes, turning them into tiny slits of blue that swept over the landscape behind me and then settled on what seemed to be my chin. He began to curl the second forelock and then let it spring back up in a corkscrew. Finally he whispered, "Can you take me there?"

"Where?"

"To your . . ."

"My what?"

"To your cave. I know where you go. I followed you, so I know that you have a cave. I would very much like to see it. Don't worry, I won't tell anyone else."

I weighed my options. I could refuse, but if he already knew I had a cave, he could go there whether I took him or not. Really, he was just asking permission. And if I didn't take him, perhaps he would get angry. And if he got angry, would he give away my secret? Tell his father? Tell my father about it? Binyamin was the only other person who knew about my cave, and so far he had kept my secret.

"Come." I turned on my heels.

"I'll follow."

I snorted, "Of course you will. It's what you want, isn't it?"

"Don't be mad, Adela. I promise I won't tell anyone else. It will still be your secret."

I didn't answer. I took him the other way around the culvert. The long way, past an old camel cart half-buried in the sand. Before entering, I hesitated. Asaf stood not a hand's breath from me. Together, we looked out at the landscape. Down below my cave, to the southwest, was the Jewish cemetery, where Grandfather Yoosef was buried, and past that was the wealthy village of Bir Zeit, where I never went, but where I heard that the imported fruit trees grew heavy with Indian mangoes and perfumed gardens sported yellow melons as big as the heads of giants. All around us the mountains rose up the color of wet wheat and old canvas sacking. To the north was the walled city of Sana'a. We could see a camel caravan coming from Amran laden with grain and khat leaves and cotton entering Bir Zeit. And there in the middle distance we espied the gravekeeper stooped over stones, while a solitary horseman rode a stallion over distant dunes, where the mauve and golden mountaintops faded into each other, like feathers on a reclining bird.

The moment for stillness passed. A breeze rustled the henna bushes. I turned to the cave, ducked, and entered. Asaf followed me in. I lit one of my little contraband lamps, along with a stub of a candle that I kept in one of the indentations in the cave walls. He looked around. As the light illuminated the space around us, I saw him smile.

"Yes, this will do, it's very nice."

"Do for what?"

"For our first home."

"What are you talking about?"

"You are my wife."

"Not yet," I said through gritted teeth.

He shrugged. "In some places in Africa, the children marry at birth. In parts of Morocco, they marry when they lose their first teeth. I see no reason why we should wait any longer." He came toward me. Quickly, I bent down and lifted one of the little pots that I used to heat water on a tiny wicking stove I had stolen from Auntie Aminah's storeroom. Before he could get any closer, I clonked him on the head.

I called him a brute and threatened to tell my mother that he had tried to violate me. He smiled, scratching his head. "Then I will tell her about this."

"And I will tell your father about Jamiya."

He pointed at my altar, my idols.

"And I will tell your mother about your little pagan gods."

"Goddesses."

"Forgive me, but I don't think she will care about the sex of your idols. Only that you have them. A Jewish girl like you—"

I put my hands on my hips and taunted Asaf back, "A Jewish boy like you, out here in the dunes, riding a horse?"

"A Jewish girl with her own cave? What will people say about you? That you meet goat boys here. That you tempt them with your wiles." He rubbed his head where I had hit him.

"My wiles? You have been spending too much time with the animals that are my brothers. Are you an animal too? Or are you a boy who mounts horses like women? That is a mare you are riding, after all?"

I don't know exactly how, but in the thicket of these crude threats, we suddenly came to a truce. And not just any truce, but a happy one. We both started laughing. We were saying things we didn't mean and didn't even understand. Our predicament suddenly seemed very funny, but funny in a way that mattered and felt safe. After all, our connection was based on protection; we needed each other to avoid confiscation. So that was the nature of our laughter. It was a balm and a joke and a trick perpetrated against the demons that overreached when they came for us. Asaf and I laughed and looked deep into each other's eyes. Did he think my eyes too big? No, I could tell that he thought they were just right. We were perfect for each other. We were each other's armor. And in that moment, we each became the other's lance, sword, and shield. We couldn't say all of this, because we were just children, so we laughed, because life was hard, and laughing was easy.

Two days later my family shared the Passover seder with Asaf and his father. At the seder, we pretended not to know each other at all. Asaf and the sons of our neighbors, who also joined us for the holiday, put on a little skit, reenacting the Exodus. Asaf played the part of Moses, defying Pharaoh, leading his people out of Egypt, raising his staff to part the Sea of Reeds.

"Oh, what a great Moses you are," my father said, complimenting him on his acting.

I thought of Moses's staff. How God had turned it into a snake, which writhed at Pharaoh's feet. This made me think of the Confiscator's jambia, and soon the fire of fear was igniting behind my eyes. The faces around the table blurred, and suddenly I was back in the market, sprawled on the ground at the feet of the Confiscator and his wife.

"Adela, what is it? Are you not well?" My sister-in-law Masudah came behind me.

"I am fine, just fine," I reassured her, forcing a big smile that soused the flames in my head. No, I was at home, all was well. I was safe. He wouldn't take me away. He couldn't, could he? When I came of age I would marry. If I did my duty and married Asaf, I would have nothing to fear, now would I?

I took the plate from my intended and examined it for clues. I needed to know: What did he like to eat? The lamb brains? The chickpea stew? Was he a boy with a big appetite? Would I be woman enough to make savory dishes to nourish and feed him?

Asaf came to my cave again two weeks after Passover. When he had tethered the horse, we sat in the cool shade of an overhanging red rock. He told me a story about a race he had watched, in which a man fell off his horse and broke his leg. The Muslim boy who won was a member of one of the far northern hilltop tribes. "You know," Asaf said, his voice tinged with what seemed a combination of apprehension and admiration, "the tribe of the great assassins."

"No," I said, "I don't know. I know nothing about any assassins." He reached into Jamiya's saddlebag and pulled out a bag of salted almonds. We sat on our haunches and shared them as he explained the intrigues of days before we were born. Asaf told me how the boy's tribe plotted against the Imam's father, who was the leader of the land when our parents were children. The assassins tried many times before they eventually succeeded in killing the Imam's father. They tried to poison his soup, to suffocate him in bed, and to break the legs of his horse as he rode at a full gallop. They even tried to kill him with henna. How? A henna dyer was paid to add a bit of coded text to the bridal application of one of his nieces. The groom was the killer. He was to receive the information that told when and where he was to kill the Imam's father by reading the soles of his bride's feet on their wedding night. But that plot was foiled too. And both the bride and groom were executed, even though the bride had known nothing about it. The assassins finally succeeded with a gunshot to the head.

Asaf finished his tale by making his hand into an imaginary gun and pulling on an invisible trigger while making a clicking sound with his tongue. After that, we were both quiet for a while. We were giving this dramatic and sad story the respect it was due. But our silence didn't last long. Next, Asaf told me about a client his father had, a Moroccan taxidermist who used spices to preserve his animals, and another, a Muslim burial master, who used spices to ward off the smell of death. I listened without asking any questions. We both reached for the last almond. Our fingers brushed together in the bag. I quickly pulled my hand out, for I knew I wasn't supposed to touch a boy who was not my brother. Especially since he was my intended. He pulled his hand out quickly too. But then he laughed, and said, "When we are married, we will share more than almonds."

I blushed, and looked down at my feet. But then I dared to peek up at him again. "Look"—I pointed at Jamiya—"she is being tormented by flies. You should take her home."

Asaf nodded, and then he did something very silly. He lay back in the sand and made an angel shape with his arms and legs. When he rose, his hair was full of sand, and his clothes dripped sand like water. He brushed himself off, ran toward Jamiya, mounted, and rode away without looking back. He took a zigzag path, riding at a slow trot. I lay back in the sand on top of his ghost angel. I let my hands fall into the wings and shut my eyes for a moment, and when I opened them again, I could no longer see him.

A few weeks later, the next time Asaf came to my cave, we drew together on the cave wall. I had some chalk stones. I drew a chalk boy and girl. He picked up a piece of chalk and drew a stick horse next to him, and one for me too.

"But I don't ride," I said.

"You will one day; it's like flying. We will ride together, race each other."

"But girls can't ride."

He shrugged. "Neither can Jews."

By the late spring, I was calling him *husband*, and he was calling me *wife*. It was a game at first, a joke even, but eventually the words seemed to change substance and become mighty on our tongues. We began to steal away whenever we could to spend time together in my cave. I always made my way to Auntie Aminah's through the backyards now, in order to hide my intentions of going to the cave. Sometimes the spinster dye mistress would be at her troughs. Once she reached for me as I ran by and made me stand in front of her. "Where are you always going, little girl?" she asked. She had been stirring a big pot of purple; I could tell because she still held her mixing staff, which dripped purple onto the sand, and her fingers were the color of caper flowers.

"To my auntie's." I looked down, blushing.

She knew I was lying. "Are you a liar or a dreamer? Neither? Or both? Well, you are not the first little girl who ran through my pots to escape one thing and find another. Just be careful you don't fall in"— she gave a little laugh—"or you will arrive at your lie or in your dream wearing a coat of many colors, and then you will be found out, and I too will be implicated in your deception." I backed away, and ran out of her yard as fast as I could. After that, I was careful to step sure-footedly through the pots of ocher and amber and red and blue and purple—all much darker in the troughs than they were on the cloth she dyed.

Asaf and I kept meeting at my cave.

"Husband, are you hungry?"

"Wife, are you well?"

"Husband, so good to see you."

"Wife, I have brought you some fava beans."

We did our best to playact the parts of devoted spouses, taking cues from our dreams and stories we had heard.

He would come in the early evening and I would serve him a little vagabond supper of scraps I had stolen from my mother's kitchen, or nuts and berries I had foraged myself. Then we would tell each other about our days, or share jokes, tell small stories before going our separate ways. I took the path around the old forge that led to the grove of citrons and into Auntie Aminah's yard; Asaf went farther west on the escarpment, emerging through a hole in the wall behind the silk merchants' stalls in the center of town.

Sometimes he would come on Jamiya, who seemed to consider me a threat for Asaf's affections. But when I dug a turnip for her out of my pocket, she took it gingerly with her big yellow teeth. In no time we were each won over by the other—I by her warm brown-eyed gentleness, she by my turnip-ness—and after that we were good friends.

Chapter 5

It was early summer of 1927. In the outside world many things were changing, though we knew nothing of them inside of Yemen. Only many years later was I able to look back and put the small events of my life in a larger context. The year of my engagement, the first transatlantic phone call was made between New York and London. Closer to home, Abdul Aziz had just been declared King of Hejaz and Sultan of Nedj, later to become the Kingdom of Saudi Arabia. Reza Kahn was crowned the new Shah of Persia. In another corner of the world, Stalin consolidated his power. But what did we know of these happenings? In Qaraah there were three weddings and nine births in Jewish households. There were the usual deaths among the old and very young, as well as a strange and incomprehensible tragedy: a scribe who killed himself after slitting the throats of his wife and three daughters.

I mourned the tragedies and celebrated the happiness of my neighbors modestly and properly, from a distance. I watched longingly as my sisters-in-law left their homes to attend henna gatherings for brides. I was always left behind, peeking out from behind my mother's disapproving shadow. I didn't spare any thought for the political or social machinations of the rest of the world. How could I? In Qaraah we were entirely cut off from global politics and modernity.

My concerns were for my father's health, my mother's temper, and the well-being of my many nieces and nephews. The Confiscator's shadow continued to loom large. I knew that I was protected from confiscation by my engagement to my cousin Asaf. I also knew that this protection was tenuous and that I was still at risk, simply because life was unpredictable and I was a Jewish girl in Yemen. Occasionally I would see the Confiscator in the market. Each time my belly clenched up and I felt fire leap in my skull. Whenever the long shadow of his maroon djellaba disappeared into a throng of marketers, I told myself, "I am safe, I am safe, I am safe" but deep down, I didn't believe it. Every so often, he came to my father's stall and ordered more fancy shoes for his wife. I had kept up my little apprenticeship with my father. Once I made the tops for the shoes. The Confiscator noticed my small stitching and complimented the delicate shape of the moon and stars I had embossed in the leather. I still hid behind my father when he came, and wondered about his wife, and whether she would be able to tell that I made those shoes, not for her, but in spite of her. If I could have, I would have learned a spell that turned dead things into living things, so I could make the leather turn into an animal that would chew on her feet and haunt her as the snakes on her husband's jambia haunted me.

In those days, I saw Binyamin Bashari rarely and never in private. He had left Torah school and was helping his father full-time in his stall, learning to make jambia. Sometimes I saw him when I went to the market to bring my father his lunch, or when I spent an afternoon with my father in his stall. We would nod at each other, and he would smile his half smile when he saw me coming, but usually I hid my face in the fold of my gargush and pretended—with a modesty I didn't really feel— that I didn't see him. When he played the khallool in his father's stall, the sinuous tones of the flute would lick at my ears and remind me of the games we used to play when we were still small children.

As for me and Asaf? We had become experts at playacting. I turned nine that summer. He was ten years old. When we saw each other in public, we pretended to be the perfect strangers everyone assumed us to be. But in my cave we were the best of friends. We spent a lot of time telling each other stories. Most of his stories were about his father's business of buying and selling ingredients for perfume. Asaf told me how, before coming to Qaraah, he and his father spent half the year traveling west to India, and the other half traveling east to sell his father's wares to perfumers in Cairo, Athens, and Istanbul. He had endless stories of their exploits on the road and sea. In return, I told Asaf my auntie's stories about the founding of Qaraah and about the myths and origins of the Jews of Yemen. He loved hearing about the jewelers of Queen Bilquis, about the miners for the Great Temple, and about the son of Noah, who came to Sana'a when the Waters of Judgment receded, and founded the city on a cloud-covered peak of the new world. We would sit in the lip of my cave, the dazzling sun dappling down on us, but our backs cool from the shady breath of the mountain behind us.

Once I was telling him about Shem, son of Noah, but toward the end of the story, my words caught in my throat.

"What is it?"

"Nothing."

"Tell me."

"No, it's silly."

"Tell me."

I didn't say any more. I didn't confess my new discovery, which was that Asaf was in my story. A companion to Shem, bending low to the still-wet earth, clearing a foundation for a home we would share. He was in all of my stories. Tall and lean, with eyes the color of good fortune. He was one of Sheba's jewelers. He was in the retinue of miners collecting gems for Solomon's Temple. How could I tell him that no story would be complete without the curve of his smile, the square set of his broad shoulders? I blushed, coughed, looked down at my hands. I didn't yet have the words for it, to explain that he was now braided into my life like a strand of wax in the candle we light to mark the transition between the Sabbath and the rest of the week. And not only into my life but also into my imagination. I would have to ask Auntie Aminah about this. She was always saying that certain embroidery stitches are charmed, and that by putting them into cloth, you give the wearer the power to change her future. She also said that the past had pockets in it, and that if you knew how, you could pick and choose the things you found in those pockets and then use them for your own purposes in the present. I never questioned her mystical pronouncements, but took them at face value. What would she say if I told her I saw Asaf in my stories? And I was there too, engaged to him in ancient days, in places neither of us had ever been, speaking a foreign tongue in which both of us were oddly fluent.

"Well, if you aren't going to finish, then it's my turn." He lay back, put his hands behind his neck. "Did I tell you about the time my father bought frangipani petals from the one-armed man in Madras? No? Well, that was the day we were both thrown into jail. I was just four years old, and they put us in a cell with murderers, pirates, and thieves." He talked and talked until the sun was low in the white belly of the sky. We left the cave late that day, and when I returned home, I was almost caught by my mother.

"I was looking everywhere for you," she berated me. "Where were you? I want you to make the lahuhua bread for dinner." I was becoming a good cook, and my mother, though never one to praise me, had been relying upon me more and more in the kitchen.

"I was at Masudah's, helping her with the baby," I lied.

"But I was just there. She said you were at Sultana's." Sultana had long black hair, heavy mannish eyebrows, and thin lips that always seemed to be puckered around some invisible lemon. Sultana wasn't ugly, but she wasn't pretty either. What she was, was kind. She would always lie for me—usually to protect me from my brothers but also to throw my mother off my trail.

"I went from Masudah's to Sultana's. I picked up some of her eggs for Auntie Aminah. I delivered them, and then I came home."

My mother stared at me. She knew I was lying, but she didn't care enough to catch me at it. Her nostrils flared, and she shook her head slightly, communicating her boredom with my excuses, her disapproval at my need to lie, and her begrudging admiration that she had raised a daughter who seemed to slip through everyone's fingers, like water. Her eyes glazed over in the middle of my explanation, and she muttered, "Well, go wash up, and then get to work on the dough."

That year we had gone many months without rain. By midsummer, people all over the northern mountains were going hungry. There had not been enough wheat in the fields, bulb flies killed what crops managed to grow in the parched soil, and a conflict between two of the lesser sheiks in the west was making it almost impossible for camel caravans, laden with dried fish from the coast or with citrus fruits from the lowland orchards, to make their way inland and north to the mountains. In the surrounding villages, people began to invoke the aid of Af Bri, angel of rain, asking that he seed the clouds from above with the water of the heavens. Some began to pray that Elohim would once again send down manna from the sky, as in the days of old. Instead of manna, locusts fell from the sky, and we celebrated. Locusts were a delicacy, and we fried them in *samneh* or roasted them on skewers and went to bed with our bellies full, sure that Elohim had heard us, and that the locust swarm was proof that the plagues of old would not smite our enemies, but feed us and lead us to salvation.

But after the locusts, the great hunger descended once more, and people from surrounding villages began to come to Qaraah in search of sustenance. Our town was blessed with the runoff from a stream called Little Lyre, so named because people said that when the stream ran full in winter, the water made the sound of a strumming psalmist, and that to drink this water was to bring harmony to one's heart. Thanks to the stream, we'd had good harvests in our durum wheat fields when the surrounding villages had none. Refugees from surrounding villages came to us before they ventured farther north to Sana'a.

One of these refugees was a skinny girl named Yael, who was maybe fifteen or sixteen and came with a babe in her arms. Yael would have been pretty, had she not been so thin. She had lovely eyes, tiger-brown with streaks of gold in them. But hunger had made most of her teeth fall out and her poor baby was afflicted with a distended belly and eyes so big they seemed to pop out of her head. Yael had made her way alone into our town, and collapsed at the little well in front of the first market stalls. She was taken to the house of the midwife. When she was revived, Yael asked for my Uncle Zecharia, and a great hubbub ensued because how in the world did a girl from the mountains know Uncle Zecharia, let alone know that he was in Qaraah? The midwife sent for him. According to the midwife, who was a great gossip and later spoke about the moment in detail, when Uncle Zecharia appeared and saw the girl, he fell to his knees and began to kiss her bony hands. Next he gathered her up, against the midwife's protestations. Uncle Zecharia shook off her complaints and carried the girl to his house and laid her on his own bed. The infant was left with the midwife, who took the poor thing to Masudah, who was nursing a new babe of her own and had milk to spare.

For three days Uncle Zecharia tended to the girl himself and refused to let anyone in his house. He didn't even let Asaf come home. So Asaf took shelter in Elihoo and Sultana's house. All anyone talked about was the poor girl's condition and Uncle Zecharia's transgression. The women at the ritual bath were all of the opinion that Yael was a mountain whore, and that Uncle Zecharia was paying her to sleep in his bed. My sister-in-law Yerushalmit said, "I suspect Zecharia knows her from his days as a merchant. She could be a daughter of the dunes . . . someone he knows from his past." Yerushalmit used the term that referred to the women who lived in desert outposts and serviced the caravanners crisscrossing the Kingdom.

Masudah took pity on the girl, and tsked and scolded Yerushalmit. "While Uncle Zecharia is being most unwise by welcoming an unmarried girl into his house, it is unseemly to speculate, and we should keep our lewd thoughts to ourselves."

But everyone kept gossiping, and finally my mother took action. On the fourth day she marched over to Uncle Zecharia's with a big pot of lamb *chouia*. She didn't even knock on the door, but barged right in, and spent three hours inside. When she came out she refused to talk to anyone, but that night I heard her say to my father, "Anyone else in their right mind would sever the agreement."

My father's voice was weary yet firm. "The son is not to be blamed for the sins of the father."

"Ach Hayyim," my mother spit out, "who knows who Asaf's mother is? For all we know, our daughter is to be chained to a bastard. But where would we find her another husband? At least this one is still alive, eh?"

I didn't understand the context, but I knew that they were talking about me, and about Asaf and about our engagement. I understood that somehow Yael's spectral presence had ignited the tinder of this horrible conversation. That night I dreamed that my life was a ball of embroidery thread, and a cat with tawny eyes like the starving girl's was batting me back and forth with her sharp claws.

Yael left Uncle Zecharia's on the fourth day. How did she find our house? I have no idea. She must have come in when we were out at the market. When we returned, we heard a noise upstairs. My mother found her in our sleeping quarters with her hands in one of the sundug boxes. She had pulled out a *lazem* necklace, the one with dangling Indian rupees and three little charm cases. I was in the kitchen, making dough for *kubaneh*. When my mother dragged poor toothless skinny Yael downstairs into the kitchen, the rage in my mother's bulging eyes was such that I was sure she would put a knife in the poor girl's heart. But instead, she overmastered her temper, cradled Yael by the cooking fire, brushed her hair back from her damp forehead, then called for me to bring some tepid stew, which she spooned between the girl's cracked lips with the tenderness of a mother feeding her own baby. But the stew couldn't nourish her back to health. Yael and her child both died the very next day. We buried them—the babe in her mother's arms—in the cemetery below my cave.

The night of the funeral, it became common knowledge that Yael was Uncle Zecharia's daughter. He had always known of her existence, and had visited her mother twice when she was still a little girl and twice since returning to Qaraah. When she had called for him to come to her at the midwife's house, she had pressed a coral toe ring into his palm, a token he had given her mother. I was sitting around a fire with Sultana and little Moshe. The men were inside chanting evening prayers in what had now become a house of mourning for two people none of us knew. My brother Menachem, who was always shirking prayers, came out of the house before the service was over and ambled over to us. He smelled like sweat and arak, which he wiped from his lips. He spat into the fire, picked up a stick, poked at the flames, and then pointed up at the sky, dark as black pudding and filled with ripe blazing stars.

"Adela," he smirked, "Uncle Zecharia is indeed the father of a great nation, his descendants more numerous than the stars in the sky."

Sultana said, "Menachem, leave her be."

I looked down at my knees. I hated Menachem, and had learned long ago that it was best to ignore him, especially when his breath smelled like drink. But Menachem wasn't finished.

"Sister," he said, "you must be very proud. After all, you are marrying into a most illustrious family. Uncle Zecharia is a bastard-maker. It seems he planted babies from Bombay to Cyprus. Why, I wouldn't be surprised if your Asaf had one hundred brothers and sisters. Just think, your children will have enough cousins to people a new world."

The morning after the funeral, Uncle Zecharia flew into a great rage, overturning a table, smashing dishes. Auntie Aminah was there. She said that Uncle Zecharia turned into a bear, but that my father became a lion, tenderly and fiercely nipping him in the neck to force him to surrender his fury, then taking his brother in his paws until the rage of grief had passed. I never doubted that my father and his brother turned into animals, for in those days metaphors were not mere decorations, but the very essence of stories, and it was not uncommon for people to become beasts, or for beasts to take on the mercies and sufferings of men.

I never asked Asaf about his dead sister and niece, how he felt about the whole sad story, how he felt about losing a sister he hadn't even known existed. But a week after the funeral, when he came to my cave, he sat for just a moment before reaching for one of my little idols—a skinny wooden one with slate-colored eyes.

"Could I have this one?" he asked in a half whisper.

"What will you do with her?"

He shrugged in the direction of the cemetery. "Maybe they wouldn't be so lonely."

"Of course, and take another one for the baby." I reached for a little idol, no bigger than my thumb, which I had made out of a piece of fallen tamarind and dressed in a piece of old blue apron. I don't know if by burying my idols, Asaf brought Yael, or her babe, or himself, some measure of comfort. Asaf and I never mentioned Yael again, but every so often, when he was in the cave, our eyes would stray to the empty place on the altar.

After Yael's death, Uncle Zecharia was different. It was as if some of his daughter's hunger infected him, and even though we had food to eat, he began to grow thin, his eyes sinking farther into those wide rheumy sockets. Almost immediately after the shiva, Uncle Zecharia decided that he would leave our town for a short journey to Sana'a, where he would stay with an old friend of my father, a rhinoceros horn trader named Aba Jerush. In Sana'a, Uncle Zecharia would replenish his basic stores of perfume ingredients. He said that he was not made for the leatherworkers' craft, and that the stink of dead flesh would kill him quicker than any earthly hunger. He insisted that if he had his basic supplies, he could mix perfumes and set up his own stall in Qaraah. The arrangement called for Asaf to move in with Elihoo and Sultana. Later Sultana told me that the night Asaf came he had a horrible nightmare and kept the household awake until the small hours before dawn.

Uncle Zecharia's short journey stretched out to one month and then two. He sent letters describing how he was waiting for a certain caravan to come in from the Hadramut with a cache of sweet myrrh, or that he would come home after a merchant arrived from the west with mastic crystals and dried karo karounde flowers.

While Uncle Zecharia was gone, no one was really looking out for Asaf, and he began to spend more and more time riding Sheik Ibn Messer's horses. Then the sheik permitted him to ride one of his mares in a race. Asaf described the race to me in great detail. At first I didn't believe him, but he later brought me proof in the form of a half Maria Theresa thaler he said the sheik awarded him as his purse. He also told me a great secret: that there were other Jewish boys who rode in Ibn Messer's races. The third son of the lime burner, the second son of the lampmaker, the youngest son of one of my father's competitors, a leatherworker, who made jambia belts too. Asaf told me to sit on the escarpment on a certain afternoon and to watch for them. I took my needlework and went past the frankincense tree, past the grove of citrons, and out onto the escarpment at the appointed time. I sat cross-legged and practiced my *Kawkab* stars. Then, just as he said they would, Asaf and the three other boys thundered past me. All the boys had their earlocks tucked into their turbans. The horses galloped with the speed of legend in their legs, as if they were the very mares of foundation, galloping away from an oasis in order to heed the call of the Prophet, proving allegiance, forsaking thirst. After this, whenever I saw those boys in the market or on their way to Torah school, they looked like all the other Jewish boys of Qaraah. But when I dreamed of them—as I often did—they did not ride horses, but were horses themselves. These horses had earlocks that hung in long curls down beside their manes, giving them a comical aspect, and when I woke up from this dream I was always laughing.

Chapter 6

That season, when Uncle Zecharia left us, there was a terrible fire at one of the larger synagogues, far away in Aden. It happened on the Sabbath before a wedding when a groom was being called to the Torah. Years later, when we ourselves moved south to Aden, I learned that six people died in the fire: the groom, the rabbi, two cousins of the groom, and two community elders. When we heard the news, I was still a girl, and the story had already rolled up and down the mountainous peaks of our land, and as it came closer to Qaraah, it picked up the dirt and sand of the ages and became a parable we marveled at. Supposedly the groom died trying to save the burning Torah. When fire licked the holy scroll, he threw his body on top of it, and soon the flames were shooting up from his writhing back, taking on phantasmagoric shapes, and ultimately spelling out one of the esoteric names for God.

Much closer, in Sana'a, there was also mourning. The RAF had sent planes from Aden to expel the Imam's troops from Audhali territory. Those men who returned described the great fire coming down from the sky, and though the Imam's men were said to have performed acts of great heroism, their deeds did not translate into parables about God. Instead, we Jews told tales of the devil and wondered who his true agents were—those who fought for the Imam, or those who strafed the clouds, those who could fly?

In Palestine, Jews were speaking modern Hebrew for the very first time, popularized by the lexicographer Eliezer Ben-Yehuda, who had revived the language almost single-handedly, naming modern things in the biblical tongue and creating words for phenomena of science and technology that we didn't even know existed. In Qaraah there was one man—Mr. Faheed Ari, a jeweler—who held the rare distinction of being the only one anyone knew who had been to Palestine and back.

He was a small, elegant man with a wrinkled box of a face and a voice too high for his personality, which was as fierce as he was dainty. He held court on lazy hot afternoons, describing the short skirts of the socialist girls from Russia who drank coffee in cafés in Tel Aviv while flirting with British soldiers. He told tales of the Arab boys in Jaffa who dove off huge, slick rocks into the Mediterranean to fish with their hands, and how the farmers of Galilee worked the land with a crude little tool, half hoe, half rake, the backs of their hands bloody from massive thorns that grew from wild roots at the base of lemon trees. Friends and neighbors gathered round. They peppered Mr. Ari with questions. They chewed khat and smoked hookahs while plotting their own escapes to Jerusalem, and lamenting the truth of the matter, which was that it would take a magic carpet to get them there, and magic was scarce in those days.

Far from all this, in our little piece of the world, Asaf and I cast our own spells. It was the autumn of 1927. The Day of Atonement had just passed. The men in synagogue had read the portion in which Jonah is swallowed by the whale. The Muslims revered Jonah as much as we Jews, calling him Dhul-Nun, the one in the whale. And just like us, the Muslim children of Qaraah drew whales in the dirt with the pointy edges of sticks. Children jumped from whale to whale, playing a game called Don't Catch Jonah. It was early afternoon; my mother thought I was at Auntie Aminah's helping her make *bint al-sahn*. But I knew that Auntie Aminah was at her friend Ela's house, helping her make baklava for her daughter's engagement party. On my way from our house to Auntie Aminah's, I stepped on three whales. I thought that the last resembled my brother Menachem, who had a round face and bulgy eyes that shifted this way and that as he appraised a room.

I ran up past the frankincense tree, past the old citrons, past the abandoned forge, around the culvert. I lit the candles in my cave. Sat and waited. It wasn't long before Asaf joined me. How did we each know when the other would be there? We just did. We were synchronized. It was as if each of us could sense that the other was coming.

Asaf came in and saluted the chalk boy and girl on the wall. Sometimes the pair of them smudged or faded, but I always redrew them. He sat down on my little divan. I had brought two old flat cushions from Auntie Aminah's storeroom and laid them on top of a little rope rug I had "borrowed" from the bottom of one of Sultana's chests.

"Come here." Asaf patted the spot next to him. I was arranging my little idols.

"Wait." I put some figs, sage, and honey in front of the idol I called Ashtoret and another I called Asherah. Then I turned to Asaf. I sat next to him on the pallet, and soon we were lying down. They say that children who have not reached maturity cannot feel the passions of men and women, but Asaf and I must have been made differently than other children, for in that moment my skin rose to his touch, and my body, though it had never known this sort of hunger, hungered for his.

We quickly sat up, stunned by this new predicament.

He put his hand on my thigh. I shuddered. And because he was an honorable boy and this game of grown-ups we were playing was really just a game, he took his hand off my leg and moved away from me. For a few moments we didn't say or do anything. But then we were drawn close. He put his hands around my waist. I laid my lips on his cheek and smelled him. Wood and rain, sage and harness oil. We kissed. His tongue pushed through my mouth. I sucked on it, hungry as a kid for a teat. He pushed me away and then drew me close again, tracing the outline of my lips with his tongue and then kissing me on my lips, my chin, my eyes, my neck, my ears. How did we stop? I have no idea. Actually I do not think we ever really stopped. Some part of me is still a child in that cave, kissing Asaf as if it were my only purpose on this earth. As if our presence in that cave were part of the balance of all creation. Our infant passion responsible for the spinning of the world, the heaving of the tides, the setting of the sun.

"Adela, I am sorry, I shouldn't have—"

"Asaf, don't say anything."

"But really, I am so sorry."

"I'm not."

"You'll come back."

"Of course."

We parted in a veil of Qaraah's ruby rays of light. He left me blushing in a beam that illuminated only the two of us behind the henna bush at the lip of my cave, while the rest of the world was shrouded in misty darkness.

After this he didn't come back to my cave for a long time. I missed him. But I was also relieved. I knew nothing of the ways of the world, and feared that what we had done would get me with child. I dreamed that a tiny baby had passed from his lips to mine and I lived many a day in terror that the baby we had made by kissing would grow ripe in my belly before I could dose myself with a concoction of dragon's-blood sap, which I had heard my sisters-in-law say that women take when the babe in their womb was not of their husband's doing. Would it kill me? I didn't care. Surely death would be better than the shame of having whored myself to my cousin.

But one month passed, and then another two. By early spring, no cave-begotten baby swelled inside me. My fears subsided. When Asaf finally returned to my cave, I was ready to greet him. I had made fig biscuits, which I kept in a little tin. And I had a flask of weak grape wine. We sat down next to each together and ate. We didn't speak or laugh. When we had finished eating, he wiped the crumbs from his face then said, "Your mother tricked my father into agreeing to our engagement."

I looked down at my lap. I had not expected this. I bowed my head, and hiding behind the dangling beads on my gargush, asked, "Why do you bring it up? The subject shames me."

He reached out, brushed his fingers on my hot cheeks, sending a tingling flutter through my body.

I spoke again, my voice quivering with anger. "Laban tricks Jacob into marrying Leah, and because of this treachery she becomes the mother of many children. The mother of most of the world."

"I am . . ." Asaf cocked his head to one side. His hand had come to rest lightly on my shoulder.

"What?"

"Adela, I am grateful to your mother. And I am not dead." He sat up, smiled, took his hand from my shoulder, and cracked his knuckles loudly, making little popping sounds. "So the curse of your girlhood must be broken. Maybe it is your little goddesses"—he nodded toward my altar—"maybe they have intervened to save my life so that you can one day become a mother too." He paused. "Like our mother, Leah. Maybe you too will be mother of most of the world."

He drew me close, kissed me on my lips over and over again. Then he laid me back on the mat. Slid his hand through the bosom slit of my dress and slowly, tenderly, brushed past the *maglab* brocade that prevented my exposure. I was embarrassed, for mine were still little buds, not yet sprouted, but when Asaf laid his hands on them, my nipples stung and swelled, and I wondered in the secret part of my soul if his hands possessed the power to call my womanhood forth.

The day we saw each other's sex was one of the last days that he came to my cave. It was chilly outside, but cozy enough among the blankets of my cave. I had laid a rug on the ground and lit a little lantern. We lay close to its heat. Soon I was naked before him. I was flooded with unfamiliar warmth as Asaf's eyes drank in my brown flesh, my mound, still hairless, a child's conch, tucked in between my legs.

I in turn had to stifle a laugh when he pulled down his pants and lay before me with a sausage between his legs. It reminded me of the *jachnun* my mother served on Sabbath lunch, a brown coil nestled between two hard-boiled eggs, themselves turned brown by the roasting of the stew. Outside, the setting sun was calling to us with its ruby rays. "Go home, go home" it said, but we ignored its warm message. He bent over me, and drew concentric circles on my flat belly, and then lower, and lower still, with his tongue. With each turn of his tongue, I twisted and arched and became a circle myself—a girl moon trapped in the orbit of a wild, unruly pleasure. When it was my turn to minister to him, I bent over my boy husband and took him in my mouth. And for all of those who say that children can't know the love of men and women, I would say— you should wonder what it was that the idols saw. Thankfully, their eyes were made of stone or wood, and they had no mouths from which to spill our secrets.

After that, Asaf stopped coming to see me, and I was lonely again. Years later, he told me that he had known even less about the ways of the world than I did, and was so afraid that he had gotten me with child when we lay together in my cave, that he could neither sleep nor eat and dreamed of fallen angels, which is what people say when their nights are tortured by visions of hell. He told me that the dreams ended only when he swore an oath to Elohim that he would not touch me again until we were married.

When we saw each other in the market or passing in one of the narrow lanes in between the salt market and the Street of Crooked Baskets, we both averted our eyes. When he came to our house for a festive meal, I avoided serving him, begging Yerushalmit to take my place at the table. But also, we spoke without speaking. The way children can speak without words, like they do in the womb before birth, listening to the conversation of angels. Over the humming incantatory swell of synagogue prayers, I listened as Asaf told me about Jamiya, about how fast he rode her, about her heaving stride, about her wild, earth-colored eyes. When we passed each other in the street, I told him about the conversations I had with the setting sun outside my cave. In my dreams, he told me about travels we would take together. And once, when we were together for a tiny seedling of a moment in the alley beside Auntie Aminah's house (I was delivering eggs, he was on an errand from my father, delivering a pair of children's shoes to a neighbor), he reached out a hand and brushed a piece of hair out of my eyes. Then he put a finger to my thirsty lips, and hushed my many questions before I could even ask them.

And then catastrophe struck. In the early spring of 1928, Uncle Zecharia returned from Sana'a. He came to my father and told him that he and Asaf would be going away together on a long journey. According to my uncle, an old client of his in Cyprus had located him in Sana'a, and asked him to deliver a quantity of *choya nakh*, the Indian roasted seashell essence used as the smoky base of several rare perfumes. "We will join the caravan of Sheik Ibn Messer's stablemaster; he is delivering horses to an illustrious customer outside of Aden and has agreed to let us travel under his protection. We will go with them as far as Aden, and then sail to India. We will spend the spring in Bombay." Uncle Zecharia cleared his throat, and then continued, "And make the eastward journey in the summer. When I return, I will be a wealthy man, for I will be paid well for this delivery."

My father protested. "What if Adela becomes a woman in Asaf's absence? The delay of the wedding could put her in danger."

"Elohim will look over your family and protect you. And anyway, the engagement itself will save little Adela from the Imam. When we return they will be married. That is, if she is a woman, of course. There is still time, Brother, she is just a child." I blushed at these words, my father and uncle discussing my body. And I burned inside, for I knew that even if I didn't have the breasts or blood to prove it, I was more than ready to be Asaf's wife.

I would like to say that we parted as innocents, but we didn't. The morning they left, Asaf met me in my cave. He drew me to him, and kissed me as a man kisses a woman—not for the first time, but for the tenth time, when shyness and astonishment have given way to hunger. His lips probed mine, burst through, and explored my mouth. Then his hands began to roam over my body. I felt my whole self rise to him, and

NOMI EVE

I returned the heat of his embrace. When he and his father rode off, I
cried so much my throat grew tight, and I had trouble breathing. My
mother dragged me into the house and made me stand over a steaming
pot of water until I could breathe.

"Ach, girl" she said in a rare show of compassion, as I collapsed
heaving into her bosom. "He will send for you in no time, and then you
will be his bride, his wife, the mother of his children." She put a hand
under my chin and lifted my wet tearful face. I could tell that she was
trying to be kind, but that she was also impatient for me to get on with
my chores.

That night I left my world and traveled to the world of strangers. I
snuck out of our house and followed the path Asaf had once shown me
to Ibn Messer's stables. His billowing tents perched on the littoral slope
behind my escarpment. It was Jamiya I was after. I had a ridiculous plan
to steal her and ride her south in pursuit of my beloved. So what if I had
never ridden before? So what if I didn't know the way? I would do what
I must to escape my abandonment. But of course I couldn't even saddle
the creature, and ended up crying in a corner of her stall. She was kind
to me, a moist, smelly animal-mother, nuzzling my face with her huge,
soft, nutty-breathed velvet mouth. Eventually I was found by a stable
servant and brought to the sheik himself. Ibn Messer looked at me, his
expression half a smile and half a frown. I was a novelty: a dirty, crying
Jewish girl.

"What is your story, little one?"

"Asaf, the boy, the Jew, is my husband. And now he is gone. I must
find him."

He raised a skeptical eyebrow, "Really? Your husband?"

"He will be my husband, when I . . . when we . . . mmph . . ." I blushed
purple and looked down at my feet.

"But child, no good would come of your giving chase. The boy and
his father are gone, you will find another to love."

My cheeks were on fire. "He is my intended. You see, we were
engaged. There is a contract."

"Little girl, don't cry. There, there."

"Please, sir," I said between sniffs, "you must know where they went.
You must tell me how to find them, they can't have gotten far."

Sheik Ibn Messer looked down at me with all the kindness of the ages radiating out of his eyes. He had an attractive face, etched by time, handsome in a way that the people of Qaraah called "hilltop handsome" for it was a quality of beauty that seemed to bring one closer to the sky and farther from the depths of Gehinom. But his eyes were dark. The sadness I saw there told me that the places where our stories met were rocky and steep. Perilous even. The servant returned, and spoke to Ibn Messer in hushed tones.

The sheik turned to me and said, "My dear, you have a friend, he has come for you. Or maybe it is your brother, come to see you safely home?"

I scrunched up my face, and was about to say, "Impossible, I came alone" when Binyamin Bashari came through the tent flap. He wouldn't look either at me or at the sheik in the flickering lamplight, but down at his feet, a deep serious blush on his wolf-muzzle face. It had been a few years since we had played together. And in such a short time, I had forgotten him, the way you can forget the most vivid parts of your childhood. But now I remembered everything. He was my friend. My playmate. He had followed me here. Had he also followed Asaf to my cave? Did he know what we did there together?

"I see you have a good sturdy chaperone, a brave lad, pure of heart, I am sure. But the night is dark. Should I send a servant with you both?"

"No, sir," I whispered, "we know the way. And if we are seen with anyone our mothers will beat us."

"I understand, little one. Go, go on your way. May the darkness shield you. And please, forget about your intended. But see to it that your mother finds you another husband soon. As soon as she can. Right? That's a good girl."

Binyamin silently took my hand. We stole across the dunes and up the escarpment. As we ran, I didn't speak to Binyamin. I didn't say, "Stop following me." I didn't say, "How did you know where I was?" I didn't say, "I didn't need you this time," because that would have been a lie. We didn't exchange a single word. And we parted behind my auntie's house, as we had parted a hundred times before when we were very small children, only this time, our journey had taken us farther than we had ever gone, and we were both forever changed for having traversed the nighttime path.

In the morning, when I awoke, I wasn't sure if I had really gone to

the stables of the sheik, or if I had just dreamed I had. Two nights later
I had a nightmare. In the morning I half remembered screaming and
kicking in the darkness with my father's cool hand on my hot brow, and
someone saying, "Sha, sha, little girl," in a voice that sounded like the
sheik's—low and melodious and full of bemused compassion.

The only token my uncle left behind in Qaraah was his tattered
deerskin Torah. I took this as a sign that they would one day return,
for who would leave an object so precious? It was one of my chores to
dust the chest in the upstairs men's salon. I knew where the key was
kept, and when no one else was in the house, I took to opening the
chest and looking at the cast-off little Torah. Sometimes I brushed my
hand on its hard curved case, even though I knew I shouldn't. Once I
even dared to take the Torah out of the chest and open it. The panel
of text that the Torah was rolled to had cracked words and moldy
dark spots over whole passages, but the poor condition didn't bother
me. I couldn't read, but I imagined my own portion of holy words. I
mouthed a strange, mixed-up parable about a girl, a cave, a boy, and
a visitation from a holy angel who did not wrestle with anyone, but
instead used his wings as a sheltering canopy under which the children
wrestled themselves.

My engagement contract was in the chest as well. I took it out several
times and let the Hebrew words wash over me like water. Sometimes I
dreamed about the contract. I dreamed that some of the words floated
up off the page and formed a wedding canopy over my head and that
other words floated up and formed Asaf, a boy made out of letters
who stood next to me and married me, as a rabbi also made of words
sanctified our union. I thought that I was the only flesh-and-blood
creature in the dream, though when Asaf put the ring on my finger, I
saw that my hand was also made of words.

I cried for weeks after Asaf and Uncle Zecharia left. My mother scolded
me for giving in to such fragile emotions. But she too gave in to her
passions.

"Your brother is a dog who sleeps in his own piss," she slandered Uncle
Zecharia. "He is an ass who eats his own shit. How dare he abandon

our daughter?" She ranted and raved at my father, and called my uncle horrible names, and so I knew that she was as perturbed as I was that my cousin and uncle had left Qaraah. In the early summer of 1928, not two months after they left, my mother dressed herself in her best antari, and plodded out of the house.

"Make your father lunch," she said, "and bring it to him before he dies of starvation."

I didn't know where she was going, and spent the afternoon doing as I was told. In the market, my father patted my head and shared his stew with me. We dipped lafeh bread in the meaty sauce. He was making a belt for a jambia, and showed me how he embossed the border with little triangles and squares. The stall smelled rich and alive and made me think of Jamiya, for her saddle had the same smell.

On my way home, I walked a wide berth around where the Confiscator and his wife had once found me sprawled with my persimmons. When I got home, my mother was there.

"Well, it's done."

"What?"

"You are free of that bastard wastrel."

"What?"

"You are free of Asaf."

"How could you call him such things?"

"What does it matter what I call him as long as he will never call you wife? Now we can betroth you to another."

"No."

"No what?"

"I won't. I refuse to marry anyone but my boy-cousin."

My mother's face contorted into a mocking grimace. "Refuse all you want. You are not mistress of your fate in this world. Perhaps you will hold the reins of fate in the World to Come."

I soon found out that my mother had gone to Rabbi Yusef Bar Yerush and paid him a whole Maria Theresa thaler to declare me an "abandoned bride," and thus no longer bound by the engagement contract my father and Uncle Zecharia had both signed. Of course she wasn't reckless enough to destroy the original document—the one that bound me to Asaf. My parents knew that it would prove crucial if my father were to die before a new groom could be found. In those days parents often commissioned small libraries of legal documents—one contradicting the other—each ready to be produced in a wink should it be needed to save a child from confiscation.

The same night my father brought the revocation home from the scribe, I stole it from out of the chest where they still kept Uncle Zecharia's deerskin Torah. While my parents slept, I threw the parchment into the hearth. As it crackled and burned, I saw strange things in the glowing flames—chief among them a vision of a dancing deer, which I took as a sign that Uncle Zecharia's Torah approved of my vandalism and that the deer who had sacrificed its hide for the words of the Law was a protective spirit, a totem of good luck and an intermediary between me and my uncertain fate. Before I returned to my pallet I thought of stealing other things—a piece of jewelry, a set of three silver spoons my mother treasured—in order to make it look as though we'd been ransacked. But in the end, I went to sleep without taking anything else or doing any further damage. That night, I dreamed of the young groom in Aden who flung himself on the Torah to protect it from burning. But in my dream it was Asaf who was the hero, and when he perished, it was the words of revocation that leapt from his body, like the mystic name writ in flames.

What I didn't know was that in addition to the revocation, she had paid the scribe to write two copies of a letter to Uncle Zecharia, informing him of the revocation. Then she paid a messenger to take one copy of this letter to Sana'a and a caravanner to take another copy to Aden—both letters addressed to associates of Uncle Zecharia. But I was ignorant of her treachery—had I known, I would have chased those letters to the far corners of the earth. Everyone would have spoken of me. I would have become a legend—a girl from Qaraah who turned herself into a mountain cat in order to overtake the messengers and dig her claws into their backs before they could tamper with her happiness. But I knew nothing of the letters, so I remained only a girl who sharpened her teeth and claws on nothing more than petty domestic trivialities. Just a few weeks after I destroyed the document, my mother went into the chest and saw that it was missing. She put me over her knees and beat my behind with a wooden spoon. Then she said, "Stupid girl, this was only a copy. There is another draft with the rabbi for safekeeping. Who do you think you are to try to thwart my plans?"

Part Two

Chapter 7

More than two years passed. I would be lying if I said that I spent those years doing anything other than praying for Asaf to come back. No one knew, of course. I kept my single-minded devotions to myself. The only ones to rebuke me were my little idols, my only true confidants, who grew tired of my doleful lamentations and urged me to stop pining for a boy who would never come back. At least that is what I imagined they said, as I offered them grain and sage and bowed my head to their altar.

Nothing remarkable happened in those years. But when I was eleven everything changed. One day my father stumbled on his way into our house, almost falling, catching himself with a surprised grunt. It was the winter of 1930. He had news to share. A letter in his hand. My mother worked at the table, stretching out jachnun dough. He explained that his younger brother, Barhun, Barhun's wife, Rahel, and their youngest daughter would be leaving their home in Aden and coming to live with us. My mother relinquished her tender hold on the dough and swore that Rahel Damari wouldn't cross her threshold, let alone come to live in her house.

"He is my brother." My father's voice rose and wavered at the same time; he was incredulous, angry.

"If they come, they won't leave," my mother yelled. "And if *she* comes here, I will leave you."

My mother had threatened many things in their twenty-four years of marriage, but never this.

"And where will you go?"

"Back to Taiz."

"You'll go nowhere, Sulamit!" My father coughed, a great heaving rattle, then grabbed my mother by the wrist and pulled her arm toward him, while at the same time almost pushing her shoulders away. They remained that way for a moment, locked in an insurmountable stasis.

"Make me stay and welcome the other Damaris and I'll poison your jachnun."

He hadn't let go of her, but she twisted her body and turned away from him. A great big glob of sputum flew from her lips and landed in the middle of the dough. It didn't soak in, but rested there like the white of an egg.

"Why?"

"They will ruin things. You'll see. They will ruin everything!"

I had been standing near the doorway. I stared at that spit, a glistening token of my mother's crude audacity. My father let go of my mother's wrists. But she wasn't the least bit cowed. She left the house slowly, arrogantly, not bothering to turn around and look back. My father and I were left alone together with that spoiled dough. Ignoring me, he sighed, went to the door, walked outside, and stood there for a moment with his hands up, as if beseeching the heavens for guidance.

I went over to the table and did what I thought my mother would do if she were in her right mind, which she clearly wasn't. I took a knife and cut out the glob of spit from the center of the jachnun. I pressed the remaining dough on top of itself and threw the spoiled dough in the slop pail. Then I took my mother's place at the table, rolling, stretching, and pressing. After all, I thought, whether the other Damaris were welcome or not, we still had to have dinner.

In my opinion, the other Damaris couldn't be coming at a better time, for I needed allies now more than ever. My aunt? If she were really a witch, then perhaps she could brew me a potion I could use to kill myself or to kill the man my mother was currently scheming to make my husband. My father still coughed and was thinner and sallower than ever. The Confiscator cast a long shadow over our lives. In the time since Asaf's departure, my mother had failed to find me a new groom. She had recently chosen Mr. Musa, the jeweler—the fattest and richest man she could find—to court me. She rightly believed that his girth and wealth would insulate him from the rumors and innuendos concerning my marriageability.

Just the week before the letter arrived from the other Damaris, she had made my father pay a visit to Mr. Musa. He was the sort of man who stayed fat even when others died of starvation. He was very old, wrinkly, smelly, and wealthy. His first wife had died childless, and his second wife was rumored to be an old toothless woman, who came to the marriage with three grown children of her own—though no one ever saw her, as she stayed confined in the house. Whoever married Mr. Musa next would be her sister-wife. According to my brother Hassan, Mr. Musa was looking for a "virgin" to make his Isaac days sweet as manna. "Isaac days" is what people called old age because Isaac, our Father, lived to be one hundred years old, the longest of the patriarchs. I had no intention of marrying a man as old as time, and swore to my mother that I would kill myself before agreeing to such a union. As usual, she paid no heed to my threats and snorted that I "would be made to marry a dog" if I continued to act "like a little bitch."

I knew that my parents made up the night that the letter came from Uncle Barhun, though the urgent sounds of their coupling were ordinary enough. As I lay on my pallet, I wondered what my aunt and cousin would look like, what clothes they would wear, and whether my cousin was skilled at cooking or sewing, or both. I wondered about my aunt. I didn't know why my mother hated her so much and I dreamed that she or my cousin could possibly help me avoid marrying Mr. Musa, as help me they surely must.

In the morning I overheard my parents discussing logistics. My brothers lived next door to us, in a little two-story house that my father had built before I was born, when my mother bore their sixth son. One by one, when they began to grow hair on their chins, my brothers had moved into the little house with the charming red roof. When they married, they moved out of it. Now only two were left—Hassan and Aaron. "Ephrim or Pinny can make room for Hassan and Aaron," my father said, referring to my two eldest brothers, both of whom had extra corners in their houses where one could lay a pallet.

"Mmpfh," my mother responded, adding, "Bad enough I have to welcome her, now you throw our own boys out of their beds?" I almost never saw Ephrim or Pinny or any of their many children. They lived on the other side of Qaraah. Later I heard my mother grumbling to Mrs. Bashari that she was on the "worse side of a bad trade. My beloved boys for that Adeni witch? Bad enough that she is coming to Qaraah, now I have to breathe the same air as her, and probably share my dinner table."

A few days later, I went to Auntie Aminah on the pretense of asking her to help me with my knitting. We bent over my wool; she tsked-tsked at my purposefully clumsy stitches and corrected my technique. I thanked her for her help, and made a few more mistakes simply so that she would have more opportunity to instruct me. But she knew that I had come for more than stitchery. She didn't disappoint and began to speak about my other aunt as if we had been in the middle of a conversation about her.

"I've never known the circumstances that led to Rahel meeting your Uncle Barhun," she said, "But what I do know is that it was a love match, not an arranged marriage. And your mother met Rahel only once—at Rahel and Barhun's wedding. Your mother came home from that trip saying that her brother-in-law had married a cow. Of course, I thought she meant that Rahel was fat and ugly, but what she really meant was that Rahel has an animal nature . . . though I do admit this was a strange way to put it."

"Are you saying that my mother called Aunt Rahel a *woman of valor*?"

This was a euphemism. It was taken from the Sabbath hymn of the same name that lists the attributes of a pious woman. But when muttered with a wink and a whisper, it referred to a woman who took pleasure in bed, not in the usual manner of wifely subservience, but with abandon, power, and passion, like men.

"Psha, girl, of course not. How would she know? I have no idea what she actually meant. An animal nature? For all I know she was referring to her stink, or her laugh. Maybe your Aunt Rahel smells like a goat or brays like a donkey. But I do think your mother is right to defy your father, right not to want them to come. Suli's fears may be justified"— Aminah and my father were the only ones who ever used my mother's nickname, Suli for Sulamit—"Your Aunt Rahel is the sort of woman who inspires gossips to flap their tongues."

"About what?"

Auntie Aminah squinted at me. "It is not for me to fill your ears with trash, filth, and misery. No, I will not repeat the rumors. But there are other reasons your mother doesn't want Rahel Damari to come. Reasons that have nothing to do with gossip. You see, with your brothers Hassan and Aaron still to be wed, she doesn't want any trouble. She doesn't know anything about Rahel Damari's daughter. She is a year older than you. What if she is a seducer? What if she is a bad influence on you and causes you to lose your morals? And what if she comes in between your brothers and their intended girls? The fact of the matter is that the child isn't engaged or married, even though she is of age. In Aden there is no fear of confiscation so there is no hurry with engagements, but of course once they are here, arrangements will have to be made."

Auntie Aminah was quiet for a moment. The clicking of our needles seemed like the chattering of insects engaged in their very own conversation. When she began again she said, "There is also the matter of Rahel Damari's profession."

"Henna?"

"Yes, henna."

"Why is this a problem?"

She snapped, "I didn't say it was a problem. Henna is henna, that's that." Startled by her rebuke, I felt my cheeks color and I looked down at my hands. I knew that was the end of our conversation. We worked the rest of the time in silence. I was knitting a pair of sleeping socks for my father. The wool was gray and knobby, but it was soft enough. I planned on giving him the socks for his birthday, just two Sabbaths hence. I didn't understand what my aunt meant. Even though I'd never had henna myself, I'd seen plenty of henna dyers, and none of them ever seemed dangerous.

All of my sisters-in-law had had Nights of Henna before their weddings. And every so often they went to one another's houses to adorn one another, either for festivals, or for no particular occasion. I had been in the room during their Nights of Henna, but was sternly forbidden to get even a tiny dab of my own. Jewish girls were always welcome in the henna house, but almost never wore elaborate patterned henna until they bled. Little girls were indulged with a smear on the palm on special occasions like marriages and births, and if a girl was very lucky, she emerged with a few elegant scribbles on her hand. But not me. I watched greedily as the women of our community adorned one another. And I would sulk home afterward, feeling so jealous that I thought my heart would burst. But my mother was adamant, and I knew better than to defy her on this.

By the time Uncle Barhun's letter arrived, even though I had never had my own henna, I knew enough about it to understand quite a lot about the process—simply from being a girl in Qaraah. I knew that for the most part, henna dyers were family members with fine, steady hands. They were knowledgeable in the usage of herbs and aromatic oils, and either volunteered their services for a bride, or agreed to the payment of a small sum for a more elaborate application. In our tradition, the hennaing of brides lasted from two to four days. The ceremony began with an application of a solid coat of henna paste up and down the bride's feet, shins, hands, and forearms. Then the bride was wrapped in special cloths known as *mehani*. The next day the cloths were unwrapped, the paste was washed off, and the bride's skin was revealed to be a deep reddish orange.

That's when the henna dyer came to perform her role. She brought with her a waxy aromatic mixture of resin, myrrh, frankincense, and iron sulfate. She heated the mixture over a small fire and then applied it with a stylus in intricate patterns. Then came the darkening of the henna with a caustic mixture of ammoniac and potash called *shaddar*. The henna dyer spread the shaddar. When it was removed, after an hour or two, the henna had turned a deep greenish-black, while the areas protected by the aromatic mixture retained their orange-red shade. The end results were elegant red designs on a background of very dark, almost black, skin. This was different from what occurred in the nonbridal henna house. When women met to adorn themselves for the new moon, for holidays, or for other special occasions, they didn't use the aromatic mixture or the shaddar. They simply applied henna with a stylus, left it to dry, and then sealed it with a coating of lemon sugar water—a much simpler process.

I shouldn't have wasted time wondering about my aunt, but since my mother was so against Rahel Damari's coming, she rose in my estimation and I imagined that she had special cosmetic gifts—like Viola, the wife of the lampmaker, who distilled the most potent perfumes, or Mary, the wife of Tomer the Scribe, who purchased only the finest imported malachite from the Timna valley, ground it into kohl, and then showed ladies how to outline their eyes to their best advantage.

The next morning, I went to visit my sister-in-law Masudah, who had recently given birth to her third son. When I came, she put an older baby, Shalom, on my lap and opened her dress to nurse his new brother. Her breasts came tumbling out, and the baby fussed for a moment before latching on to an enormous brown nipple. The baby on my lap reached for a clump of my hair. I let him curl his little fingers and tug so hard it hurt. I kissed his little upturned nose, and breathed in deep the yeasty, milky smell of him before I asked Masudah to tell me something about Aunt Rahel.

She didn't answer me immediately. She bit her lip, let out a big sigh. Then she looked at me intently. When she finally spoke she said, "Your Aunt Rahel was the most famous henna dyer in Aden. And not only in Aden. When she and Uncle Barhun were first married, they lived in Sana'a, so she is famous there too. She did the henna for so many brides that they used to call a bride she hennaed 'one of Rahel's blooms.' Your Uncle Barhun not only permits but also encourages her to practice her craft. She is even known to henna Muslim brides—the daughters of sheiks and the daughters of Turkish functionaries." Masudah knew this because she too was from a village near Aden and had grown up in the same community where Rahel attended brides. "Why, I had hoped she would do my henna when we were wed, but of course, I was married here in Qaraah, so it was not to be."

As for my girl cousin and the threat she posed to my brothers' morals, I had to laugh at the thought. I was sure my cousin was an elegant, sensitive creature and would want nothing to do with my brothers. My brothers were the real animals—goats crossed with gazelles, hairy beasts that rutted in the fields and grew skittish at their own shadows. At least this is how I thought of them when I was just a girl and they were already men.

Over the following days, I continued on my quest for information. My brother Aaron was thick, short, bucktoothed, and irritable. He cracked his knuckles and sneered at the mention of Uncle Barhun.

"Uncle Barhun is coming here to mooch off our father. You'll see, he'll sponge Father dry. And with all those daughters, there'll be nothing left for your dowry."

"But why are they coming?" I probed for answers. "I thought that Uncle Barhun's business was profitable." Of my father's two brothers, I knew that Uncle Barhun was the wealthier—at least he had been before the current misfortune, whatever it was.

"Umph . . ." Hassan was a taller, uglier version of Aaron. He had a finger in his mouth and was working on dislodging a piece of candied ginger from his molars. He gave up and wiped his fingers on his dirty *shamle.* "He's a coward and a simpleton, almost got himself killed in Aden, and is fleeing like a ratty dog."

Hassan had a tear in his left nostril, from an accident when he was a boy. While playing with some boys in a quarry, he had tripped, fallen, and ripped his nose open on a sharp piece of volcanic rock. The wound festered and had to be excised. When it healed, he was left with only half a nostril, and people called him Half Nose.

I tried to get more information out of my brothers, but they either knew nothing, or refused to satisfy my curiosity. When I asked Auntie Aminah why the other Damaris were suddenly descending on Qaraah, she just shrugged, and answered with uncharacteristic defeat. She was usually chock-full of information, but now she confessed to being left in the dark.

"Who tells an old woman about business dealings? No one. If you find out, little girl, make sure to come tell me."

It was my father who finally explained it to me. My mother had sent me to his market stall with a lunchtime bowl of stew. We sat together as he ate. The market was quiet, as it typically was in the middle of the day. My father's stall always smelled of cured calf's skin, shoemaker's pitch, beeswax. He had been working on a pair of *ghof* sandals for one of the Muslim town councilmen. The sandals were stitched with turquoise and silver threads. Stitching the leather was not difficult work, but it made my father's fingertips burn from pushing in the thick needle. I knew because when I helped him, my own fingertips stung and sometimes they even cracked and bled from the effort. When I arrived, my father was rubbing beeswax on his hands. I sat on one of the big leather pillow-stools, waiting for my father to finish his lunch. I must have felt very bold that day, for I opened my mouth and asked why exactly it was that the other Damaris were coming to live with us. My father looked at me the way I imagined a teacher must look at a boy in Torah school when he asks for knowledge reserved for others. He made a sound as if he would speak, then he stopped. When he opened his mouth again he spoke to me in a way I hadn't heard before, as if I weren't just a child, or a young girl, but someone who actually deserved answers to big questions.

"It's like this, Daughter," he began. "In Aden, the coffee-export trade is ruled by a few foreign establishments, most notably the Barde et Cie corporation from Lyon. But the foreign traders mostly concentrate on the larger business of exporting beans to Europe. It's left to the small merchants, like your uncle, to perpetuate the petty trade among the Red Sea dhow captains who buy and sell coffee in between Aden, Djibouti, and Berbera. Your Uncle Barhun was one of these petty traders, with a stall in the market in Little Aden and a connection to a small but profitable interest in the Barde et Cie domestic coffee exchange. Just after the New Year, Barhun was cheated by a customer, and when he lodged a complaint with the British customs functionary at the port, the cheating customer hired men to beat Barhun, and to destroy his small warehouse, torching it in the middle of the night. He was lucky to escape with his life," my father said, exhaling. The look on his face was terribly pained, as if he had witnessed the beating himself. "And of course he will be welcome here. He can depend upon us for refuge."

I had no idea what happened in the next month to change my mother's mind. But as the date of the other Damaris' arrival approached, my mother not only agreed *not* to leave my father but also roundly declared to the women at the well that she knew it was her duty to greet the Damaris and treat them as kin. Another child might have thought this about-face strange, but my mother was temperamental, and it was not uncommon for her to swear one thing and do another.

Chapter 8

Two weeks after the arrival of Uncle Barhun's letter, Mr. Musa came to Sabbath lunch. I served him his jachnun and *hilbeh* and precious hard-boiled eggs. For the entire meal, he spoke in proverbs. By the time the coffee was served and the men began to chew their khat, he had already proclaimed, "Work like an ant and you'll eat sugar"; "Who dies today is safe from tomorrow's sin"; and "A monkey in its mother's eye is like a gazelle." He picked his teeth as I cleared his dishes. After I was done helping with lunch, I went out back and sat underneath our frankincense tree. In no time at all, Mr. Musa found me. I tried to walk away. He followed. I slipped through the opening in the wall leading to the dye mistress's yard. He followed me again, and I looked over my shoulder, surprised that such a fat, decrepit man could fit through the narrow passage. I'm sure he would have continued to chase me, but instead of going farther, I turned to face him.

"Mr. Musa," I said, "please leave me alone. I am unchaperoned, it is unseemly for you to—" but before I finished my sentence, he grabbed me by the crook of my arm and began to paw at the front of my dress.

"Let me go," I hissed, but he pulled me toward him. I smelled his foul onion breath. My heart raced in my chest. I noticed a wart on his right cheek, white hairs sprouting out of his nose. He bent toward me, puckered his gray, flaky lips, and almost pressed them into my own. But before he could force himself upon me, he screamed and fell cursing into a big trough full of purple dye.

"That's right, little girl" the dye mistress said. She was standing behind Mr. Musa with one hand on a hip. "You tell that horrible man to leave you alone."

She had come out of her house, snuck up behind Mr. Musa, and hit him over the head with a clay pot.

Mr. Musa dragged himself out of the trough. The dip had dyed his earlocks—dripping bruised wormy streaks on his pouchy cheeks. His shamle was dyed purple, and his huge belly looked like a swollen eggplant over his pants. As he slogged out of the yard cursing the two of us, I couldn't help but laugh, covering my mouth with my hands.

"Remember, it is no shame for a girl not to be wed." The dye mistress put down the pot next to the trough. She came and stood next to me, and patted my forearm. "There can even be happiness in a spinster's lot. Look at me." She spread out her hands, gesturing to the kaleidoscope of troughs and to the many-hued pieces of cloth hanging from lines around the edge of the yard. "If Jacob our Father asked, I could make Joseph another coat of many colors. I am blessed with my work. If you ever need a profession to earn your keep, you come to me and I will teach you my craft."

People gossiped about what had happened. They said that Mr. Musa had imbibed too much Sabbath arak at lunch and mistook the dye mistress's yard for ours, tripping on a crack in the path. Only I knew that he had followed me there, and that the dye mistress had saved me from his thuggish advances. The day before the other Damaris arrived, I left her a small basket of aromatic soap in between her troughs. Then I sat for a little while, losing myself in the colors of all the drying cloth. Saffrons and blues and reds and yellows and, of course, purples. I looked at the vat that had proved Mr. Musa's undoing. The deep purple was almost black, so dark that my face, reflected only barely, seemed to float on the surface of a starless, moonless sky. I felt so melancholy and filled with longing for Asaf. I wondered where Asaf was at that very moment. If he was on land or at sea. In Africa, Arabia, or Asia? If he was eating or praying, or striking a bargain with a purveyor of rare perfumes. I wondered if he knew that I still slept with his little amulet under my pillow. I thought about what the dye mistress had done—how she had protected me. I saw myself. I was wearing Jacob's coat of many colors. I lifted my arms and every tint of the rainbow shimmered down from my arms. I was cloaked in glory like a bird with incandescent wings.

My father called for me. "Adele, where are you? Adela, Adeellla . . ." I dropped a little stone into the trough, breaking the taut canvas for my visions. I left the sanctuary of the dye mistress's yard just as her father was coming outside. A cheerful little green bird perched on his arm twittered and sang as the old blind man whistled—the two seemingly engaged in a very pleasant conversation.

When I got back home my father was standing by the rear window. My mother was sitting on the low stool in front of the hearth.

It was strange to see her sitting in the middle of the day.

"What is it, Mother?"

"You should know, Daughter . . ."

"Know what?"

"Mr. Musa has graciously agreed to marry you. You will be formally engaged before this coming Sabbath. And he will marry you two Sabbaths after you first bleed. You are already eleven, almost twelve, so it can't be long hence."

His onion breath. Those fat, flaky lips. His hands pawing at me. And who was the wife at home? I had never seen her, not once at the market and never at synagogue, but I had overheard my brothers cawing that Mr. Musa's wife was an invalid and that he married her because her strange infirmities inflamed his nighttime sorties, his elephantine thrusts.

"But . . ."

"But what?" My mother's voice was gritty with impatience and frustration.

I spoke so low it was almost a whisper. "But we are not suited for each other."

I heard a sound come out of my father's throat. A cross between a gasp, a cough, and a sigh. He walked out the door, and I heard him saddle up Pishtish the donkey.

"What did you say?"

"Mr. Musa and I. Surely you know that we are not the least bit friends."

Did she laugh? Or did she cry with me, her sobs watering my own? Is this a chronicle or a parable? A history or a heartbeat? *Sha, sha, little girl. Sha, sha. Don't cry. Crying will not change your fate, now, will it? Will it?*

It happened, as she said it would, just two days later.

"Don't cry, Adela. Do you think you are the first girl to be promised to a man she doesn't favor? Such is the way of the world," my mother hissed at me, tugging at my gargush; then she spit on her fingers and dabbed at an invisible spot on my right cheek.

"Leave her be, Suli." My father had just come into the house. He sat down heavily at the table and began to cough. When he caught his breath, he said, "Mr. Musa will be here in fifteen minutes. The rabbi is on his way." Then he looked at me and said, "Adela, the Confiscator ordered two new pairs of shoes this morning. And he asked after your health. I told him that you were to be engaged today, and you know what he did? He ordered a third pair in your honor. *Use the proceeds for a dowry gift for your little girl*, he said. And that is what I will do. I will buy you a lazem necklace for your wedding day." He looked down at his hands as he said this—as if he knew that the finery was of no use to me, and that the Confiscator's words were nothing but a reminder of the yoke we wore.

I almost didn't say anything, but then I asked, "What shoes did he order?"

My father smiled. "Bashmag sandals and holiday shoes with a little heel. He asked for the tulip border design. Your favorite."

I went and sat on his lap, as I used to when I was a very little girl, and for a few moments before the ceremony, I imagined that I wasn't facedown in the dirt of my life, but standing on the high, clear crest of the mountain of it. I had been eight years old when I was engaged to Asaf, now I was almost twelve and engaged to a man old enough to be my grandfather. My father kissed my hair. Patted my back. He whispered into my ear, "You can come and help me with the shoes if you'd like. Your hands are nimble, and I always enjoy your company, little rabbit. Sha, sha, Adeloosh, all will be well." He wiped away my tears with the corner of his sleeve, and held me tight as I burrowed my face in his neck.

Mr. Musa humored my mother and wore the triangle amulet neck ring for the ceremony—the same one that all of my brothers had worn at their engagements, the same one that Asaf had worn when we were engaged as small children. It was much too small for his fat neck so he wore it on a chain, hanging low over his fat belly. During the ceremony I had repulsive thoughts. I imagined that the baby teeth in the amulet belonged to a demon baby who would bite Mr. Musa, drawing blood, maybe even severing his jugular. When the rabbi pronounced us engaged, I imagined that the nails in the amulet were being hammered into his fingers, and when my father signed our engagement document, I imagined that the mercury was in his eyes, making him a true monster, with silver eyeballs, a groom so grotesque my revulsion was more than justified.

Afterward, I drank all the arak from the leftover glasses. Soon I was retching, heaving, and crying all at once out in the garden, my face a mess of snot and vomit and tears.

Masudah held my hair back. Sultana brought a cool cloth for my face. When my mother came she took one look at me and went into the house. She came back out with an amber vial and uncorked it. "Drink this," she ordered. I took two sips, and she said, "Not enough."

"But Mother, I can't." She reached out, held my nose, tilted back my head, and before I could struggle I had swallowed the rest of the contents of the vial.

"You will vomit for another hour or so, but in the morning, your head will be clear." She turned around, stomped away, and left me there with my sisters-in-law. They took care of me. In the morning, I awoke with my body so empty and my head so clear I could see my life backward and forward, and I was convinced of one true thing: no matter what else happened to me in my life, I wouldn't marry Mr. Musa.

Kicking my feet. Wiggling my dusty toes. Sweating under my gargush. It was five days after my engagement. I had finished my chores, and was sitting on the fence in front of our house. My head was stuffed with jagged thoughts. Should I kill myself to avoid the disastrous marriage that awaited me? Or run away, which would amount to the same thing, as there was nowhere to run but into the desert? I was imagining the way my bones would look—askew in the sand, picked clean by hungry buzzards—when I first spotted my uncle. *Clop clop clop, creak creak, jangle jangle.* The donkey cart announced their arrival. Barhun Damari was riding sidesaddle on a sturdy black donkey. How did I know it was he? I felt a tug. My life being pulled this way and that. As if he were holding not only those reigns, but also my fate in the sure grip of his thumb and forefingers.

Another two donkeys were pulling a cart filled with furniture and crates of belongings. Riding behind the cart on a fourth donkey was a woman I assumed was my aunt. Riding in the back of the cart was my cousin, Hani Damari. She jumped out the moment she saw me, and came skipping down the road and into my life, changing it forever.

Hani, with her sensual, puckered lips and already womanly hips that
swung from side to side.

By the time I had jumped off the rail to run and greet them, Hani was
already in front of our house. She was much taller than I. Dark eyes, full
lips, a broad nose that made her look a bit like a she-tiger. She was the
prettiest girl I had ever seen.

"Oh how I have missed knowing you! Tell me everything about you!
Tell me now, right now!" She cooed and petted me. This girl, the youngest
of four living sisters, was an expert in the intimate art of sisterhood. She
wrapped herself around me, enveloping me in her chestnut-colored
arms, smelling of cloves and roses and hibiscus and cinnamon. She didn't
wear a gargush; her hair was covered with a black and brown kerchief
instead, and she wore a black traveling tunic and gray pants.

"Adela, you must forgive Hani," Uncle Barhun said affectionately.
"We have been on the road too long, and she has become like a wild
animal. Hopefully here in Qaraah she will be domesticated. Eh? More
like you, a little lady. With this perhaps you could help?" He looked like
my father, and like Uncle Zecharia, but he was infinitely more handsome
than either of them. He had all of his teeth. His nose was roguishly
crooked. And his complexion was smooth, except for a puckered scar
under his right eye that looked fresh, for the skin around it was still
pink, and the scar itself had that shiny sheen of a newly formed layer
of flesh.

Alerted by the commotion, my father had come out of the house.
Uncle Barhun smiled broadly when my father held out his arms, face
alight. My father also smiled a wide happy smile, showing his black
front teeth and missing left incisor. As they hugged, then parted, then
hugged again, my father made a series of sounds, like an "aha aha,"
crossed with a laugh and a tender throaty exclamation, which, when
combined, all sounded to me like the celebratory cackling of a well-fed
buzzard. I was embarrassed by my father's sounds, and looked away,
showing that I didn't really belong to him, at least not the way Hani
belonged to her handsome, elegant father.

Aunt Rahel had hung back while my cousin had surged forward,
but when she finally emerged from behind Uncle Barhun's broad
shoulders, I was confused. I squinted. I looked her right in the eyes,
and then away, for I was embarrassed, and I could see that she too was
unsure of herself. I looked back. I thought that she must be the wrong

aunt, for there seemed absolutely nothing extraordinary about her. She was just a typical woman, small-hipped, with good-enough teeth and pretty-enough black eyes, but with none of the beauty or vivacity that blazed from her daughter. I had imagined my Indian aunt billowing into our lives dressed in a brilliant sari, perhaps of gold or yellow silk. But instead she wore common garb—a gray cotton dress and black trousers without a stitch of embroidery. The only bit of color was the magenta and green embroidery on her cuffs. Like her daughter, she didn't wear a gargush, but her head was covered with a simple black scarf. I peeked at her again. She had a nondescript face, one you could easily overlook in a crowd. She *was* Indian and so her skin was a different shade of brown than our toasted sesame complexions, more like tea left to steep overnight.

"Come, Rahel," Uncle Barhun said, but she barely moved.

"Come," he said again, urging, but not criticizing. "Come say hello to Adela. Adela, this is your aunt."

"So you are Adela?"

"I am."

"Hello, Adela."

"Welcome, Aunt Rahel."

She reached up to touch my cheek, a tender gesture. As her hand fluttered back down, I noticed Aunt Rahel's henna—the red geometric flurry that covered her fingers, the backs of her hands. The elements were arranged in patterns I had never seen before. They seemed to tell stories at once simple and incomprehensible. But other than her henna, nothing about her seemed—at least on the surface—intriguing or mysterious.

Hani thrust her hand into mine, asking me one hundred questions all at once about the fairy tales I knew, the secrets I didn't, the stories I would maybe be so kind as to finish for her, for she had come to a point in the plot that needed a fresh perspective.

When the cart arrived, my mother had come out of the house. From the very first moment, she was rude to Rahel and less than deferential to Barhun. "Here," she said, showing Rahel the path that led to the well. "There"—she pointed the way to the wadi where we washed clothes— "behind the stump of the thorn tree." She shrugged in the direction of the outhouse. She snorted out skimpy little answers in a bitter voice, barely looking Rahel in the eye, and letting it be known from the outset that a wide gully existed between our families, one that she wouldn't cross willingly. As for Uncle Barhun, she wouldn't look at him directly. When he tried to compliment her cooking, hospitality, or housekeeping, she barely nodded, and then looked away peevishly. Later, my parents would fight over this. My father even struck my mother on the left cheek, leaving an ugly welt. And I saw my mother spit again—not in dough, but in his face.

Yet that first night, they didn't pay any attention to each other at all. My father acted as if he didn't notice my mother's rude behavior, and welcomed his brother and sister-in-law with the giddy smile of a man who had kneeled down to drink in a river and instead of his own reflection, sees his own boyhood staring back at him from the mossy depths. My father laughed, drank too much arak, and sat next to Barhun with an arm draped over his shoulder. Barhun towered over his big brother, but was gracious enough to sink down in the pillows and slouch so that my father didn't have to reach too high in order to embrace him.

Almost immediately, my mother ordered me to take Hani next door and help her unpack and change out of her traveling garb. Hani shed her clothes, and I must have made a sound. She turned to look at me, but instead of chastising me for insulting her modesty, she giggled and then held up her hands and showed me her forearms, palms, fingers, and then her feet and ankles, proud of their abundant adornment.

I learned that night that the only way to know that girl, to know her truly, was to know her henna. Hani's clothes may have been plain, but she was the fanciest creature I had ever seen. Hani and her big sisters, the other Damari girls, wore henna all the time. That first day I had no idea why they were always decorated—though of course there was a reason. With the other Damaris there were always reasons, and stories behind the reasons, and reasons behind the stories. But I didn't need to know why. At least not yet. That first time she stood before me, revealing the designs on her naked skin, lush and swirling with age-old geometric mysteries, all I wanted to do was admire her, drink her in.

And she was so proud. Shamelessly, and with guileless pride, she pointed out special embellishments in the designs—a single seashell, a tiny swirling conch on each of her fingertips. She spread open her hands, so that I could see each one. Big stars on her palms and interlacing rosettes on her ankles. Eyes of God on the tops of her feet. The leaves of a laurel tree wrapped like a wreath around her elegant wrists.

As she showed off, I noticed not only Hani's henna but also her body. Lithe, dark like her mother, with full pear-shaped buttocks, lighter breasts, sparrow-wing hips, a concave belly. When she took off her kerchief I saw that she had the most marvelous hair—curly and dark like coffee, with glints of red and gold glistening on the ends of corkscrews. She was tall, like her father, and although she looked mostly like her mother, only prettier, she had something of Uncle Barhun's strong features in the powerful current of her face. I lost myself in the inscriptive bounty of her henna, and in her unabashed nakedness. The dazzling henna designs played tricks on my eyes and made her look simultaneously more exposed and more hidden, as if her henna was at once transparent and opaque.

"Don't blush, little cousin." Hani pulled on a clean shift and wrapped her arms around me. "And don't be jealous; soon enough my mother and I will henna you too." She reached out and wiped big fat tears out of my eyes, tears I hadn't even known were there. Why was I crying? Because Hani and her henna changed everything. I didn't know that then, of course, but I did know immediately and viscerally that henna was what separated me from this new blazing star of a cousin, and that if I was to be one of her tribe, I would also need to wear those tattoos.

I learned many things that first night. "Why aren't you married already?" I asked, for surely she was of age. "Shouldn't you already have wed?" While the others were still eating, a dinner of chicken stew, eggs, olives, and hilbeh, Hani took me aside, clutched my arm, and told me that she was in love with a boy she left behind in Aden. "His name is Ovadia, Ovadia Shabazzi, and he is the son of a book trader."

"You are in love? Do your mother and father know about him?" I was gape-mouthed, full of questions, heady with the flush of being taken into confidence, but mostly I was astonished. I had never heard of a girl arranging her own marriage. She laughed, an arrogant throaty laugh.

"Of course they know, and I will have their blessing. But it doesn't matter whether I do or don't. I will marry him, you'll see. And what is the rush?"

"The Imam—"

"Psha, if the Imam comes for me, Ovadia will vouch for an engagement. And if not him, there is Yusof Bin Turo, the schoolmaster's son, or Amnon Dishdashta, the son of the warehouse manager in Little Aden. Any of them would marry me in a second—and not only to save me from your dreadful Imam," Hani said with disdain. Then she scrunched up her face, put a hand under my chin. "And what about you, little girl? I hear that you were engaged to be married to another one of our cousins. What is his name? Asaf? But he ran off and left you? My father tells me that he is our eldest uncle's youngest son."

With the mention of Asaf's name, I felt a flash of panic, as if his leaving had actually coincided with Hani's arrival. My longing for him felt fresh and raw.

"No," I insisted, "he didn't abandon me. He had to leave; his father made him go."

"And you haven't heard from him?"

I shook my head.

"And now what is this? You are betrothed to an old man? To be his second wife?"

Tears fell down my cheeks.

"Don't worry." Hani dabbed my tears with her own sleeve. "You are only eleven, right? Many girls don't bleed until they are thirteen. Maybe this Musa person will die and you can come with us back to Aden one day, where you can pick your own groom and write your own fortune in the blood of your marriage bed."

I flinched, shuddered, my whole body possessed by a powerful force that traveled up my spine and made my face hot, my skin cold.

"Oh, poor little bird." She petted my arm, and spoke in purring, comforting tones. "Don't worry. Perhaps the Imam will be assassinated and his successor will revoke the Orphans Decree. Then the decree will be lifted, and children need no longer marry . . . Look how shocked you are!" Hani laughed. "Poor dear, you are starved for audacity. Don't worry, I will toughen you up."

I couldn't help but smile. The truth is, I wasn't shocked at all. Just relieved. Relieved that this brazen girl had arrived to be my bulwark against the future. I had never heard girls speaking so subversively. Where had she come from? What kind of creature was she really?

* * *

While our parents were drinking coffee, smoking hookahs, and eating baklava, we girls sucked on ginger candy and cracked sunflower seeds. Hani lay languidly back on the big embroidered pillows that smelled of wheat husks and woodsmoke. She wore a little puckered pouch on a leather thong around her waist.

"Adela, sweet girl, would you like to sort through my treasures?"

She took off the pouch, opened it, and let the contents come tumbling out in her lap. Out came a miniature set of dolls. They had shiny white cowrie beads for heads, cork bodies, and translucent aquamarine beads for hands and legs, all held together by metal wire. Hani picked up the dolls one by one and handed them to me. "This one is the mother; you can see that she has six children. This is the baby, my favorite. I will have double that many children, maybe even more."

I nodded, agreeing with her, though I didn't know what I was agreeing to. There was also a tiny, mottled, chipped sapphire in the pouch, "from a one-eyed man in the market who said he was a Kashmiri, but I think he was a Turk." A sprig of something that smelled like wall rue and a tiny book of psalms, which I think surprised me the most. Hani picked it up and paged to Psalm 102. "Here," she said, "this is one of my favorites, *I am like a pelican of the wilderness; I am become as an owl of the waste places.*" I couldn't read and marveled at Hani's command of letters. Like all the girls in Qaraah, I memorized prayers, but couldn't read a single letter, let alone a whole psalm.

That night, after showing me her treasures, Hani told me about her sisters. The two eldest, the twins, were buried under an acacia tree in Aden. Edna, the next one, was married to a scribe and was mother to three daughters already. The next one, Hamama, could tell the future. And Nogema was married to a British gentleman and dreamed of studying history, like an English girl, and becoming a teacher.

When the other Damaris left us for the night, I slept on my pallet, as usual, in the room with my parents. But in the middle of the night, I got up. I shed my blankets, stood at the window, looking at what was now their little house. I stared into their dark window and thought of the stories Hani had told me about their travels, *We came across a lost girl who claimed she was from Shahara. We almost took her with us, but she was crazy—screaming about scorpions and pulling out her own hair. And did I tell you about the Ethiopian lout in Al Ma'afer who fell down drunk in the road?*

My head was still suffused with the dreamy lazy feeling I got from sipping my father's arak. Hani's hands had been in my hair, making a long braid, and then lifting it up and kissing the nape of my neck. Was that me giggling when my whole body shivered? Her hands, petting me, reassuring me that I was one of them. Those other Damaris. *One of us sisters, now, truly.* Or did I just imagine that is what she said?

Over the next week, my new aunt went about transforming the little house with the red roof. When I stepped inside, I marveled. Could it be the same place? My brothers' smelly lair? And had all these delicate treasures been packed and piled up on the donkey carts? Rahel Damari had not arrived wearing silver ornaments or exotic clothing, but her house was a sight to behold. On the biggest wall she hung a dark green velvet tapestry decorated with lotus flowers and jungle animals, all embroidered with silver and gold thread. On the opposite wall she had hung a tapestry embroidered with a double satin stitch of gold, maroon, yellow, and indigo. In the center of the cloth was a circle of colorful women holding hands, their joined bodies forming a large flower. On tables and the backs of chairs she'd laid patchwork pieces of maroon silk adorned with cowrie shells and iridescent beetles' wings. A lush carpet with bluish-red palmettes covered the floor. I took off my shoes and walked across it barefoot; I had never before felt anything so soft. There were high-necked jars of rosewater perfume, a samovar with a pomegranate finial and two brass dragon handles, a collection of eight ivory elephants that held each other's tails, biggest to smallest. My mother hated finery, refused to adorn the walls, and laid the floor with the plainest dull brown hemp rug. We had only two decorations: a single small tapestry showing two little jade hummingbirds flying toward an orange fruit, and an engraving of the Portuguese warships in the port of Aden that my father had received as a gift from a customer who had mistakenly believed that my father had an interest in maritime lore. The dullness of our own house rebuked me for my own plainness, assuring me that I belonged in the emptiness, and not over here, in the other Damaris' lush jungle. But the colorful walls and soft floor weren't all there was to marvel at. Aunt Rahel had set up a laboratory on three little tables, with her vials of essential oils—tea tree, lavender, rose— and her pots of honey, red wine, baskets of lemons and limes, and all the many pouches and glass bottles of spices she added to her brews—vanilla, nutmeg, cardamom, cinnamon, peppers, and rosemary leaves.

Aunt Rahel had been out by the grinding stones. Now she came inside, and saw me standing there. She came up behind me, put a hand on my back, and gently urged me forward. "Uncork anything you want, little niece. Breathe in deep, Adela, ahhh, it's good, isn't it? I tell myself that the mixture of all my herbs and oils together is what Eden must have smelled like on the sixth day of Creation. When Elohim had made everything but us. What do you think it smells like? What is your opinion?"

Chapter 9

It didn't take long for the rumors to follow Aunt Rahel to Qaraah. Late one day, about a month after her family's arrival, Hani ran to our house, out of breath, tears running down her face. There was a wild look in her eyes, and her hair was falling out of her kerchief. In our doorway she seemed to struggle with herself. Clutched in her hands was a henna stylus, which she threw down to the ground, discarding it like a sword with a blunt tip, a weapon that would do no good in actual battle. She heaved, taking big gulps of air. My mother pulled her through the doorway. Then they sat together on the wheat-husk pillows. Hani cried in my mother's lap like a small child, racked with sobs. My mother, with the distasteful but dutiful motions of a reluctant nurse attending a leper, ran her fingers through Hani's hair. "Sha, sha," she said, "sha, sha, all will be well," consoling her in a way I don't remember ever being comforted.

When she could speak, Hani explained, "We were at the wadi, my mother and I, and a woman we didn't know approached us. She was cursing and threatening to burn mother with a hot poker if she dunked her bucket in the water."

"Why? Why would she do that?" I was astonished, outraged. How could someone insult Aunt Rahel? Shame her in public?

Hani glared at me, her chest still heaving. Crumpled up on my mother, she was twisted, holding her side to quiet the stitch in it. But her eyes were narrowed, darker than usual, and filled with disappointment. I had failed. But failed at what? I heard my voice, running ahead, repeating myself, prattling like a baby, "Why would she insult your mother?"

Hani's eyes said, *How could you not know? How could you be so stupid to even ask?* My mother must have seen how Hani looked at me. She puffed herself up and patted Hani's brow. "Sha, sha, Hanele," she said, and I could see that she was glad for this proof that Hani hadn't entirely taken me into her confidence.

That night, no one in our family mentioned the shameful incident. Everyone spoke loudly, and about trivial things. Uncle Barhun was mostly silent and reserved, and he looked "seams out," which is how my auntie always said people look when they refuse to show the world their true emotions. Aunt Rahel wasn't there; she had stayed in the little house with the red roof, and didn't emerge until late the next day. When she did, her face was pale and drawn, her eyes red, and she barely spoke as we all cooked, served, and ate supper.

Auntie Aminah heard the story from one of the women at the little well. The next day we sat knee to knee, sunk comfortably together on the rug and pillows by her sewing table. She was hard at work, unraveling an old sweater to be reused for wool for winter socks. She explained it to me quickly, spitting out the words as if they had a bitter taste. "The woman at the wadi was Mrs. Bar Yonah, the potash man's wife. She had been to a wedding ceremony in Sana'a many years ago, where it was rumored that your Aunt Rahel had seduced the groom . . . That's right, the groom, a boy of sixteen. According to Mrs. Bar Yonah, the wedding was almost canceled, the boy dishonored, the girl left a virgin. But, as the accusations couldn't be verified, the wedding went forth. But now, years later, Mrs. Bar Yonah recognized Rahel Damari, dropped her bucket, and launched into her vicious tirade."

Auntie Aminah finished speaking and took a deep whistling breath through her nose, then let out a rattling cough. She had come to a hard knot. I reached for the sweater to help her.

"Do you think it's true?"

"Adela . . ."

"It can't be true—"

"Adela . . ."

"What, Auntie?"

"Adela, there are some women who attract lies like a thumb dipped in honey. And then there are other women who are the bees, and sting for spite. And then there are other women who are the honey, the nectar, the sweetness that drives men and women mad for want of it."

"And which is Aunt Rahel?"

Auntie Aminah reached out and took my hand in her own. Her knuckles were thick, the skin of the back of her hand wrinkled and soft, the color of old sun-kissed leather.

"Which do *you* think she is?"

I opened my mouth to defend my new aunt, but then I closed it without issuing either a defense or an indictment of her character. I asked, "But why doesn't Uncle Barhun defend her honor? Why doesn't he make an indictment? Take Malkah Bar Yonah to court? Surely he has due reason? After all, it is a husband's right to defend his wife from slander." Auntie Aminah shook her head. "Your uncle will not publicly defend your aunt. But not because he doesn't trust her, or think she is an honorable wife."

"Then why not?"

"Adela, everyone knows that henna is not permanent, it fades with time. So will these accusations. But to air them in public, to make a complaint to the court, will only set the dye deeper into the soul of anyone who listens."

We sat in silence for the rest of my visit. We continued to untangle the sweater, until it was entirely deconstructed and lay like a heap of shredded rags in our laps. I left Auntie Aminah's, and walked slowly home, going through the backyards, even though there was no reason for me to hide. When I got to the dye mistress's house, she was crouching by one of her pots, stirring a vat of orange. She smiled when she saw me. I noticed that a few strands of the hair peeking out of her gargush were white. I wondered how old she was. She seemed to be Masudah's age, thirty-three. But she also seemed younger, because she had never had babies. At the same time, her graying hair made her seem older. Her body was lithe, her hips tiny. "Where have you been, little girl? Not hiding anymore? Hmmm, well, I think I know the reason for that frown. The mess with your new aunt at the wadi? Of course I know. Everyone knows everything in Qaraah. Well, don't you worry; soon enough the gossips will have something else to chatter about."

I said, "She is innocent. I know she is."

"Of course she is, dearie."

I passed out of her yard. But instead of going straight inside the house, I stayed out back and sat in the saddle of the old frankincense tree. I examined what I knew. Since arriving in Qaraah, Aunt Rahel had been nothing but kind to me and to everyone she met. Other than her henna, there was nothing startling about her. The only thing unusual about their family was that she and Uncle Barhun seemed to actually love each other. I had never before seen a husband drape his arm around a wife's waist, or call her "my beloved," as Uncle Barhun called my aunt. As for the accusations? Surely if Aunt Rahel was a loose woman, Uncle Barhun would throw her out of the house, divorce her, or at least beat her. Why, I knew of women who had been beaten to death by their husbands for a lesser offense.

I resolved to find out everything I could about Aunt Rahel. I couldn't ask Hani, because if she had wanted to tell me herself, she would have, and I couldn't ask my mother, as she would slap me for even wanting to know, and I couldn't ask my father, for I feared that whatever mysteries there were to know about my aunt could be explained only by mothers, sisters, or aunts.

The next afternoon, after I finished my chores, I went to visit my sister-in-law Masudah. Masudah had two babies on her lap, ten-month-old Suri, and her newborn, Shalom. She handed me Suri, who had a tiny upturned nose and very long dark eyelashes. Her cheeks were big and rosy, like her mother's. Around her neck was a strand of cubical amber beads. Masudah had bought them from a Muslim bride. Jewish brides didn't wear amber, yet Jewish mothers sought out the beads and draped them on their babies, to borrow the protection that the stranger magic could confer. Little Suri reached a hand up and pulled my hair. I uncurled her fingers from my locks and kissed them. Then I leaned back with her on the pillows of the divan and let her play with the cowries on my dress. I loved Masudah's house. It was an airy, lighthearted place filled with a bustle of children, toys, a riot of color. Masudah had a red rug on the floor, blue and green tapestries on the walls, as well as drawings that she drew—pictures of people or places in Aden, where she was from. I loved looking at Masudah's pictures. She was very good at faces and expressions. She had sketched me a couple of times, but I liked her pictures of other people much better than my own portraits. She didn't only make the drawings, she also made the paper herself.

There was nowhere to buy paper in Qaraah, and Sana'an paper was very expensive. Once or twice a year, Masudah boiled a big vat of rags in lime and then rolled the rags up into balls and kept them damp in a barrel behind her house. The water fermented the rags and helped break them up. After several months, she took them out and beat them to a pulp. Usually my brother Dov would do the heavy beating for her—he even fixed up a barrel with a blade in the bottom that you could turn using a handle on the outside. This made the work much easier. They would put the fermented pulp inside and turn the handle until the mixture was a creamy paste. When the paste was ready, she mixed it with fine sawdust that she procured from a carpenter. Then she poured it into a rectangular sieve and pressed it with a heavy wooden block to squeeze out extra water. She put the "sheet" between layers of felted cotton and squeezed it again and again and laid the sheets out in the sun to dry.

Masudah and my brother lived near the ritual bath. Women were always trooping by, either on their way to or returning from their monthly dip. Masudah liked to look out her window and see who was coming or going. She always laughed that she knew who was expecting long before anyone else, because if a woman didn't visit the ritual bath, it was a sure sign that a baby was on the way. But Masudah generally kept confidences, and gossiped only when she had a compelling reason.

"Mmumph—" I opened my mouth and shut it again.

"What is it, Adela?"

"Nothing."

We sat in silence. I didn't know whether to ask directly or to take a roundabout approach. Finally I opted for directness.

"Masudah, what can you tell me about the scandals that nip at the hem of Aunt Rahel's skirts?"

More silence. When Masudah finally spoke, she was direct too.

She said, "What the woman at the wadi said was nothing more than lies and slander. Your Aunt Rahel is not a seductress. She is an honorable woman. But I am not surprised that such a thing happened—what I mean is, I am not surprised that someone objected to Rahel's presence."

"Why?"

Again silence. I waited, dandling the baby on my lap.

"Adela."

"What?"

"What I am saying is that your aunt is the sort of woman people blame. For everything. They blame her equally for good or for evil."

"Blame her for good? That makes no sense."

"Sense? There is no sense. There is only blame, blame, and more blame for all the good or evil that befalls a soul. Adela," she sighed, "let me tell you two stories. I can see that it is no use *not* telling you. Who am I to deny you what everyone else already knows? These stories are not secrets. But we do not prattle about them. I don't want to hear you repeating them to anyone. Understand?" She took a deep breath, shifted the rooting baby at her bosom, and began.

"Many years ago, Rahel hennaed the hands and feet of a laboring woman. The woman gave birth to triplets, all of whom lived. After the blessed event, people began to whisper that Rahel was not a proper Jewish woman at all, but a priestess of Anath, masquerading as a Jew. Those spreading the rumors insinuated that Rahel had called on the old goddess herself to multiply the babies in the mother's womb and to see them safely born."

She paused, switched the baby to her other breast.

"And now the second story . . ." Before she continued, she gave me a remonstrative look, which let me know that even though she was being generous with information, she was uncomfortable with the subject, and cross with me for asking her to venture forth into it.

"This story is in many ways the opposite of the first. Last year, a bride whom Aunt Rahel had hennaed gave birth to a two-headed baby. A pathetic creature. Both the baby and the mother died, of course, and some would say that it was God's mercy to send them to the World to Come. But the family of the bride blamed Rahel. They said that instead of inscribing charms and murmuring incantations against the owl-footed demoness Lilitu, she had called Lilitu forth, and that because of her dark arts, the demon mother had possessed the bride, and caused her to bear the two-headed demon infant."

"But that's—"

"Sha, Adela, let me finish."

"I don't understand."

"What I am saying is—"

"That Aunt Rahel is a sorceress?"

"Of course not. What I am saying is that even if there hadn't been trouble for Uncle Barhun, they would have had to leave Aden anyway. It wasn't . . ."

"Wasn't what?"

"Wasn't safe for her there anymore."

Masudah reached for my arm, and gripped my wrist tightly. "Know this, Adela . . . regardless of what anyone else says about her, your Aunt Rahel is an honorable woman, and the best henna dyer in all of Yemen."

Suri tugged so hard on my hair that I had to pry open her little fingers. I kissed the little palm of her hand. "Masudah?"

"What?"

"Are there other stories about Aunt Rahel?"

She wrinkled her nose. "Don't be greedy for bad news, little girl." She put a hand under my chin, while spearing me with a gaze that was both rebuking and forgiving. Then she put the baby down in his basket and went to make us tea.

After all the trouble, Aunt Rahel didn't go often to the wadi where the other women gathered, and she never lingered in the market, gossiping as other women were wont to do. I continued to wonder about her. But when I dared to ask more questions, I never received answers, only more rude innuendo and conflicting stories cackled by the women at the well.

Chapter 10

"What goodies do you have for me today, sweet Adela? Have you brought some of that yummy citron jelly? It is so tart. Makes my lips pucker up, my mouth water."

His voice was low, phlegmy. He smelled tart and wormy, like moldering melon rinds. I backed up against the wall and held the basket out in front of me for Mr. Musa to take it. Every time, it was the same. He reached for the basket and put it down at my feet. Then he reached up under my antari, shoved aside my underlinen, and pleasured himself, while I stood there shaking. He thrust his fat fingers inside me while I grimaced in pain, swallowed my cries, and watched his face contort into an ugly mask of pleasure. Afterward he wiped his hands on his shamle and then patted me on the head, like a dog.

This was my nightmare.

I dreamed it over and over. And in the morning, I would wait until my parents were out of our room and I would take off all my clothes and examine my body for dreaded signs that womanhood was approaching. To be a woman was to be a wife. To be a wife was to be possessed by Musa. To be possessed by Musa was to be as good as dead. Two months after the other Damaris arrived in Qaraah, I found a hair on my pubis, and I yanked it out. It was early spring and I cursed my own body for sprouting this scrubby mountain grass. When my nipples grew dark and wide, I tried to press them back into my chest. When that didn't work, I cut a length of cloth and bound myself each morning. If I didn't give my breasts room to grow, I reasoned, perhaps they wouldn't swell and betray me to marriage. Sometimes a hard little nut of a thought flashed in my head: When I was engaged to Asaf, I wanted to be a woman right away. Now that I was engaged to Musa, I wanted to stay a girl forever.

In my waking life, as in my dream, I did visit Mr. Musa's house. But, thank Elohim, he was never there, as he was always at his stall in the market. My mother insisted that I go to his house on Friday mornings before Sabbath, and deliver a jar of our citron jelly and a share of our kubaneh bread. My new cousin, Hani Damari, came with me. Mr. Musa's wife always answered the door, swathed from head to toe like a Muslim woman, even though everyone knew she was a Jewess from a village to the west of Sana'a. All I ever saw of her were her eyes, tiny little blue slits of light peeking out of her coverings. Those eyes didn't look old, and they didn't look crazy or like they belonged to an invalid. She seemed young enough to be one of my sisters-in-law and walked by herself without a cane. The stories about her had been false. She never invited us in, and all she did was reach for the basket and whisper a quiet "Thank you, little sister" in the dialect of her people. She didn't have any grown children, but a single baby, a little boy with a snub nose whom she carried in the crook of her arm.

One Friday, when we were walking home, Hani asked, "Do you think Musa hits her to give her pain, or to give himself pleasure?"

I balked, "What do you mean? What a horrible thing to say." I was blushing.

"Well," Hani said, "clearly she covers her face to hide bruises, and she doesn't appear in public so people won't gossip about her injuries. And when a man hits a wife, sometimes it is for punishment, but sometimes it is to open the gates of paradise. For him, I mean. For her? Well, a man's paradise can be a woman's hell."

"How do you know such things?"

Hani snorted. "My older sisters taught me more than my aleph bet. And I will teach you, so you will know the ways of the world. The dark ways, as well as the light. For it is not enough to know just one of them."

"If those are the ways of the world, I am sure I don't want to know them. When I am married to Mr. Musa, if he hits me like that, I will cut off his grapes." I spoke with crude bravado, pretending to be audacious, even though I wasn't.

"Oh, Adela." Hani stopped, wrapped her arms around me, and kissed my nose. "Don't worry. Mr. Musa will not hit you."

"How do you know?"

"Because he won't marry you." Hani spoke with authority. "You will be free of him."

"What is to stop him?"

She smiled a coy, all-knowing smile but wouldn't say any more.

"What is to stop him? Can you tell fortunes? Free of him?" I gulped. "I will never be free. Have you heard my father cough? If my father goes to the World to Come before I am married to Mr. Musa, I will be confiscated, and if he doesn't? Well, I don't think Mrs. Musa looks very free, do you?"

Hani looked down at her feet, and then looked up at me. She had a strange expression, as if she half knew something that I would like to know the whole of.

A few days after this conversation, I went next door, to the little house with the red roof. I was delivering some soap that I had just finished making with my sister-in-law Sultana. I knocked, but no one answered. I knocked again, and still no answer. The door swung open under my hand. I found myself walking in, breathing in the scent of Eden on the sixth day, and soon I was standing in front of Aunt Rahel's herbs and unguents. All those little colored bottles and the satchels filled with mashed roots and dried leaves. I picked one up, and then another. I couldn't make out any of the writing on the little vials, because I didn't know how to read. But I knew enough about roots and herbs, from listening to my sisters-in-law discuss the treatments they found for their many female maladies, to know that a storehouse of herbs always contained bitter little treasures that were like coins—two-sided, deadly when taken in certain doses, healing when taken in others. My eyes fell hungrily on my aunt's stores. I breathed in deeply, wondering how I could discern what I needed from this wheaty, earthy amalgam. But as I couldn't tell one from the other, I just reached out and grabbed a little embroidered satchel with a cinch top. I had almost slipped it into the sleeve pocket of my antari when I heard a noise.

Aunt Rahel had walked in, quiet as a cat. She stood before me, her eyes flashing over the vial in my hand. She reached for it, appraised it, and raised an eyebrow.

"What do you need, Adela? What ails you?"

I opened my mouth. I was going to lie. I was going to say, "Aunt Rahel, I am interested in learning about healing. Will you teach me which herb stops a fever? Which stops blood? Which causes vomiting? Which reduces swelling?" But when I looked into my aunt's eyes, I saw oceans and deserts. I saw a world not yet created, and worlds that had died long before I was born. In other words, I saw eternity, and in eternity, I also saw myself. So I told her the truth. I said, "Aunt Rahel, I need a deadly poison."

Aunt Rahel was not like other women. She didn't say, "Child, it is an abomination to speak of such things." She didn't hug me to her bosom either and comfort me, trying to lift me out of my morbid sense of doom. She said, "Do you plan on killing yourself or some other?"

I let out a big sigh. "To kill Mr. Musa I would have to poison the citron jelly that I deliver for the Sabbath. And that would mean that if they had a taste of it, his wife and baby would die too. And I would not like to hurt them. So unfortunately I have to kill myself." I was relieved to give voice to what had been weighing so heavily on my mind.

"Adela, you have several options." She reached behind the bottles and pulled one out. "The distillation of this herb is toxic. It is best mixed with wine to mask the bitter taste. But be leery of it; sometimes it only works halfway, and to halfway kill someone makes one a murderer twice over. Another option is this powder. But that will cause you horrible agony and convulsions that last six days. Another option is a diffusion of the contents of this little green jar. Lovely, isn't it?" She uncorked it, sniffed, and then put it under my nose. "Smells like salty apricots, don't you think? I got it from a trader from the east. Puts a sufferer to sleep, and escorts her tenderly over the threshold of death. Better you die in your sleep and dream your way into the World to Come. But before you act too hastily, may I ask you why you want to possess such bitter knowledge?"

"Look, I will be a woman soon." I stuck out my chest, and showed her my swelling little bosoms. "And I have awful pains. My belly feels like it has been punched. Like I have a bruise in my womb. I am afraid that my blood will come before the new moon. And then I will have to marry Mr. Musa."

She examined me with her eyes. Then made me open my antari, so she could look at my nipples. She even made me raise my skirt and lower my linens. Then she told me to cover up again and said, "No, you will not become a woman for some time. And by then Mr. Musa will be dead."

I balked. "But he is not ill."

"Oh no, you are wrong; he is a very sick man. He has a terminal malady of the liver, I suspect, and perhaps also a blockage of the heart."

I wasn't used to people speaking of livers or hearts, unless they were referring to the slaughtering of goats or chickens. I almost laughed. Her diagnosis made me think of fat Mr. Musa slung out on a butcher's table, his organs glistening under the threat of a cleaver.

"How do you know this? Are you a doctor, Aunt Rahel?" I had once heard a story of a lady doctor in Aden, a British woman who helped bring babies into the world. But Aunt Rahel didn't answer, and then I heard myself turning mean and saucy. "Or are you a sorceress, like my mother says?" The words were already out of my mouth before I knew what I was uttering. My face got hot, and I tried to hide in the folds of my gargush.

She shook her head again, this time with a pained half smile. I could see that she wasn't the least bit angry, even though she had every right to be. "No," she said, "I am not that either." She had the little embroidered satchel on her palm, the one I had chosen. "Adela, perhaps you are the sorceress among us, because you yourself reached for my most deadly mixture. You brew tea from these dried leaves and it kills in five sips. But perhaps you knew this already. Maybe you already have all the knowledge you will ever need to save yourself." She tucked the little satchel back in its spot—just to the right of a long fluted green glass vial, and to the left of a big basket of dried henna leaves.

I left the little house with the red roof and walked home thinking about poor Mrs. Musa. Was Hani right? Was the poor girl hiding bruises under her antari? A split lip? A blackened eye? And how would I really behave if Mr. Musa hit me? Would I cower? Or fight back? I had never fought anyone, and when my mother beat me, I curled up deep inside myself until the blows had passed. I thought about Aunt Rahel's vials and pouches.

Later she would prove herself to be a woman of healing. When one of Masudah's sons fell and a branch stabbed his thigh, making a deep slash, she rubbed on a poultice and wrapped the wound with linen. When one of Masudah's babies got a bad cough, she gave Masudah a decoction of powder in wine, which eased his cries, and in the morning he was well again. When my brother Elihoo got a blistering, oozing sore on his lip that festered, she gave him a paste of henna and tea, and the sore was gone in two days. Eventually women I didn't know visited Aunt Rahel and would leave with little pouches tucked in their dresses. I supposed Aunt Rahel was sharing her cooking spices. But Aunt Aminah—who never hesitated to give me a proper education—

told me that Rahel gave the women love charms, and "worts and roots to sprinkle on their husbands' stew to assure potency."

But then, in the early days of the Damaris' time in Qaraah, we still didn't know what she was capable of. That night I lay awake in bed for a long time thinking about her herbs and potions, and about convulsions that would leave me strangling on my own tongue, foaming at the mouth. The next day when Hani came into our house, I was at the table, shucking walnuts with the big silver cracker. I said, "Hani, your mother cured my bellyache. Please tell her that I feel so much better."

That night in my dreams I slept on a soft carpet like Hani's mother's. My own boudoir was curtained by fuchsia and azure silks from China and wood blocked drapes from Zanzibar.

Chapter 11

I continued to deliver Sabbath baskets to poor Mrs. Musa. Three months after my engagement, she invited me in. That's when she took off her veil, and I saw that Hani had been correct. One week her right eye was black, another week, she had a bruised cheek. Another day she opened the door missing a front tooth. I grew to dread these visits, thinking that one day she would come to the door a corpse, and I would still hand her the basket and she would still say, "Thank you, little sister" even though she was already departed for the World to Come.

Once I tried to tell my mother about Mrs. Musa's injuries, but she rolled her eyes and said, "I hear that she is a clumsy girl, that she falls on her way to the well. Also, she has bad eyesight and bumps into things." She wiped her shiny brow with a kerchief and said, "You will be a help to her, and will be able to do the chores that her poor eyes make onerous."

More time passed. My breasts swelled, my hips grew rounder. In the market, from afar, I examined Mr. Musa for signs of the illness that Aunt Rahel had diagnosed. His skin did look yellow to me. And the man was shorter of breath. Perhaps Aunt Rahel was right. But would my body wait for Mr. Musa to die? Or would I become a woman before he was dead in the ground?

It was late spring when I awoke with pain gripping my belly so badly I was nauseated. Surely this meant my blood was coming. As I carried water from the little well, I sweated more than usual. As I ground wheat, my head throbbed, and all day long the pain in my belly grew worse and worse. Soon, sleepiness came over me. I swooned when trying to straighten up the kitchen. I lay down on my pallet and closed my eyes. In the morning there was a wad of rags between my legs. It was soaked through with my blood. My mother helped me to the chamber pot, and she washed me herself, sponging the blood from my thighs. Then she helped me back to my pallet.

"I am sorry, Mother."

"For what?"

I shook my head. I didn't know what I was apologizing for.

"You have nothing to be sorry for other than becoming a woman." She scrunched her face, left me, and returned a few minutes later with Aunt Rahel, who bent over me, smelled my breath, put her hands on my heart, and then lower, quickly undressed me, exploring my body.

"Ooooh," I moaned, when she pressed my belly. "Not there, not there."

I tried my apology again. "Aunt, I am sorry."

She put a hand on my sweaty forehead. "You asked me if I was a sorceress or a doctor. I told you I was neither."

"So what are you?"

She cocked her head to one side. Bit her top lip, and then said, "The ancient mothers believed that a girl's menarche rearranged her organs, putting the womb in the heart and the heart in the mouth."

"So my heart is in my mouth now?"

She shrugged. "Do you feel rearranged?"

"No, I feel like I am one of the ancients. I hurt everywhere. Like I have become an old woman overnight."

"Not an old woman, but a baby one. You are a baby woman, poor thing. You will feel better and worse tomorrow. You have indeed become a woman. Here, drink some of this." She handed me a small flask. "It will help with your cramps. But it won't help with anything else. Mr. Musa isn't dead yet. But he will die soon, leaving you a widow, but I am sorry to say, already a wife. Your blood came quicker than his death. I am so sorry. I wish there were something I could do for you, but there isn't, there simply isn't."

My cousin's and sisters-in-law's preparations for me were elaborate. In the two weeks before my wedding, they dressed me up and practiced prettying me. They plucked the hair under my arms, rubbed my whole body with pumice, and then powdered and scented me with myrrh, spikenard, and coriander oil. Sultana shampooed my hair with lavender soap and waxed my eyebrows with beeswax, then darkened them with burnt matchsticks. Hani stained my lips with geranium and poppy petals and rouged my cheeks with a cream Masudah cooked out of vinegar, isinglass, nutmeg, honey, and red sandalwood. Aunt Rahel made me drink a tea brewed out of a root she called kava kava. She said it would give me fortitude and calm my nerves. Masudah gave me new amulets to hide in my sleeve pockets and put under my pillow. Yerushalmit gave me a coral bracelet that she said was my mother's. Hani experimented braiding my hair in an elaborate coiffure.

I let them pummel and pound me into a bride. But we all knew the truth of it—I was miserable, and my wedding day was no real cause for celebration.

"Will Elohim send a ram in my place?" I blurted out as Sultana rubbed kohl on my eyebrows.

Yerushalmit snapped, "Haughty girl, who are you to compare yourself to Isaac our Father? You are no sacrifice."

Yerushalmit had been younger than I when she married my brother Mordechai. She had no patience for my complaints.

"Leave her be." Masudah wiped the tears off my face with her apron. "Sha, sha, little girl, now we have to clean you up and prettify you all over again." She turned to Yerushalmit and shot her dagger eyes. "All brides blaspheme. Elohim is merciful and has nothing but forgiveness for virgins taken by old men. Sha, sha, all will be well in the end." Then Masudah hugged me to her big bosom and whispered little lewd things in my ears that I never thought I would hear from my sister-in-law— ugly bedroom tricks on how to make my husband "finish his work before it even started" so I would not have to "suffer like a cart horse under the yoke of him." In those final days leading up to my wedding, the only thing that aroused in me any emotion other than dread was the fact that I would finally get to have my own henna. I couldn't help but feel a twinge of excitement. As I was to be a bride, my mother couldn't deny me a Night of Henna. To do so would be against the custom of our people and would arouse talk of the evil eye. She may have been a spiteful woman, but even my mother wouldn't launch her only daughter into matrimony under a cloud of ill omen.

But the promise of henna wasn't enough. Three days before my wedding, I stole away. I ran through the dye mistress's yard to Auntie Aminah's, and then back past the frankincense tree. I hadn't been to my cave in a very long time. I ducked into the entrance and found it almost as I had left it. The chalk boy and girl were faded, and the chalk horse was missing snout and ears. I picked up a chalk stone and redrew the outlines, and then I backed against the wall and fit myself into the image of the girl who held my place in the darkness. I reached for the chalk boy's hand, and I shut my eyes and prayed that Asaf would come back for me now, right now. That he would miraculously appear, rescuing me from Mr. Musa. I missed Asaf. I missed him so much that for a moment I became emptier than the chalk girl. I was a shadow of myself, aching with longing for my boy cousin.

I left the cave and returned to my parents' house. The next day, I waited until I knew that the other Damaris were out of their house, and I stole inside. I stood looking at Aunt Rahel's potions and tonics. My eyes fell on those she had described as deadly. There, the little embroidered satchel. I reached for it, took it in my hand. Outside, a cock crowed, a dog barked, and a goat bleated, but the most powerful sound was that of my beating heart, my own animal noise joining their earthy chorus. Do I kill myself? Or kill Mr. Musa? I raised the satchel to my nose and sniffed—turnip root, goat dung, jasmine flowers, burnt olive oil, freshly baked bread. The satchel smelled of everything and nothing. The dog barked again, and I fled the little house clasping that little parcel of death in my hand, burning a dark star in the middle of my palm.

The next morning, I rose before my parents and lit a small fire on the outside cookstove. I boiled water and took the satchel from my sleeve pocket. What would it be like to die? And what would it be like to lie in unsanctified ground? Would I be lonely? Of course you will be, I told myself. Lonely as bleached bones. I opened the satchel. The strange smells wafted out and I breathed them all in, packing the scent of far away and long ago deep into my lungs. Then I felt movement behind me. I turned. The dye mistress was there. She had come into our yard. She squatted and whispered something in my ear. She said, "Adela Damari, I have brought you a present." In the buttery dawn light, she unfurled a black and red lafeh cloth, fresh from the drying line. "This is my present to you." She nodded at the satchel, and I cinched it up, then took the cloth from her. A married woman's lafeh, for me to wear over my gargush.

"Thank you, but I take no joy in my wedding."

"Of course you don't, but still, you must act the part. I often take no joy in my spinsterhood; I have no babes to fill my arms, and yet by acting the part of it, I convince myself that I am not lonely. And sometimes it works."

I let her kiss me on both cheeks, and then she left me alone. I folded up the lafeh cloth. Then I swung Aunt Rahel's satchel from my fingers, letting it swish back and forth in the air. I watched it swing, realizing that I would not kill myself, not yet at least, and that I would marry Mr. Musa, pretending that I was still a flesh-and-blood girl, when really I had traded places with a girl of chalk. I put Aunt Rahel's satchel back in my sleeve pocket. I went back inside the house thinking about all the different kinds of loneliness there were in the world, and wondering if my own loneliness would smell like turnip root, goat dung, jasmine flowers, burnt olive oil, freshly baked bread, or like the dye mistress's troughs—colorful wells of water that she scented with roses to mask the stench of stagnation.

The next day was a Friday. My wedding was called for two days hence. That morning, my mother packed up the bread and jelly for me to bring to Mr. Musa, but when I was on the path to Musa's, Hani ran up behind me and grabbed the basket from me. "I will deliver it," she said with a wink. "You go hide away at your Auntie Aminah's house."

"I don't understand. Why . . . ?"

"I know you dread it, so I will do it for you. After you are married, there will be nothing that I can do to save you from that house, but today at least, I can relieve you of this errand."

I relinquished the basket, and watched her walk down the road. Then I turned on my heels and stole away to my auntie's, grateful to Hani that I didn't have to look into Mrs. Musa's sad eyes and see my own reflection there, at least not yet.

A few hours later, after I'd returned home, pretending to have delivered the basket, my brother Ephrim thrust his shaggy head in the door. Ephrim was always the most disheveled of my brothers, and today he looked like a lion with a tangled, overgrown mane. He flared his nostrils, growling, "Where is our father? Tell me Adela, where is he?"

I pointed to the back of the house. My father had not gone to work that day. He hadn't felt well for a few days, and was now sitting behind the house reading scripture wrapped in a blanket. Ephrim went out and said something. I heard my father make a noise—a cross between a moan and a broken-backed laugh.

My mother joined the men behind the house. Then more of my brothers arrived. Finally, my mother came inside. She reached out, took off my gargush, and ran her hands through my elaborate braids, unraveling them. I felt her thick fingers tugging my hair from the root, but I didn't cry out. When the braids were undone, she said, "Mr. Musa is dead. He was murdered. That poor girl did it—his wife. She stabbed him when he came home for lunch. Then she killed herself too. Her corpse has two black eyes and a broken nose. The babe has already been confiscated. Those black eyes? That broken nose. His last gift to her, I suppose. And his death? Well, that is her gift to you, though what kind of gift it is I don't know, for it will surely open a pit under your feet and you will tumble headlong into confiscation, just like the babe." To my surprise, she bent down and kissed me on the lips. I laughed when she pulled away, and then she slapped me. I clamped my mouth shut, but I kept laughing. She slapped me again. "Laughter tempts the devil," she spat through clenched teeth. When my brothers filled the house, I was curled up in a corner, nursing my stinging cheek. Their eyes told me that they pitied me. I was a cat they had kicked many times, but now they were half-sorry I was lame.

That night, my mother and father had their old argument.

"There is no one for Adela to marry." My mother said the words slowly, as if they took her on a long journey and tired her out.

"We will find someone for her. It is our obligation. We can't give up." My father sounded defeated.

"Her fate is her own now. If we live forever, perhaps she can do as the dye mistress has done and marry herself."

I buried my face under my rag pillow and pretended to cry myself to sleep. I cried to please my mother. I wanted her to think that I was crying for myself, and for dead Mrs. Musa and for her confiscated child, and for Asaf, the boy I had already loved and lost through no fault of my own. But the truth was that I was crying out of relief. That night my sleep was restful. I had escaped a terrible bondage. But when I awoke in the morning, the reality of my tenuous situation assailed me. Still, I was grateful that I had escaped marriage to fat old lecherous Mr. Musa.

* * *

Mr. Musa was buried the next day. The night after the funeral, I dreamed that I saw his wife. In my dream, she wasn't veiled anymore, and she had no bruises. She was dressed in the antari and gargush of a married woman. She had the same sweet snub nose as her baby and her eyes were laughing. Her cheeks were two high rosy apples. She was traveling on a donkey cart, leaving Qaraah, returning to the western village where she was from, taking her baby away before the Confiscator could sniff him out. "Good-bye, little sister," she sang in her singsongy village dialect, "good-bye." I dreamed that I kissed her hand to show her that we were indeed sisters, even though we had never truly shared the brute who had beat her, and pawed me in the dye mistress's yard.

After Mr. Musa's death, I became "a leftover nut," which is what our people call a girl who has no husband in the offing. My parents gave up finding me another groom. My father's cough grew worse and worse; everyone assumed that he would die, and that the Confiscator would eventually come for me. Only I knew otherwise. Every so often, when I was alone in our house, I took out Aunt Rahel's embroidered satchel, untied the cinch, and sniffed the bitter flakes of root. It didn't smell to me like Eden on the sixth day, but on the day the snake reared his head. It smelled of death, decay, and all manner of miseries. It also smelled of freedom. I knew that taking my own life was against the sacred law of our people, but I also didn't think that anyone would judge me poorly for my actions. After all, what else was there for me to do but take matters into my own hands, if my father should die, leaving me an orphan? I usually took out the satchel after seeing the Confiscator in the market—when he would come to my father's stall to order yet another pair of shoes for his wife. Or I would turn to the satchel after hearing a chilling story of a confiscation from the women at the well. I never saw the Confiscator's wife again, but I often heard her silvery ribbon voice in my head, as she made her plans to steal me for her own.

Chapter 12

My one regret after Mr. Musa's funeral was that I had not had my Night of Henna, and so my hands and feet were still unadorned. Hani and her mother were always decorated. Before coming to Qaraah, Aunt Rahel had been paid to henna brides and give ordinary women fancy applications, but here in Qaraah, no one would let her touch them, so she cloistered herself with her daughter and performed her rites in private. Their henna usually lasted two to three weeks. But they didn't always rehenna immediately. Sometimes they waited until Aunt Rahel deemed that it was time. I don't know how she decided when to henna, and when to wait—whether she consulted an astrological calendar or just chose the dates at whim. Once they hennaed on the new moon. Once they waited so long that their henna had faded completely, and their hands and feet were blank, like mine.

My sisters-in-law now regularly joined them for their applications. I was sometimes allowed to watch, but not to participate. My mother forbade me from getting so much as a dot of henna from my aunt's stylus.

Other than this, the next period of my life, free of matrimonial prospects, was quietly wonderful. With Mr. Musa out of the way, I was at liberty to tend and stoke the fires of my loyalty to Asaf. I was convinced, despite a complete lack of evidence, that he would return for me. I confided my hopes to Hani, who cheerfully kept me company in my girlhood. I view this time as a temporary reprieve from worry and dread. Hani and I spent most of our time together. By now, I had heard so many stories about her sisters in Aden– about Edna, Hamama, and Nogema—that I felt as if I myself half knew them. But I had heard almost nothing about the two Damari girls who had died, Naama and Asisah. I didn't even know *how* they'd died. No one in the family spoke about them, especially not in the presence of Aunt Rahel. But that was to change, approximately one month after Mr. Musa's funeral. I was sitting with Hani outside the synagogue in the early evening of a fast day. Our fathers had prayed all day, and our mothers had stayed home cooking for the end of the fast. We had been sent to the synagogue to track when prayers were almost over. Then we were to run home and let our mothers know that it was time to serve the meal. The twins, Marta and Freda Paradesi, were walking by the synagogue, arm in arm. They were two years older than I. Both had recently been married. They leaned together as they walked, and whispered to each other conspiratorially.

"Naama and Asisah were like that," Hani commented, pointing toward Marta and Freda.

"Identical?"

"They belonged to each other more than they ever belonged to anyone else."

Freda wore her hair swept up and a freckle by her hairline became visible; otherwise, they were like two sunflower seeds, indistinguishable one from the other. Hani watched them unabashedly, then she hugged her knees and told me a story as elegiac as the prayers of our fathers escaping through the synagogue window.

"When our twins, Naama and Asisah, were little, they were chatty, happy girls," she began. "I don't remember this much, but my sister Edna says it was so. When they turned ten, they both became sad and quiet. Then they got quieter. Finally, they stopped talking to anyone but each other. Months went by and they had become so quiet it was hard to know they were even there. Sometimes we would bump into them— we younger sisters—and we would be surprised, for we hadn't even known they were in the house. Before either even became a woman, we lost them. My parents saw that they were missing and looked for them everywhere. Three days later, a shepherd found them at the bottom of a wadi surrounded by steep cliffs. There was a path to the cliffs from behind the tannery. Sometimes we would go there, in a group of course, to make bonfires. But we never went close to the edge. Did they fall or jump? I have always been certain that they jumped, holding hands, as they did everything. Edna and Nogema think they fell. Hamama is sure they were pushed, but she is always suspicious and suspects malevolence where there is really only sorrow.

"For a long time after they died, my mother was quiet too. Sometimes we sisters were afraid that she would follow their ghosts up that mountain pass and fall, jump, or push herself in their wake. But when the year was up, she began to talk again, and then even to laugh sometimes. It is because of that tragedy that we were allowed to henna from the time we were little girls. A year after their deaths, my mother gathered us to her. She said, 'My eldest daughters never wore henna, and now they are dead. The rest of you will wear henna, and you will live forever, won't you?' She kissed each of us and cried down onto our faces, and drew on our skin marks of *beracha*, blessing, and the triple and quadruple diamond protections against devils, demons, and djinn. When I die, I will go to heaven and find Naama and Asisah and I will give them my husband's kisses, his embraces, and my children will be their children too. This is what I dream sometimes, that they are up there waiting for me, and that the bottom of that valley is really just the floor of heaven, or at least, it is one floor, for surely heaven is everywhere, don't you think?"

A few nights after Hani told me about the twins, we women were washing up from dinner. Aunt Rahel pointed to Hani's hands, where the henna had become a faded gray scrim. "Soon we will reapply. Hani, try to dream up a new design. Or we will just improvise. Eh? Like usual."

Just before the other Damaris left our house, Hani lingered at the door and comforted me.

"Don't fret, Adela." She took my hand, threading her fingers through mine. "By the next time, I am sure your mother will have a change of heart."

"And if she doesn't?"

"Then by the next time. There is always a next time. But don't think about it; you will join us and have fun anyway. A henna party is always fun, regardless of whether one gets henna or not."

"Mmph . . . fun for you maybe. But for me? I am nothing but jealous."

"Oh, Adela, your time will come, you'll see." She flung an arm around my shoulders. The coins of my gargush tinkled against her kerchief. She turned and gave me a quick peck on the cheek, and then she poked me in the ribs with her free hand. I laughed. With Hani it was hard not to laugh.

The door was barely shut behind the other Damaris when my mother issued one of her customary threats. She had overheard Hani, and wasn't taking any chances that I would defy her.

"Don't you dare come home with henna on your hands," she hissed. "If you do, I will scald your skin, or scrape it with a knife to remove it." My mother always made it clear that though she was letting me keep company with my new cousin, I was not for one moment to think I was one of her sisters. I knew she was serious. Once my second-eldest brother, Elihoo, ran away and spent three nights living with acrobats and clowns traveling with a caravan from Kashmir. After my father dragged him home, my mother put leather thongs around his wrists and tied him to a fence post, making him stay there two days and nights, until the straps had cut into his skin and he was so hungry he began to gnaw on the leather. My mother never made idle threats, and was willing to shed the blood of her own children if she believed they deserved it.

The next afternoon, after I had finished my chores, Hani took my hand. Aunt Rahel had found henna bushes on the ridge behind the ritual bath, near Masudah's house. We foraged together, while Hani showed me what to look for. "These are the leaves we want," she said, stripping the plant of green leaves with a little red vein down the center.

I pointed to the blood lines. "They look like crimson pieces of thread."

"And that's what we want, the leaves with the brightest veins."

She smashed a leaf on a stone, showed me the color on her nail. She reached out and took the fingers on my right hand and rubbed the color on my fingertips. Then she ran ahead and dared me to chase her.

"You can't pick leaves and then store them for months and use them later for henna. They have to be newly picked."

"Why?"

"Old leaves lack the most important quality of henna."

"Good color?"

"No, silly, steadfastness. Old leaves don't leave a decent stain."

After a while, we had stripped all the bushes of the good leaves. I had an idea.

"Hani, I know where there are more bushes."

"Take me." She smiled.

"It's a secret."

"I swear I won't tell anyone."

I took her the back way, through the dye mistress's yard. We ran up past the frankincense tree, past the citrons, down the escarpment, and over the culvert. I was proud and excited to show Hani my cave, but as we approached, I was suddenly filled with regret. Other than that quick visit before I was supposed to marry Musa, I had utterly neglected my cave in favor of my cousin. What kind of friend was I? Would my little goddesses remember me? I felt ashamed that I didn't even have any wheat or sage in my pockets to lay on their altar. But the second I stood in front of the cave opening, my feelings of shame receded. I knew then that my cave would always welcome me, and that I would always feel more at home there than I ever would in my parents' house.

When we ducked inside, Hani didn't bow low enough.

"Ow!" she exclaimed as she hit the top of her head.

"Sorry, you have to watch that."

She frowned, rubbing her forehead. I lit my lamp; the wick flicked into life, illuminated her face, and then pressed both of our shadows into the wall. She moved around my little cave, touching all my treasures. When she got to my idols, she said, "Adela, your mother would skin you alive for these. But I am impressed. This proves what I have suspected about you. That you are fearless and reckless and bold. Your cave is the best place in the world. I want to live here. Do we ever have to leave? Let us stay and grow old here."

We heard a sound outside. Hani squealed, sure we were about to be discovered. I peeked out and saw a horseman riding toward Bir Zeit. My heart leapt, and then just as quickly fell at the sight. In the time since Asaf had left, every horseman in the desert could be he. Every hoofbeat vibrated with the song of our reunion, and when it wasn't he, as it never was, Asaf receded just a little bit further into the mist of memory and possibility.

"Let's go."

"So soon?"

"We'll come back, I promise. But Hani . . ."

"What?"

"Please don't tell anyone—"

"I understand. If too many people know, it won't be yours anymore," Hani said, giving words to what I was feeling. She moved over to me, reassuring me, interlacing her fingers with mine. Then she nodded at the chalk girl and boy on the wall near the entrance and at Asaf's chalk horse. They had faded again but were still visible—little ghosts left to haunt the cave in my absence. "What sweet little friends you drew," she said. "How do you do, little girl? Little boy? My name is Hani, I am pleased to meet you." She leaned forward and kissed each of them on their faces, where their lips would have been, had they had features.

Just as she straightened up again, I heard a rustling outside in the henna bushes. A shiver ran down my spine. Who could have found us? I turned and found Binyamin Bashari ducking into the cave. It had been many months since we had seen each other last, other than from a distance, in the market. He had grown so tall, and he no longer wore the tattered sharwal and tunic of his childhood but the gray shamle of a man, and a nicely wrapped black turban on his head. His face had grown in to his wolf-muzzle jaw. But still, he had an exotic look, as if he had come from elsewhere, even though he was a Qaraah boy born and bred.

Hani had backed up into the darkness of the cave when he entered. Now she stepped forward and cocked her head to one side, appraising him. She had taken to wearing a gargush like a northern girl, and when she did so, the coins tinkled and glinted in the little ray of sun that came through the cave entrance. She seemed unsure. I saw a flash of fear pass over her eyes, and then curiosity, and then she must have understood— though no words had been exchanged—that Binyamin also belonged to the cave or, at least, that he belonged to me. That's when her face changed and she began to look coyly at Binyamin. She reached a hand up to twirl a lock of hair that had come loose from her gargush. "I know you," she said. "You are the jambia maker's son. What are you doing here?"

Binyamin didn't answer her. He hadn't said anything yet. She looked from Binyamin to me and then back again.

"Oh Adela, what kind of secret cave is this? No, don't worry, I will keep your 'secret.'" And she pointed to the chalk boy and girl on the cave wall. "So this is you," she said to Binyamin, "a flesh-and-blood boy in my cousin's pretty little lair." She laughed and wagged a finger at me. "All this time, Adela, how could you keep this, *keep him* from me?" She said this in a full, loud voice, and then nodded toward Binyamin as if he were a statue and couldn't hear her.

"No, Hani," I protested, "you're mistaken. Binyamin is engaged to another. It's not like that between us at all."

"Oh, really?"

Binyamin was blushing crimson from his neck to his turban, "Adela . . . I . . . I . . ." He stammered my name again and his eyes locked onto mine. We were children of the high northern sun, and in that moment he spoke to me as the sun would—with a fierce blaze that scorched in places I didn't know could burn. But not another sound passed his lips. Before I found my own voice, Binyamin turned around, ducked down, and left.

When he was gone, Hani rushed over to me, put her warm hand on my cool arm. "Tell me everything about him. He is not really handsome, but he is certainly interesting-looking—and so strong, a tree-trunk boy, so sturdy, he looks like he could lift up half of this mountain. And he is your friend? You say he is engaged? Pfe, what a shame. But perhaps the girl will die. Do you know anything about her health? Do you know her? Is she pretty? Or ugly? Maybe she is just a little twig of a thing that will break underneath him?"

I didn't answer. I was angry at Hani for teasing Binyamin, for making him so uncomfortable. Hani put her arm around my shoulders, kissed my ear. "Silly Adela, say something." She poked a finger in my ribs and tried to tickle me, but I pulled away.

"Don't be so cruel and hateful!" For the very first time, I yelled at her. We'd never once fought, but now I was filled with rage. "How can you say such things? Elohim forgive you, and protect Binyamin's intended from the evil eye." I flashed my own dark eyes at Hani, but then she again flung an arm over me, kissed me, and begged my forgiveness. My anger quickly melted away.

"He is just an old friend," I heard myself saying. "We played together as small children."

For the second time Hani pointed to the chalk girl and boy. "What a shame he is not engaged to you. What a sweet couple you make on the wall."

The truth burst out of me. "No, that is Asaf. Our mutual cousin Asaf Damari is the boy on the wall. After we were engaged to each other, he visited me here when we were just children. We playacted at being husband and wife. But Binyamin was always just my friend. He and I were innocents together as small children."

Hani took a quiet moment to digest this jumble of revelations, then the coyness returned to her voice. "Well, be careful not to *play* with the jambia maker's son now that you are a woman. If you bear his child, everyone will know it is his. He doesn't look like anyone else, does he?" I blushed, my face as crimson as Binyamin's had been.

"Hani, really, we were just friends." But as I said these words, I felt like a hypocrite, and the image of me and Asaf in this cave came unbidden to my mind and left me feeling as if I had deceived my girl cousin about several things, even though I hadn't lied to her about anything.

When we returned from my cave, Hani and I added our bounty of extra leaves to the cache Aunt Rahel had collected. Aunt Rahel nodded approvingly. "Good," she said, "now we have more than enough." She laid the leaves out in the sun, and then took out already dried leaves and began to macerate them with mortar and pestle, working rhythmically, with a swift turn of the wrist that quickly pulverized the leaves into tiny flakes, and then into pieces so small they looked like specks of green-gray dust.

Soon after that day, Binyamin left Qaraah forever. His intended had become a woman, and he went to marry her and to live with her people in Sana'a. When I heard news of his departure I realized that he must have followed me to my cave to say good-bye. Something told me— perhaps those womanish senses that were rising in me—that perhaps he had the same regrets as my mother that we could not be married. I murmured a little prayer beseeching Elohim to watch over Binyamin on his journey, then I daydreamed of when we were children, how Binyamin had slipped his hand into mine, how he would run with me, our pounding feet together blotting out the hiss of the Confiscator's serpents.

The day after I showed Hani my cave, after I had finished my chores, I sat with Aunt Rahel and Hani. I watched as mother and daughter adorned each other with fresh designs and then let the henna set by painting over the designs with a paste of lemon and sugar. I felt shy and out of place, though Hani didn't make me feel that way. *Come closer, Adela, come sit by me, look, this is how we do it, you dip the stylus, the ink has to be loose, but not so loose it will drip down her hand. . . .* Hani was already adept at applying henna. Her mother would let Hani do her hands and feet, tutoring her all the while. Sometimes mother and daughter consulted Aunt Rahel's henna book, a little red leather notebook in which she had written hundreds of henna elements down the left-hand sides of the pages. The book was a real marvel. I had never seen a book that wasn't a holy text before. I didn't even know that books existed that weren't dedicated to psalms, prayer, or scripture. Really, I had never considered such an unlikely thing. Every single page and blank spot of paper was written on. Some of the elements were as tiny as a dot or a single slash, a half triangle, a swirl within a swirl. Next to the elements Rahel wrote the corresponding meanings. Hani read to me—explaining how two little wavy lines signified water and abundance. A whole page of different paisleys all stood for mango fruit. Next to the paisleys, Aunt Rahel had written, "Paisleys—mango, the Buddha's fruit, contemplation, paradise, repose." I was surprised that a Jewish woman would reference a pagan god, but the more I flipped the pages, and the more my cousin read and explained what was written on them, the more I saw that the henna elements did not spring only from the seeds of our own Jewish traditions: there were Chinese lotus leaves for fertility, Turkish carnations for luck. Even New Zealand Maori designs, fierce and angular. Next to them Rahel had written, "Hero warriors. Not for brides."

Aunt Rahel let Hani practice, never minding if she made a mistake or tried her own variations. She took joy in Hani's experimentation but also scolded a lazy line, an uninspired cufflet, a blankness that should have been filled in. My aunt and cousin told stories as they decorated each other. Scary stories . . . *Once there was a dead god who lived in a place where the wind blew the flesh off the bones of men.* Love stories . . . *Once there was a flute maker in the Suk el-Thuluth who fell in love with a maiden from Abyssinia.* When they had finished inscribing each other, Aunt Rahel sang a song of the sister and brother Canaanite goddess and god, Anath and Baal, and their enemy the Mot, god of darkness. Aunt Rahel sang of mythic intrigue, romance, war, gore, retribution. In her song, henna was everything. It was worn for battle, applied for seduction, smeared on breasts, hands, and feet. Anath waded knee deep in the blood of her brother's slayers. Chopped off their heads and put them in a bag she wore on her belt. My head grew dizzy. My heart beat in time with the supple melody. In Rahel's song, henna was blood and blood was henna. My aunt and cousin lay back on pillows, waiting for their henna to set. I lay back with them, languid and hot, holding my hands delicately, pretending that I too was decorated, that I too had swirls and lines on my skin.

After the singing was over, we ate a small feast of nuts and dried fruit. I inched closer, and I listened to everything, hoping to be gathered into the soft circle of their arms. But still, *I* knew I was an intruder. On the ground next to me was the pot of henna paste. It smelled wheaty and earthen, like the very clay of the pot.

Toward the end of the night, I looked up at my aunt and was startled. She looked different. She was radiant. She was a queen riding on an elephant in a distant jungle. Hani was her princess. I looked around. The tapestries on the wall began to shift forms, and the animals peeked out from behind trees whose names I didn't know. Though she was ordinary in the outside world, here in the henna house, Rahel Damari was exquisite. My aunt. An artist of flesh, an acolyte of flowers. I left drunk with their laughter, their breathy whispers, their triumphs of art and intimacy. When I crawled onto my lonely pallet, I wished with all my heart that the walls between our houses would dissolve, and that I could cross the distance between us, curl up next to Hani, her hennaed arms wrapped around my own, our hennaed feet entwined like vines. In my dreams, I was as decorated as they were. But in the morning I woke up blank and lonely. I hurried through my chores and then ran out of our house to join her as quickly as I could.

Throughout the summer of 1930, when I turned twelve years old, my new girl-cousin kept me busy. Hani taught me six different step dances. She tutored me in herbs—for she was following in the footsteps of her mother as a healer. And best of all, she taught me my Hebrew letters. She explained that she and her sisters were all fluent in Hebrew, Judeo-Arabic, and Arabic. Uncle Barhun bragged affectionately that his girls were born reading, and that they read words before they walked, whole sentences before they ran. My cousin told me that in Aden it wasn't unusual for fathers to teach their daughters to read. Why, there were even schools for girls, and Uncle Barhun not only sent his daughters to the Selim School for Girls but also tutored them himself in French, a smattering of dockside Hindustani, and some pidgin Italian too—all of which he had learned in order to conduct his business dealings with customers at Aden port and the gentlemen from Barde et Cie.

Compared to Hani, I was miserably ignorant. My mother had taught me my Arabic letters and numbers when I was old enough to be sent to the market—rudimentary literacy was useful for grocery lists and making change—but I didn't know the Hebrew alphabet, the aleph bet. It had never occurred to me that I would learn. Hani changed all of that. She took a stick and drew letters in the earth. She made me repeat their sounds after her.

"See, Adela," she said, pointing to the letters that spelled out my name, "*aleph* א, *dalet* ד, *lamed* ל, *heh* ה." She gave me her stick and I traced her letters. Then I wrote my name over and over again. She praised my steady hand, corrected my mistakes. And when I was done learning my name, she wrote the entire aleph bet, all twenty-two letters. I started from *aleph* א, and on the third day had them all memorized. Hani also showed me the secrets behind the shapes of the letters. She said that every letter came from a picture, and that if you remember the picture, it is easier to remember the letter itself.

"*Aleph* is an ox, see how we can draw the face of an ox? And *bet* is a house, see how the shape of the letter makes a shelter, a little house?"

When I asked why a girl needed to know such things, she opened her big eyes even wider than usual and said, "Adela, every daughter of God is a spark of light, and when we gather together at the end of time, all of our sparks will illuminate the World to Come."

"Really?"

"Silly, I'm just teasing you. But it is better to learn than not to learn, don't you think? And anyway, knowledge makes us less susceptible to despair. I heard this once, from an old woman in the coffee marketplace of Aden, and I have decided to believe it."

She chased me up a hill and drew a big *gimel* ג in the earth, *gimel, gamal, camel* . . .

A few nights later, when my father saw me scratching the Hebrew letters of my own name in the dirt by the grinding stones, he smiled and said, "Adela, you are as smart as a boy."

This remark stung, because if it meant that I was as smart as my brothers, I was still destined for idiocy. But I didn't dwell on it, for I was immersed in my own joy. Hani had indeed rescued me from my dreary life, and I was reveling in the light of her company. I was happy, truly happy, for the first time since Asaf had left. My father rarely coughed these days. And when he did, it was a quiet little cough, not the familiar rumble that shook his whole body and left his eyes gray and his lips white with spittle.

But my happiness was not complete, for my mother would still not let me fully participate in the Damaris' henna ceremonies. I was desperate to have decorated hands and feet, like them, and one day even scratched a design into my left forearm, with the sharpened edge of a twig. I didn't draw blood, but the white lines that emerged from my skin gave me away and my mother rubbed rancid butter on my skin and didn't let me see my cousin for three days.

Chapter 13

Summer gave way to autumn, and with autumn came our preparations for the New Year. Our New Year marked the end of the yearly cycle of Torah readings and the beginning of a new cycle. I remember thinking about how every year we Jews read the same stories, and how my life felt like it too was a familiar story writ on a parchment. The same portions happened over and over again. I woke in the morning and helped my mother cook, clean, and do marketing. And then I woke another morning to the same cooking, cleaning, and marketing. One day was exactly like the next. Perhaps things would have continued just the way they were, an endless cycle, had Sultana and her son Moshe not fallen ill. It happened in the days between the New Year and the Day of Atonement. Sultana was stricken first. Sick with fevers and rashes, she would neither eat nor drink. She grew delirious. Masudah cared for little Moshe, who was now five years old. But then Moshe wouldn't eat either. He tugged on his left ear and screamed in pain. His body was racked with violent coughs and he could barely breathe. He was wakeful and hot, too tired to even cry.

In my family there are many versions of this story. In one, Sultana and Moshe nearly died, but at the last minute, Aunt Rahel burst into Elihoo's house and came to their aid, saving both mother and child from certain death. In another version, Aunt Rahel insisted on being allowed to help but was forbidden to enter the sickroom, barred by my brother Elihoo, who had heard the stories about Aunt Rahel and refused to allow her to tend his family. In this version, Aunt Rahel tried three times, knocking on the door, even opening it herself, each time being rebuffed until the final time, when she was given passage. Another version was that my mother herself humbled Elihoo, telling her son that he was but a gnat in the bog of the universe and that she was a spider, spinner of webs. In other words, she let him understand that he had no authority when it came to the life of a child of her own blood. Then she went to Aunt Rahel. Did my mother beg Aunt Rahel to come? I am sure she didn't have to. Whatever bargains my mother made were between herself and God.

When Aunt Rahel arrived, she found Sultana greatly improved, but Moshe . . . Moshe was more dead than alive. He was breathing rapidly and his heart was pounding so quickly in his chest he was more like a bird than a boy. Hani later described the treatment to me. Aunt Rahel examined his little chest, listened to his breathing, looked at the color of his tongue and the consistency of his sputum. Then she prepared tonics. She sliced an onion and put it in a bowl with pure honey; after an hour she had him drink the syrup. She also gave him parsnip juice and a tonic of sesame and linseed. She rubbed peppermint oil on his back and pressed a cotton sack filled with warm, damp wheat to his left ear. I went to visit and to see if there was anything I could do to help. When I arrived, Aunt Rahel was holding Moshe and praying. But it wasn't a prayer I knew. She was asking *Ayin HaChayim*, the Wellspring of Life, to redeem Moshe, to save him from his illness.

Aunt Rahel stayed with Sultana and Moshe all night. In the morning the crisis had passed. Moshe slept soundly in his mother's arms. His chest had cleared, his fever had broken, his ear had drained its noxious fluid. Rahel hadn't even hennaed him. "Sometimes henna comes first," Hani explained to me when I asked her about the role of henna in treatments. "Sometimes it comes last, and sometimes it is not even needed."

Before the other Damaris came, my life was empty of questions. Now, everything set me wondering. When Moshe had his sixth birthday, a few weeks later, Sultana proudly walked with him to the bigger well. The other women gathered around and cooed at how tall he had become, they listened to him tell jokes, they cheered his perfect openmouthed grin. Sultana's smile was a sight to behold.

I wondered how Aunt Rahel helped save Moshe. Was she calling on God? Or on God by a different name? Did Elohim answer if you called him Ayin HaChayim? I supposed so, for the boy had lived. But why had I not recognized the words? A few weeks after Moshe's sixth birthday, Aunt Rahel prepared her pot of henna paste. I sat at the grinding stones and watched Hani wash her skin and then help her mother sort through her array of moisturizing oils and unguents. My mother came out of our house and summoned me. I followed her inside. She put a piece of dough in my hands and told me to make the evening bread. When I had finished rolling and stretching and stretching and rolling, she said, "Enough, enough" as if I had forced myself upon her, as if I had asked for the work. Then she said, "Well, go already."

"To where?"

She looked out the window, at the house with the red roof.

"To them" she said, spitting out the word *them* but then softening. "To your cousin."

She had never referred to Hani as "my cousin" before. She usually said "the *other* Damari girl" with a bitter emphasis on the word *other*. I knew that something in our relationship had shifted.

"And may I—"

"Yes, you may let *them* . . ."

Them—the word danced in the air, twisted, arched, and unraveled. I didn't need her to finish her sentence, I ran so fast. Flying to Hani and Aunt Rahel, as if they were birds about to take flight, I, the littlest bird, flapped my wings frantically, heedless of anything but an ancestral urge to join them on their seasonal journey.

"What is it, Adela?" Hani was holding a pot of henna paste, adding a dilute tincture of coffee water drop by drop. I held up my hands, and then I turned them slightly front to back, as if I were sanctifying a Sabbath flame. She knew. She clapped and shouted. Held out her arms to me, imprinting a permanent design of joy on my skin, my soul, even before the ink was fully prepared.

Rahel Damari presided over my first henna ceremony but let Hani do the actual inscribing. I felt so lucky as her stylus tickled my skin. My sisters-in-law Yerushalmit and Masudah were there too. They joined Aunt Rahel and Hani in singing a song of Anath and Baal—I heard my voice mingling with their voices. Aunt Rahel led a song about the matriarchs and heroines of scripture. About our mother Miriam and her tambourine, about our mother Sarah's laughter, about Esther's courage, Deborah's wisdom, Ruth's loyalty, Judith's daring, Eve's beauty. The tickle of the stylus on my skin gave me gooseflesh. I laughed when Hani got to my pulse points. She laughed with me. Plaited my hair. Rubbed rose balm on my shoulders. Rubbed my feet and sang me a song that seemed to braid through itself like the strands of a havdalah candle. I didn't say a word. I must have been a bore and a disappointment to them all, though they never made me feel that way. Not for a single second.

Aunt Rahel inspected each design, made criticisms and comments, and helped with smudges. "Oh, Adela, you are so beautiful!" The paste dried quickly. I could feel it growing tight and purposeful on my skin. Once all of our hands were decorated, Sultana lifted a tambourine, and all our voices joined in song. We sang a song of the hill-country women who bear baskets on their heads but keep their spines straight as arrows as they traverse the distance between market and home. That first night I was a novitiate. Soon, like the others, I would learn about the stars in the heavens by reading the astronomical tables they inscribed on my feet, shins, and fingers. Soon, I would grow to believe that I myself was an actual text, and that my skin *without* henna was like a holy book without words—a shameful, almost blasphemous, thing. Without henna, I wouldn't know how to read myself. With henna, I was as sacred as a sanctified Torah. With henna, I was the carrier of ancient tales—a living girl-scroll replete with tales of sorrow, joy, and salvation. After the singing, we lay back on the fragrant pillows and dozed. When I woke up, everyone gathered around to see my hands. Hani had given me a pattern of roses and lilies. The tendrils and petals wove their way from the insides of my wrists to my pinky fingers, and wrapped themselves into my palms.

I left the house with the red roof a different sort of Adela from the girl who had gone in. When I walked into our house, my mother was at the fire, frying lungs for dinner. She turned around, saw my arms. She didn't tell me they were beautiful. She pretended that nothing was different about me. But instead of making me help with dinner, she said, "Go to Sultana and return her second coffee grinder, ours has been fixed." The grinder was in a basket by the door.

"I'll be back quickly."

"Take your time."

I knew that she was excusing me from dinner preparations so that I wouldn't ruin my fresh henna, which still had to set. I wanted to thank her, but I knew it wasn't what she wanted. For my mother, my silence in the face of her kindness was thanks enough. The next day at the market I waved my arms extravagantly, insouciantly, in every direction. Women cooed and clucked at my adornment. There were some, though, who had strong opinions. The candlemaker's wife told me in no uncertain terms that the henna on my arms marked me as a slut, and that I should soak my hands in lemon to bleach the color off before my reputation was ruined. The lampmaker's wife told her to shut her mouth, and said that I was as pretty as a picture.

After I had danced around town with my abundantly decorated arms and feet, I realized that Aunt Rahel was the one my mother had been thanking. I was just the vehicle. My arms and legs, hands and feet spread the news that Sulamit Damari, respected matron and wife of Hayyim Shalom Damari, the leather worker, was proclaiming her sister-in-law's worthiness and daring any other woman in Qaraah to slander her name. My skin was writ with my mother's testimony. My body bore a pledge of honor from one woman to another.

I didn't know it then, but my mother *had* forgiven Rahel for being who she was—a woman of henna, with ancient charms on her lips, bloodred hands, and the stories of so many brides tucked up into her skirts. But at the same time, my mother *had not* forgiven Rahel for a more private sin—a sin that became a bone in my mother's throat, something she choked on every single time she looked at my aunt.

That night my father and Uncle Barhun sat out by the fire between our houses while my mother was at Auntie Aminah's, who had been unwell and needed help when the pains in her back made breathing most difficult. I thought about the first night the other Damaris came to live with us in Qaraah. I remembered how, when Hani took off her traveling clothes, I was stunned by her beauty and how her henna made her seem both more dressed and more naked. Now, desperate to see my own adorned skin, and alone in the house, I took off my dress and pants and let myself be recklessly naked for just a moment. The light of the fire from the courtyard filtered through the curtains and cast a yellow glow on my body. I was a traveler now too, walking the road with them from Aden, coming north through desert and dune and narrow mountain pass. I held up my scriptural hands, curled my decorated toes, and thought, *I am one of them now, truly.*

Soon after I received my first henna, my father's cough worsened. He took to his bed, breathing in big gulping wheezy gasps. But then Aunt Rahel gave him a tonic and a steam treatment and he recovered a measure of his strength. After that, anytime he suffered a "relapse" she would treat him again. He called her Nurse Rahel. My mother grumbled when he said it, but she also found little ways to thank her sister-in-law, like sending me over with a pot of kubaneh for Sabbath, or a tray of sweet nut pastries for a festive meal. After Aunt Rahel saved Sultana and Moshe, the women of Qaraah stopped speaking ill of her and soon they remembered that she was an expert at the art that they all admired. It wasn't long before she had no trouble getting work as a henna dyer. This is how Aunt Rahel came to henna the hands of the daughter of Ibn Roush, a leatherworker like my father. She also hennaed the hands and feet of a toothless old woman who had miraculously survived a fall off a roof and wanted to celebrate her redemption. And once Rahel started, more and more came for her. She quickly regained her reputation as the best henna dyer to be found. Jewish brides came to her as well as Muslim ones. Soon she was able to charge a premium for her services. Most of the women we knew from Qaraah, but some came to contract her services from the surrounding villages, and some from as far away as Sana'a. They sent messengers to the little house with the red roof, or made the pilgrimage themselves, holding out their hands, showing the width of their palms, and sitting with Aunt Rahel in the stone courtyard between our houses, discussing patterns, intensity of colors, redolence of herbal tinctures.

Hani would accompany Rahel to her "jobs," working as her helper and apprentice. Hani became known in Qaraah for a vivid and unusual star pattern that we began referring to as "Hani's constellations." No one else could achieve the same effect, not even Aunt Rahel. Hani's henna stars and planets seemed to radiate off the skin with their own vivid light. And the women who wore Hani's constellations noticed that each time they looked at them, they saw different arrangements of the stars and found the shapes of new animals and old heroes that would appear and fade into each other, and then reappear as different shapes entirely.

And what about that magic? Sometimes it seemed to me that Hani believed in scriptural charms and amulets, believed that what she drew on our skin had power to ward off evil, cosmetics with ulterior motives. But other times it seemed that she thought her art was nothing more than elegant scribbles—beauteous designs.

Aunt Rahel's reputation grew and grew. On more than one occasion she was even called on to henna the daughters and nieces of the Imam himself. The brides she hennaed—both the Jews and the Muslim girls—began once more to be referred to as Rahel's Blooms. She used special mixes for her applications and the result was that her designs sank deeper into the skin and lasted longer than henna done by less skillful hands. It was whispered that Rahel's Blooms not only enjoyed sensuous love affairs but also experienced a pleasure in their marriages that lasted so long that the painted flowers on their palms wilted before they stopped screaming in ecstasy. This was always said with a nod and a twinkle in the eye at the point in the next henna ceremony when the women had drunk their share of spiced wine, and the steam of the fire and the *clink clink* of the shinshilla cymbals and the damp sea-urchin scent of the incense colluded in making everyone lazy and inclined to confuse fantasies with secrets, and say such things as would make even the most seasoned matron blush.

If you ask people who remember those days, some will insist that strange things happened once Rahel Damari started to work in earnest. It was said that the men of Qaraah grew too potent for their own good and began rutting in the streets like goats and rams. Others said that it was the women who grew lusty and were not ashamed of their own desires, which took strange forms, and made them drowsy during the day, unable to cook, or clean, or even care for their many children. But there are others who remember those days differently, and swear that none of these things happened, and that the coming of the other Damaris had absolutely no effect upon the marital lives of the community. I myself have no idea what was true, for when I was old enough to ask, the truth of the matter had dried up, like the lava from the ancient mountain volcanoes, lording a petrified history over us like giants of ash and smoke.

Chapter 14

In midautumn, a month or so after my first henna, my mother's thick shadow fell over my hands. I was sitting in the courtyard between our house and the other Damaris' house.

"Umph, you have no talent for their work."

I was used to my mother's criticism, and knew better than to respond. I didn't even look up.

"Really, you are clumsy; you'll never succeed at it."

I gritted my teeth and ignored her. I had begun to take up the stylus myself, tentatively practicing my own lines on scraps of cured calf skin. At first I tried to hide my new habit, but it is hard to hide henna. I tried to work under the frankincense tree behind Auntie Aminah's house, but I needed water, because my henna was too thick, and the water was out front, in the basins. I then tried to work next door, by the dye mistress's pots, but she was nosy and kept looking over my shoulder to make aesthetic suggestions. I moved to behind the chicken coop, but my brother Dov saw me and mocked me in a loud voice, scaring the chickens. I stopped hiding and started working in the small courtyard between our house and the little house with the red roof. And that's when my mother saw me. She'd come out of the house, walked over to where I was sitting, and peered over my shoulder.

I kept at it. I was trying very hard to make a seashell. The whirl of the bottom curve was tricky. My hand wavered and blurred the henna, leaving a blotch.

"Umph," she said again. But she didn't leave. I dipped my stylus again and made another shell. Again, I botched it. My mother shifted her feet but still didn't move away. I heard her breathing, clearing her throat. She never wore henna, not even at very special celebrations. I suppose it was her way of distinguishing herself from them, rebuking their ornate lives with her own austerity.

"No, you have no talent for their work." She squatted in front of me, held out her palms, and winced as if she were showing me a tender place, a spot pricked by a deep splinter. She curled her fingers into fists and then opened them again, revealing work-weathered skin overlaid with the skein of her life lines.

"If you are going to improve, you need to practice on something other than dead animal skin, no?"

The first time I put the henna stylus to my mother's skin, my hands shook, my lines blurred, my heart pounded so loudly I was sure she could hear it. I was in a most precarious position. No matter what I did, she would be angry, and would yell, and would use henna as just another way to let me know that I had no real place in her heart. I brought the stylus to her skin so slowly that the henna clumped before I could apply it. I tried again. When I felt the stylus press into her skin, I braced myself. Surely she was toying with me and would smack my ears, swipe the stylus from my hand. But nothing happened. So I drew a line, another line, a wave, a wave, a curl. The littlest flower. She held her hand taut and even let out a little giggle to show that it tickled. She didn't chastise my artless sloppiness. And when I was finished that first day she held her hands up to her face, puffed out her lower lip, and even nodded her head in mild approval. The next time I was less nervous. After that, the only time my hands wavered was because I was not sure what to draw next, not because I expected to be condemned by her for my efforts. At first my mother washed the henna paste off before it could dry, but eventually, she let me set it with lemon and sugar water, and left it on. Sometimes she even wrapped her hands at night after I had hennaed them in order to let the color sink even deeper into her skin. And then she went about her work vividly adorned. When someone in the market or in synagogue would comment on her henna, she would say, "Ech, my Adela is lazy with a stylus, but it is all I can do to help her get better, no? It is a mother's lot to suffer her daughter's deficiencies." But I always knew that she wouldn't have worn my henna if she weren't proud of my efforts.

Hani was delighted to be my teacher. "Good henna relies upon intensity," she said. "The darker the bride's henna, the longer a couple's love will last."

She showed me how my squiggles were too weak and my angular

lines too sharp. She taught me how to make her favorite designs—fish, shells, and peacocks—and then laughed indulgently when my fish looked like snakes and my shells looked like ears and my peacocks looked like pigeon wings.

She bored me to tears with a lecture on Egyptian and Sudanese henna traditions but was relentlessly patient when I kept confusing squares with circles and diamonds with teardrops for ankle cuffs and wrist bracelets. And she was my tutor in variations of the Eye of God, the most powerful design to ward off evil.

Almost every henna tradition has its own version of the Eye. Hani began with the most straightforward, a Berber charm of three concentric triangles, with a cross in the center to deflect evil in all four directions. She explained the symbolic meaning behind even the simplest henna marks. "These ripples" she said, pointing to my pathetic and squished attempt at waves, "signify the purification of water, and the abundance of all life." She wrinkled up her nose. "But maybe your water is not so abundant yet, just a trickle, a little thirsty stream?" She tugged on my hair and smiled, to show me that her teasing was good-natured.

Each sign had a corresponding connotation. A squiggle was a wave in the ocean, but it was also a cupped palm, a gesture of greeting, or of harvest plenty, or both. I memorized thirty or so of the most important "elements" and their corresponding meanings. I practiced combining the elements to create traditional forms (arabesque, peacock, garland, nightingale, fish, sunburst, paisley cuff, and so on). I marveled at how a single line or dot, replicated with artistry and expertise, could create a design so intricate. Learning how to apply henna made me look at the world differently. Where before I had seen pebbles, pine needles, blades of straw, I now saw shadows and lines that were the sinew and bone of pictures yet to be drawn.

Hani was delighted that I wanted to learn. She gave me practical tips: "You hold your subject's hand in your own, start on the left and finish on the right. That way, you don't smear the side of your own hand as you work." She showed me how, when making ankle designs, one must paint three-fourths of the way around, and then go back to the beginning to meet the line from the other side. "Otherwise, there is a good chance your lines won't meet, and instead of a bracelet, you will have inscribed an endless line, which you will have to finish off somehow, probably with another rotation."

One day, she took my arm and put it over her shoulder. She was taller than I, and my arm sloped up, my hand burrowed in her hair.

"In order to do the inside part of the arm, have your friend rest her arm over your own shoulder as you work." Hani always called henna subjects "friends" even though a henna artist is often hired to decorate the skin of strangers. She pretended that she was holding a stylus and showed me how she would decorate the skin between my armpit and elbow. We were very close together. Before she let me go, she leaned forward and kissed me on the lips. Then she proceeded to tickle me so that I doubled over with laughter. When I had recovered she said, "Silly Adela, you are adorable. Look at you. You've seen me do this one hundred times, and now you are wide-eyed and curious."

My own henna skills? In spite of Hani's patient tutelage, I was not very good, but after a while I was proficient enough to have my own flair. I mastered the basic vocabulary. Most designs are linking ones, with one line touching the line next to it, garlands and chains joined in concentric dances, which link a girl to herself, a woman to her mother, a mother to her grandmother, who wear the designs too. My lines were never as elegant as Hani's. But my swirls always flowed together in a pleasing manner. My garlands of flowers or hearts or triangles or wings or seashells were always continuous in a way that seemed to suggest that the arm or the hand was only a starting point, and that the design repeated itself in swirls of infinity.

One day Auntie Aminah came to visit. My mother was stirring a stew. I had hennaed my mother's hands with a pattern inspired by the cuff stitching on a pair of fancy leggings—paisley tears and interlocking triangles as well as concentric circles and little stars. I noticed Auntie Aminah looking at my mother's hands gripping the stirring spoon. When I walked her home she was unusually quiet. I was quiet too. When we reached her house, she took my hand in hers, kissed my fingertips.

"Adela, your mother was wrong."

"Wrong about what?"

"Hani has not influenced you at all. You are your very own person. An original girl. I am proud of you."

I held up my hennaed hands. "Auntie, surely I am a copycat, mimicking my cousin's skill, stealing her interests and talents."

"Dear, there is a difference between mimicry and inspiration."

"Humph. I have no idea what you mean."

But my auntie could see that I was smiling, proud and grateful for her compliment. Because I did know what she meant. I knew even then that my designs were different from Hani's and Aunt Rahel's, and that I drew from a different place, my artistic eye trained on a different horizon.

Aunt Rahel did not show me designs or correct my artistic mistakes, but invited me into her "laboratory." She was teaching me some recipes and letting me watch as she "cooked" the henna to the right consistency. By midwinter, I had grown quite adept at forming henna elements. Now Aunt Rahel promised to show me how to make the henna paste a more vibrant shade of red by adding a brandy infusion. We made an appointment at Hanukkah time. I remember that it was Hanukkah because she had told me to come over after I had finished preparing the *zalaviyye* pancakes for our holiday meal. I finished cooking and then walked through the courtyard and into the little house, but no one was there. Instead of leaving, I decided to wait. Hani was with Masudah, helping her with her babies. Uncle Barhun had gone to the market with my father. I sat back on the jasmine-scented pillows and felt something bulging beneath them. I reached underneath and pulled out a little leather satchel. I held it up and realized that it was Hani's, the one she had brought to Qaraah, tied around her waist. I hadn't seen it since. Without thinking, I tugged at the leather thong that cinched its neck closed. Then I hesitated; for a moment I felt as if I shouldn't. But Hani had never been stingy with her treasures. I opened it up. There were the dolls with their shiny white cowrie beads for heads, cork bodies, and translucent aquamarine beads for hands and legs. I lifted them up one by one, fingering their cold smooth faces. But the bag wasn't empty. I upended it onto my lap. The chipped sapphire came rolling out. I pressed my fingers into the defects of the stone. The old sprig of wall rue had been replaced by a sachet of crushed rosemary. And there was the book of psalms. I flipped through the pages. When Hani had taught me to read, she had used this very book of psalms for instructional material. Now I could read myself. I mouthed the words as they flew past my fingertips. *And He rode upon a cherub, and did fly; yea, He did swoop down upon the wings of the wind.* As I flipped through, something caught my eye at the very back of the book. On the last page, in the margins, up and down Psalm 150, were graffiti. In her precise, neat hand, Hani had made a grid and filled it in with the Hebrew alphabet, the aleph bet.

Corresponding to each letter was a tiny henna element. I was stunned. She had written in the sacred book, as if it were no more holy than a piece of butcher's paper. There are twenty-two letters in the Hebrew alphabet and there were twenty-two henna elements in the list, the most rudimentary ones, slashes and humps and dots, swirls, circles. On their own these elements are meaningless, but when joined together by a skilled henna artist, they become a blooming hibiscus, a thorny vine of roses, a venomous snake, or the Eye of God itself. I ran my finger down the page, my fingertips touching each Hebrew letter and its twin henna element. When I had finished, I half expected to have wiped off the letters—as if they were little fruits that I could collect from a tree, or berries on a bush no one had ever seen before—and to have my hands full of Hani's cryptic henna work. But my hands were empty and the page was still full. I knew these elements well by now. They were the building blocks of complex designs, little picture-bricks in the sturdy house of henna work. I scanned again, with my finger traveling down from aleph to taf. The last henna element was a thick sideways hook like a thumbnail clipping. This element is useful in windmill designs, each curve a different blade on the swirl. Just as I was beginning to lose myself in this strange new language, I heard a noise. Aunt Rahel.

"Oh my dear," she said, "I am so sorry that I left you waiting!"

Quickly, I shoved the dolls, the sachet, and the sapphire back into the bag. Without thinking, I took the little leather-bound book of psalms and secreted it in my skirt pocket. By the time Aunt Rahel was standing before me, the leather satchel was back beneath the pillow.

"Now where were we? Oh yes, I was going to show you how to make a brandy variation in order to deepen the color red. Your father was kind enough to get me the brandy. Here, smell it. Strong eh? Well, we had better get started, we have much to do."

She began by adding coffee water to crushed henna leaves. As she mixed, adding the water drop by drop, she told me stories about the many brides she had hennaed. I had heard some of them before, for Aunt Rahel often told them in the henna house, when the fire was low, and designs complete, the paste setting on our skin.

"There was the bride who laughed like a crow," she said, "and the one who cursed, and fainted. And the silly little bride who shuddered, as if she were being beaten. And a nervous one who drank so much date wine, she farted and burped during the ceremony, and almost fell asleep before it was over. And then there was a dainty bride, with fine black hair. As I hennaed her feet, she whispered that she was going to die on her wedding night. She'd had a vivid premonition."

"Did she?"

"Of course. Of course, she did, two months after the chuppah. Adela, all premonitions on a bride's Night of Henna come true."

"Really?"

She looked over at me with a sly smile. "Only if you want them to. And then there was that skinny thing—what was her name? Oh yes, Beena, her name was Beena, and she had knobby elbows, a crooked nose, and buckteeth."

I remember being surprised by Aunt Rahel's stories, by how irreverent they were. She didn't hesitate to make fun of brides, or to laugh at their fear.

"Auntie Rahel, is it proper?"

"Is what proper?"

"To laugh at them, to find amusement in their suffering?"

"Silly Adela, what do you think? That a henna dyer is a confessor? A friend? A confidant? No, the henna dyer is engaged to offer a service. Not to fawn over or flatter the girls who wear the bridal gargush. And anyway, a good henna dyer must maintain a sense of distance from her subject, otherwise—"

"Otherwise what?"

"She risks absorbing their sadness, their sacrifices. That's where the danger lies. For the sadness of a bride is more permanent a dye than henna. And no woman could stand to saturate herself with all the emotions of so many brides. A lifetime of brides would stain a soul."

I still remember those story-brides exactly as Aunt Rahel described them. The women given to pay monetary debts. The women given to become stepmothers to a dozen children even though they were still children themselves. I remember Rahel's tales of ugly brides bartered for so many goats, and her descriptions of the weird bug-eyed, thin-lipped creatures given in deference to ancient agreements between families who had traded boys and girls back and forth so many times and through so many generations that their lineages were a macramé tapestry, every fresh wedding a new knot on the brocade.

And then there were the brides who actually loved their grooms. When Aunt Rahel spoke of them, her voice slowed down, became deeper. I came to understand that these stories were rare.

"When there is love, the stylus is swift, magical," she said. "The honey and almond pastries set out for us to eat are sweeter."

"And the songs?"

"The songs we sing to the brides sound louder, as if there are extra voices in the room; brides who love their grooms let me—they let me anoint them with oil, massage them, make them smell like a fragrant field of jasmine flowers."

"And the ones who don't love their grooms?"

"Brides who don't love endure these rituals, and even, sadly, begrudge me for participating in their enslavement. But brides who love welcome my ministrations and even let me confide my special secrets."

As I macerated leaves, mixed an herbal infusion, or measured scent according to Aunt Rahel's instructions, every so often my hand would bump against the book in my pocket. It made me feel as if I had a secret. But I also knew that I had nothing to hide and that if Hani were there, I would show her. "Look," I would say, "I found your book."

When the concoction was almost finished, I asked Aunt Rahel something I had been wondering about for a long time.

"Aunt Rahel," I said, "your henna designs are so beautiful. But they disappear so quickly, a few weeks, poof, they are gone. They have no . . . no . . . posterity." I searched for the word, which felt very grown-up on my tongue. "Why don't you ever draw or paint on paper?" I asked her. "Like Masudah. She makes her own paper and draws pictures from her home, from Aden. You could too. You could draw all your patterns. That way the designs would last."

"Phe, Adela, paper is for men."

"Skin is for women?"

"Parchment is skin. The Torah is written on the skin of an animal. So, you see, skin has holiness."

"But no permanence?"

"Adela, if you look for permanence in this life, you will be sorely disappointed."

"Well, at least there is your book."

"What book?"

"Your henna book, with the elements; maybe one day it will be in a museum."

"Eh?"

"I heard about museums from my father," I explained. "He said that in Istanbul they have museums of ancient civilization. They have displays of artifacts from the time of Abraham our Father. He said that it is possible to see a bowl or a spoon or a necklace made of iridescent glass beads, perhaps worn by Sarah our Mother herself. What I am saying is that I would like to build my own museum."

"And what will be in it, this . . . museum?" Aunt Rahel smiled.

"Your henna work. Your patterns. The designs you collect, and those you create."

"No, not my work."

"Then whose?"

"They are not mine to claim. The patterns, the elements. The recipes. They belong to all of us. To any woman who has ever held a stylus in her hand."

That night when I was alone, I took Hani's book of psalms out of my skirt pocket and studied the list of elements and their corresponding letters. I rummaged a piece of thin kitchen paper from the pantry, the kind we used to wrap meat. I copied the letters and their corresponding elements, checking over the list three times to make sure I hadn't made any mistakes. Before falling asleep, I tried to memorize as many as I could. Aleph was a wavy line. Bet was a left-to-right slash. Gimel, an open-bottom triangle. Dalet, a left-open triangle. I folded up the paper and put it in the drawer where I kept my underclothes, under a cotton shift. I put Hani's book under my pillow. When I finally fell asleep, I dreamed of Hani's little cowrie dolls. But in my dream they were all in pieces. The heads had become detached from their bodies. Their hands were broken off. Their legs were all in a tangle at the bottom of the satchel.

In the morning I made some excuse to go next door. The house was empty. Aunt Rahel and Hani were at the market. I didn't know where Uncle Barhun was. Quickly, I dug underneath the pillows and retrieved the leather satchel. I put the book of psalms back where it belonged. When I came out, my mother was in our doorway. I remembered that I had promised her I would mix more *hawaij*. My mother rarely complimented my cooking, but more and more she asked me to make dishes, spices, and breads that she usually made herself. I knew that everyone liked my hawaij because I added saffron and extra cardamom.

My mother squinted, appraised me. There were wedge-like lines on her forehead and deep wrinkles coming from her eyes.

"You will ruin that dress. So much turmeric will stain more than your fingers."

"What?"

"Take it off; you can't make hawaij wearing a nice dress, can you?"

"Of course not."

"Well, go change. Go already. You should be halfway finished with your chores by now."

By the time Aunt Rahel and Hani returned from the market, my fingers were yellow from the turmeric, and I was tired from all my chores. After the hawaij, I had spent time at the grinding stones smashing corn for meal for dumplings, and then I had collected and delivered eggs to Auntie Aminah. I was a mess. My braids were falling out of my gargush, my apron was stained, my face sweaty.

Hani smiled at me. "You've been hard at work. Let's go wash you up, and then I'll braid your hair."

We walked from the grinding stones to the washbasin, and I splashed water on my face. Then we walked to Auntie Aminah's house and sat under her frankincense tree, while Hani brushed and braided my hair. I shut my eyes as she tugged my head backward. I imagined that Hani's sisters, the cousins I knew only from her stories, were there with us. Naama and Asisah, the dead twins, were there as shadow-selves; Edna was in front of me, Hamama and Nogema behind us, and we were part of a chain of girls braiding one another's hair, a chain so long that every girl in the whole world was another link, her nimble fingers tugging, tucking, weaving, and telling tales.

"There, now you won't feel so hot." I had thick heavy hair, and it was a relief to have it off my neck. We sat there for a few more moments not speaking and then we got up to go. As we approached the dye mistress's yard, we could hear her humming a tune about swallows and springtime. Hani began to hum along. I began to hum too. The dye mistress was at her troughs. She stopped humming when we walked by and we exchanged casual pleasantries. I followed Hani through the wall, to our houses. I thought of her henna alphabet. I wondered if I should ask her about it, and if I did, if she would be amused that I had found it, or angry at me for opening her bag, invading her privacy. I was never a girl reluctant to speak my mind, but when I opened my mouth to ask her about it, no words came out.

She stopped, leaned against the donkey's hitching post. "What, Adela? What is it?"

I think that is the first moment I ever really saw her. Her hair was falling loose from her gargush. Strands of gold and red, embedded in her chestnut locks, glinted in the sun. Or maybe what I mean to say is that for the first time I really understood her. As if she too had been a code that suddenly cracked. I have often thought of her at that moment. So pretty. Her head cocked to one side, as if she were listening to the music of scripture, the desert song of ancient days.

"What is it?"

"Nothing." I suddenly felt fear, a prickly chill at the back of my neck. "But . . ."

"But what?"

A thought had just occurred to me. How had I trusted her to write on *my* skin? A verse of scripture popped into my head. *The words of Elohim are pure words, as silver tried in a crucible on the earth, refined seven times.* My skin prickled. She looked away from me, up into the sky. I followed her gaze. A pair of sooty falcons was soaring overhead. The air was hot and thick, there was no wind. And then I had the worst thought of all. Hani had delivered Mr. Musa's basket the day he died. What had she once said? *He won't marry you. You will be free of him.*

Had she cursed Mr. Musa by delivering the basket? Had evil murderous charms been written on her skin when she handed the kubaneh to Mrs. Musa? Charms that made Mrs. Musa kill her husband?

"Nothing. I am tired. Forgive me." I walked on, forcing myself to speak normally, and not let my voice betray my horrible suspicions. "I will see you at dinner, Hani."

I went inside, shut the door, and leaned against it. I thought of the story Asaf had told me so long ago—the one about the groom who tried to assassinate the Imam by reading the henna code on his bride's feet. I thought about the stories Masudah had told me about Aunt Rahel. How people said she cursed brides and made them bear monsters. Or that she blessed brides and was said to be in congress with the goddess Anath. Henna dyers arrange their designs into pictorial amulets and ancient imagistic charms to ward off evil. But these charms and amulets are not alphabetical. They are language without language. What would happen if people knew that Hani had devised her own alphabet, and was perhaps writing insults instead of blessings? If they knew that she had hidden intentions, an agenda all her own, what would they think of her? What would they do to her? Would they run her out of town? Shame her? Or worse?

I didn't meet Hani's gaze at the meal. That night around the fire, her hennaed hands, and the hands of my sisters-in-law, my aunt, and my own hands flitted and worked as usual. We were embroidering, cracking nuts, weaving on a hand loom, cupping to show a quantity of a recipe's measure, gesturing to show the size of a large drum someone saw at the market. I watched everyone's hands in the orange glow of the firelight. The henna on everyone's skin seemed to shift this way and that, and to glimmer like lengths of shimmering silk. The more I watched, the more the henna seemed enchanted. The elements unwound themselves from ancient patterns, and rearranged themselves into stories no one had dared to tell me before. I imagined that I saw Hani's code curled in every slant and circle. I was transfixed. I couldn't decipher anything, and yet, was sure that there was something to be deciphered.

"Adela, Adela, did you hear me?" Hani touched me on the shoulder. "Didn't you hear?" She repeated the punch line to her joke.

I smiled, and pretended to join in the conversation. But inside, I had a thousand unanswered questions. How had I not noticed it before? How had I not seen the code adorning her life line? And if it was really there, how would I ever be able to read it? I had just learned to read Hebrew; how could I read a code of swirls and lines and stars?

Before she left, Hani said, "You must get good sleep tonight, Adela. You don't seem like yourself. I hope you aren't getting sick. If you don't feel well tomorrow, you must come to Mother for some of her special bayberry tea."

I lay on my pallet making resolutions: I would memorize the alphabetical correspondences and keep my eye out for any stray elements on hands and feet that Hani had hennaed. I told myself that if she were using the code on anyone, I would catch her and go to Aunt Rahel. And that if she had used the code against me before, well, there was nothing I could do, but she would certainly never use her dark skills on me again.

But, by the light of day, I found that I wasn't upset anymore. I reminded myself that I didn't believe a whit in dark magic, and that it was ridiculous to think that charms scribbled on a girl's hand could cause a man's death. I reassured myself that Hani had always been kind to me. I told myself that I had overreacted and that her henna alphabet was probably an old discarded game. Nothing but a scrap of nonsense. And I was even a bit enamored of the idea that Hani and I now shared a secret . . . or at least, that I knew her secret. I told myself that I would keep my eyes open, but I had no reason to suspect that she was up to no good.

Chapter 15

In the late spring of 1931, several months after I'd found Hani's coded henna alphabet, a Jewish girl was found murdered near the camel caravan depot. The men went to search the hills for the murderer, and we girls were not allowed to walk alone. Many of the young men of Qaraah took to patrolling. The patrols were meant to keep us all safe, but we girls scoffed at the boys, and mocked their bravado and bluster behind their backs. Our foraging trips to gather henna were curtailed. My aunt's henna supplies dwindled and she had to resort to purchasing her henna leaves from a stall in the market. We no longer went to wash clothes in the wadi unless traveling in a large group. Hani and I avoided my cave, leaving my goddesses once more abandoned. Two weeks after the first murder, a Muslim girl was found dead, the daughter of a horse breeder. She was found behind the camel market, disposed of just like the first girl, naked, with her throat slashed and clods of earth in her mouth. We grew even more fearful. We stopped going to the well unless a brother, father, or uncle went with us. When my father accompanied us, he often offered to carry water himself. Uncle Barhun carried water too, and sometimes both my father and uncle came with us and would amuse us on the long walk to and from the well with stories from their youth, in which Barhun was often getting lost, and my father tasked with finding him.

My brother Hassan, Half Nose, had hated me from the time I was a baby. "He couldn't have had a reason," Sultana said, "for you were both too young for reasons." She told me that when I was born, and he was just four years old, he would add extra blankets to my cradle so I would sweat in the summer and take them off in the winter so I would shiver. He dumped salt in my food so that I would cry and spit it out and go hungry. He pinched my toes and maligned me to our mother. In short, he made my life miserable whenever he had the chance.

When it came to looking for the murderer, Hassan joined every expedition he could. Everyone knew that Hassan was no hero, and volunteered only because it was his way of shirking his duties. He was lazy, a reluctant worker. He had been apprenticed to a lampmaker when he was just a small boy. By volunteering to look for the murderer, he got himself out of the workshop and into the dunes around Qaraah—freedom to do what he wished.

One afternoon, I was at the breadboard, pounding dough for supper, and my mother was at the fire, clarifying butter for samneh, when the door opened. Hassan strode in, lips open, crooked teeth sharp and menacing, face stretched in a punishing leer.

"Look what I found!" he growled.

I saw with a flash of panic that he was holding two of my idols.

"I was out patrolling," he continued, "and I came across a cave above the old iron forge. Inside was an altar, a pagan altar. I found ten little idols arranged for devotions. They belong to your daughter—a little witch." He glowered at me. "For all we know, she conjured the devil who killed those girls. I found all manner of things in the cave that implicate her. Cast-off pots, rugs, and trinkets from our household. Look, Father's leather." He pinched a piece of leather around the middle of one of the idols. I had made a little apron for Anath, my newest idol, out of a scrap of leather from my father's shop. The edges were marked with my father's distinctive triangle and circle pattern.

My mother had put down her wooden spoon and was now standing with her hands on her hips. Hassan kept talking. "That little harpy. Maybe Adela has cursed every one of us." He held up the idols. I noticed that his face was a strange shade, pale and greenish, and he looked like he was going to be sick.

My mother turned and lifted the butter pot off the fire. She placed it very deliberately on the cooling stone. Then she wiped her hands on her apron and reached out and took the idols. At that very moment, Hassan put his hand up to his mouth and ran out the door. We could hear him vomiting, retching into the earth. When he came back in, my mother threw a rag at him and made a disgusted face. "Clean yourself up," she ordered. Hassan dabbed miserably at his glistening lips as my mother held one of my idols, examining it, lifting up her clothes. I had made her a skirt out of a scrap of blue cloth from our darning basket—the same cloth that was now on our table, set for dinner. My mother raised the idol to her face. Her nostrils flared, as if she were smelling something spoiled, acrid. Then she threw it into the hearth fire. The flames danced around the smooth body, licking it, and scorching the cloth. She put the other idol on the breadboard and then began to beat me. I had suffered enough beatings at her hand to know how to brace myself against her anger. But this was different. Her slaps were harder, and kept coming, blow after blow on my face, my shoulders, and then into my belly, her fingers curled in a fist. I still had a piece of dough in my hand, and I squeezed it hard, focusing my entire soul on that little piece of dough. *Maybe I will become the dough*, I thought, *maybe I will leave this world and return as a bit of simple sustenance.*

How long did it go on? For as long as it took for that idol to catch and crackle. For as long as it took for Hassan to wipe his face, sit himself down on the divan pillows, and lean back in a languid pose, declaring himself both judge and audience. My mother must have paused in her attack to throw the second idol into the fire, though I don't remember a break in her fury. The little Anath idol caught slower than the older idol, its body holding on to its integrity for a few moments before the flames pounced. And still my mother kept beating me. But then the door opened, and Hani was there. Hassan made a scraping sound with his throat, as if the mere sight of her made him feel like vomiting again. My mother, her hand raised to me, gaining purchase before coming down again on my cheek, spat out the words "Out girl, this is none of your business," but Hani didn't listen. Later she told me that she had had a premonition, and that the idols themselves appeared to her in a vision, telling her that they were burning, like Moses' bush. Sultana said that Hani didn't have a vision, but was walking by our door and heard my mother yelling. Masudah said that it didn't matter why Hani came, only that she did, and that once she was inside, the idols in the fire told her everything she needed to know. She ran right past Hassan, and put herself in between me and my mother. "Oh, Aunt Suli," she said, dropping down to her knees, "don't blame Adela. The idols are mine. I made them. They are all mine. And so is the altar. I bring them offerings. Adela has never even been to my cave. She has nothing to do with my foolishness."

Hassan was shaking his head, saying, "Mother, don't be tricked. If anything, they are in league together. Beat them both. They are both little witches."

"Get your uncle," she snarled to Hassan. "Tell him to come. To come now for his degenerate daughter."

Hani continued to defend me. "Auntie Sulamita, Adela would never do such things. She is a pious girl. Why, every morning she prays, and when she catches me gossiping, she warns me against the dangers of the evil tongue. She reminds me to say the prayer of Motzi before breaking bread and is in every way a modest Jewish girl. Why, if she had known of my idols, I am sure she would have thrown them into the fire herself."

My mother looked back and forth between me and Hani. Then she sat down heavily on the stool by the hearth. She bunched up her apron and ran a hand through her hair, gray and wiry, which had come loose from her gargush and was hanging in front of her eyes. I was peeking up at her from where I was curled up on the floor, my face stinging, my belly bruised, my whole body shaking from the assault.

I do not know if my mother wholly believed Hani, or if she merely colluded with her. That is, if she let Hani lift the burden of my guilt, and wrap it around herself like a prayer shawl, a holy garment upon which we could all embroider our threats, sacrileges, and suspicions. My mother had blackened my right eye and split my lip. She did not apologize in words, but put me to bed with an onion poultice on my back and potato peelings on my eyes. She sat up by my side, changing the poultices every few hours throughout the night. My father complained to my mother about how she had treated me, but he did not yell or raise a hand to her, which I assume was a concession. After all, she had warned from the very beginning that *the other Damari girl* was a bad influence. Now she had proof. In the morning I was sore and ugly. My right eye was almost swollen shut. But my parents coddled me. My father went to the market and brought me a coral bracelet, a lavish indulgence that I took from him, incredulous, and put on my wrist right away. My mother, in a rare show of remorse, cooked me my favorite lentil soup and fed me herself, as if I were a baby.

Uncle Barhun and Aunt Rahel punished Hani by having her devote herself to prayer. They made her sit and read psalms in the synagogue every afternoon for weeks. And after that, she was ordered to sit with the women who watch over dead female bodies, saying psalms until they are buried. With this final punishment, even my mother objected, complaining that it was "a morbid task for a girl." She railed to my father against my aunt and uncle's treatment of Hani, which I found astonishing, as she had seen nothing wrong with beating me, her own daughter, for the same crime.

When I asked Auntie Aminah about it, she said, "Your mother would have beaten you and been done with it. For all her faults, she would not have continued to punish you after that beating, however harsh her blows. But your Aunt Rahel and Uncle Barhun know what it means to be haunted by other people's beliefs and suppositions, and wish no such strife for their daughter. They make her pray in public in order to save her from herself."

After I had recovered from my beating, I heard many stories about what had really happened when Hassan found my cave. Some seemed credible, others fantastical. Masudah told the lewdest story, which gave it credence, for she was not one to speak of such things ordinarily. She said that after my beating she overheard Hassan crying to her husband, my brother Dov. Hassan told Dov that he found the cave because when he was patrolling nearby, he had heard a sweet melody coming from inside. He was drawn there, unable to resist the allure of the unearthly music. Inside, he encountered a siren—a woman who was also not a woman—and that she made love to him like a man, subjecting him to unholy carnal feats until he begged for mercy.

Sultana rolled her eyes, furrowed her mannish eyebrows, and said that she too had overheard gossip. "There was no siren," she said, "only a shepherd boy and girl, taking each other in front of the altar. Hassan hid and watched them and grew aroused. When they saw him touching himself they laughed and mocked him, causing his manhood to shrivel. He fled that place like a little girl, his balls withered in their sacs."

Yerushalmit heard a woman in the ritual bath tell a different story. Supposedly Hassan came across an old sage in the cave. The sage invited Hassan for tea and then cackled that he was a demon, and that since Hassan had shared his drink, he would be a demon too. "When he came to your parents' house, he was deranged with fear. Didn't he vomit? Well, that was the demon's tea, stirring up his insides."

I don't know if any of this ever happened. But I know that Hassan was different after my beating and Hani's punishment. He was humbler, and much less horrible. Not long after he found my cave, he married a poor young widow with five children, a woman everyone overlooked, but upon whom he doted. He became a good husband and stepfather, though he never sired children of his own. He applied himself in earnest to learning the lampmaker's trade. He even stopped hating me, and would go out of his way to compliment my cooking and my stitchery and to ask my opinion on matters of consequence.

In the blaze of midsummer, just days before the ninth of Av, when we wear sackcloth and ashes and cry from morning till night to commemorate the destruction of the Temple, a man was caught on the paths above the little well, forcing himself on a girl whose clothes he had already torn to shreds. The girl's anguished screams had alerted a pair of brickmakers working at a nearby kiln and they came to her rescue. Bloodstained clothing was found at the man's house. He confessed to the earlier crimes. The murderer was hung in the scrubyard behind the southern cistern. The community breathed a sigh of relief, though it was still some time before mothers let their daughters walk unescorted to the well, and we could not go out collecting henna without looking over our shoulders and feeling our hair stand on end at the rustling of leaves or the snap of a twig.

With the murderer gone, everyone relaxed. I watched my mother bathe in the wadi for the first time in months with a smile on her thin lips, the water running in cold rivulets down her graying hair. I watched the midwife hitch up her dress and run around our town, mopping her brow as she went from one house to another. Aunt Rahel helped her, and Hani and my sister-in-law Sultana did too—for the midwife couldn't be everywhere at once. It seemed that many mothers had crossed their legs and held their babies in while the murderer was still afoot, and now that he was caught, they'd agreed to let their babies come into the world. My father rarely danced, but now I watched him dance on the Sabbath eve, his arms flung with casual languor around Uncle Barhun's shoulders as they moved together to the beat of the tabl drum played by my brother Dov. Even the Imam's men, when they came on a patrol from Sana'a, seemed more relaxed. Though I suppose this was just coincidental, for what did they really care about the capture of a murderer who killed young girls? But still, they harassed us less. A jeweler who had been fined and imprisoned for building a fifth story on his house, making it taller than the houses of the Muslims in Qaraah, was released from jail.

A boy who had been imprisoned for refusing to carry a corpse out of the house of a Muslim neighbor was also released, and a girl left orphaned when her parents both died of diphtheria was saved from the Orphans Decree. They let an aunt adopt her, even though she could afford to pay but a paltry bribe.

Chapter 16

I carefully considered how to thank Hani, and finally went to Masudah and asked her for some sheets of her paper. This was an extravagant request, but she didn't seem surprised. She agreed even before I had finished bargaining for it. "I'll come every day and help you with the children," I said. "I'll mix your hawaij and bake your Sabbath jachnun throughout the summer."

She tsked. "Take however many pieces you want. Just promise me that you won't be using it to give your mother any more excuses to beat you. I don't want to be party to your punishment. Promise me? Yes, that's a good girl. Go, go get what you want; you know where I keep it."

Then I asked my father for a few pieces of leather. He told me I could use any scraps I could glean from the floor of his shop. I spent an afternoon sorting through the pile until I found a few good-size pieces. I cut the leather into rectangles and used my father's blunt needles to sew the pieces together, adding a little nub of a sandwich panel the size of two joints of my pinky finger between the two larger pieces. I sewed a stiff linen "spine" onto the nub. I glued Masudah's paper onto the spines of the books with some thick animal glue that I boiled myself using a piece of hide I bought from the butcher. I had taken ten sheets of paper, which I cut in half. This gave me two "books" of ten leaves, each with twenty pages. My books were no bigger than a book of psalms, just a little larger than the palm of my hand. I took some silk thread, and reinforced the glue with strong stitches. The leather was embossed with my father's triangle and square signature, the same signature that had implicated me. I left some of the pattern down the sides of the front cover for decoration.

When my books were finished, I took a henna stylus and I mixed henna with black gall. I chose the better-made book, the second one

I had stitched together. In the very center of the inside back cover, I wrote, in Hebrew, "To Hani Damari, from your cousin Adela Damari." I formed the letters carefully, exactly as Hani had taught me. Underneath our names, I wrote "Qaraah, Kingdom of Yemen, 1931." I drew a vine of roses underneath. The leather, calf's hide, was very soft and smooth, the color of sugary coffee with goat's milk. It was the kind of leather my father used to make the insides of women's slippers.

Hani was at the grinding stones when I approached her. I held the present hidden behind my back. She looked up, smiled. "Come sit with me."

I crouched beside her. "Here," I said, "I made this for you."

She put down the grinding stones and took the book, which I had wrapped in a piece of yellow cloth and tied with a bow that the dye mistress had dipped for me herself, dipping it three times so that it would come out a bright vermilion.

"What is this?" Her face brightened. She turned the little package over. "What is this for?"

"It's for you. My way of thanking you for what you did for me."

"I didn't do anything you wouldn't have done for me."

"But I won't ever have the chance."

"What do you mean?"

"I won't have to save you, the way you saved me."

"Now you sound like my sister Hamama."

"What do you mean?"

"Hamama can see the future. Can you?"

"Of course not. But there is only one cave, and my idols are broken. If I ever save you, it won't be for what was hidden, and what was holy."

"If your mother could hear you, she would beat you all over again."

I shrugged, but then I put my hand in a fist and I beat my heart with it, like men do on the Day of Atonement, striking heart with fist in penance for all manner of sins.

"What was most holy to me about the cave was gone long ago. My mother was angry about the wrong idols."

Hani screwed up her face, and then covered my hand with her own and pulled it down from my heart. "You have nothing to atone for, Adela. Hope is not a sin, and neither is fidelity."

I nodded toward the present. She pulled the bow and opened my gift.

Her eyes widened, her lips opened in a huge smile. She ran a hand over the cover, and then flipped through the pages.

I said, "It bothers me that henna fades. Your work is so beautiful. It should be preserved. Your mother has a henna book; I thought that you might like one too. You could write all the elements you know, and make up new ones. You could draw your best designs, add notes and henna recipes. It's just a rough, homemade book, but it should last. The glue is strong, and I stitched and restitched all the pages twice."

She reached the last page and read the inscription. Then she closed the cover and wrapped it back up, tying a tight bow with the cloth. We sat together at the grinding stones for a long time. The evening sun began to set, laying its crimson rays down on top of our conversation. She thanked me many times for my gift, and I thanked her many times for saving me from my mother. Later that night, when I lay down on my pallet, I dreamed of that conversation. I dreamed that our words left our mouths and transcribed themselves into the pages of the book. When I awoke, the dream was still cleaving to my soul, hovering there, only now Hani and I were far away from Qaraah, far away from Yemen, in a country whose name I didn't know. In Hani's hands was the gift I had made for her, she held it while I read from it with a pointer whose tip was a shiny silver finger, of the sort our fathers used on Sabbath days when they were reading from the Torah.

And the book I kept for myself? I did not know yet what I would write in it. I had slipped it in my drawer, under my underclothes, on top of the code sheet I had copied from Hani and next to the little embroidered satchel of poison I had stolen from Aunt Rahel. Before I covered it up with linens and leggings, I flipped open the blank pages. For a brief moment I was reminded of that first night after Asaf left Aden. I had dreamed that he was a groom of words, and that I had married him under a canopy of words, and that when he had spoken the wedding blessings, binding me to him, I had turned into words too. I shut the book and covered it with clothes, hiding it as much from myself as from my mother.

Chapter 17

Six months after I gave Hani the book, a young man came to Qaraah and swept her off her feet. It was midwinter of 1932. The other Damaris had been with us in Qaraah for two years. My body was growing into womanhood, but next to Hani, who was voluptuous and beautiful, I felt like a homely little girl. The groom wasn't her old love, Ovadia Shabazzi. This young man's name was David Haza, and he arrived along with his father one day with no warning just before afternoon prayers. David Haza had a kind face, straight teeth, full lips, and a well-tended beard. His wide hazel eyes were just a bit too far apart, his cheekbones were very pronounced, and his nose was like an arrow, but these defects combined to make him handsome in an original way. His father, Mr. Moises Haza, was an old trading partner of Uncle Barhun. Mr. Haza looked nothing like his son, who was trim and smart in his British suit. The father was fat and doughy. We had not seen such an overfed man in a long time. He had kindly crescent-shaped eyes and was completely bald but for the grizzled fuzz growing out of his ears. His bulk was generously and elegantly wrapped in Turkish silks. When Mr. Haza raised an arm, the folds of the gold and yellow cloth billowed. He wore a maroon tarbush, his beard was pointy and reached midway to his chest, in the Turkish fashion.

David was an apprentice scribe and would be studying in Aden under the great Torah scribe Rabbi Aryeh Ben Ari.

"My son can write a whole page of Talmud without even half a mistake," Mr. Haza bragged endearingly about David's talent. But David was modest. Every time Mr. Haza tried to expound on his accomplishments, David would turn the conversation to minor exploits of their travels.

"In the soap market in Aleppo we saw an African man eat knives," he would say, or "In Aqaba we were in a hammam with a British mystery writer writing a book about the murder of a diplomat at the hands of a camel thief."

Hani listened rapt as David spoke, and he was always stealing glances at her. Whenever their eyes met, they blushed and quickly looked away, though there was no hiding the obviousness of their attraction.

"The road to Qaraah was harder than we expected, and took us much longer than we had hoped," Mr. Haza explained.

My father offered an extra room in my brother Dov and sister-in-law Sultana's house. "You will stay with us as long as you need, and rest up for your future travels." David looked shyly up at Hani when she served him at table, and the next day he went out of his way to put himself in her path when she was coming from the well, so he could gallantly offer to carry her burden of water.

I teased Hani. "What about the son of the bookseller? Isn't he waiting for you?"

Hani grimaced. "That dolt? I certainly hope not. My sister Nogema writes me that he is fat now, and can barely see, his eyes are so bad. He stumbles around the market on the way to his father's stall." She was cruel the way she said it, as if she actually wanted the son of the bookseller to fall in a trough of filth. But I found myself laughing along with her as she added, "So what if I loved him when we were children? I also loved a dog then, a black flop-eared puppy, and I can't be expected to marry that little dog, can I?"

"But why are they here?" I asked. "No one comes to Qaraah without good reason."

Hani smiled and licked her lips. Her eyes sparkled with the wisdom of one who possesses superior information. "Mr. Haza is an Adeni, like us," she explained, "but he left Aden long before we did, and lived for many years in Istanbul, where he managed a warehouse and owned shares in the mercantile house of Fey and Absev. Now he is on his way back to Aden. My father told me that the Fey and Absev Company wants Mr. Haza to oversee their southern distribution point. They promised him a generous number of shares in their Aden establishment. Mr. Haza needs a partner and told the Fey and Absev men about Father, and they agreed he could offer Father the position. Mr. Haza had heard through mutual friends that Father was in Qaraah. He came to see if he could talk Father into returning to Aden, and joining with him in what he promises will be a lucrative partnership."

Tears sprang to my eyes. Hani patted my hand and said, "I am sure we won't go. And if we do, we will take you with us."

I managed a smile through my tears at her kind lies. But inside I sobbed, thinking, *First Asaf and now you? Am I to be abandoned once again?*

Over the next few weeks, we grew well acquainted with the Hazas. From the East Mr. Moises Haza had brought with him the habit of standing on his head. It really was astonishing that such a big, round person could balance like that. He was a kind and generous man, who even upside down radiated a sense of charming good humor—as if he were going to tell upside-down jokes, or at least laugh with you about things that were hilarious even right side up. He explained that he had picked up his habit of daily inversion in Istanbul and that it improved "conversation, salivary health, and cardiac circulation." Every evening before prayers, Mr. Haza took out a reed mat, unrolled it in the courtyard, knelt down, put his forehead to the ground, and then did a series of kicks that resulted in his thick bowed legs pointing toward the sky with pointed toes. He wisely changed out of his Turkish pants for the exercise, which would have billowed down around his middle, and wore instead black trousers tucked into thick black socks. He maintained an expression of serenity the entire time, not even widening his eyes or pursing his lips. Only the tips of his ears belied his exertion, turning red as a pepper. But still he didn't come down. He stayed upside down for as long as it took for a "goat to eat his grouts," which seemed to be anywhere between five and ten minutes. When he finally righted himself, the blood flowed back out of his ears, turning them pale again, and his face flushed with a healthy glow. He would then move on to knee bends, marching fist thrusts, lunges, and jumping kicks. Sometimes, in between exercises, he would spend a few moments loudly and ostentatiously cracking his knuckles and neck.

Children grew besotted by Mr. Haza and were soon imitating his exercises and following him around, asking him to show them the correct posture for inversion. They began against a wall, but soon graduated to freestanding headstands, like him. It became a familiar sight to see the children and Mr. Haza planted upside down "like so many turnips," as my father would say. He was mightily amused by the spectacle and would tease the children who swayed or shook, and do his best to resist the urge to flick their toes and make them fall.

One week after their arrival, I counted no fewer than six children upside down in the courtyard. Their faces were red, their cheeks puffed out—only the littlest, Masudah's youngest boy, skinny, determined Pinchas, was accomplishing the trick with the balletic grace and casual serenity of bald Mr. Haza, their teacher, the master inverter.

Mr. Haza made the proper inquiries as to Hani's status. And when it was ascertained that she was indeed unpromised to any other, Uncle Barhun held a private meeting with Hani. Her father told her that he considered David Haza to be a prince of a young man. Hani told her father that if this prince would overlook the fact that she was no princess, she would agree to be his wife. Uncle Barhun relayed Hani's willingness to Mr. Haza. The next day there was a beautiful letter, a single *chet*, ח, the first letter of Hani's name, calligraphed in the earth outside the little red-roofed house. The letter had been written with a sharp stick, and everyone walked around it, giving it wide berth. There was much tittering because of the chet.

Masudah said, "A chet has the same shape as a marriage canopy; surely it is a token of engagement."

It was Sultana who made everyone laugh—and made Hani blush. "The only mystical thing David the apprentice scribe is saying by drawing Hani's chet into the earth is"—she paused for effect—"that he would like to dip his quill in the blood of her maidenhood!"

After that, Hani's marriage was swiftly arranged. Though, of course, her transgression with the idols (which was really my transgression) had to be broached. Uncle Barhun explained to Mr. Haza that Hani had committed a serious sin against Elohim. He related the sad story of the cave and the idols, sparing no details except those of my beating. Mr. Haza's response was so wonderful that it was repeated many times among us females. He said, "If our foremothers, Rahel and Leah, saw fit to steal their household gods from Laban, I myself have no prejudice against a daughter-in-law who cleaves to the ways of the ancients. And my son shall consider himself as blessed as our Father Jacob to be so fortunately wed."

It was clear that Mr. Haza never really considered Hani to be a sinner, for he had a twinkle in his eye when he offered to whittle her some replacements. She was all too happy to play the role of penitent and piously told Mr. Haza that she regretted her childish mistake, but she said it in a voice we all knew well—the same funny lilt she used when telling jokes, or having a small laugh at her own expense.

In preparation for Hani's engagement ceremony, Aunt Rahel gave her new henna. None of us was the least bit surprised when mother gave daughter the henna of nightingales, with the birds' elegant necks arching up over her shins, and their tail feathers draped over the tops of her feet, signifying the lightness of her step as she flitted about, as if her heart too would take flight at the slightest provocation. I opted for a design called Grapes of Thebes, and so did my little niece Remelia, who was so overjoyed with her application, and with how grown-up it made her feel to sit among the women in the henna house, that she became giddy and foolish and tripped over her own gangly limbs like a foolish colt, smearing the design of a pretty cluster of grapes that ran up the back of her right hand. Masudah fixed it for her, as Remelia sat shamefacedly looking at her knees.

"It is no shame to smear your henna," Sultana comforted her.

"That's right; we've all done it at one time or another," Yerushalmit added.

With this, Remelia cheered and her round cheeks once more filled with the rosy blush that marked her as Masudah's daughter. When Aunt Rahel was finished with Hani's henna, she excused herself and kindly took the little ones with her. Remelia went too, gathering up her younger brother and sister, though when she passed through the door it was with a regretful backward glance and a bitten lip that bespoke her wishes to stay and listen. Aunt Rahel wasn't the least bit prudish, and had shared many a bawdy story herself. But when it came time for her own daughters to be married, she generally left the storytelling to others, and now absented herself from the gathering so that Hani would not have to blush in front of her mother.

It was Yerushalmit who did the honors. Yerushalmit had flung off her mean and prudish ways and turned into the lewdest storyteller in the henna house. Yerushalmit wasn't pretty. She had a narrow little face, her nose was both crooked and pointy, and her pockmarked chin jutted out too far under her mouth. But she had a happy, lilting voice, and when she spoke she gave her words an extra helping of expression. It was always fun to listen to her. You knew you would be pulled along by the tale and surprised by a twist in the end. After we all had our henna, and were waiting for the paste to dry, she commanded our attention.

"In honor of Hani, the virgin, and David, the apprentice scribe, I lay before you a story that I will call 'The Scribe Lover.'" We all nodded our approval. Yerushalmit prided herself on matching her stories with the true details of a courting couple.

She began, "Once there was a scribe in the Kingdom of Yemen, in a village where the sand was like the vellum of the Torah. Wherever the people of the village walked, they pressed sacred words into the dunes, and these words sprouted a harvest of delicacies that nourished their bodies and minds for generations. In this holy place lived a young scribe who married his sweetheart. On their wedding night, he laid before his bride the following declaration: 'Beloved, now that we are wed, it is important for you to know that my most difficult and important task as a scribe is to write the sacred names of Elohim with perfection in the Torah. I tell you this because I see little difference between my duty as a scribe and my duty as a husband.' 'What could you possibly mean?' asked his bride. 'Lie back, my love, and let me show you.' She did as he instructed. He parted her legs like Elohim parted the Red Sea, and then he used his tongue like a quill to write the names of Elohim *down there*. Names such as Emet, Truth, and HaRachaman, the Merciful One; Magen Avraham, Shield of Abraham; Boreh, Creator; and Eyeh Asher Ayeh, I Will Be Who I Will Be. All the while, the bride writhed and moaned, and begged him to keep 'writing.'"

Yerushalmit had gotten to her favorite part of the story. Her voice rose. "When the poor girl could take it no longer, she sat up in bed, then lay down again. She covered her eyes with her hand and murmured a prayer of thanks for her good fortune, and then begged Elohim for the strength to endure it. Her lover bowed over her. She reached out and traced his lips with the tip of her finger. Then he lowered himself again and wrote one more mystical name for God on her sanctified flesh. What did he write? *Ein Sof*, Without End, the name that refers to Elohim's infinite presence. And her pleasure became that of the holy name: Without End, the infinite of all infinites. Forever and ever."

We all erupted in laughter. Hani was holding up her hands, blowing on the paste to help it dry. She was laughing too, and when our laughter died down she played the coquette, amusing us all with her alluring bravado.

"Yerushalmit," she purred, "promise me something—that you will sneak into David's room at night and whisper this marvelous story in his ear as he sleeps. Do it in the third hour after midnight, when the angels open the soul to suggestion. Promise me. Yes? For what a waste it will be if only girlish ears hear it."

"Of course, my dear, of course." Yerushalmit sat back and made a show of examining her own henna. She had a big smile on her face and it was clear to see that she was proud of her efforts. Masudah snorted, "Oh, Yerushalmit, how do you think of such things?"

Yerushalmit winked. "When I am doing my most boring household tasks—shelling beans or darning socks—I let my mind wander."

"Such wandering, it's a wonder you feed your husband and keep house." Sultana chuckled. "Mordechai must appreciate his good fortune, when he gets home and finds that you've been daydreaming yourself into a state of *readiness*."

We laughed, enjoying ourselves and reveling in the celebration. "Who knows"—Masudah gestured at Hani—"maybe David will write the holy names on your wedding night."

Hani herself added a last word. "Or maybe he will write the Shem HaMephorash."

We all tittered. She was referring to the seventy-six-letter name for Elohim that the kabbalists use only on rare occasions to refer to the most secret mysteries of creation.

"Seventy-six letters?" Yerushalmit cackled. "Show me a virgin bride who could bear such devotion!"

That night I lay down to bed with the laughter of the women of my family echoing in my head. I smiled into the darkness. Hani, David, and Mr. Haza wouldn't be leaving Qaraah for another six months, the delay having something to do with the commencement of David's studies and the beginning of Mr. Haza's contract with Fey and Absev. My uncle Barhun was still undecided as to whether or not he would accept Mr. Haza's offer of partnership and return with Aunt Rahel to Aden. Six months seemed like a very long time. Their departure was still so far off in the distance as to seem unreal. I lay on my pallet suffused with optimism, happiness, and hope—as if some of their love had rubbed off on me, as if some of their luck was actually my own. And if it wasn't, well, I still had Aunt Rahel's satchel of herbs hidden away safely with Hani's coded henna alphabet.

Chapter 18

Hani's wedding was set for the fifth day of the week before the third Sabbath in the month of Sivan. This was June in the world outside the Kingdom, 1932. I was almost fourteen years old. We hadn't had rain in many weeks and people feared that another drought was upon us. The daisies and mustard flowers weren't blooming in the dunes, and our meals were meager, but our hearts were light with the prospect of the celebration. Sivan was the month when Elohim descended to Sinai to give the Torah to his people. This was considered an especially auspicious time for a marriage, because when God gave the Torah to the Jewish people, it was as if he married them too.

Three weeks before the wedding, Aunt Rahel was scheduled to travel to Sana'a to henna a Muslim bride. Hani had always traveled with her mother, but this time she couldn't go, as it was too close to her own wedding. Aunt Rahel asked my parents to let me come as her helper. My mother balked, scoffing at the idea. I was pounding dough for lahuhua, so I heard it all, though I dared not look up from the board. I peeked out of the corner of my eye and watched Aunt Rahel make her case. She said, "Adela has never seen anything of the world. Let me take her with me; I will take care of her. We will return in just three days. One day for travel each way, one day in Sana'a." My mother wiped her hands on her apron. Then she shook her head with a leering, almost laughing expression on her face. "No, sister," she said, "you will not take my daughter to Sana'a."

I had never heard my mother call my aunt *sister* before, and while it would seem that the word conveyed warmth and connection, in my mother's mouth it was sodden with the opposite: malice and scorn, like a sponge that had soaked up all her suspicions. "Adela will stay here with me." I pressed the heel of my hand into the dough, grinding it so hard that my hand hit the board underneath and the dough splayed out on either side of my palm.

Two days went by. I heard from Masudah that my mother told her she would just as soon send me to Sodom alone as send me to Sana'a with Aunt Rahel.

Masudah offered advice. "Don't be mad at your mother for denying you the opportunity to accompany your aunt," she said, trying to make peace. "She is only trying to do what she thinks is best for you." I had come storming into her house. I was so angry, I couldn't sleep or eat. My anger loosened my tongue, and I heard myself speaking in an almost unrecognizable voice.

"I don't hate my mother, Masudah, but I don't love her either."

"Sha, girl!" Masudah widened her eyes, signaling for me to bite my tongue. Her kitchen, as always, was filled with children. Remelia was shelling fava beans. Her younger sister, Tamar, was sitting right next to her. The two didn't even pretend not to listen, staring at me with bald admiration.

"So you think it is wise? Just? Fair? That my mother won't even spare me for a few days to go and breathe the air on a different mountain?"

Masudah came right up in front of me and took my face into her hands. "Adela, go home, make a little amulet box, and beg a scribe to write you a name for Elohim that no one has ever heard before. Put it in the box, and sleep with it under your pillow. Maybe in the morning you will forget your spite. I say this for your own good, not your mother's. Spite will curdle a girl's womb, and even though you aren't yet wed, no good can come of the anger I see in your eyes."

I backed away from Masudah, took a deep showy breath, and then forced a smile. "Oh, Masudah, I am my own amulet box, and the name for Elohim is already written on the inside of my eyelids. I have already forgotten my anger, you see. Just speaking my ridiculous words aloud has caused me to remember to honor my mother. Don't worry about me. I will be fine."

I wasn't fine, but I was good at pretending. I left Masudah's and went home, where I found Aunt Rahel sitting in the lap of the big frankincense tree with her traveling case between her legs. In the case were little baskets and boxes—some with lids, some open with little drawstring pouches inside. I could see that she had been sorting through the materials she brought with her when she was contracted to do henna.

"Adela," she said, looking up at me, "you are to come with me to Sana'a after all. Go inside and check that your clothes are clean. You must bring your new antari, and of course your leggings with the cowries and coral. You must look your best. We will leave in three days."

"But ... ?"

"Don't worry. Just go. Ask for a bag. And then come to me. I must give you new henna. I will be waiting for you."

"But Aunt Rahel—"

"Don't fret. Just do as I say."

Was she defying my mother? I could never go without permission. Inside, my mother was at the table cutting a scrawny little onion. Though she rarely cried from this work, tears were running down her face. When she saw me, she wiped them away with the back of a weathered hand.

"Aunt Rahel told me to—"

She cut me off. "So," she said, "so it is to be. Go, go to my lesser cupboard, pull out a bag, pack it with a change of clothes. And take my carnelian ring, wear it on your third or second finger, whichever fits. And make sure you wash yourself and your hair before you travel. You can't go with hair that looks like a nest, can you?"

Three days later she bid me farewell for the first time in my life. Uncle Barhun had hitched the donkeys to the carriage. They were swishing their tails with shut eyes, sleeping standing up. Aunt Rahel was helping him load her baskets of supplies. It was just before dawn, the sky a starless blue-black. My mother held me by the shoulders, hissed into my ear, "Don't drink or eat in the henna house, not a bite or a sip. No matter how hungry or thirsty you may be. Swear it to me, Daughter, or I won't let you go."

I nodded.

"Eh?"

I was wearing her carnelian bridal ring on the second finger of my right hand. I knew that my mother believed that this ring had special magical properties, as she had been wearing it on three separate occasions when she almost died—once from illness, once from childbirth, once from a falling roof in a storm. I knew that she wanted me to wear the ring because she was afraid I would be poisoned. She believed that Muslims were always trying to poison Jews, slit their throats, or smother them with a pillow. She didn't believe this frivolously. Before the Imam came to power, it wasn't unusual for minor disputes between Muslim and Jew to be resolved with the fatal slash of a knife or a dose of aconite slipped into a cup of coffee—administered while the Turkish functionary guard looked the other way. Those days were past but not forgotten in the Kingdom.

"I promise, Mother," I said. "Not a bite."

Aunt Rahel put her arm on my shoulder. Her hands were covered with Hani's magnificent star pattern. It seemed to me that the stars that weren't in the sky that dusky morning were on her skin, as if my aunt had actually reached up and scooped out the very lights of heaven. I also had new henna. Aunt Rahel had given me a pattern called Eastern Fig and Western Lily. She had hennaed me all the way up to my elbows. The design was dense and elaborate. In the morning dark, it looked as though I were wearing gloves.

"Don't worry, Sulamita, we will keep her safe and return her to you without a bruise or blemish."

My mother stalked away before we were fully loaded and prepared to go. My father came out to the carriage to bid us farewell.

"When you return, you will tell me all about the great city, eh, Daughter? You will sit with me in my stall, like when you were little, and tell me stories of your adventure."

"Of course I will, Father." I went to hug him, but he pushed me away, and then coughed into the cloth that he kept in his sleeve pocket. Aunt Rahel pursed her lips, and said, "Brother, are you taking the tonic I gave you?"

My father nodded. "Of course I am"—he coughed again—"but perhaps when you return you can brew me a fresh dose."

I flung myself on my father, despite his protestations. As I hugged him, I felt his bones rattle with another cough, and I thought of the little embroidered satchel of poison in my drawer. The old dread gripped my heart, and the long face of the Confiscator flashed through my head, bringing bitter bile up to my throat. I wondered if I would be burying my father and brewing my own tonic before Hani was even wed. I reluctantly let go of my father, climbed up on the carriage, and left Qaraah for the first time in my life.

I did eventually learn why my mother relented and let me go with Aunt Rahel. From whom did I hear the truth? Maybe from a ghost—come back from her grave to speak truths that could not otherwise be spoken by the living. Maybe I heard it from out of the mouth of one of the many blue-green lizards that kept us company on our trek south when we finally left Qaraah for Aden. Or maybe I heard it in the henna house, in a voice that was many voices—that of all my sisters-in-law, who would spill secrets as they inscribed one another with pretty pictures and amulet words.

The story goes like this: Before I was born, my mother and father traveled south to Aden to attend Barhun and Rahel's wedding. At the Night of Henna, my mother drank too much date wine and let herself be taken behind the curtain by a friend of Rahel's who liked women more than men. My mother lay with this woman of her own volition, and was heard to utter sighs of pleasure. And this is why my mother harbored such hatred for Aunt Rahel, because my aunt held the secret of my mother's indiscretion like an asp to her breast. In all the time they were in Qaraah, Rahel never whispered a word of it—that is, until my mother refused to let me go to Sana'a. Then Rahel reminded my mother. She said, "Remember when we were young, Sulamita, and it wasn't so difficult to distinguish pleasure from pain, pain from ordinary life, and ordinary life from the life that is to come?"

"What are you talking about?" my mother asked.

"My Night of Henna." Then Rahel lowered her voice and whispered the other woman's name—that of my mother's lover. That is all she did, whisper it, but it was enough. My mother knew that Rahel Damari held her reputation in the palm of her hand. She let me go so that Rahel would speak of it no more.

I was not astonished when I heard this story. I knew that my mother was neither the first nor the last woman to take her pleasure in the henna house. And I also knew enough about the ways of the world to pity my mother for having been shamed by matters of the flesh. But I was surprised that Aunt Rahel would spend the coin of my mother's shame to pry me from Qaraah. It later occurred to me that I had very little to do with it. Perhaps Rahel was simply tired of having my mother lord her resentment over her. Maybe, after so many years, she wanted to let my mother know that she was growing weary of keeping her secret. And if the secret could purchase a little bit of freedom for me, well, my aunt was willing to speak the words that had long gone unspoken.

Chapter 19

We entered Sana'a late in the day through an arched gate in the city wall. What did I see there? Beggars in tattered black djellabas; decommissioned Turkish soldiers in fezzes and grimy uniforms sitting on overturned boxes playing *sheshbesh*; brown turbaned boys laughing and loitering in front of a mosque; old men spitting wads of khat onto the dirty street as our carriage rolled by. I watched with eyes "the size of little moons," Aunt Rahel later told me, laughing. I saw toothless fortune-tellers squatting over pads of incense; wealthy-looking Muslim gentlemen in thobe skirts and dark suit jackets leaning into each other, and holding each other by the crook of the arm as they walked purposefully by the side of the road. I saw red- and orange- and vermilion-clad women swathed in *abaya* and *sharshaf* swaying through the throng, baskets filled with market goods flung over their shoulders, or balanced on their heads. And the buildings? Ocher-colored, with white arched windows. On all sides of us thousands and thousands of buildings rose up like the spires of a buried castle. They were so tall, I craned my neck but could not see the tops. Eight, nine, ten stories into the air, with red-brick and white-gypsum designs around domed windows and rooftop lattices. And so many mosques! Their domes and minarets gleamed in the sun. We passed by caravansaries with mules and donkeys braying in stalls. The city seemed a geometric puzzle assembling and reassembling itself before my eyes. The beseeching songs of the muezzin rising up from minarets; throaty men hawking rubber novelties; an angry soldier calling after a boy who had stolen a bag of nuts; the pitiful *caw caw* of a crow in a cage; the high-pitched complaining of three children stumbling after their mother as she disappeared through the muddy puddles of a dark narrow alley that smelled of shit and piss. I didn't care if the place stank. I wanted to see everything, but as we made our way through town, I caught myself slouching down in the carriage, and suddenly I felt very small. Sana'a's loudness and largeness made me feel like a miniature version of myself, as if I were tiny, a doll-sized girl who hailed from an earth of more modest proportions.

We entered the Qu'al Yahud by the Al-Boonia gate. Inside the Jewish Quarter, the curled earlocks of the men and boys and the black gargushim of the women and girls alerted me that I was once again among my own people. Houses were marked with Stars of David and were only four or five stories high compared to the nine- or ten-story towers in the rest of the city. Uncle Barhun clucked his tongue and urged the donkeys forward past a ritual bath, a synagogue, and a neat courtyard off which radiated lane after lane of bustling stalls and shops. We were to spend the night with the family of a locksmith Uncle Barhun knew, who would provide our lodging in return for a modest payment.

In the morning, we rose early. After we had checked our bags and seen that all our materials were in order, Auntie Rahel braided my hair and painted my face with black gall—giving me three dots on each cheek and a triangle on my chin. She put turmeric powder on my eyelids and a smear of indigo higher, under my eyebrows. Then she dabbed hyacinth perfume on my pulse points. She had brought big silver hoops for my ears, a beautiful lazem necklace with Maria Theresa thalers and rupees dangling from the red coral beads, and six silver bracelets—three for each wrist. I felt very grown-up in such finery.

We made our way out of the Qu'al Yahud to the house of the parents of the bride. The celebrations for the Night of Henna were already well under way and had spilled outside. There were red-nosed musicians, rushing caterers, and neighbors who had already come to deliver their good wishes to the bride in the form of huge trays of candied sweets that filled the air with the allure of caramelized sugar and attracted so many bees that they seemed to be accompanying the music from the tabl drums with their syncopated hum and buzz. Even though we had eaten that morning, I felt almost faint with hunger, for it had been many weeks since I had eaten my fill. Now, everywhere I looked, I saw overflowing trays of fruits, sweets, and savories. I wondered if the drought hadn't affected Sana'a, or if this bride was so wealthy that her family could afford to pay a premium on rare delicacies. Uncle Barhun helped us unload our baskets and then he left to attend to some business back in the Qu'al Yahud. Aunt Rahel and I were ushered into the ladies' salon on the second floor. We were introduced to the women assembled there by the bride's mother-in-law, and then led over to where the bride was sitting.

The bride was a beautiful creature with perfect teeth, high cheekbones, plump lips. She was ensconced in a wooden throne cushioned with red velvet and bedecked with chains of fragrant rue flowers. Her bridal "undergarments" revealed a generous bosom, a soft belly, big hips. She wore nothing but the undergarments—a sleeveless white dress and silver and red short trousers—so that Aunt Rahel could easily paint her hands, arms, feet, and legs. She wasn't wearing a conical gargush—as a Jewish bride would have—but a tight-fitting gold and red scarf with rupee bangles over her forehead. She had on big silver hooped earrings and three rows of coral and amber beads around her neck. So that Aunt Rahel could do her work, she wasn't yet wearing her bracelets or rings, but I knew that by the time she was dressed in her finery, her arms would be mostly covered with jewelry. Cousins and sisters surrounded her throne. One of the women was very pregnant and she had a black and red lafeh scarf tied around her big belly. I wondered if this lafeh came from the dye mistress who lived next door to us. The bride's henna "base coat" had been applied the day before. The fresh henna was protected by strips of cloth, called mehani, wound around her limbs. The mehani strips hadn't been removed yet, and I knew that our first task would be to unwrap the bride's hands and feet.

I hung back, behind Aunt Rahel. The bride was singing. "La, la la, la la," her husky voice tripped up and down an octave. In between la la la's, she would giggle, and the girls all around her would laugh along with her, as if to the punch line of a private joke. No one noticed us at first. For those first few moments, I was acutely aware that I was a Jewish girl among Muslim women. Of course, I knew Muslim women in Qaraah, but I was never in their homes. We saw one another at the well or at the market. We were not intimate like this. My skin pricked and I felt my mother's fears climb my spine, leaving me queasy with an anxiety not really my own. Then the bride saw my aunt and said, "So you are to paint me?" The Sana'an bride squinted and appraised my aunt, cocking her head a bit to the right.

"I am." Aunt Rahel's voice was low and soothing.

"Well, I am very ticklish, so you will have to put up with my writhing and wriggling."

"No worries, daughter, I have a light touch." Auntie Rahel smiled. "Some say they don't even feel my stylus on their skin."

"Ticklish on a wedding night is not a bad thing," one of the sisters piped in. The bride giggled. "Yes, but it is my groom who should do the honors."

They all laughed, and then someone fed the bride a fat white lychee nut, and someone else wiped the juice running down her chin.

The women were nothing but kind to me. They complimented my black-gall makeup and my henna. They cooed and petted my arms and invited me to eat and drink, but I heard my mother's voice in my head and declined their date wine and honey balls of semolina dough, their mango and melon slices—piled like orange and green smiles on a tray—in spite of my growling hunger.

Aunt Rahel addressed the bride. "Please, hold up your hands, like this . . ." She held her own arms up, stiffly in front of her. The bride followed suit.

"Take the end," Rahel instructed me. Slowly we unwound the mehani cloth from the bride's arms. She stayed as still as a statue as we tugged—my hands looping over and under her arms, close to her torso and then around her pretty feet, such elegant little toes, lifting them up gracefully so that we could unwrap her heels, her arches, her ankles, her shins. When all the mehani cloths lay in a heap on the floor, Aunt Rahel began handling the bride's limbs as if they were her own—turning a wrist, squinting to inspect a forearm, ducking down to espy the soles of her feet. The bride let herself be inspected and admired like a rag doll. Then Aunt Rahel stepped back and nodded her approval. There was clapping and laughing and ululations, *kulululu*, the women trilled their tongues to warn off any lingering demons. Everyone was happy. The henna was a henna of good fortune! The leaves had done their work, for her brown skin was rust red with a hint of vermilion, shades of blood orange, all scented with roses, jasmine, and high notes of honey. Aunt Rahel nodded her head again in approval and then wasted no time getting to work.

She began by measuring out the ingredients for her waxy mixture—resin, myrrh, frankincense, and iron sulfate—mixing them together, and heating them in a high-sided pan over a fire until it was like molten wax. She also added sage and mint extract. Once she had brought the earthy mixture to the right consistency, she scooped out a small amount and put it into a wooden bowl; then she handed me the spoon and told me to keep stirring, lest it clump. After I had stirred for ten minutes she said, "Go to the bride and show her this." She handed me a little oval clay pot, the size of my palm. I opened it, and inside saw that there was a miniature naked clay lady, with big breasts and a round belly. She was lying side by side with a naked man whose member was so long that it snaked out from between his legs, and in between hers. I did as my aunt instructed. Soon the bride and her sisters were tittering over the fertility amulet. Meanwhile, Aunt Rahel crouched on the floor by the bride's right foot, dipped her stylus into the little bowl, and began to draw on the balls of her feet. Later, when I asked her why she had begun with the most ticklish part of the bride's body, Aunt Rahel said, "If I can do her feet without tormenting her, then I can do everywhere else. I start there, to show her that she has nothing to fear from my touch."

Aunt Rahel finished the ball of the bride's left foot before the girl even noticed that the work had started. When she realized that she'd been tricked she laughed. "You bring such wonderful 'toys' and have the softest touch, Mrs. Damari, you are a mistress distracter and a magician with your hands." Aunt Rahel thanked the bride for her compliment and kept working. She was executing a variation on a traditional grain of wheat design, alternating the stylized grains with waves and crescents in a tight spiral. Every so often she would hand me the bowl and I would fill it with more of the mixture. Every ten minutes or so, I stirred the mixture and checked the consistency. In this way, we passed three hours. And just as the bride's attendants fed her little bits of meat, bread, and sweets, so too I fed Aunt Rahel, urging her to take a sip of tea, a bite of date pastry, a piece of melon. But I didn't eat a thing. I heeded my mother's injunction, despite my growling belly.

By the time the bride's feet, shins, hands, and forearms were covered it was already late afternoon. Now it was time for the shaddar. Aunt Rahel mixed a paste of ammoniac and potash. She spread this paste on top of the waxy mixture. The bride grimaced when it was being applied, but by now she was feeling the effect of all the sips of spiced wine her sisters had given her, and she didn't complain that the shaddar was cold, or that it smelled like moldy ashes, or that it was giving her a headache.

I knew that brides often complained about the "ordeal" of henna, and Aunt Rahel would say, "It is a bride's prerogative to complain about the shackles of beauty."

One hour later, Aunt Rahel rubbed off the shaddar. When the paste was all off, I saw that the henna had turned a dark greenish-black, but everywhere Aunt Rahel had applied the waxy mixture was still reddish-orange. The result was an intricate brocade of red against the darkened skin. The design had within it elements of *labbeh* necklace patterns— double-sided crescents, pears, flowers, and spheres that danced on her hands and forearms and were joined together by little links. The bride started singing her funny little song again. *La, la, la, la, la,* she sang, with her sisters and cousins joining in. I bowed low and shuffled backward, as all the women in the room gathered around to coo and trill their tongues at the success of the application.

All around me were delicious smells coming from overflowing trays on tables around the sides of the room. My belly grumbled, and my head hurt, but I ate nothing—that is, I almost ate nothing. Just before we left, I stole a few bites of a persimmon. I was so hungry, I couldn't resist. The fruit's mellow flesh dissolved on my tongue. I took another bite, and another. Many years later, when I heard the Greek myth of Persephone and Hades, I thought of my mother's warning, and how strange it was that at the henna house that day, I ate forbidden fruit just like Demeter's daughter. I wondered if perhaps I too later had suffered for giving in to my hunger. But at the time, I was so hungry, I barely noticed that I had disobeyed my mother at all.

We left Sana'a at dawn the next day. As we rode away, I crooked my neck back and saw the city not as a series of structures made by man but as a pattern for henna. The jutting towers and graceful minarets, the arches of the gates, and the encircling girth of the walls combined into a henna of history, a henna of conquerors and conquered, a henna of brides and grooms.

"What are you thinking of, dear girl?" Aunt Rahel brushed a few strands of hair out of my eyes. I thought for a moment before I spoke. I was very grateful to my aunt, and wanted to give her a snippet of conversation that would make her feel that I was worthy of this gift of a journey. And I was also feeling mischievous, unbound from ordinary life. I spoke in a whisper, so that Uncle Barhun couldn't hear me.

"I am wondering about your little 'toy,' and if the real groom is as

well endowed as the groom of clay that the bride was so eager to fondle."
Aunt Rahel's eyes flashed in a conspiratorial smile. "Oh *reeeeally*?" She
giggled. "I had thought you weren't paying attention."

When we returned, my father was faring better and coughed only at
night when he lay in bed. During the day, he seemed full of a careless
vigor, but also half out of step with himself, as if a younger version of
himself had climbed into his skin, making him clumsy from the inside
out. But no one paid much attention. The bustle of Hani's wedding
preparations occupied us all. We made marvelous concoctions out
of our meager stores. We women cleaned and sewed and darned and
baked. By the time of Hani's Night of Henna, all of us were exhausted.
Even my mother contributed. She generously gave of her stored beans,
coffee, and honey sugar, and opened her larder to let Aunt Rahel take
a precious jar of stewed persimmons for the wedding feast. And on the
day before the Night of Henna, she lent Hani a pair of tomb bracelets,
which had been part of her own dowry. Tomb bracelets, named for the
little tomb-sized protrusions all the way around, were an essential part
of any wedding outfit, and were supposed to help scare away the evil
eye by shielding the bride with opposite tokens of grim fate. Hani kissed
my mother for the bracelets, and my mother let herself receive a hug,
stiff under the embrace. In her own queer bitter way, my mother had
forgiven Hani for the idols, and joined in the festivities and preparations
with no hesitation, as if Hani were a favored daughter, and not a niece
of whom she had always been suspicious.

Hani's Night of Henna? Aunt Rahel came in with the pot of henna
on the candle tray and swung her hips to the music. She approached
Hani, resplendent in her bridal gargush. She danced in front of her for
a few moments, swaying her hips so that the candles on the tray cast
jumping shadows on the walls. Then Aunt Rahel smeared a single dab
of henna at the center of each of Hani's palms. We all rubbed henna on
her forearms and I joined in, spreading the musky paste over her shins
and feet as Aunt Rahel danced with the other women, our neighbors
and friends, who had gathered to see Hani become a bride. When the
paste had set, we wrapped Hani in mehani cloths, and then began to
feast. We ate and drank and danced until well after dark.

The next day, after we had unwrapped the cloths, Hani entertained us all with songs and jokes. She was a laughing, chatty bride on her throne in her white shift, her orange and gold leggings. The henna house was different that night. The colors of the women's dresses were brighter, the sounds of the shinshilla cymbals and the khallool were louder, the food was both sweeter and spicier. Yerushalmit told stories. Masudah plaited Hani's hair. I took my turn with the tabl drum and heard myself thrumming out a strong, sure beat. And Aunt Rahel's art? When she finished decorating her youngest daughter, and we rubbed the shaddar off her skin, Hani was revealed to us as the most beautiful bride anyone had ever seen. Aunt Rahel hadn't just given her an ordinary decoration, she had improvised at every point; every petal had a hundred tiny petals inside of it, tendrils never ended, paisleys held within them miniature worlds, and whimsical flourishes were Eyes of God in disguise. Hani held out her hands and laughed with delight. She and David were married the next day. I stood on tiptoe trying to get a glimpse of them under the bridal canopy. I couldn't hear David as he said, "With this ring I make thee holy unto me," but I heard him stomp the glass to scare away ghosts and demons, and then we all raised our voices in celebration of the sanctification of their union.

Chapter 20

Our little town, Qaraah, was nestled like a bird in the winged embrace of the Naquum Mountains and, being so high up, escaped most of the cursed plagues that were such scourges to the lower-lying villages and towns. At least that is what we all liked to believe, that we were safer. That the mountain breezes coming south from Amran or west from Marib swept cholera and typhus germs west to the Red Sea or south all the way to the Gulf of Aden before they could settle in and destroy whole families. But the breezes betrayed us that year, for we were afflicted by all manner of pestilence. Illnesses no one had ever seen before ravaged whole families. Overnight, in one of those acts of nature that cause men to believe that the world is not as it seems, the Little Lyre river dried up. The big and little wells ran dry. An attempt was made by the men of the community to dig a new well on the eastern edge of town, and the effort commenced with gusto. But even as the men worked, we all knew that the well wouldn't water our fields or make the millet and sorghum sprout. We began to feel the effects of the drought. Our family suffered losses just like everyone else's. Masudah lost a son—four-year-old Binny. Yerushalmit, who had never before been pregnant, now suffered a miraculous pregnancy, and a tragic birth. She vomited every day until she delivered. She grew so skinny, she looked like a skeleton with a little melon between her hips. Her front teeth fell out in her fifth month, and then she lost twins, two little boys. When she got up from her sickbed, she would speak only with her hand in front of her mouth, and her eyes had receded so far in her head that she could barely see. And that wasn't all. Sultana's mother and sister died, and she fell into despair, temporarily unable to care for Moshe. In those dark days, we ate sparingly, paid many visits to houses of mourning, and grew even skinnier. I often went to bed hungry, and dreamed of the days when we had so much food that I could steal some away and make feasts for myself and Asaf in my cave and no one was the wiser.

Our sorrows only multiplied. Auntie Aminah died in late autumn. Masudah found her, collapsed in a corner of her kitchen, when she went to help her dip Sabbath candles. She said, "Auntie Aminah died with a dolly in her hand." I ran to her house when I heard, but I was too late to kiss her on the lips before she was taken to be cleaned and prepared for the World to Come. Left behind on the floor was the Muslim bride dolly she had been making for one of Masudah's many children. It wore a red and yellow polka-dotted kerchief and orange glass beads for necklaces, but the pink brocade dress was only half-finished. The doll had little black bead eyes and a sewn-on mouth. I sat in the corner hugging it and crying. When I gathered myself up, I took the doll with me, swearing I would finish the stitching myself.

A few weeks later, my mother's friend Devorah suffered an attack in the ritual bath, lost control of her bowels, and soiled the pure water with a gush of foul sickness. After that, no woman could cleanse herself from the impurity of her menses, and if they couldn't cleanse themselves, they couldn't lie with their husbands, and if they couldn't lie with their husbands, well, everyone knows what misfortune comes from a husband who is not sated, let alone scores of them. People lamented that such a misfortune would besmirch our town for years to come. My mother's old friend Devorah died three days into her sickness. My mother went to help dress her in her *lulwi* dress. When she came back from dressing Devorah and saying psalms over her corpse, my mother stripped out of her antari. Her eyes were red, and she cried big gulping tears as I rubbed her naked body with mint soap that we moistened in boiled cooking water. Then I patted her down with rosewater. I had never given my mother a standing bath before, and she showed absolutely no modesty as I touched and rubbed to rid her of the stink of the death house. When we were finished, she donned a clean dress and trousers and put the soiled garments in a closed sack in the storeroom for washing when there was more water.

Other deaths followed. The tinsmith's wife, the slaughterer's son, the young daughter of a teacher in the Talmud Torah, the wife of the couple who had moved into Auntie Aminah's house, a lampmaker, a harnessmaker, and the eldest daughter of the glassblower—all succumbed to a malady of the belly that came from drinking bad water.

The new well was blamed, but what were we supposed to do? The other wells were almost dry.

After Devorah's death, during that foul gray midwinter, my mother fell into an ill temper. From my parents' nightly arguing, I understood that ever since I went to Sana'a with Aunt Rahel, my mother had refused to lie with my father. Their arguments grew more bitter. I buried my head in my pillow as my mother hissed at Father to stop pawing at her. But, as I shared a corner of their room, I heard everything.

My mother growled, "Pleasure yourself like a dog, rut up against a tree, coat your member with samneh and have one of the donkeys lick you until you spurt. But don't come close to me or I will cut off your hand before you grab again for my tits."

In the morning, my parents continued their fight. My mother declared her intention to leave us. "I'll leave you and go to Taiz, and stay with my sister and her husband. Then we will be rid of each other." My father didn't seem to care very much about this threat, for his mind was on more pressing business.

"Just tonight, Suli," he said, "lie with me tonight, and then I won't bother you anymore." My mother pulled herself up to her full height. She flared her nostrils, and stretched her lips, her gums a gray purple, her voice coming out in a combination of a croak and a shout. "You paw at me in the night again, and I will cut off more than your hands. Come close to me no more. I am not your wife anymore. I am done with the burden of you. Done!"

What happened to my mother? Sometimes I dream that she made good on her threat. That she left Qaraah and traveled south to her sister, carrying nothing but a single basket of provisions slung over her shoulder. In my dream, I watch her but I don't call after her. Not because the cry wasn't in my throat, but because I knew she wouldn't turn her head, and that she was leaving me perhaps even more than she was leaving my father.

Other times I dream that I was the one who found her, that I rolled over on my pallet and saw her dead face staring at me, and since it was a dream, I dreamed that I tried to wake her up, over and over, but that she wouldn't wake up, and I was trapped in an existence in which all I had to do was to keep trying to rouse her from the clutches of the demon who tempts sinners to offer themselves willingly to the World to Come.

But really it was Aunt Rahel who found her. She came across my mother by the frankincense tree, her limbs twisted in a thick rigor that shaped her into the form of gimel, ג, the third letter of the alphabet, a contortion that made her death both strange and legible. Rahel let out an anguished shriek. I had been at the market and was on my way home, close by already, when I heard my aunt yelling. Hani had been in the little house with the red roof, and the dye mistress was in her yard, dipping cloth. They both came too. When I reached the yard, the other women tried to prevent me from stepping forward, but I saw my own dark fortune written on their faces and refused to let them stop me. I dropped to my knees by my mother's side. I watched myself reaching out, straightening her gargush, which had slipped down over one eye. Her flesh was cold and tacky. She was a fierce woman, and it was clear that she had wrestled with death. The expression on her stilled face was one of outrage and disappointment, as if death had proven itself to be a craven foe, yet one who prevailed despite her obvious moral superiority. I had been crouching beside her on my haunches, but I felt arms under my armpits, pulling me up. I was still wearing my mother's carnelian ring. After my trip to Sana'a with Aunt Rahel, she had never asked for it back. As my cousin and sisters-in-law pulled me to standing, I closed my fingers in a fist and stroked the stone with my thumb. I must have swayed. Hani steadied me. Then Aunt Rahel reeled me into her bosom, and stroked my hair as I cried in front of everyone—big heaving sobs that left me spent and light-headed. When I pried myself loose of her, I saw confused faces. Somehow the others had appeared. My father, my brothers, my cousin, and sisters-in-law. They looked at me as if I were half a stranger. And I was just as confused as the rest. Who knew I would cry for her like that? Wiping my eyes on the sleeve of my antari, I blushed, turned my head, and hid in the shoulder folds of my gargush.

My father and brothers buried my mother under a broad, thorny acacia tree down in the graveyard below the escarpment, in view of my cave. My brothers joined my father in the obligation of saying the Prayer for Sanctification three times a day. We were all treated with solemn respect by the rest of our family. My cousin, sisters-in-law, and aunt cooked for us and watched over us. Throughout the seven days of our shiva, I sat under the frankincense tree, in the very spot where my mother had passed from this world into the World to Come. My tears mingled with the fragrant resin tears of the tree. I felt as if the tree had become one of my idols, a huge Anath or Asherah come to keep me company. I cried in fits and starts, and wasn't sure if I was crying for the mother I had just lost, or for the mother I had never really had.

Hani sat with me the entire week. Once, when I was doubled over with sobbing, she tried to comfort me. "Your mother did love you," she said. "I heard her bragging at the little well about your *malawach*, and when I embroidered her a square for a pillow, she took one look and said. 'Adela's handiwork is better than yours.' Why, I even once heard her praising your skill with leather, complimenting your helpfulness to your father."

I let Hani prattle on, though her words brought me little comfort.

Chapter 21

"So, was I right to wonder all those years ago? Do those strange eyes of yours see more of the world, or less of it?"

I looked down at my feet, modestly covering my face with the side of my gargush. I tried not to blush, but I knew my face blazed with fear. The Confiscator still carried the same jambia with the two jeweled serpents wrapped around the handle, a band of rubies at the thumb point, and an embossed hawk's head on the lip of the hilt. Whenever the man spoke, the snakes looked at me, opened their fanged mouths, and hissed.

"Don't be afraid, little girl, I mean you no harm."

I was back in my father's stall, helping him almost every day. In the two months since my mother's death, my father's cough had grown much worse. He took more and more of Aunt Rahel's tonic, but it did no good. He was very weak and could barely make it through a day's work. So I helped him. Sometimes my brothers helped too—especially my brother Hassan—but they were generally busy with their own toil and had little time to spare for my father. On this day, my father was in the back, sorting supplies. I was embossing triangles on flaps of leather that would be used for little purses. The Confiscator had been standing at the entrance to the stall. Now he came around, and hovered over me. His shadow fell over my hands. "You do more than just help your father with sales and supplies," he said. "I can tell. Your nimble hands do the work of boys. You are skilled with the knife and awl. Those eyes of yours help you to see more than others."

I took a deep breath and slowly raised my head, the coins of my gargush tinkling. The Confiscator's long face had grown old. His skin was a dry riverbed, wrinkled and cracked by the swelling and receding of years.

HENNA HOUSE

"I suppose, sir . . . I suppose I see what everyone else sees." I heard my voice, high and soft, as if from far away.

"And what is that?"

"I see ordinary life."

"And what is ordinary about life?"

"Sir, why ask a Jewish girl?"

"Because what is ordinary about your life is extraordinary to me. As my answers would be to you. And we have much to learn from each other."

I grew bold. "Are you a philosopher?"

"Are you?"

I looked down at my shoes again, and hid once more in the folds of my gargush.

My father came out from the back. When he saw the Confiscator he almost dropped the pile of soft skins in his hands. "Sir, I am so sorry. Please forgive me that you have had to suffer the prattling of a little girl."

The Confiscator laughed. "She doesn't prattle, she philosophizes. This one is a deep thinker."

"Beg pardon, sir, beg pardon. How can I serve you? More shoes for your lovely wife? Eh, I am at your service."

The Confiscator ordered two pairs of shoes for his wife—a fancy pair and an everyday one. After the Confiscator left, my father began to work on the fancy pair immediately. He instructed me to cut the pattern for the everyday bashmag sandals, and I did as I was told.

That night, my father and Uncle Barhun went to a meeting at the synagogue. Before he left, he said, "Adela, we will leave Qaraah, and the Confiscator will not torment you anymore."

I said, "I am not afraid of him."

"Ach, Adela, there is no need to pretend."

"Father . . ."

"What is it, Daughter?"

"His knife—"

"His jambia?"

"How is it that a man can carry silver snakes, and they never turn around and bite him?"

To this I got not an answer, but an embrace. My father smelled of cured leather, cracked nuts, and hookah smoke, a comforting amalgam of smells. He closed the door behind him and went to a meeting. I sat

181

back on the wheat-husk pillows and imagined myself a Muslim girl. What would my name be? Who would marry me? What would it be like to pray to Allah and not Elohim? And if I were confiscated, would I be married to an old man or a young man? A kind one or a monster? And would I ever see my family again?

The meeting lasted for many hours. It concerned our departure from the village. One by one, the families of Qaraah had come to a common decision—to leave our little town and to seek health and good fortune elsewhere. It was not easy to leave. A Jew had to get permission from the Imam's functionary. And that usually meant that a man had to either abandon his property or sell it to a Muslim for far less than it was worth. So the embarkation on a new life had to be undertaken with minimal funds. The most skilled among our community were prohibited from leaving unless they each taught their trade to a Muslim first. Our best jewelers and jambia makers had the hardest time of it and they despaired that their loved ones would die in this wretched place before permission would be granted. On top of all that, the road itself was dangerous. It made no sense to travel north, where the drought was even worse, and passage south meant going through the territory where the Imam's soldiers fought tribesmen in proxy battles with the British. One risked getting caught in the cross fire. It was impossible to know exactly where the fighting was taking place. But in spite of these hurdles, many families succeeded in prying themselves loose from the northern mountains to risk a venture south.

More often than not, a bribe secured the passes that were needed. My father, Mr. Haza, and Uncle Barhun had gathered together a decent enough sum to bribe the Imam's functionary in charge of the Jews of Qaraah. Their intention was to go to Aden, where Uncle Barhun and Mr. Haza had business connections. The night my father went to the meeting, we were waiting for our passage papers and prepared to leave in a month's time. At the meeting, the men traded strategies for procuring the papers and discussed the best routes south.

When my father returned, I gave him a bowl of chouia. Usually I put pepper in my chouia, but I made it bland for my father, as the pepper made his cough worse.

"Thank you, Adela," he said as he began to eat. Every few bites, he had to put down his spoon to cough. Even the bland stew was hard for him to swallow. As he caught his breath, I began. "Father . . ."

"Eh?"

"Before the other Damaris came to Qaraah, Masudah told me that Aunt Rahel had had . . . er . . . troubles in Aden. That there were families who blamed her for their own misfortunes. If this is true, how can Aunt Rahel and Uncle Barhun return there?"

My father put down his spoon and wiped his face. He took a deep breath. I could hear the rattling of his chest.

"What you say is true. There were troubles in the past. But your uncle has had word that the families who accused your aunt have left Aden. She has also pledged not to do any henna in Aden, save that of her own kin."

A fit of coughing racked him and he bent over as if a fist was wrapped around his middle, squeezing him too tight for breath. I ran for Aunt Rahel, and she came to give him a steam treatment, draping his shoulders with a blanket, helping him huddle over a pot of boiling water.

I watched my aunt minister to him. Her henna was old, and the lines and swirls on her skin looked like ugly scars in the dim lantern light.

Ten days later, in early March of 1933, my father died in his sleep. When Aunt Rahel came to see his dead body, she held me. My sobs were craggy and painful; my chest heaved and a stitch racked my side. I gasped and gulped and moaned and felt myself spinning. In one instant my grief was large and I was infinitesimal. In another, my grief was a shard of light, and I a vessel too porous to contain it. Aunt Rahel wrapped her arms around me and said, "I am so sorry, my darling. So sorry. When we lived in Aden, I apprenticed with a lady doctor. I learned what I could from her, but I didn't learn enough."

We buried my father secretly, by moonlight in the ravine behind Yehezkiel the Goat's old abandoned forge. Aunt Rahel prepared his body. Masudah sewed his shroud. My brothers dug the grave.

When we returned from the burial, Aunt Rahel, Uncle Barhun, and Hani took me into their house. Aunt Rahel said, "You must not cry anymore, Adela. You must pretend that your father is still with us. Permission for our travels should come before the passage of two Sabbaths." She held my hands as she spoke. I stared into her faded henna and saw there the form of a burning bush, which I took as a sign that despite evidence to the contrary, Elohim had not completely forsaken me.

"Tonight you must begin to pack your things for the journey." She reached out and wiped my tears with the corner of her apron. "You will need to be ready to leave at any time, but you will stay in your house until then. Hani will stay with you. The house must appear as though nothing has changed. You understand that we cannot sit shiva for your father. We cannot let the Confiscator know that you are an orphan. We must act as if your father is still alive in the house, as if you are ministering to him—feeding him soup, bringing him small comforts."

My aunt was talking about "propping up" a corpse. Jewish families sometimes attempted it when there was no other way to protect an orphan from confiscation. But it almost never worked.

Uncle Barhun spoke next. "Darling Adela, if the Confiscator finds out that you are an orphan before our traveling papers arrive, we will present your old engagement contract to Asaf Damari. But if the Confiscator refuses to honor it, we will marry you off immediately."

"To whom?" Aunt Rahel looked pointedly at her husband. "The matter is not so simple."

Uncle Barhun put his hand to his beard and spoke without hesitation. "To David. Hani's husband can take her as a second wife."

Hani and I looked at each other, and for a moment my heart stopped beating, for in her eyes was a sickle knife of hate, a cunning blade that would carve out my heart. And then her eyes changed back to loving orbs and she was all over me, as on the first day we met, touching my hair, kissing my eyes, caressing my shoulders.

"Yes, of course. It will be David, it will be David."

David Haza was not with us then. He was elsewhere, perhaps with his father, who was also not privy to the conversation. Later, I learned that David Haza himself had put forth this solution. That he had gone to my uncle and suggested it even before my father died.

"I will marry little Adela if she is ever vulnerable to confiscation," David had told my uncle. And my uncle had held the weight of this solution in his hands, and felt the true measure of his son-in-law's goodness. For this was both a sacrifice and a bounty on David's soul—a bounty that Hani would not suffer to pay back.

Hani threaded her fingers through mine and kissed me on the lips and reassured me in little whispers that she would link her fate to my own and thus save me from confiscation.

"Mother, I will take Adela to pack."

We walked across the courtyard into my parents' empty house. The first thing I did was to go up to the second floor. I found the key to my mother's chest. There on top was my contract to Mr. Musa, next to it was my old contract to Asaf, and there was the deerskin Torah, like a corpse sharing a too-small grave. I wrapped my hand around the parchment that bore my name and Asaf's. That's when I suffered a fleeting memory. A flash of his face.

"Can you take me there?"

"Where?"

"To your . . ."

"My what?"

"To your cave. I know where you go. I followed you, so I know that you have a cave. I would very much like to see it. Don't worry, I won't tell anyone else."

"What is it, Adela?" Hani had come over, and put her hand on top of my own.

"Nothing,"

"But I saw you; you shuddered."

"I am fine. Here are the documents. I suppose I should wrap the contract with my things. The Torah we will leave for the men to handle."

Slowly, we gathered my mother's jewelry, her best antari, and other garments too precious to leave behind.

"There won't be enough room for everything, so you must choose carefully." Hani's voice came from the bedroom, and my heart fluttered in my chest when I saw her at the drawer where I kept my undergarments.

I ran across the room and placed myself between Hani and the drawer—my drawer of secrets, which held Aunt Rahel's satchel of poison and my copy of Hani's code. I remembered how I had suspected that Hani used the code to write curses. It struck me as preposterous now and I blanched at the thought. But still, something pricked at the back of my neck. I wondered what my predicament would look like spelled out in Hani's secret language. It would probably look beautiful. A girl engaged, abandoned, almost widowed, and now orphaned. Loops and swirls, delicate petals, little florets. How could I be all of these things, and still only fourteen years old?

"I will pack my linens."

"Of course, Adela, of course." She quickly moved over to the cupboard where I kept my two dresses. "I will fold your good antari, yes?" She was at the bigger set of drawers. "And you must take all these shoes, especially the newest sandals, which were such a nice gift from your father."

Hani sat up with me until the small hours of the morning. My mourning took the form of sick-bellied wakefulness. Unable to sleep, I was a girl again, hiding behind the supply shelves in my father's stall. I told Hani about the Confiscator and his snakes and that when he first came to my father's stall I was just a child. I told her about his wife, how I made part of her shoes, and hoped they would come to life, eating her feet before she could steal me.

"Hani, if he comes for me, I want you to know that I will not marry your husband."

"Hush, Adela, we will be gone in under a week. And when we get to Aden, I am sure Asaf will be there, returned from his travels, waiting to make you his wife." I let her lie to me because I was so tired. And I lied to her too. A lie of omission. I didn't tell her why she would never have to share her husband with me. I didn't tell her about her mother's little embroidered satchel, and about the bitter root inside of it. I planned that after she went to sleep I would steep it into tea and drink the whole thing down in one gulp. But Hani never left me, and I had no opportunity to steep my doom, stew my salvation. She stroked my forehead, whispering one of my auntie's old stories, of the sons of Noah on the mountaintop of Sana'a, and soon I was asleep. In the darkest part of the night, I roused to hear my cousin arguing with her mother and I knew that they were outside on the little path between our houses and that Hani was refusing the prospect of giving up a piece of her own husband to me. I fell back asleep with my head full of their noise, or maybe it was a gathering of bitch cats in the yard, sharpening their claws on the shreds of a sad little mouse who had been unlucky enough to wander into their domain.

The next night, when everyone had gone to bed, and Hani was asleep on my pallet, I took out the embroidered pouch. I lit a fire and steeped the tea. Then I drank the five-sip dose. When sleepiness came upon me, I muttered the words to the Shema, as I was going to the World to Come and would affirm my faith in Elohim, even though I was not worthy of salvation.

I shut my eyes and fell into a deep ravine. At the bottom was the Confiscator, older than he had been when he had last walked into my father's stall, older than any man I had ever seen, a patriarch older than time. Then he receded and I tumbled backward into the dye mistress's troughs, backward off the escarpment, backward off the ledge of an unfurled scroll of scripture and into an endless abyss. At the bottom of the abyss was a raging river. I became a tiny pebble in the water. I was tossed by waves, smashed against boulders. Finally, I came to rest in the sandy shallows, where I was swallowed by a fish who swam with me out to the depths of a dark ocean.

When I awoke, not dead, Aunt Rahel and Hani were bending over me. Aunt Rahel had a warm cloth on my forehead. Hani's face was blotchy; she had been crying.

I struggled to find words. My tongue was thick in my mouth. "What . . . ?"

Aunt Rahel was holding the little embroidered pouch.

"You brewed this to kill yourself?"

I nodded, and when I did my head hurt. "But I'm not dead."

She half smiled, half frowned. "Oh no, you wouldn't have killed yourself with that little root. I could never let you. Everything I told you about it was a lie. The root is harmless. It did its job—nothing more than put you to sleep for a day and a night, and give you queer dreams."

Did I hate her or love her even more for this confession? A little bit of both, I suppose.

On the fourth day of my father's not-shiva, I left the house and ran past the frankincense tree in Aunt Aminah's old yard. I made my way past the old grove of citrons, and past Yehezkiel the Goat's abandoned forge. I took the path down the escarpment and around the culvert. I hadn't been back to my cave in over a year—since it had been discovered and defiled by my brother. The henna bush at the lip had grown dense and woody. I squeezed myself behind it and ducked to enter. The stone altar was still there, but the cross-eyed lafeh scarf was not, so the stone was bare. Of course my idols were all gone, along with my rustic utensils, little rope-braid rugs, and pilfered furnishings—some scattered, broken knickknacks were strewn about on the floor. It gave me a sad, unraveled feeling to see my cave like this, and I wondered if the cave saw me in much the same way—a girl who had been filled with possibility, and was now empty of all comfort.

I didn't have much time, so I quickly got to work. I had brought black gall with me, along with chalk and candles. I lit two of the candles and put them into notches in the wall. On the wall behind my little improvised divan, I redrew the boy and girl. But this time I drew the girl dressed like a bride, her conical gargush reaching all the way up to the heavens. The boy was dressed like a groom, in a wide-sleeved *jallayah*, with a silk scarf over his head. I redrew the horse next to the boy. And I made it so that the girl pointed to herself with one hand, and to the boy with the other. I wrote Asaf's name under the boy, and my own under the girl. To signify where we were going, I wrote very clearly *Aden*. The only difference between the Adela I left on the cave wall, and the Adela Asaf had known was that I gave the cave-Adela henna, to show Asaf that I was a woman now. I drew little barley sheaths on her hands, to signify that this was a drawing of a marriage and that I, like other Jewish brides, would borrow the stranger magic of my Muslim sisters to protect me on my journey from maiden to wife. And I drew circles within circles within circles—the symbols of eternity—on my forearms and on my forehead. Those circles were a double message. I was telling Asaf that my love for him was eternal, but also that I was now shameless and bold, and that I wanted him to know that I had not forgotten the circles he had once dared to inscribe on my body when we were small children in this cave, rehearsing the roles our parents had cast us in.

When I finished drawing I sat down on the cave floor and sobbed. My tears ran out of my eyes, trailed down my cheeks, dripped from my chin, and dropped into the crevices of my cave, down through cracks and crannies where they joined the secret river that flows out of Eden and into the World to Come. Then I grew calm, and quiet. I wiped my face on my kerchief, blew out the candles, and looked one last time wistfully around at my old place of refuge and hope. Then I shook off my despair and left my cave forever—with the same regrets as one would have when leaving a bosom friend, and a hollow sense of emptiness now that I would not have her as a confidant and sister.

On the sixth day of my father's not-shiva, the Confiscator came to my father's stall to pick up his wife's shoes. My brother Hassan was with me. Together we had finished both the bashmag sandals and the fancy pair he had ordered. I had pressed the florets into the toe and softened the back panel by rubbing it back and forth across the end of the anvil. They were in all ways perfect, and just as my father would have made them.

"Your father?"

"Doing business at the tannery." Hassan was a bad liar. His torn nostril quivered when he spoke.

The Confiscator raised a quizzical eyebrow at me. "I have known this imp since she was a little girl. She would not lie to me. Tell me, A-del-aa," he said. He still dragged out my name, as he had since before I could remember. "How is your father's health?"

"My father is quite well, sir. He will regret that he missed your appearance."

The Confiscator nodded and paid my brother, but before he walked out of the stall he said, "I understand that you lost your mother recently. What a pity." He turned to leave, but before crossing the threshold of the stall, he turned around and winked at me, then continued on his way. I knew his wink meant that he didn't believe Hassan's lie. He had seen into our souls and read the bald truth—that our father had gone to the World to Come.

Was I brave? No. My bowels betrayed me, and I shat myself in fear right there in the market. My brother stripped my linens, wrapped me in a blanket, carried me home cradled in his arms like a baby, even though I was a grown woman. Then he gave me into the loving arms of my sisters-in-law, cousin, and aunt to clean and comfort me.

That evening, unknown to me, Uncle Barhun bribed the Imam's functionary into giving us our traveling papers. At midnight I was shaken awake, and soon I found myself bundled onto the back of the donkey carriage. Most of the family was there, packed into four heavily laden carriages. As I tried to get my bearings, it dawned on me that we were escaping, but I don't know what surprised me more—that I was leaving the only home I'd ever known in the dead of night, or that my aunt and uncle would take such a risk for me. The penalty for their crime? My uncle could be beaten, jailed for many years, or worse. The Confiscator was not known for his mercy and had wide leeway to punish those who dared betray his authority. No one spoke as we wound our way through the penumbral little lanes of our neighborhood. Not a single word. We passed by the synagogue, and through the salt market. Qaraah was silent but for the barking of a far-off dog. Then, just as we were about to reach the camel caravan depot, on the southern road out of town, we heard hoofbeats behind us. Hani pushed me down, covered me with her cloak. I curled up at her feet and she piled bundles on top of me. I felt my heart beating in every single corner of my body—my little fingers, my knees, my hips, my belly, my mouth. Through the bundles, I heard the hoofbeats coming closer, and then closer. I tried to imagine myself a speck of dust, a grain of sand. I squeezed my eyes shut but the darkness in my head tortured me with images of the Confiscator's jambia, his serpents, which in my terror I imagined writhing around my legs, and then upward to my torso, squeezing the life out of me. Uncle Barhun urged our donkeys on. Pishtish began to canter, but still the hoofbeats grew louder and louder. And then they were upon us. Did I die then? I think so. I think the Confiscator's serpents squeezed the life out of me.

But my death was short-lived. And when I awoke, I found that I wasn't dead at all. Rather, I had fainted dead away and missed learning that it was my brother Dov. Under cover of darkness, he had borrowed a Muslim neighbor's fastest horse and chased us down. In a satchel on his back, he carried the little deerskin Torah, which had been left behind in the scurry to depart. I didn't know it yet, but Dov and Masudah and their children were staying behind. Dov handed the Torah to my uncle for safekeeping and then bid our party farewell. I found this all out in the morning. My faint had ushered me into merciful dreamless sleep. When I finally came to, the sun was rising in the sky, and the landscape of my youth had been replaced by the scrubby sands of a desert I didn't recognize. Hani pulled me up next to her, and together we dared to smile and almost laugh. We kissed each other and embraced, and she laid her hand on top of my own. I took my free hand and lifted her hand up and put it on my lap. As the carriage wheels squeaked, and the donkeys' tails swished, I traced a meandering path on her palm, a path beginning with the coming of the other Damaris to Qaraah, and ending in this astonishing journey of redemption.

Part Three

Chapter 22

We were not the only Jews trekking down through the mountains. Drought had hit hard throughout the Kingdom, and what had begun as a trickle of refugees had become a flood. We saw many families we knew along the way. Hope lay in the south and the largesse of the British. Some, like us, had contacts and relatives in Aden. We were lucky, for we never once fell into the path of either the Imam's or the tribesmen's armies, nor were we ever close to any of their skirmishes.

Those first nights on the road I barely slept. I kept waking up and seeing a ghost—a girl with my face, squatting in the dust next to my pallet. She rocked back and forth on her heels and accused me with narrowed eyes. I didn't know it then, but I was looking at a cast-off version of myself—the Adela I was leaving behind. Sometimes in my dreams, I still see her, this left-behind Adela. She cries out to me. She begs me not to leave. She tugs on my ears and tells me that the tragedy that later befell my family would not have happened if only I had stayed. But when I awake, I tell myself that this is foolish. Even if I had stayed in Qaraah, the design would be the same, as it was already fixed in fate, set by lemon juice, writ in indelible scribbles.

"Did you hear that?" My brother Hassan usually trotted in the back of our caravan.

"What?" My brother Elihoo rode in the middle, but he often doubled back to consult with Hassan.

"Hoofbeats behind us."

I usually traveled in the third and last carriage, or I walked beside it.

"No, I hear nothing."

"Listen."

We all stopped and tried not to breathe. One of the donkeys made a belching sound. Another whinnied. A carriage wheel creaked.

"At least one rider, maybe two."

"No, Brother, this time there is no one."

It was my brother Hassan who kept hearing the hoofbeats, and my brothers Elihoo, Mordechai, and Pinny who kept hearing nothing. Menachem was the smallest and meekest of my brothers, and he was always taking Hassan's side in an argument. "Hassan is right; there are riders on our tail." Menachem spat when he said this, and then rode to the middle of the caravan. A coward, he would hide behind the women.

Though we tried to pretend we hadn't heard anything, the truth is that we all heard whatever most frightened us. I heard the hoofbeats of the Confiscator's horse, still convinced he was coming after me. Uncle Barhun also heard the hoofbeats of the Confiscator's horse – because he had stolen me away. But he also heard the hooves of the Imam's functionary's horse. None of us knew that Barhun had paid the bribe for our departure papers in counterfeit thalers, and that, until we reached Aden, he feared being followed and arrested for the crime. My sisters-in-law Sultana and Yerushalmit heard a monster who was rumored to live under the wide-open sky and prey upon travelers, eating their faces off with their three rows of teeth. Aunt Rahel heard the hoofbeats of an angry husband. Had one of her brides died in childbirth? Was a baby born with a cleft palate? It had been a long time since she had had any troubles, but she was never fully at ease. And here on the road, all of us were out of our element. As for Hani? What did she hear? Did she have special reasons of her own to fear that someone was giving chase? If she did, she kept her own confidence.

"Are you sure you didn't hear something?" Hassan wiped his sweaty brow with the back of his hand.

"Well, yes, now I hear a carriage." Menachem squinted and cocked his head, trying to get an extra earful of sound.

Then we all heard it, and until the carriage or the horseman had passed, we were jumpy and cross with one another. This time it was just another family of Jews from a village east of Sana'a and we all breathed easily again. Eventually we descended into a basin girded by black-gray mountains. The sun bleached the gritty sand so that every stone looked like the white of an open eye and every felled branch like a piece of a cast-off skeleton. My thoughts were unbound. My mourning became a lesser kind of burden, and I became dreamy, distracted. I found myself half-giddy with the newfound freedom from fear of confiscation. No, the Confiscator wouldn't find me here. We were far from Qaraah. I was safe for sure. I laughed for no reason and found beauty in every parched bit of landscape.

Uncle Barhun and my brothers Menachem and Elihoo went into the nearby city for its Fourth Day market, purchasing some much-needed meat and oil and hard-boiled eggs for the children. We were a big group. Five of my brothers and nine of their children had come with us. The youngest children were a pair of twins—two boys, my brother Pinny's new wife Salma's first living children. They were eight months old when we traveled and we women all happily traded those sweet, wiggly babies back and forth on the journey, strapping them to our backs when we walked, cradling them in our laps when we rode. Masudah and Dov had stayed behind because Masudah was expecting her ninth baby and was too far along to travel, but she had sent Remelia with us. When I realized that Masudah wasn't with us, I cried out as if I'd been kicked in the gut. Aunt Rahel promised that Masudah and her family would join us once she was safely delivered. But I didn't believe my aunt—not because I thought she was lying, but because when I realized Masudah wasn't on one of the carriages, I had tasted burnt almonds in my mouth, even though I hadn't eaten anything bitter. When I told Hani, she said that her sister Hamama, who understood the future better than she understood the present or the past, would say that the bitter taste in my mouth was a bite of future sadness. She would say that Masudah was lost to us all, even though she wasn't really lost yet.

That night Masudah came to me in my dreams. She held me by the shoulders and said, through clenched teeth, "Adela, promise me that on the way down, Remelia will sleep by your side and that you will look after her always. You promise? No, no tears, little girl, no tears." I dreamed that I buried my face in her bosom and sobbed. When I awoke the moon was still high in the sky. Remelia was sleeping by herself near Sultana. I picked up my sleeping blanket and lay down next to her. And when she roused, crying for her mother, I comforted her, and after that we slept together for the rest of the journey.

We spent a quiet Sabbath with three other families banded together in a dry culvert near a grove of craggy olive trees. The men gathered to pray to Elohim. The chill of midwinter had dissipated, and the air was warm. Rain fell, drenching us, but also bringing with it the sprouting of welcome greenery. We women pooled our food and foraged for wild grasses and tree nuts, but in the morning we left our camps at different hours and departed separately, for we knew that by traveling in too large a group, we risked attracting unwanted attention on the road.

Sometimes the men walked by the side of the carriages. Often we females and the children walked too. Sultana's Moshe was a sturdy nine by now, old enough to ride or walk with the men. When the men walked, they took turns carrying Uncle Zecharia's deerskin Torah, for it was our tradition that a Torah should be cradled like a babe in arms when transported. Usually Hani's David carried it. He said that when we got to Aden he would make it his mission to assess its true state of disrepair, and that perhaps as part of his apprenticeship as a scribe, he could undertake its restoration. David had a lovely voice and he sang as he bore the Torah down the mountains. Sometimes the other men joined him, and their voices enveloped us all, as our feet pressed their lilting tones into the earth. The deerskin Torah, with its ruddy parchment, played an important role on that strange journey. Every second and fifth day, and every Sabbath morning, Uncle Barhun and the rest of the men would gather around and read the weekly portion. And if other Jews were traveling with us on those days, they gathered around too, and treated that broken Torah with unabashed reverence— as if it were the original copy of the Words of the Law itself, written by Moses our Father in the desert. For it was a great relief for a tired road-weary soul to quench his thirst on the spiritual drink of the words of the holy portion.

Once we reached the environs of Wadi Kha, we shrugged off our fear of capture. The wadi connects the midlands to the Red Sea. We had climbed out of the plains and were high above Wadi Kha, which flowed through a narrow slash in a vast gorge. We stopped and marveled at the water, and I know I wasn't the only one who wished I could dip a hand in, grasping for a moment a palmful of the water that would precede us in our trek south. Down on one of the higher banks of the wadi we glimpsed a wonderful site—tribesmen dressed only in loincloths, wading in. They were expert swimmers and flipped and dove like sea creatures, their long hair released from their turbans.

We slept that night not far from a place where legend tells that Ali, son-in-law of Mohammed, left a footprint on a large round rock. There were pilgrims camped nearby, and when they lifted their voices in prayer, I found myself wondering in whose steps we were following. I also wondered how we could learn to read the marks left by ancient travelers on the stones of this earth. The journey was rough, but pleasurable too. For the first time in my life I slept under the constellations and bathed under a waterfall. From a distance I saw a British woman riding in an open car—her blond hair blowing out from under her kerchief. I ate the meat from a deer caught by my brother Hassan with a stone-launched trap and roasted on an open fire. On the road from Yarim to Ibb, we watched Nubians pass us on a camel caravan laden with goods from Egypt. My brother Menachem tamed a caracal that followed after our carriage for a whole week.

We all became very companionable: Uncle Barhun told stories from the childhood he had shared with my dear father, Aunt Rahel shared stories of India, and Mr. Haza took us traveling as he walked us through the streets and alleys of Istanbul. Hani's David was revealed to have the best songs. Yerushalmit surprised us by knowing the names of all the birds in the sky. Sultana's husband, my brother Elihoo, proved to be a talented whistler. Young Remelia had the best jokes. Yerushalmit even let her hand fall from in front of her mouth and spun wonderful stories of an underwater kingdom. Hani was the best at spotting animals— graceful ibex, foxes, shy gazelles, sturdy oryxes, rabbits and porcupines and badgers camouflaged against the dunes that we passed along the way. And as for me? I baked our bread in ovens I constructed—quite ingeniously, I was told—out of stones I found wherever we camped. And I added spices and herbs I found along the way: wild sage, thyme, rosemary, wild onion that had a peppery taste. I also helped with the nighttime stews and the morning cups of coffee-husk brew and fenugreek porridge.

I lay awake many nights of that strange journey. The stars were closer to earth in those days, or at least they seemed to be. In my drowsy discomfort I sometimes reached up and tried to pluck them like daisies. But instead of starlight, I got only an emptiness that revealed itself in the form of glowing Eyes of God in the center of my palms. We wore no henna while we traveled, for we did not have the leisure to spend a morning devoted to adornment. But I saw henna everywhere—in the patterns in the rocks, in the trails of snakes left in the sand, in the tracks of foxes, ibex, and voles. In the sleeping forms of my sisters-in-law and their husbands. In the curled fists and rosebud lips of the children we met on the road. In the meandering shapes of dry riverbeds.

Chapter 23

Toward the end of our journey we met up with a curious group of travelers—a large extended family of Habbani Jews camped by the banks of the Khoreiba River. They were very far from their homeland in the Hadramut, where the Habbanim had lived since King Herod dispatched a brigade of Judeans to fight with the Roman legions in Arabia. The Hadramut was the name for the land bound by Aden to the west, Oman to the east, the Red Sea to the south, and the Rub' al Khali to the north. It was the scorched hem of the skirt on the southeasternmost tip of Arabia. It was puzzling to find the Habbanim here—north and west of Aden—in such a beautiful spot. The gray-gold rocky mountains rose up on all sides, but the land around the river was jungle-green, dense with big-leafed trees, draped in flowered creepers, a welcome respite from the desert landscape. Yellow and orange butterflies danced through the air, and birds of every color flitted and chirped overhead. The family was camped in little reed huts. Their patriarch was a tall man whose naked muscular chest was shiny with oil under a blue prayer shawl, draped over one shoulder. In the Muslim style, he wore a big curved jambia on a belt around his waist. To cover his sex, he had on only an indigo-colored loincloth. His thick curly hair was tied with a thong, and he wore no earlocks, which was strange. I had never seen a Jewish man without earlocks. His face was sharp, his features angular, eyebrows very bushy, mustache clipped.

I had never seen Habbanim before, and had to stop myself from staring at the almost-naked men, though it was the women who most intrigued me. They were adorned head to toe in the most beautiful jewelry I had ever seen. All of it had been made by the patriarch, their husband, and father. At least this is what they led us to understand.

They had so many necklaces; it looked as if their heads were being held up by the tiny metal links of their chains, not by their own flesh and bones. They wore filigreed disks on thick chains, as well as six or seven beaded necklaces, layered one on top of the other, all hung with amulet boxes. Their wrists were adorned with thick silver bracelets, five or six on each arm, set with carnelians and coral. And they had rings on every finger. Their hair was plaited in graceful manes of tiny braids that hung free around their shoulders, topped only by little embroidered diadems on their foreheads instead of gargushim or kerchiefs. Even the youngest girls were dressed like this, like wild little desert brides. On their foreheads some of the women and girls wore black-gall dots. Others wore kohl under dark eyes, or triangle markings on their cheeks and mouths, just the way Aunt Rahel had marked me when we went to Sana'a. We came to understand that three of the women were wives of the patriarch, who was a skilled silversmith, and that most of the thirteen or fourteen children belonged to him as well.

When my uncle asked them what they were doing so far from their homeland, the patriarch unburdened himself of a story. He had welcomed us with coffee and porridge and sat on a big rock not far from the river's edge chewing khat. Uncle Barhun and the rest of the men sat down on other rocks. We women hung back, listening. He spoke Hadrami Judeo-Arabic, which meant that his pronunciation was different from ours, but for the most part, we could understand him.

He said, "An Englishman came to our homes near Abr, three summers ago. He was a representative of the Crown government, and came to build dams in the Hadramut, to help stave off the dreaded droughts that plague our land. This man, an engineer, had a wife back in Aden, and he was much impressed by the jewelry I produced in my little workshop. He was so enamored of my skill that he promised me that if I came to Aden, he would see that I was situated and compensated for my work. I could not refuse such an offer. We went to Aden, and spent two years as the favorites of the high officials of the British petroleum refinery. But it turned out that the engineer was a liar, and I was never fully compensated. The British engineers who purchased my work to give to their wives and lovers back home never paid me. Now we are tired

of the city, and of the Englishmen's lies. We have come north in order
to live under the stars. We plan on returning home sometime before
Hanukkah."

Later that night I overheard my brothers speaking. They assumed
that the man was lying and that he was returning to his home in the
Hadramut a wealthy man. Elihoo said, "He doesn't want to tell us
that he prospered. He fears we will rob him. He is right to be wary of
strangers he meets on the road."

We camped not far from them, and enjoyed their hospitality, and the
river's green, rushing welcome for a few nights. I had heard stories of
the Habbanim from Auntie Aminah—how they were fierce warriors,
and how they were sometimes hired by the great sultans of the north
as mercenaries. According to Auntie Aminah, the men "fought with
names": if a Habbani Jew was threatened, he would simply lift a finger
and draw a Hebrew letter in the air. The letter became a weapon that
speared the heart of his enemy. She also said that Habbanis were the
only Jews in Yemen allowed to wear jambia, because no imam or sultan
would dare disarm them.

We spent the next morning gathering herbs and berries and
replenishing our bladders of water, for the water from the river was
sweet. Then we were invited by the Habbanim to share their lunch of
peppery soup and bread. After eating, our men joined theirs to pray the
afternoon liturgy. Some of the Habbani women and girls sat in a circle,
embroidering a big green cloth that they told me would be used for a
wedding canopy. One of the older girls in the family was to be married
in a few weeks. I brought handwork and sat on a flat rock, close to one
of the Habbani huts. A few of the little girls were playing near where I
was sitting. After a few minutes of work, I absentmindedly put down
my embroidery and picked up a stick. I crouched down and doodled
some letters in the sandy earth, *vav* and *zayin*. One of the little girls
inched over to see what I was drawing. She had heavy-lidded eyes, long
lashes, a snub nose, and plump lips. The black-gall markings on her
cheeks were little upside-down triangles. She had thick silver hoops in
her ears and many necklaces and bracelets. After watching me for a
minute, she reached out her arm, let it hover for a second or two in the
air, and then gently put her hand over my own. Her bracelets slid down
her arm, making a tinkling sound, which added to the gentle music of
the flowing river water. She had a ring on each finger, except for her

thumbs. Her palm was warm on my hand, but the rings were cold on my knuckles.

"Nu," she said, "Sister-whoever-you-are, let me do it with you." She held onto me like a little monkey.

I smiled. "You want to write with me?"

She shrugged. "Let me do it with you," she repeated.

I thought for a moment and then I wrote א, *aleph*. Her hand fast on my own. Then *samech*, ס, and *peh*, פ. I let the stick rest between my legs. She was squatting by our letters, and now rocked back and forth on her heels.

"What is your name?"

"Esther."

"Pretty name for a pretty girl. Would you like to see your name? Yes? Come here, darling; put your hand back on mine. That's right." Together we wrote her name, אֶסְתֵּר, and then I drew a little crown over it. "Like Queen Esther, you too may wear a crown." She squealed with delight and called to her sisters. Soon I had written the names of four little girls in the earth, and one by one they had put their hands over mine, helping me form the letters. Over in the culvert, the voices of the men gliding up and down the liturgy reached us in an emphatic crescendo. A tall woman with heavy-lidded turtle eyes came over and clucked for her daughter—little Esther, who had started me on my naming game. The girl went to her mother and then disappeared behind her.

"What is it? What are you doing?" The woman squatted down by the scribbled harvest of names.

"Just showing the girls how to write their names."

"Eh?"

"Just their names, nothing more. See, there it is, *Esther*." I pointed to the first name, the one with the crown. The woman squinted, puffed out her cheeks, then thrust her tongue through a blank spot in her teeth. She made a tsking sound. My heart fluttered, for she looked angry, and I knew that my mother would chastise me for making trouble with strangers we met on the road. But then I remembered—with the shock of the newly bereft—that my mother was dead and would never chastise me again. I suffered a terrible pang at this knowledge, for in the strange way that a captive will grow to love her captor, I would miss my mother's constant rages and disapproval. I looked over to where our men were praying with their men. I was sure that the Habbani men had learned to read as little boys. But these women and girls were as ignorant as I had been before the other Damaris came to Qaraah. Had I overstepped? The woman's face warmed in a broad, openmouthed smile. She pointed to her own chest, thumping the red, yellow, and green embroidery under her many necklaces.

"Rosa," she said, "my name is Rosa." She put out her thin callused hand, encased in an ornate sarcophagus of rings and bracelets. She clutched onto mine, over the stick. I was startled. "Rosa," she repeated. "I am Rosa."

She wanted a lesson too.

"And I am Adela," I said. "Here; I will show you how to write your name." I formed the *resh* ר and *vav* ו then *zayin* ז and *heh* ה, and when I was finished, I added a little flower next to it. All the while she held onto me like a rag doll—slack-wristed—so that I could move for the two of us without any resistance. Rosa called to one of her sister-wives, a younger woman with a high forehead, a nose like an upside-down arrow, long lashes atop piercing eyes, and a birthmark on her chin. Her name was Hemda, and I wrote her name too. Hemda called to her daughters, four leggy girls who looked like miniature versions of their mother.

Hani came to see what I was doing. As soon as she understood the "lesson," she picked up a stick and began to write, just as I was writing, with an extra hand atop her own.

"So we have a school?" Hani asked, smiling and squatting behind the smallest girl, a little jewel with green eyes who had a zigzag scar on one cheek. "How wonderful. The School of the Road we can call it. The School of the Road for Girls." She took the hand of the little girl with green eyes, closing her own fingers over the child's little beringed fingers. "Like this, baby," she cooed. "You write the *tet* ט from the top left to the top right, not the other way around." I looked at them together, the little Habbani girl and Hani. Hani had her mother's coffee-bronze Indian skin. The Habbani girl was much darker and finer boned. Hani was round and soft, and her hair had golden glints in it. The Habbani girl's hair was obsidian black—braids oiled and gleaming. Hani was curled over the child, her own necklace—a single wrought amulet box—gently touching the back of the child's head. They looked like two mismatched species, as if a lioness had adopted the cub of a mountain panther. By the time we finished, we had written the names of at least ten women and girls in the sand. Each girl guarded her own name. Some picked up their own sticks and began to copy the shapes of the letters. Two little girls got in a fight because one accidentally stepped on the other's name. The mothers also picked up sticks. Hani and I walked among them, correcting and complimenting their efforts.

The next day I was at the water's edge. We women had bathed, and now I was dipping my feet. The Habbanim all went barefoot, and I was enjoying the break from my sandals, which had been cutting into my heels.

"Sister-whoever-you-are?"

I felt a tug on my dress. It was little Esther.

"What is it, sweetie?"

She pointed over to the closest of the reed huts. Her mother was outside, looking in our direction. "My mother wants you." She tugged again, but I needed no further invitation. As we walked together, she slipped her little hand into my own. The rings made her fingers heavy. I noticed her henna. It was an Eye of God, but not one I recognized. I hadn't noticed it the day before. It was such a strange and alluring pattern. I told myself that I would ask Hani to look at it. Perhaps she would know its origin. When the girl closed her hand, it seemed to be winking, and when she opened it, the diamond-shaped eye seemed to twinkle.

We had reached the little hut.

"What is it? Oh, the henna?" Rosa had seen me looking at her daughter's hands. "When she was just a year old, she survived a fall from a rock about as high as that one." Rosa pointed to a cliffside overhang.

"She hit her head, and didn't wake up for a week. While she slept, a traveler gave her this henna. My Esther finally opened her eyes the very moment the henna had set. The traveler was a henna dyer from Lahaj. She had beautiful eyes. Eyes that looked like this." Rosa pointed to the ultramarine stone on one of her bracelets. A vivid blue with tiny specks of gold throughout. "She was very skilled. She saved my daughter. And now I reapply this henna every month. It is her lucky charm. I can show you how to do it. The henna dyer taught me how to draw the eye so that it moves—she said, 'Your girl is looking at the other side of the world, but this eye will look back at her, and lead her back to you.' And so it came to pass. Just as the henna set, Esther woke up, and suffered no ill effects from her fall. Would you like me to show you? Yes? But you must give me something in return."

"But I don't have anything to give—"

"Sha, you are rich enough. You have your own bounty. I will give you Esther's Eye if you give me *your letters*. Draw the aleph bet for me, and teach me the names of *all* the letters. Will you do that? An Eye for an alphabet, heh? I think that is a good trade."

I smiled. "Of course."

"Good. Let us start with the henna. It is a powerful charm. The henna dyer told me that for those who are sleeping, it wakes them up, and for those who are awake already, it sharpens their vision, though I must admit that my own eyes are poor—I have worn the special Eye many times, and my eyes are just as weak when I wear the charm as when I don't. But I don't question its power. Sometimes I think that the sharper vision is for the inner eye. I dream clearer when I wear it, and I have even had visions of the future, as if I can see beyond my own life span."

She went into her little hut and came out with a henna pot and stylus. I put out my palm for her, and she put the stylus to my life line. But as it pricked, I hesitated, pulled back.

"Wait," I said, "I have an idea. Would you wait for me? Please? I will be right back." I ran over to our carriage and rummaged through my little bag of belongings. At the very bottom was the book I had made for myself when I made a book for Hani, using Masudah's paper. I returned to Rosa with my book. "Please draw it in here"—I opened to the first page—"not on my hand."

She cocked her head sideways, squinted, and espied my book with a skeptical biting of her lips.

"Maybe, ummm . . ." I stalled. "Maybe my eyes are too sharp already. Or maybe I am afraid of what I will see. Don't be offended, Mrs. Rosa." I put my hand over hers. Her bracelets had fallen all the way down to her wrist, and her rings were so thick on every finger that scarcely any skin showed through. With the other hand I thrust the book a little closer to her. One of her necklaces, with a cylindrical amulet box, brushed the edge of it. She drew back, as if she had touched something foul or hot.

"Please?"

She shook her head. "You are a silly girl. You want to keep henna forever. But you can't trap henna. It is not the same on a piece of pulp. It belongs on a hand or a foot. On a girl or a woman. Not in a book. But don't worry. I will oblige you. I will draw it wherever you wish. Because I am an obliging woman and you are a nice decent girl . . . well, a nice decent *silly* girl. I can see that. And I can also see that you have no motives other than a search for knowledge. And knowledge is a blessing. But if the eyes stare at you funny, or glare, or ask you questions you can't answer, don't blame me. I can't be responsible for what the design will do when trapped on the dead animal flesh between the covers of your Torah."

"It isn't a Torah—"

"Not yet, it isn't. But it will be. Don't fret. I won't tell anyone your secret."

"But I don't have a secret."

She smiled. "Here, give it to me, let us begin."

She sat on one of the stones and traded the henna stylus for a quill with a black-gall nub. It didn't take her long to draw the design. When she was finished, it was easy to see the differences between our regular Eye of God and this one—hers had waves, where ours had straight lines. Hers had tiny triangles within triangles, where ours relied more on circles for the outer border. And the diamond eye in the center of hers was smaller and thicker-lined than the one Hani had taught me to make. Even so, these differences did not lend the Habbani woman's Eye of God its power. It was something else. Like Hani's constellation of stars, there were simply some patterns that had life and another dimension, other than color and form. Was it breath? Soul? Blood? Or some other essential additive that enlivened the henna, made it shimmer and talk and twinkle?

When she was finished, I put small rocks on the corners of the splayed pages and left the book open to dry. Then I went over to one of the thorny mimosas, bent down, and rummaged for a sharp fallen branch. I wrote the entire aleph bet in a straight row in the dirt, as it would appear on a page. When I was done, Rosa put her hands on her hips, squinted. "What can you tell me about them?"

"About whom?" I looked around.

"Them!" She pointed to the letters. "Pretend they are people and we are gossiping fools. *Tell me who they are.*"

"Oh, them." I smiled at the thought of the letters as people, having their own lives and personalities. Having faults and successes and domestic dramas. Things to gossip about. "Yes," I said. "I can tell you what I know about *them*."

"Good, and don't leave out any tidbits or scandals."

"If I had tidbits and scandals, I would happily share them with you. But all I have are the tiniest stubs of stories."

She shrugged. "Oh, just go on, go on already."

I began to relate what Hani had told me about the aleph bet when she taught me how to read. How the form of each letter comes from an ancient picture. And how this picture itself came from an essential part of the lives of the people who first drew the letters.

"Aleph is the head of an ox." Next to the א, I drew an ox head *b*, and I pointed out how with the addition or subtraction of a few lines, the letter derived from the picture. "*Bet* is a house"—ב ◻—"*Gimel* is a foot"—ג ㄥ—"*Vav* is a tent peg"—ו Y—"and *zayin* is a plow"—ז ⚎—and I showed her the shepherd's staff in *lamed*—ל J.

While I was drawing, Rosa and little Esther squatted next to me. Esther took her second finger and began copying my letters in miniature. Rosa rocked back and forth on her heels.

I had gotten almost to the end of the alphabet when Rosa shook her head and snorted, "No, that just won't do." She got up, stepped forward, and stamped out the beginning of my alphabet, leaving a blurry, illegible smudge underfoot. Esther scampered back and took a perch on one of the big rocks behind us.

"But it is as I have said. The letters correspond to pictures. I am not making anything up."

"Yes, but the pictures are the wrong ones."

I cocked my head, squinted at the remaining letters, wondering what they looked like to her. Were her eyes that bad? Maybe my drawings were incomprehensible to her.

"What I am saying is that they are not *our* letters." She thumped her chest, pointed to me, and then back at herself. "*Our* letters would show this—" She reached for little Esther, pulling her from the rock and gesturing to the enchanting curve of the child's cheek. "Or that—" She pointed over to the acacia, where one of her companions was nursing a babe. The child's legs kicked, and with one hand, he was playing with his toes.

Rosa puckered her lips. "Draw me the letter that shows the lips of a babe pursed to suckle." Then she reached for her own breast, cupped a hand, and lifted it up. "Or the fullness of the breast at which he sucks. Now, that is something I could read, a letter drawn from my life. And you know what? It would read me back. Tell *my* stories." Another one of the women stood up, and came to join us from under the acacia. She was older than Rosa, maybe even old enough to be her mother, though they didn't look anything alike. She bent down over my letters, the ones Rosa hadn't smudged. Her dress was a flowing expanse of dusky black between her legs. She had a dot on her forehead and a ring in her nose, and big hoops in her ears. Her nose was like an eagle's, pointy and sharp.

She nodded her agreement and smiled, adding in a soft high voice, "Those letters"—she pointed to the collection of Hebrew letters in the earth—"come out of men like globs of spit, or spurts of wet heat from their phalluses. But where is the letter that could show this?" She put her hand in between her legs, crudely, over her own sex. Then she pointed at the letter vav, which took the shape of a straight line. "That letter is a staff or a man's member, or perhaps it is his weapon, his spear? See the pointy tip? It is a man's tool. Used for man's business. But where is the letter that shows the sweet doorway to the Garden of Eden?" Once again, she put her hand in between her legs. "The letter that shows how we welcome men in and out of this world?"

Rosa cackled her agreement, and then added, "And where is the flower letter that shows this?" She raised her hands and showed me her henna, the lush garden of blossoms on her palms.

"Adela, that is your name? Adela, the letters you draw belong to *them*." She gestured to where the men were smoking hookahs and chewing khat. "Next time we meet, on the road between somewhere and nowhere, show me *our* alphabet." She thumped her chest. "Teach me *our* language"—she motioned toward her companion with the eagle nose, her sister with the babe at her breast—"and then we can teach each other how to speak it."

I fumbled for words and stood there for a moment not saying anything. Then I remembered Aunt Aminah's tale and said, "But ladies, I have heard marvelous stories about *your* men using letters for weapons. How they draw letters in the air, fell their enemies without shedding blood. What could be more powerful than that?"

Once again Rosa shook her head. "Sha, don't be ridiculous. Our men fight with spears and shovels, knives and clubs. Fierce, yes. Dangerous? Of course. But legends don't win wars, and neither do letters. And if you think they do, then you are the one who needs lessons, not us."

At this they both laughed, sharing a joke at my expense. I thought for a moment, and then I squatted once more. I drew a *kaf*, כ **ﬡ** , the letter that takes its form from a cupped palm.

"You are right, some of the letters are men's letters," I said. "But there are also female ones. This one is an open palm, see? A hand that can pet a cheek or offer a quenching drink of water. And here is *mem*." I drew מ and **ﬦ**. "This one is water, see the ripples, how they come from waves? We women have within us the spirit of the tides and waves. *Mem* is our letter every month when we flow like the waters. And this one, *tet*" —ט **⊗**— "is a basket, a market basket slung over our shoulders, perhaps filled with potatoes or onions we will use to make our evening soup. And this one is *peh*"—פ כ. "Look, it is a mouth, maybe a mother's mouth calling her child in for dinner or singing to her as she falls asleep in our arms."

Rosa's and the eagle-nosed woman's faces both burst into easy smiles. They clapped their hands. "Wonderful," Rosa said, and the other woman added, "Good, good. At least we will have something to start with."

We left early the next morning. I turned just as we were about to round the bend that would take us to the road out of the river valley. I saw Rosa and Esther standing by the closest of their reed huts, watching us depart. Little Esther yelled to me, "Good-bye, sister-whoever-you-are." I waved, making my hand into a kaf, the cupped palm letter כ **ﬡ**. Rosa waved too. And for a brief moment our cupped palms were an entire alphabet unto themselves, a system of writing that did not represent, but actually *created*, the entire world.

For the rest of that day, I thought of what Rosa said. And as I listened to my own voice and to the voices of my aunt and cousin and sisters-in-law and their children, I wondered what we would all sound like if Eve our Mother or Esther our Queen, or Miriam our Prophetess or Rosa the Habbani Jewess had been holding the stick that formed the letters that made up *our* words. But I also thought of the legend of the Habbani warriors, fighting with words. I believed everything Auntie Aminah had ever told me. I wondered how I could form my letters so that they would come out of my mouth not as air but as blades or bullets. I wondered what it would feel like to speak a weapon, and to forge a word.

Chapter 24

We approached Aden two weeks later, a month and a half after we first left Qaraah. It was the springtime of 1933. We went through the main pass, down through a deep gorge, past an old Jewish cemetery with graves facing north, to Zion. We descended slowly, and then made our way through streets choked with bulky lorries, imported British automobiles, their green and yellow and red bodies pale under gauzy layers of grime, and Indian army trucks with British or Indian soldiers or Aden Protectorate Levies shoving their boots out the back. I was shocked by all this, my first experience with the truly modern world. I felt overwhelmed by the cars and the iron lampposts and the paved roads. Sana'a had been a medieval circus compared to this panoply of twentieth-century life. And Qaraah? Qaraah was a dusty-winged moth pinned to the distant past. Here was modernity. Acrid exhaust like the taste of forge smoke coated my tongue. Heavy machinery rolled by us on the road. Camels, donkeys, and horses all shared the road in a jostle of metal and flesh and voices yelling "*yalla, yalla, yalla,*" everyone hurrying each other along.

During our journey, I'd asked Uncle Barhun to tell me about Aden. From him, I'd learned that Aden is the southernmost settlement on the Arabian Peninsula—the ancient terminus for all camel caravans traveling south through Arabia, as well as the deep harbor seaport through which ships traveling between Europe and the Far East—laden with heavy goods, mercenaries, and soldiers—had passed since Roman days. Equidistant from the Suez Canal, Bombay, and Zanzibar, Aden was perfectly located to ensure its international importance. By the time we arrived, its fortunes had risen and fallen many times but it was ascendant again, the busiest port in the entire British Empire. The Royal Marines had landed in Aden in 1839 to stop pirates from attacking

British ships en route to India. With the growing importance of India in the Empire, the British needed a safe and dependable coaling station en route to the Raj. Also, the opening of the Suez Canal made Aden a linchpin in British military communications. Before British rule, Aden had been occupied by the Portuguese, the Ottomans, and the Sultanate of Lahaj. My uncle explained that each of these rulers had left its mark. He said that like a coin minted by many masters, Aden was textured, and while it looked to the future, it was also mired deep in the past.

We rode past hotels with expansive verandas and official-looking buildings. Then we passed a hospital, a big synagogue, a ritual bath, a school, and rows and rows of little shops leaning into one another like companionable fellows. The light in Aden was neither the ruby-red haze of Qaraah or the yellow butter of Sana'a, but bone white, as if the air itself had been bleached by the sun. We continued past streets named with English letters and finally stopped in front of a three-story house. A young woman who looked like Hani, but older and tinier, came running out of it. Edna burst into tears and threw herself at her mother, Aunt Rahel. Only twenty years old, she was already mother to four girls and one dead boy. "Oh, Mother, oh, Mother." She let out a high waterfall sound—a laugh that had a sob for a scar. "Oh, Mother, how I've missed you all." Or was it a sob that had a laugh for a beating heart? Edna thrust her youngest child—a curly starry-eyed poem of a girl named Noemi—into Aunt Rahel's arms.

"Oh, darling, she is a perfect cherub!" Aunt Rahel smothered the baby with kisses while Uncle Barhun took Edna's face in his hands, squeezed her cheeks, kissed her forehead, and shook her husband's hand—then quickly gave up with such formalities and hugged him as he would a son.

"We have been long on the road, and too long gone from Aden. Feed us like cart horses and water us like plants. We are parched and hungry, and I fear that we have grown uncivilized on our journey and we will make a mess of your tables for lack of manners."

"Oh, Father, we have been preparing for your arrival. Come in; I have three feasts waiting for you, each one more scrumptious than the next."

Soon my new cousins were embracing me. I felt as though I knew them already, from Hani's stories, even though we were meeting for the very first time.

"Oh, look at her pretty hair." This was Edna, who I knew cared the most about beauty, but was so kindhearted that she would never begrudge a girl (myself included) her lack of it, instead managing to see even the most homely of souls as beautiful in spite of themselves.

"When is your birthday, darling? And for whom were you named?" This was Nogema, who Hani had told me was always full of questions, the family historian.

"Tell me everything about you! Tell me now, right now!" This was Hamama, who always needed to know things, but also seemed already to know them before they even happened.

I let myself be petted and cooed over. They all knew of my recent loss of both mother and father and spoke the customary words of mourning. I thanked them for their blessing, and then found myself taking stock of these new wonderful creatures. Hamama was younger than Edna, but she was taller, had a fuller figure, and a chipped front tooth. I was to learn that the henna she wore always had some version of the Eye of God hidden in surprising places. Edna, the eldest, was the most petite. Her voice was also the highest, and I would soon learn that she was the best singer. She favored delicate little conch shells in her henna designs. Nogema was only thirteen months older than Hani, and looked most like her—both had full bosoms and generous hips, but weren't as tall or voluptuous as Hamama. Nogema was partial to interlocking laurel leaves in her henna, and her forearms were awash in them. She had an alluring birthmark below her left nostril, a broader face than Hani's, darker shadows under her eyes, and a sprinkling of freckles across her nose. Hani's hair was the curliest. Hamama's was the longest, reaching all the way down her back. Edna's was the lightest, with more gold and red than brown in it. These sisters were dressed in unremarkable Adeni clothes—black and gray trousers and white tunic shirts. They wore red and blue and yellow shimmering kerchiefs and their hair peeked out of the front and cascaded out the back, so that the magnificent scarves seemed to only caress their hair, not hold it at bay.

The men all helped unload our carriages. David Haza and Nogema's husband saw to the donkeys. Little Noemi was shy of her aunt, but Hani bent down and whispered something into her ear. Then Noemi reached up her arms and let out a little laugh. She let Hani pick her up. Aunt Rahel threaded her hand into Edna's. I walked behind them into the house. They spoke with their heads bent together. Before the day was out, the entire other Damari clan went to visit the graves of their lost twins, Naama and Asisah. And after that Aunt Rahel went often to the old acacia tree, whose boughs were indeed stooped so low to the earth they seemed to be embracing the graves, not just shading them.

That night we ate a stew made of a white fish. I had never tasted fresh fish before, and did not much like the feel of it in my mouth, but I was hungry and ate my fill. Late that first night, I sat with all four sisters on the pillows in Hamama's house. Their children had long since fallen asleep, and were arrayed at our feet like so many sleeping doves. I was too tired and too dumbstruck by the twists and turns of the road to join in. I also didn't know the rhythm, the cadence of their connection; they had been weaving their voices together since before they could speak or toddle. So I was mostly quiet and lost myself in the tendrils of their henna. But then Hamama took my face in her hands, kissed me full on the lips, and brushed the hair out of my eyes.

"So what is this I hear? You were once engaged to be married to our cousin Asaf?"

Her voice was lower, huskier than Hani's. "And he left on a long journey? How many years ago? Four? Five? Well, no worries, little chick, he will come to Aden before you leave it."

I felt a shock in my heart, and stammered, "How . . . how do you know?"

She shrugged and crinkled up her nose in a smile. "Some people have a good sense of time, others a good sense of direction. I was born with a good sense of the stories we live. Sometimes I see ends, sometimes I see beginnings, but usually I see flashes that don't fit in anywhere. But for you, my darling Adela, I see a boy making his way past the grave of Cain and I know that he is coming here to Aden, and that he is as much your cousin as you are mine."

My face grew hot, and I blushed and turned away. If what she said was true, my deepest wish would be fulfilled, but perhaps Hamama spoke nonsense? How could I know if she was a true soothsayer, or if she was just clever and sly enough to say exactly what I wanted to hear?

I lay awake that night, tossing and turning, struggling with my own memories, desires, and prayers. Deep in the night, I thought I heard music. Aunt Rahel had told me the legend of Cain. She said that after Cain murdered Abel, he was cursed by God to wander the earth. When Cain stopped wandering, he founded Aden. In his shame and exile he grew lonely. When the loneliness in his heart became unbearable, Satan appeared to Cain and gave him a reed instrument. Cain played on this little flute, and the shadows lifted from his heart. Cain's grave sat at the entrance to Aden, just above the narrow mountain pass through which we, like all travelers from the north, entered the city. That night, our first in Aden, the night Hamama prophesied Asaf's return, it seemed to me that for reasons I could never fathom, Cain himself was serenading my dreams.

We were quickly situated. At the time I had no idea why we were so generously treated. Years later I learned that Mr. Haza was not only speaking the truth about the Fey and Absev Company but also had another source of income. He spied for the British in Aden and had been all over the midlands before coming to Qaraah. He had supplied the British with information concerning the Sultan of Lahaj's plotting to retake Aden for Yemen. Mr. Haza had been handsomely paid for his covert services. Together, Fey and Absev and the British government settled our entire family in Crater. Uncle Barhun, Aunt Rahel, Remelia, and I were given a little three-story house just next door to Edna and Hamama, who shared a house with their husbands. Yerushalmit's and Sultana's families shared a house around a southwest corner. Hani, David, and Mr. Haza moved into a house around another corner. We were all within five blocks of one another. Uncle Barhun became Mr. Haza's partner. They managed a warehouse for Fey and Absev in Steamer Point and did business down at the harbor—running the Red Sea dhow coffee trade for their bosses in Istanbul. David began his studies with the great scribe Rabbi Aryeh Ben Ari. He also undertook the repair of the deerskin Torah, which Rabbi Ben Ari had inspected and declared "a true treasure, most worthy of restoration." My brothers all found work in their various trades, and we counted ourselves as lucky that we were not among the impoverished refugees from the north who bunked in big sweltering open rooms on the floor of the charity hostel and who begged in the streets of Crater, hands open for alms, eyes half-closed with the shame of it.

One thing I needed to grow accustomed to was the heat. In Qaraah, we had benefited from mountain breezes, but my first summer in Aden, I learned that the heat was unrelenting. Hot sandy winds from the north called *shamal* taught me to walk through the streets with a scarf over my face. And then came the *kawi*—cauterizing sandstorms that blinded horses and clogged up carburetors, causing lorries to stall in the middle of the road. When I commented on the heat, Aunt Rahel teased me.

"Adela, don't you know? There is a furnace buried in the bowels of Mount Sirah, and on the Day of Judgment it will burst forth, scorching souls to hell." I learned quickly that people liked to joke about the heat in Aden. And that they rarely spoke about it without slipping a noose of dark humor around their words. The only way to stay cool was to admit that the heat was a monstrous adversary, one that would ultimately win. Edna told me another legend of a man who sent a rope down a well in Aden.

"When he pulled it up, the end was scorched," she said. "He sent it down again, this time with a bucket. When he pulled up the bucket, the water was steaming. But his thirst was so great he took a drink, boiling his guts."

At night, we would all go up onto the flat roof and try to sleep. The house was only three stories, but it was sturdily built and had a little garden in the rear where onions, potatoes, squash, and clematis vines grew. I lay awake deep into the night, sweating from every pore in my body. Sometimes when I opened my eyes my vision was blurry from the sweat on my eyelids. Oh, had I ever been so hot? Remelia was breathing heavily next to me, little beads of sweat above her upper lip. My aunt and uncle slumbered a few yards away. I flipped over my pillow to get the cool side, and lay there for what seemed like hours, unable to sleep, staring at the stars. I no longer felt the fire of fear in my head; the Confiscator couldn't reach me here. But I did suffer from an ache in my heart that made me dull and sluggish. I was homesick for a blighted place. I missed the dusty prayers that sustained us when the wells ran dry. I missed Masudah and her many children. I missed the dye mistress. I missed those I had already lost for good—Auntie Aminah, my father, even my mother. Here in the new-old city, I was unmoored. It was as if I risked floating up and becoming a star myself, but one with little light to shed on the glories and wonders of old creation. When the sun rose, the city came to life. The muezzin called men to prayer. Cats ran behind fishmongers, mewling for scraps. Donkey carts creaked through the streets. Lorries belched on their route between Crater and Steamer Point. Women called to their children to get away from the sides of the rooftops.

* * *

Soon after arriving in Aden, we received the dreadful news that
Masudah had died in childbirth and that illness had carried off three
of her youngest children, the rest fostered out as her husband, Dov,
my eldest brother, had lost his mind. The children weren't in danger
of confiscation, because even though he couldn't care for his sons and
daughters, Dov still lived, and children would not be taken away from
a living father. What can I say about my mourning for Masudah and
her brood? I can tell you that it never ended, and that somewhere in
my soul, I still cry for her, that other-mother of mine, whose warm
touch taught me kindness and love, when my own mother had none
to give. Poor Remelia suffered terribly and never smiled in quite the
same way again. We sent for Masudah's remaining children. There
were six of them, and they were brought down through the mountains
by a charitable neighboring family. They lived in all of our houses, but
mostly they lived with Yerushalmit, who took Masudah's offspring into
her heart with a natural grace that smoothed over the rawest edges of
the tragedy.

Several months after the arrival of Masudah's children, Hani bore
her first child, a daughter she named Mara. It was late autumn of 1933.
I was fifteen years old, and Hani was sixteen. I was with her during
the birth and was the third to hold the babe—after Aunt Rahel and
Nogema, who helped the midwife in the delivery. Hani gave me the
baby after she had suckled her for the first time.

"There," she sighed, "a dolly for you to play with. If we were back in
Qaraah, I would let you bring her to your cave, so you could pretend
she was your own." I tucked little Mara into the crook of my arm, and
rocked her back and forth. Hani's words had caught me off guard. I
didn't know if she was being mean or playful, but since she had just
given birth, I forgave her if she was pointing out the fact that I had no
husband, no baby of my own in the offing. I kissed Mara in between her
little eyebrows.

"She has your eyes," I said to Hani, but Hani had already fallen
asleep, exhausted from the trials of delivery. I sat for the next hour
telling Mara everything I knew about life, which wasn't much at all,
because I left out the parts about Asaf and my cave—they were entirely
unsuitable subjects for a newborn, though Hani's taunting had riled

up my memories, and even as I kept my tongue, I saw myself as I had been then: a girl who married a prince she had conjured out of sky and earth.

After Mara's birth, there were others. Nogema bore a fourth son, who died the day before his circumcision. Hamama bore twin boys who both lived. Sultana's son Moshe entered the King George V Jewish School for Boys and received many compliments from the headmaster, who called him "a genius little scholar." Remelia went for a time to live with Masudah's sister, her aunt in Lahaj, but returned complaining shamefacedly that her aunt's husband groped her under her dress and made other advances too mortifying to even mention. Throughout this time, more and more Jews were coming down from the Kingdom, filling the streets of Crater. These refugees were essentially stuck in Aden. They had nowhere to go. If they had their druthers, most would have gone to Palestine. But entrance into the port of Jaffa was severely restricted by the British. Only able-bodied folk under the age of thirty-five who could pay their own passage plus a sizable fee were permitted into the Holy Land. So the refugees glutted up Aden, overflowing the hostel built to house them.

Aunt Rahel began to take a personal interest in the refugees from the Kingdom, and volunteered in the hostel as a nurse and midwife. "After all," she said, "it is our luck that we are prosperous and have a place here in Aden. These people are our brethren, and we must care for them like brothers and sisters."

Sometimes Hani would leave her infant daughter with me or one of her sisters, and join her mother at the hostel. But while Aunt Rahel would nurse the refugees, Hani would bring a little pot and stylus and do their henna. When my sister-in-law Yerushalmit asked her why she was "dirtying her hands with the refugees," Hani glowered, replying, "Yerushalmit, it is as my mother says: these women are our sisters. And a woman can bear greater burdens if she can look in her hands and see the world there. A woman can live in her hands, if she needs to."

Aunt Rahel nodded her approval. "Hani is as much a nurse as I am," she said. "She prescribes patterns and elements—paisleys, rose petals, lotus tendrils, conch shells, and three-dot borders on pulse points. Such medicine heals in its own fashion."

* * *

Cleaning. Cooking. Marketing. I helped my aunt keep house for my uncle, but there was also Remelia, and the three of us made quick work of meals and household chores. As time passed, the dullness and heartache inside of me was replaced by a hunger I recognized: the urge to get outside of myself, the urge to ramble and explore. As when I was a girl, I began to wander. My cave was far, far away, my idols smashed, burned, and abandoned, but I still felt the same pull that I had felt as a child. I was a dutiful Jewess on the outside, but inside my heart, I was in search of a new altar at which to bow my head and bend my knee.

I'd learned that the city consisted of four main neighborhoods. In Ma'alla in the Northeast—a former fishing village—the Brits built a customs house and garrisoned their troops. Steamer Point, or Tawahi, to the west, is where they built a new deepwater port. The climate was cooler in Steamer Point, and so it became the locus of English political and mercantile activity with government buildings, housing for high officials, consulates, banking houses, shipping offices, as well as a public park with a statue of Queen Victoria and duty-free stores, catering to sailors and foreign visitors. There was also Sheik Othman, an Arab village north of Ma'alla, whose artesian wells supplied water to Aden. And Crater, the largest neighborhood, built in the crater of an extinct volcano, on the far eastern side of the Aden peninsula. The only way into Crater was through the main pass, which cut through rocky mountains.

Soon after arriving in Aden, I'd developed a regular route. I left our house and walked down B Street, across the Street of Answers, right at the Street of Questions. Another right, past the palace of the Great Banin Messa, departed and beloved president of the Jews of Aden, past the Prince of Wales Hospital, past streets F, G, and H. Finally I reached the Selim School for Girls. What a marvel! Hani had told me about the girls' schools in Aden, but until I saw them for myself I couldn't believe that such places actually existed. I found my window, leaned against the wall underneath it, and listened to the teacher inside speak to her class. I eventually learned that her name was Mrs. Sylvia Townsend. Her deep voice was like a plow—a good firm tool that makes purposeful ruts in the earth. I went almost every day for two months and listened underneath that window. Occasionally I followed Mrs. Townsend away from the building. She had red hair and a lipsticked mouth like a mountain poppy blooming wide open. She had big teeth. Freckles everywhere, even on her eyelids. A big peachy woman, like two Yemenite women put together. Not fat, just broad. I followed Mrs. Townsend through the market and watched her buy orange persimmons, roasted almonds, and a container of imported hand cream from one of the cosmetics ladies whose stalls were swathed in chemical perfumy vapors. I sat outside the window of the Selim School for Girls and listened to her goad her students, encourage them, drill them, praise them, and celebrate their accomplishments. One day Mrs. Townsend sent a student outside to bring me in. The first thing she said to me was, "I knew you were there all along, and I have finally taken pity on your poor curious soul. How old are you? Are you married? Where do you live? What does your father do? How long have you been in Aden?"

"Dear lady, how is it that you speak our language so well?"

"I learned it the hard way. Walking on my knuckles like an ape through a jungle of Levantine grammar. My husband's secretary taught me. A rare bird of a boy—an Adeni Jew with a British father."

She taught almost exclusively in the language of the Jewish population, Yemeni-Judeo Arabic, a mixture of Hebrew, Aramaic, and Yemenite Arabic. Of course she spoke her own language, English, and in the market, I had heard her haggling in Arabic with an ostrich-feather merchant. I explained to Mrs. Townsend that I myself had been taught to write by my cousin, and how I had taken a stick in my hand and taught the Habbani girls and women their letters. I told her that teaching the Habbanim was like a charm sewn into my soul, a special magic stitch; that I often dreamed of the riverbank, of the letters in the earth, of their hands on my hands. She nodded her big pink head, bit her red lips. She thought for a moment. Then she pointed to my hennaed hands. "Adela, your name is Adela? I will make you a bargain. You give me henna and I will let you sit inside the school. In my classroom. And then, if you would like, you can help with the littlest girls—teaching them their letters." She pointed again to my hands. "I want you to give me an application. An honest-to-goodness application. Yes? Do you know how? How to do it properly? You have good technique? Good. I have always wanted to wear henna. This is what we call *a fair trade*. My husband will laugh. He will say, 'Sylvie, now you have really gone native.' And he will be right." She screwed up her face and let out a belly laugh. When she was done laughing she said, "Tomorrow afternoon? I teach until lunch. But you know that already. Meet me after class, and we will take the lorry to Steamer Point."

On my way home from the market I thought of the Habbani woman—Rosa—and how she had traded me henna for letters. And now I was trading henna for letters again. Would I be a teacher? *A fair trade*, the British teacher had said, and it dawned on me that my father, who made his living trading the skin of animals for money, would not have seen it that way. Henna is just color and shape. Letters are just shape and ink. But this was a trade of color for ink, and shape for shape. I had to agree with Mrs. Townsend; it seemed a fair trade indeed. Would she really let me stand in the front of a room of girls and teach? The thought left me giddy. I didn't pay attention to where I was going and walked straight into a boy with a basket of seeded loaves on his head. He scowled at me, dodging to the side, a maneuver that almost tipped his burden.

The next day I met Mrs. Townsend on the steps of the school and let her pay one rupee for my ticket to Steamer Point. She lived in a neat white stucco house not far from the crescent of shops near Victoria Park. I held her pale, pinkish palm in my own, pressed a stylus to her life line, and drew for her my very own variation of one of Hamama's amulet water inscriptions. A woman of such learning deserved a powerful design, I thought, a design that would eddy around her palm and flow into her blood. When it was finished, she held up her hands and appraised her own worth.

She said, "My, what a long way I have come from Tottenham Court. What will my Gordon say?" She pointed to a framed photograph of a square-jawed British gentleman.

"You must teach me. You simply must teach me how you do it." A few weeks later she convened a little class in her house, and that is how I came to teach five British ladies—all of them wives of British engineers or bureaucrats—the basics of the art of henna.

Ever since coming to Aden, my aunt, cousins, and I met on the New Moon to readorn ourselves. Sometimes my sisters-in-law joined us. When next we met for henna at Edna's house, just a few days after I'd taught Mrs. Townsend and her friends, I told everyone what I had done. I told the story of the trade, of Mrs. Sylvia Townsend interrogating me, and of the stale little flat biscuits she served her friends.

Sultana said, "Adela, your mother would beat you for such impudence. She would insist that you never again do such a thing as that."

But Hani nodded her approval, clapped her hands, and said, "Adela, you are brilliant. British ladies wearing henna. Maybe we can make a special pair of gloves, mark them with henna designs, and put them on the Statue of Queen Victoria in the park at Steamer Point. Wouldn't that be hilarious? Visiting dignitaries would think that she'd *gone native*."

Nogema screwed up her mouth. "Adela, they must have their own designs. Your ladies . . . I heard once that there are rings of stones on the British Isles. You must encourage them to incorporate the ring stones into their designs. It is important to honor one's own origin and landscape."

Hamama didn't approve at all. She was uncustomarily gloomy when she scrunched up her face in disdain. "Pale skin clashes with henna. The contrast is too great, and the evil eye confuses the henna for blood. No good can come of it."

That night I thought about what Hamama had said, about the British ladies' pale skin and henna. In Qaraah, almost everyone was a toasted sesame brown. But here I had become used to seeing people of different shades: coal-black Nubians who worked down at the docks, dark-chocolate Somali women who served in the wealthier Arab and Jewish houses, burnt-umber Ceylonese coffee traders who came and went from Uncle Barhun's house, sepia-toned Indian customs collectors who levied taxes for the Crown, and their wives—Indian ladies in billowing Calcutta silk having tea on the veranda of the Aden Inn. The Arab fishermen and boatmen who lived in Sheik Othman, their skin the color of honeyed walnuts, and their wives swathed in black *balto* with their faces the same honeyed color, peeking out from behind their kerchiefs as they did their marketing and walked through town. There were the tourists from Europe and Great Britain, people like Mrs. Townsend with skin as white as a cooked whole egg, or as pink as the downy belly of a newborn kitten. They sipped lemon ices on the veranda of the Hôtel de l'Europe while pointing at Abyssinian monks, bare-chested Somali fishermen in loincloths, and Arab tribesmen from the north in robes so long they seemed to carry all the secrets of the desert in the folds of their flowing djellabas.

I wondered why Hamama was bothered by the clash of dark henna on pale skin. I lay on my pallet tossing and turning. I thought about all the different colors of the people of Aden, and the different contrast that henna would present on each of their bodies. Hamama was right—the henna on Mrs. Townsend's skin *did* look like blood, a skein or a web of it. But Aunt Rahel and my cousins had never shied away from henna's bloody imagery. After all, Anath slays Mot and wades in his blood. Why did it matter if the British ladies' hands looked as if they had been dipped in the same river that we ourselves conjured? I was not superstitious like Hamama. But neither did I take henna for granted. I fell asleep puzzling over this question. I had a feeling that Mrs. Townsend would dismiss Hamama's warning as "utter nonsense." But still, I felt as if I should warn her. Though when I awoke in the morning, it seemed silly, and I knew that I would keep Hamama's misgivings to myself.

Chapter 25

It was five or six days later, when my uncle came home from morning prayers with a grim look on his face that bespoke misfortune.

"What is it, Uncle?"

"An accident at the Selim School. A ceiling in one of the classrooms collapsed. One of the teachers was killed, another injured."

The old fire flared up behind my face and I ran out the door before my uncle could say another word. Police lorries clogged up the front entrance to the school. Uniformed men were rushing in, hauling out debris on their backs. Girls were everywhere, wailing, holding one another, saying psalms. The tragedy had unfolded just as teachers were arriving. Thank Elohim, no students were in the building yet. Parents had gathered with their daughters. One father had dropped to the ground and prayed loudly, praising Elohim that none of the girls had been inside when the ceiling fell.

I made my way behind a big group of girls. I opened my mouth to ask them, *Which teacher is it?* But I couldn't speak.

Out of the corner of my eye, I saw the square-jawed gentleman from Mrs. Townsend's photo. He was distraught and was being shepherded away from the building by two other men, their arms flung protectively around his shoulders.

I backed away, afraid to turn my body on the catastrophe. Afraid of who might come after me if I let down my guard. In my head echoed Masudah's old words, *What I am saying is that your aunt is the sort of woman people blame. For everything. They blame her equally for good or for evil.* I tore myself away and ran back home.

When I reached Aunt Rahel and Uncle Barhun's house, I ran out back to the necessary. My bowels loosened and I felt myself being emptied of every shred of anything save my fear. How had Hamama known? And was it my fault? What if the teacher's husband came for me and demanded answers? What if others came and accused me of witchcraft? I took to my pallet and didn't get up for the rest of the day, not even to help prepare dinner.

That evening Aunt Rahel sat by my pallet and stroked my forehead. "No, it wasn't your teacher," she said, "not your teacher who died, but another."

"How do you know?"

"I made inquiries. I knew that you did the henna of one of the teachers, and when I heard of the catastrophe, I needed to be sure so we would know . . ."

"Know what?"

"What we were dealing with."

"Aunt Rahel . . ."

"My dear?"

"Do you believe that henna can bring misfortune?"

"No, but I know that there are those who mistake our art for something that it isn't."

"I am afraid. Hamama disapproved, I shouldn't have—"

"Don't be afraid, my darling. I have a friend who is a nurse at the hospital, and she reassured me that the British teacher is in full possession of her senses and doesn't blame anyone but the mortar and bricks that fell on her leg. Visit her, see for yourself. Her leg is broken, but it was easily set. She will recover with no permanent harm."

"I'm not sure I can. What if she accuses me?"

"She won't. From what I have learned of this woman, she is much wiser than my daughter."

"But Hamama sees the future."

"No, Hamama sees possibilities, and when they come true, we mistake them for prophecies."

I didn't go to the hospital, but I did send a little present to Mrs. Townsend. I purchased some leather at the market and made her a little purse. I would have embossed it with a pretty design, but I had no real tools, and my fingers bled as I worked a thick needle through the hide. I wrapped the purse in vermilion cloth and left it for her at the hospital entrance. I wrote a little note: "I am sorry for your misfortune, your friend Adela Damari." I don't know if she even received it, for I heard that not long after her accident, she and her husband left Aden on a steamer to England and never came back. As for me? I despaired of becoming a teacher and avoided the Selim School, walking a wide berth around it on my marketing path.

After that, I went down to the dock at Crater Harbor almost every day. Late winter had given way to early spring. The dock seemed more crowded than ever, bustling with travelers and merchants from all over the world. Secretly, I disagreed with Aunt Rahel. I had come to the conclusion that if Hamama had known that the British teacher would come to a misfortune, surely she was right about Asaf's arrival as well. And what if Asaf came to Aden and I missed him? What if he were to walk the streets of Crater and pass right by me as I was pounding *malawach* with the heel of my hand, inside Uncle Barhun's house? The thought that my fate might pass me by sickened me, but it also renewed my resolve. If Asaf were to come to Aden, I would find him.

Soon after I started going down to the harbor, Hani began to tease me. "It's not the boats but the boys you watch. The ones who come down the gangplank. Poor Adela, promise me you won't wait forever for Asaf. He could be on the other side of the world. He could be married or dead or living a dissolute life somewhere in Australia or Africa."

"I don't know what you are talking about," I lied. "I just go to the docks because it is interesting. I like to see the boats, and to imagine where they are from. Where they are going."

"You don't have to lie to me, Adela."

"I'm not." I flattened my voice, and narrowed my eyes, but it was hard to be angry with Hani. Motherhood agreed with her. Her daughter, Mara, was a delight. Hani strapped her on her back and carried her around Crater, happier and more full of life than everyone else.

"You should let me introduce you to one of David's friends. His fellow student scribes. Here in Aden, a girl is allowed to meet her groom before marriage, and even to have a say in it. Without the Imam breathing down our necks, there are even love matches. There is one boy from Tunisia, another from Taiz. Both would be suitable candidates. David says they are both *handy with their quills,* though I assume he is referring to their mastery of letters and not to their expertise in more important matters. What a shame." She laughed at her own joke, her voice trilling over the thought of playing matchmaker for me.

"No, Hani, I'm not interested."

"You are becoming an old maid."

"I'm only fifteen," I bristled, swallowing my words. I was feeling my age like a noose around my neck. Time had become a crowbar that had kept me away from Asaf for years now.

Hani shrugged. "Our Mother Sarah may have given birth at the ripe old age of ninety-one, but I wouldn't want to be a baggy old mother. You should pay heed, my darling Adela. And don't wait on that good-for-nothing cousin of ours forever."

I ignored Hani and kept my vigil. Every day, after I did my chores and marketing and helped with the cooking, I went down to the harbor and squinted at the ships coming in. When they docked, and their crews and passengers disembarked, I scanned the faces of new arrivals. Every few days I was sure I saw him. Once or twice I even yelled his name. But then he was too tall, or too short, or not as handsome, his nose too straight, his eyes lacking sparkle. I would end my watch as lonely as the day he left Aden, when I had been just nine years old. But then the next afternoon, another boat would come, the hull would slosh through the water, the boat boys would yell at one another to get out of the way, gulls would caw sloppy celebrations over their bounty of fish heads dropped between dock and harbor by careless fishermen, another ship would disgorge its crew and passengers, and my heart would hope anew.

Chapter 26

By the spring of 1934, a full year after we arrived in Aden, my habit of walking the streets of Crater and standing watch over the ships as they entered the harbor had become ingrained. It was as if my bones knew where to lead me. No matter where else I set out for, I always ended up down at the docks. One morning, as I kept my sentinel, eyeing the boats and observing the activity of the busy port, a little British boy approached me. He was no more than three or four years old and had a smattering of freckles on his adorable upturned nose. He tugged on the bottom of my antari. I bent down and let him run his fingers through the coins on my gargush. He had funny little ears that stuck out and he smelled like vanilla syrup. The little boy stood back up and went back to his mother. He was wearing pale blue britches, a little linen suit coat, and a jaunty red cap. His mother had skin as pale as milk, and a blond cloud of hair swept up in a sleek knot.

I smiled, then I raised my hand and waved. Hani had given me new henna—a new Egyptian Eye of God that winked out at both of them from the middle of my palms. The mother blanched when she saw it and pulled her son away.

I dropped my hands by my sides and made fists, cupping my henna, protecting it from the British woman's glare. I supposed I looked very strange to her. Perhaps she was newly come to Aden and not yet accustomed to the place or its people. Like the refugees in the hostel, I still wore my antari and my gargush in Aden, even though that conventional dress set me apart from the Adeni Jews, who wore modern European clothing and looked down their noses at my "primitive" garb.

"Yalla yalla, out of the way, out of the way." A team of six African men trudged by me with trunks on their backs, thick ropes bracing the leather boxes to their foreheads. I skittered out of the way, picking up

my skirt to avoid a big patch of mud. I took one look back toward the
sea. A large gray ship was due tomorrow, a German freighter. Was Asaf
on it? And if he was, would he recognize me? With a start, I put my
hand to my head and tugged at my gargush. Would he think me too
primitive now that he had seen something of the world? Should I stop
wearing it? Would it be better to look like a sophisticated Adeni girl? I
lingered a little longer and then took the uneven wooden steps up from
the harbor. When I entered the dockside market, on my way back to
Uncle Barhun and Aunt Rahel's house, I heard loud angry voices. At
first I thought there was a disagreement in one of the stalls. But then the
voices grew louder and multiplied. I picked up my pace but the yelling
followed me, and seemed to be coming from every direction. At the
end of a row of shops, I turned and saw a large group of young Muslim
men gathering. Several were in suit jackets and turbans. A few were in
army uniforms. Others were dockworkers, wearing nothing other than
breeches.

I saw them yelling and shaking their fists in the air, becoming a roiling
group, so many different faces contorted in fury. More and more men
seemed to come from out of the alleyways. Soon the market was filled
with an angry mob. At first I hesitated; I wasn't sure what to do, where
to go. But then I broke into a run. Looking back, I saw with horror that
behind me, Jewish shopkeepers were being pulled out of their stalls and
beaten in the lanes. I fled, making my way through the market, but then
tripped on a rut in the path. I scrambled back to my feet. Somewhere
to my left I saw the British mother; she was holding her child, her lips
curled in a snarl of fear, her eyes wide as moons. She was being jostled
by the frantic crowd and then she was pushed backward and the child
flew from her arms. The woman screamed. I tried to scramble toward
where the boy had disappeared, and then I stepped on something slick
and when I looked down, I saw with horror that I was standing in a pool
of blood leaking out of the boy's trampled skull. His eyes were open but
unseeing. His neck was bent sideways in an odd angle. All around me
bodies were pressing and pushing. I tried to run, but was thrust into
the mass of people. I tripped again, felt my shoulder hit the dirt, feet all
around me. I realized that if I didn't move, I would be trampled like the
boy. Suddenly hands reached down, grabbing me around my waist. A
stranger pulled me up and dragged me into an alley, his hands pressing
me farther into the darkness. I was sure that either my life was over, or

that I would emerge from the alley a torn and ruined girl. I struggled, reaching up and raking my nails across the young man's face. In the alley darkness, I could see that he was in a British army uniform. He let out a little *aaagh!* when my nails pierced his flesh, but he swallowed the sound. He reached for my wrists and pinned them behind my back. And then a whisper. "Adela." My name. How could he know my name?

"Adela, it's me." I looked up. "It's me, don't make a fuss. Let's not let them know we're here. It's not safe. Hush now." He held me tightly. Instinctively, I continued to struggle. The alley was dark, and my senses were distorted from the violence of the mob in the market. I questioned my own eyes. My ears. Could it be? Could it really be? The wolf pup of my girlhood? *Binyamin!* A man now. Deep-set eyes, high cheeks, full lips. His eyebrow and upper cheek were bloody from where I had dug my nails in. From the street I heard a scream. My legs grew weak, my racing heart burst with fear. I began to shake. That poor boy, I thought, that poor little dead boy. I heard another scream, someone begging for mercy. I reached out and put my hands in Binyamin's hands. I felt Hani's Eyes of God press into his life line. And for a moment, my henna was the mark of the old warrior Goddess Anath wading through rivers of blood to lay claim to her brother-lover. I must have made a little sound—a surprised gasp—because Binyamin let out a hushed sigh onto the top of my head. He squeezed my hands. We stayed like that, shaking and embracing and trying to melt into the darkness of the alley as the roaring mob passed us by.

What was happening?

It was not the first time that the Jews of Aden were attacked, nor would it be the last. This time the origin of the pogrom would be traced to a poorly thrown stone down at the docks. The Adeni Jews were among the greatest scribes and scholars in history. Throughout the ages, the Adeni sages had kept up-to-date on the intellectual outpouring of European scholarship by posting scouts to stand in the harbor and wait for ships to come from Germany or France. When a ship in Crater harbor arrived bearing Jewish merchants en route to India, the scribes of Aden would borrow the scholarly texts and copy them while the ship was in harbor. The rabbis of Europe often asked the wealthy Jewish merchants to carry texts to and from Arabian ports. In this way, the

Jews of Aden not only amassed great libraries, and felt the breath of the sages on their faces, but also sent their own scholarship west, ensuring an intermingling of ideas in communities otherwise distant.

Although it had been many centuries since the great Rashi's commentaries on the Talmud were acquired from passing boats, the illustrious scribal houses of Aden still kept up the tradition of sending a novice to wait at the harbor for the arrival of ships from the West. Especially those ships known to be carrying Jewish merchants. And so that is how all the trouble began. A novice scribe named Selah Bir Ami had been waiting in the sun at the docks of Crater Harbor. He had been there since morning prayers and he was hungry. Selah Bir Ami had no money to purchase a crusty roll or a piece of fruit, and was doomed to wait until his replacement came—and the boy was not expected until long after lunch. A ship was due to come in from France, and the last time a ship had come in, a rival scribal house had had an apprentice there, and they had been the ones to copy the Responsa of the Great Chatam Sofer. On the passenger manifest of this ship was none other than a Mr. August Lohn, whose library was among the most important of Bavaria. Supposedly, he had brought with him a copy of Rabbi Samson Raphael Hirsch's commentary on the Bible—with the generous understanding that he would leave it in Aden and pick it up on the way home, after his sojourn in Bombay. But Selah Bir Ami was bored. He had been at the docks four hours already. He was hot and thirsty. He began throwing stones. This is a well-known fact—for an Australian botanist who came off a ship from Socotra saw him. According to the botanist, Selah picked up a handful of pebbles and threw them at the gulls fishing in the shallows. But one of those stones accidentally landed near a group of three young Arab men mending sails on the beach. No one actually saw Selah Bir Ami hit one of the Muslims in the eye, and no one treated the young man for an injury, but there is little doubt that the stone-throwing ignited the incident. The botanist watched aghast as the three Muslim dockworkers charged the boy, knocked him off the pillar, and beat him to death in the sand, bashing in his skull with a big rock. Their unchecked fury was contagious, and it spread through the harbor like a kerosene fire.

Hani and David's house was the closest. When we reached their door and pounded, Hani opened it, grabbed me, and pulled me in. When she saw I wasn't alone, she urged Binyamin to follow us over the threshold. He refused. "I must make my way back to my barracks," he insisted.

"But Binyamin," I protested, "it's not safe!"

He shook his head and motioned to the lapels of his British army uniform. "My uniform will keep me safe from the thugs."

He turned on his heels and departed. Hani bolted the door behind him. She was pale, shaking.

"Where were you, Adela? Down by the docks? I feared for your life! Thank Elohim you are safe. But who was that? How do you know him?"

"He was my friend, Hani, my old friend Binyamin Bashari from Qaraah."

"Ah," she remembered, "the boy from the cave, all dressed up like a Brit. But enough prattling. It's not safe down here." I followed Hani upstairs to the roof, where the family had sought refuge. Little Mara was already there, sitting on Nogema's lap. Nogema and her sons were there too, three little boys. But her husband—the British Petroleum man— was at work in the refinery.

The riots lasted for three terrible days. We later learned that in addition to Selah Bir Ami, three other Jews had been killed that morning. The mob slit the throat of a butcher with his own knife. A lampmaker was trampled and died in the Prince of Wales Hospital, and a young jeweler was shot defending his shop from looters. And of course there was that poor little British boy. By nightfall thirty additional Adeni Jews had been injured. Two more succumbed to their injuries the next day. Seven Jewish houses were burned, twenty market stalls ravaged. I joined Hani and Nogema and her boys in the center of the roof, but every so often I went to the edge and looked down at the mayhem below.

From her roof across the street, Hamama yelled to us. She was frantic for her husband. He had been at his stall when the riot started. Was he okay? Was he even alive? We had no way of knowing. Hani shushed her. "We must be quiet," she said. "We must not let them know we are up here." I looked about—all around us the roofs had filled with Jews like us, taking refuge. When I think back to that day, I see us as shipwreck survivors. The roofs were our rafts, the streets a shark-infested ocean, our prayers the gentle waves that buoyed us aloft until the storm had passed.

Thank Elohim, the rest of our family was safe. My sisters-in-law and their children all escaped unscathed. My brother Menachem's nose was broken and Nogema's husband was bashed in the head with a club, but he recovered. Uncle Barhun and Mr. Haza were safe in their warehouse. Aunt Rahel had taken refuge with a neighbor. Hani's husband, David, and his fellow students took shelter on the roof of a nearby mosque— the cleric had opened his door to so many Jews that day that ever after he was known as "righteous Absalom." He never paid for a pair of shoes, a tailored djellaba, or a basket of fruit again—that is, until the Jews left Aden forever. We didn't come down from the roof until the next morning. The Aden Protectorate Levies were sent to restore order, but not before the riots had mostly died out.

Years later, when the Muslims of Aden rioted again and the Jewish community of Aden was viciously and irreparably attacked—leaving eighty souls dead, scores wounded—people would remember the earlier catastrophe. They would say, "It is just like when that boy was throwing rocks at birds."

I would remember too. I would remember how Binyamin Bashari had pressed me into the alley wall, and how I struggled against him until I realized who he was. I would remember how in our fear, the alley became a kind of cave, a sister to my mountain aerie, holding us in the cupped hand of kindness until we garnered the courage to emerge.

Binyamin came to visit me a week after the riots. We sat in my aunt and uncle's parlor. Remelia darned socks across the room. We were quiet together for a long time. As a boy Binyamin never had many words, but now I could see he was full to the brim with them. He needed to speak, but it was hard for him.

He opened his mouth, shut it again. More silence. And then finally he spoke.

"That day . . . that day I came to say good-bye to you in your cave . . . I didn't want to leave home without saying good-bye."

"I know. And I have always regretted that we never really took leave of each other. Hani . . . Hani got in the way, didn't she?"

Binyamin shook his head.

"Your wife?" I said softly. "How does she fare?"

"My wife died giving birth to her first child. The child died too, two years ago in Sana'a."

"May you be comforted amongst the mourners of Zion."

He nodded his thanks at my recitation of the ritual words. Then he confessed to me that although he mourned for the child, he had not loved his wife. That from the very beginning she belittled him for being unsophisticated, for coming from a mountain village. She had eyes only for a neighbor, a jeweler—and Binyamin suspected that the baby she had carried wasn't even his own. He was ashamed of these dark confidences and he spoke looking down, his cheeks under his beard flushed in the moonlight.

"I am so sorry for your sorrows, my friend," I murmured, then added, "What a lucky coincidence that we are now both in Aden together. Now tell me, why are you in a British uniform?"

He didn't answer and seemed suddenly very self-conscious, fingering the top button of his uniform and then adjusting his cap. That's when I noticed that he had cut off his earlocks. Before this, I had assumed they were hidden under his cap, but now I saw that they weren't there at all. All boys and men from the Kingdom had long earlocks, but some Adeni Jews didn't. My brothers still wore theirs, as did Uncle Barhun. I took a good look at Binyamin. Without his earlocks he looked bolder, and freer, as if someone had filled in his features with more vivid strokes and colors.

When he finally spoke he said, "I am sorry for *your* losses. You lost both mother and father in such a short time."

I nodded. "Elohim spared them the long journey south."

"And your cousin, did he, did he ever . . ."

"Come back for me?"

"You aren't wearing a ring . . . or a lafeh cloth. . . ."

I blushed that he had noticed these things about me. Now it was my turn to look down at my feet. I heard my own voice, as if from far away, and for the first time since coming to Aden I heard myself speak the truth about Asaf. "I wait for Asaf every day down by Crater Harbor, but he never comes for me. Who knows, maybe when the Messiah comes to Aden I will be very forward, and I will ask if He has seen my intended in some other corner of the world. But no, I don't want to talk about Asaf Damari. Tell me why you are here. And why are you in that important uniform?"

He patted his lapels and broke into a wide smile. "I am in the service of a British major who has a fondness for the traditions of the East. He found me in Sana'a and brought me to Aden. I am part of a troop of

Yemeni musicians in a little ceremonial unit that performs for visiting dignitaries. Would you believe I played my khallool for the Prince of Wales's cousin?"

We sat for a little while in silence. Then Binyamin took out a handkerchief and wiped his sweaty brow. He explained that he had been down at the docks on an errand for his major when the violence broke out. He was running to get out of the way of the mob when he saw me. "I called your name first, but you didn't hear me. I wasn't even sure it was you. You forgive me, don't you? For pushing you into the alley like that."

"I forgive you, Binyamin Bashari. If you'll forgive me for ruining your face."

He reached up and patted the sore spot on his face. "Ruined? Is it that horrible?"

We were sitting quite close together, and I shifted slightly away, but then I broke custom and leaned back toward him. I reached up to pat the red streaks on his face where I had raked my nails. I touched him softly, and murmured, "No, not horrible at all."

Chapter 27

Two weeks after the riots, Binyamin Bashari came for Sabbath dinner at my aunt and uncle's house. The riots had cast a pall over the Jews of Crater, but I was not gloomy at all. In fact, I found myself walking with a little bounce in my step. It was Aunt Rahel who urged Uncle Barhun to invite "the young gentleman from Qaraah." At dinner, Uncle Barhun peppered Binyamin with questions.

"Does your major meet with Mr. Ah-Tabib of the Zionist committee? And is he encouraging regarding the refugee situation?" My uncle had recently become involved with the Committee for Jewish Settlement in Palestine. Uncle Barhun made up his mind to either like or dislike the British officers in Aden depending on their views on the subject. He had even refused to do business with an officer who was heard saying that the refugee problem could be settled quickly and efficiently by having the Jews sent to settle the Red Sea Islands—barren, waterless chunks of black stone. We knew that there were British officers who scorned us Jews and would just as soon see us tumbled into the sea. But there were also those who looked sympathetically on the plight of the Jews of Yemen, and saw themselves as having a rare historical and geographical opportunity to help us escape the grip of the Imam and the drought and poverty of the north by aiding in our efforts to go to Palestine, where at least our fate would be of our own making.

Binyamin reassured my uncle that his major was sympathetic to the plight of the Jews, then steered the conversation to other subjects—the decommissioning of the lighthouse on Perim Island, a triple murder among the camel drivers who brought firewood into Aden, and finally, the impending visit to Aden by a cousin of the King of Sweden. After grace, Binyamin took his leave of us, promising my aunt that he would come back to share our table. He was true to his word, and was the perfect suitor. When he came to court me he blushed and mangled his words, he cracked his knuckles, and acted in all ways uncomfortable and desperately in love. But in private, in those tiny moments when we had a cushioned alcove to ourselves, with only a cousin or a sister-in-law minding her own business on the other side of the room, he wasn't any of these things. He was confident, kind, and full of all the words he didn't have as a boy. He looked me in the eye and said that he wanted to move to Palestine. That he longed for a home he had never known. That the Torah he had learned as a boy seemed like a road map to him, and his heart was the compass, pointing to Jerusalem. He told me that he had a recurring dream in which he was walking through a city of golden stones, holding a big ring of keys.

"And where do the keys let you enter?"

He shrugged. "It's a mystery. But in the dream I'm not bothered by it. I walk with curiosity and confidence down a street named for the Angels of Redemption, under an arch, around twisty corners, past bakeries and shoe shops and spice stalls. I turn right and left and right again. As if I know where to go."

"Do you?"

"What?"

"Know where to go?"

He smiled his wolfish grin. "I have always been told that I have a good sense of direction."

"When I was a little girl, I always wandered."

"And you never got lost, did you?"

"You know I didn't because you followed me."

He shrugged. "My brothers beat me, my father was a drunkard . . . Following you was a game I played. I told myself that somewhere in the dunes was a secret city and only you possessed the key to it."

"Keys again?"

"I suppose I've been dreaming about keys for a long time."

Soon after this conversation, I dreamed that Binyamin came to my house with a big ring of keys. "These," he said, "unlock the secret doors of Aden." He took me on a patchwork tour, unmoored from geography. We explored the Memorial Building, where the British war dead were honored; we entered the bedrooms and ballrooms of the Grand Royal Hotel, the private officers' cinema in Steamer Point, the inner recesses of the concert hall in Crescent, and the back rooms of the belching refinery in Little Aden. And when I thought we were finished, Binyamin took out one more key. It unlocked the great lighthouse in Crater Harbor. I followed Binyamin up the narrow twisty stairs. He showed me how the great mechanism on the lens lit up the night. We stayed there a long time, spotting ships coming into harbor, as well as the dancing tails of mermaids who surfaced ever so briefly before swimming east to India.

Binyamin courted me throughout that summer, and through the autumn. My memories of those days are of a series of sweet little gifts. One day I was making dough for lafeh bread when Remelia answered the door. She called for me to come. Binyamin stood in the doorway looking awkward and yet very proud of himself. A half smile turned one side of his mouth up. He shifted back and forth on his feet and thrust a basket of dates at me. "These are for you." I accepted the gift, imagining that the dates were music notes, and he was handing me a basket of melodies.

"What is it?" He looked concerned. My strange vision must have flashed across my face.

"Nothing. Thank you. Thank you so much." I gave him a big, unambiguous smile. "I was wondering, will you bring your khallool and play for us sometime? My uncle would so love to hear your music."

Later that night when I ate the dates, I had the same feeling. That I was eating music, delicious music.

He came again the next Friday afternoon with a jar of spicy pickles for our dinner table. And a few days after that with a jar of honey. Once when he came, Hani was over and we were making jachnun together. When he had left she said, "When you marry him, I will give you a special henna. He will lose himself in the tendrils running up your thighs." She poked and pinched me until I doubled over in a knot of laughter.

"Really, Adela," she said, "when he first came upon us in your cave, all those years ago, I thought Binyamin Bashari was an animal turned into a boy, a desert creature come to eat you up. But now I see that he has grown quite civilized, and I love him for you, because he has taken you from your vigil at the lonely harbor and turned you into a girl who primps and blushes." At this, I blushed even redder, then grew angry, for although I knew I had left my post—and replaced my hope of Asaf's return with hope for a proposal from Binyamin—I felt guilty. In some ways it felt as if I were carelessly relinquishing a holy obligation that had been bestowed on me, not by the Imam nor my parents, but by some other meddling force that spelled out my fate in smoky letters in the sky.

"Achh, don't go all gloomy on me. If Asaf were going to come back for you, he would have been here by now." Hani rolled out another piece of dough, pounding it with the heel of her hand. "And anyway, we are no longer backward villagers of the Kingdom; we are modern girls"—she winked—"and modern girls can choose their own paths."

The next week, Binyamin was once again invited to share our Sabbath table. Toward the end of the meal, there was some unpleasantness with my brother Menachem. Menachem had always been pious, but in Aden he had become even more so, and he was suspicious of Binyamin for shearing his earlocks. The men had been discussing the refugee problem—how the Brits claimed to be protecting the Jews of Aden, yet they wouldn't let us immigrate freely into Palestine.

"The Brits lie," Menachem said bitterly. "If we have rights here, then why won't they let us enter into Palestine without quotas?" Menachem pointed to the broken cord in his guftan coat.

"I'll tell you why. It's because too many of us forget that the Temple wasn't destroyed only in the past but is being destroyed even now, continuously. Our mistreatment by the British is punishment for our own spiritual laxness. Whose? Jews who don't keep the Commandments, Jews like you who are ashamed of looking Jewish. Why don't you wear earlocks, Binyamin? Why do you cut your hair? Such impiety is a grave dishonor."

"I mean no offense, Menachem. And I pray whether I wear earlocks or not."

"But I don't see you in synagogue. Don't tell me that you pray with the British soldiers." His face twisted into a mocking glare. "There aren't enough Jews in your little regiment to make a minyan."

It was true. Binyamin rarely went to synagogue with my uncle and brothers. When he came for a Sabbath meal he didn't walk with them around the corner to join in community devotions. He told me that sometimes he prayed privately in the mornings, and that he was more comfortable saying his prayers alone than in public. I didn't mind. I knew that Binyamin and I were of the same opinion. We felt that

Elohim was everywhere—in the black rocky shoals of Crater Harbor, on the banks of the Khoreiba River, in the symbolic break of corded hems, and in a far-off cave found by a girl who prayed in the way she was born to pray. In other words, we both believed that the forms of our prayers were ours and ours alone to fashion.

The next time Binyamin came, he didn't have a little present but an invitation:

"Can you meet me at the fair at Sheik Othman the day after tomorrow?"

"Alone? I don't think—"

"Bring one of your sisters-in-law, or Remelia, or one of your cousins."

I looked into his eyes. Dark brown with flashes of amber. I was possessed by the urge to touch his face, to feel his bones under his flesh, his soft lips, those warm tuneful eyes deep set in their sockets.

"You'll come?"

I took a deep breath.

Chapter 28

The fair at Sheik Othman was a lorry ride west from Crater. I had never been there before. When I asked Hani, her face lit up. She said, "Mara will love the festival. And we can use her as our excuse to go."

The next day, Remelia dragged me to Hani's house after we had finished our marketing. When we walked inside, I realized that I was being treated to a new henna application. I could smell the wheaty henna paste in the pot and the fruity rosewater in fluted glass flasks that Hani would use to wash my hands before beginning her work. My last application—over three weeks old—was a faded gray scrim. I sat down on Hani's low cushions and thoroughly enjoyed myself as she teased me by pretending to have no idea what to draw. She flipped her hair, which was loose, as she was inside her own home and not wearing her kerchief. I noticed that it seemed even curlier than it had been before she had had Mara. She flashed her eyes and looked into my palms for a long time. When she began to draw, I saw that she was giving me the same rose and lily pattern she had given me on my very first henna. But there were other elements in it too: little waves that signified the Red Sea, and twisty mountain paths that signified our journey south, and a little corrugated swirl that was the sign of the secret angel who watched over courting couples.

Binyamin was where he said he would be—standing next to the entrance to the fairgrounds. We spent a pleasant hour walking through the attractions. We watched a puppet show that thrilled Mara, who clapped her hands and let out delightful little laughs at the puppets' clumsy clownish exploits. Binyamin took a turn in the shooting gallery. Then we went to watch the tamboora dancers representing all the many tribes of the midlands and western Hadramut. Binyamin explained how the long-necked tamboora endowed magical properties on those who danced to it. Hani cheekily asked him if his khallool had a similar effect. "Of course it does," he replied, "but my magic has a renegade flair, and I can't predict the effect it will have on those who dare to dance to it."

"How does your major feel about that?" I looked at him sideways, smiling.

"My major has two left feet, so there is no worry that he will get himself in trouble at my expense."

We walked through the rhythmic throng, stopping occasionally to watch a performance. We played a game of Lucky Dip and a game of Ring Toss. Hani and Mara rode on an elephant. Then Binyamin steered us toward the Ferris wheel. Years have passed since that afternoon and I have since been on Ferris wheels the size of ten-story buildings, but back then, when I was still a girl in Aden, the Ferris wheel in the festival at Sheik Othman was a true marvel—though by today's standards it would be looked upon as nothing more than a pile of matchsticks. It was fabricated entirely of wood, and had three cars. When on top, the riders were approximately one story above the ground. The entire contraption was turned by a giant wheel that was hitched to a team of oxen. There were several three-seat wheels, which turned at various speeds, depending on the perk and vigor of each wheel's oxen. Hani and Mara went in the first car, Binyamin and I climbed into the next.

Every time we reached the top my heart jumped to my throat, and when we swooped down again it came back up, up and down, up and down. Binyamin kept paying extra rupees for extra turns. On our eighth turn, the wheel stopped when we were on the top. We swung there as the operator let Hani and Mara off. But the next couple haggled about the price, and so we were left swinging as they settled the matter. Tamboora music floated over to us from behind the roulette tables.

"Do you know what that is?" Binyamin pointed to the arena. From where we were, we could see the audience and the dancers. The crowd consisted of British officers' families, Indian bureaucrats and their wives, a handful of tourists from Europe and Australia, and an assemblage of local Arabs and Jews from Aden and the environs. The men in the troop began to dance a slow beat, and then a frenzy. One by one they took out their jambia from their sheaths and cut themselves—in the palm, on the face, on the bottom of a bare foot—and all the while they kept dancing.

"The dance of the jambia." I grimaced. "I have heard of this ritual, though I have never seen it."

"Some call it barbarism," Binyamin said. "My major disapproves, and is hoping to eradicate the custom."

"Do you think he will succeed?"

"Those men have been dancing that dance since the dawn of the seventh day, when man was created."

"Do you mean to say that Adam our Father danced the dance of the jambia in Eden?"

"No, I mean it just as a figure of speech. I don't believe that Adam our Father was ever in Eden. I am a rationalist, and I believe that men were descended from apes, not men from men."

"Men were never descended from men," I teased him, "or do you not know the ways of the world?"

He took up my challenge. "Perhaps I need a wife to teach me."

I let this suggestion float in the air. But it did not stay there. With those words, the Ferris wheel became gigantic, lifting us higher than Mount Sirah, until we were on top of a spinning wheel of mythic proportions. Our hands touched and our fingers entwined. He espied my new henna, lifting my hands up to examine them. He traced the intricate wonder of the petals, paisleys, and tendrils on my wrists. I shivered under his touch as he patted a little paisley drop on one of my knuckles. From down below some of the jambia dancers had begun to scream. "Look," I said. I took my hand away from his, pointed. A few of the dancers had broken loose from the arena. "Where do they run to, bleeding like that?"

Binyamin shrugged. "I suppose to the well at the fairgrounds' entrance, to douse the pain."

"What did you mean to say? About the major . . ."

"Men have always mixed blood with music and magic. No British major will be able to take the dance out of their legs or the knives out of their hands." Darkness flashed over his face. His eyebrows hunched together, he huffed in exasperation. "Ach," he said, "what a shame that our conversation should be so serious. It's not . . ."

"Not what?"

"Not at all what I had intended."

The wheel began to move again.

"Adela?"

Open lips. Soft mouth.
Yes. Oh. Yes.

That Sabbath, Binyamin came once more to my uncle's house. We went out into the garden after grace. He took my hand. Raised it to his lips. Brushed his lips against my knuckles. His finger traced my life line, and then doubled back on the tiny shallow tributary lines that flow up to my fingers and down to my wrist, which inscribe the filigree fortunes of love, hope, trust, and honor. I felt the rose vines on my forearms come to life, as if they were growing, spreading out, wrapping themselves around my arms. He kissed my fingertips. The tiny buds on the backs of my hands burst into bloom. I had heard tell of this in the henna house, how henna can come to life if bidden by the conjuring of a love match. Bride for groom, groom for bride. His forefinger was on my palm, on my life line, and then up to my wrist, my forearm, and then he was holding me by both shoulders and pressing his lips to mine.

In the morning, I rolled onto my back and lifted my arms to inspect my henna. I expected living flowers and sinuous green vines, but my henna lay once more flat and maroon on my skin, and the pulsing life of my nighttime longings seemed to have left no trace of whispers or magic. Had I dreamed it? Or lived it? And had Binyamin Bashari and I really spent a night such as that in the garden? Years later, Binyamin told me that the day after we stood together in the garden, he asked his major for permission to leave his unit and for help in obtaining visas to enter Palestine. He planned to ask me to marry him, and hoped that we would travel together to Jerusalem to make our home there.

If only that night had lasted forever. Could I have saved Hani and Asaf by staying true to Binyamin? Or would my beloved cousins have doomed themselves anyway? I search in the thicket of the past for answers that are always out of reach. In my dreams, I follow Binyamin back to his barracks, whispering frantically in his ear that we must consummate our love before daybreak. He takes me in his arms—but the dream dissolves, and my history of betrayal begets its own betrayal with the coming dawn.

Chapter 29

Asaf came at Hanukkah time, when the windows of the houses of the Jews of Crater were filled with hanging oil lamps, lit to commemorate the miracle of the tiny drop of oil that blazed for eight days, resanctifying the soiled Temple.

I was sixteen and he was seventeen years old. Eight years had passed since our engagement. In one version of the story of my life, Asaf became a dove that flew through the window of Uncle Barhun's house, perched on my shoulder, and pecked my ear, drawing not blood but honey. In another version of the story, when he came to Uncle Barhun's house, knocking on the door, I didn't know who he was. I mistook him for a stranger, and refused to acknowledge that in another life, on a far-off mountain, we had played husband and wife. And in yet another version, I knew him immediately, and pretended to be overjoyed to see him, but in my heart I was distraught, for anyone could see that he had come too late, and that my heart now belonged to another.

Uncle Barhun was immediately fetched from the warehouse on Steamer Point. My uncle didn't recognize his nephew, as they had never before met. When he had gathered up his wits and realized that he was standing on one of the good latitudes of life—a spiritual line that demarks charm from curse, gifts from retributions—my uncle's face quivered. He flushed red as a beet, tears came to his eyes, and he sank to his knees, exclaiming with such loud joy that everyone in the street came running to see the commotion.

When he had sufficiently recovered, Barhun said, "You are my dear brother's son, and now you are my son too."

Asaf was taller than Barhun, but Asaf tilted his head respectfully in a way that made it seem as if he were not looking down, but up, at his uncle. Soon everyone was crowding into our house—Aunt Rahel and my brothers and sisters-in-law, my cousin, and their husbands and all the children—they all came to see Asaf, our very own Hanukkah miracle.

There was a resemblance between Asaf and Uncle Barhun. Aunt Rahel was the first to mention it. She said, "This boy is your mirror-child, Barhun," shaking her head in wonder. "Coined as if from the mint of you." It was true. Both had heart-shaped faces, high foreheads, curly black hair. Uncle Barhun's was thinning, but Asaf's tumbled out of his cap. I hadn't noticed the resemblance when Uncle Barhun first came to Qaraah, but of course the Asaf I remembered was a boy, and the Asaf now in front of me was a man. His face had grown into itself. I took an accounting. Their noses were crooked (Asaf's upturned nose had been broken in the intervening years, but now it was as roguishly charming as Barhun's), their lips were thin. Why, each even had a scar on his brow. It was as if they had weathered the same storms, even though they had only just met. But there was something else. Asaf, like my uncle, was unabashedly handsome.

The night Asaf arrived I was supposed to meet Binyamin for a walk in Steamer Point, but I sent word that I couldn't come because I was busy with household duties. The next day, I made another excuse—that I had to help Nogema, who was pregnant. On the third day, Asaf caught me looking wistfully out the window. We were alone in the house. Aunt Rahel was out back in the garden.

He bent toward me and asked, "What are you sorry about, Adela?"

"Nothing," I lied. "I am sorry about nothing."

"Your expression tells me otherwise."

I didn't look at him when I asked, "Have you heard about the dance of the jambia?"

"No, I haven't."

"A native custom, it's gruesome but impossible not to watch."

He gently touched my chin, tenderly forcing me to look at him. "What makes you think about it?"

"My mind is just wandering, that's all."

"You always were a dreamer, Adela."

"What are you talking about?"

"In your cave, you would imagine whole worlds, wouldn't you?"

"No, I would imagine only this world, and the way I fit into it."

"Do you remember, Adela, when we—"

I cut him off. "I remember nothing of those days, Asaf. How about you? Do you trust *your* memories?"

He didn't answer me. I let him kiss me, even though it wasn't the least bit proper. His lips were rough against my own and he smelled like his travels—spicy and foreign and improvised.

I was false to Binyamin. A coward, too. I broke off my connection to him by messenger. We were not yet engaged, so it was as simple as that. My brother Hassan went to him in the barracks in Ma'alla at my behest. Hassan did me an act of great kindness by sparing me the details of their exchange. After it had been accomplished, Hassan said, "The musician is an ugly man, Sister. A crude Esau to our Asaf's fair Jacob. You chose well. And our dear mother, may her memory be a blessing, would approve of your steadfastness. You do her a great honor by staying true to the old contract and marrying our cousin, which was, after all, her intention."

Hani was the only one to question my choice. She took me aside, held me close by the shoulders, and spoke to me in urgent tones. "Are you sure, Adela? Is this really what you want?"

"Of course it is."

"Don't lie to me."

"I'm not." I began to feel angry. "Hani," I said, "I've always loved Asaf, before you ever knew me. He was there . . . he was there first."

Then I almost told her that when we first met, Asaf was wearing a red cap and we were both missing our two front teeth. I almost told her about the first time I ever saw him riding Jamiya, and about how he had once played a valiant boy-Moses at our Passover seder. I wanted to tell Hani that Asaf and I had been innocents together and that it was our sweet innocence that filled my heart now and that bound me to him—not what came after. But none of these words reached my lips. Instead, I remained silent, and pulled away from her. Hurt and disapproval flashed across Hani's face; then some other unruly emotion that I couldn't quite recognize flickered in her eyes, but finally she took a deep breath, kissed my cheek, smiled, and purred, "Forgive me, Adela. I will never question your choice again. I promise."

Why did I really agree to marry Asaf? Because for so long I had worn my engagement like armor, shielding me from the Confiscator's reach. And because my mother came to me in a dream. She pinched me under the arms, bared her gums, and railed at me, threatening me with all manner of mortal punishments. She said, "Asaf Damari came back for you. He honored his commitment, and who are you to spit on the sacred promises of the past?"

How had it all transpired? I will pause in my story, because it is time for a full accounting. Here is what Asaf told me. He left Qaraah with his father in 1927, when I was nine and Asaf was ten. They went south by donkey, to Aden. From Aden they took a steamer to Port Salalah in Oman, and from Oman they sailed to Bombay. They traveled inland, and spent months on the continent collecting spices, unguents, and rare ingredients. They purchased the prized *choya nakh* essence in Uttar Pradesh, then turned around and began the long trek west. They took sail on the Sabbath of Miketz, when scripture tells us that Pharaoh had two dreams, and only our Father Joseph could interpret them. When they reached Aden, Asaf and his father sailed on a dhow for Eritrea. But in Eritrea misfortune struck, and Uncle Zecharia suffered an attack that left half his body paralyzed and killed him within a week. Asaf buried his father in Africa on land he purchased from a farmer for a small quantity of Red Sea coral. The farmer kept cows, and when Asaf was digging the grave, the cows kept him company, lowing softly as he pried the parched yellow earth loose from the rocky sediment below. Asaf continued the journey alone, trading some of his stores for passage on a felucca that sailed north on the Nile, through Egypt. Then he bought himself passage on a steamer to Palestine. He stayed in Jaffa for almost a month before sailing on a British ship to Cyprus, and from there to Turkey. He had with him, tucked in the folds of his cloak, several vials of precious *onycha* oil, distilled from Red Sea mollusks. This oil was a powerful aromatic fixative Asaf was delivering to a perfumer in Turkey, who would use it to make incense and unguents to be sold in an atelier in Paris. In Istanbul, the perfumer took a liking to Asaf and asked if he would like to stay and work in his shop. Weary of traveling, he accepted the offer, living in the back of the perfumer's shop, learning his craft. When he eventually left, he traveled even farther east, landing finally on the Greek island of Corfu, where he lived with the family of an olive farmer, bartering work in the groves for lodging and food. After a year on Corfu, he decided it was time to return for me. He regretted that he had not returned sooner, for he was possessed by wild fears and bad dreams on his journey and was certain that his bride either belonged to another, or had already gone to the World to Come.

He reached Qaraah two years after my family and I left for Aden. What he found was wretched—my parents were both dead, Masudah was dead, my brother Dov, Masudah's husband, had lost his mind, and we were gone. The village itself was a dried-up husk of itself, a ghost-village with few inhabitants left. Asaf went through our empty house. He stood in the alcove where my pallet had been. He squatted in the place where we had taken our meals. He stood before the emptiness of my mother's big chest on the second floor—the chest that had held his father's Torah—and then he went outside and sat under the frankincense tree. Under the tree he lost himself, and cried out my name. The dye mistress heard him and gestured to him from her yard. She had stayed behind to care for her elderly father, who refused to leave Qaraah. She gave Asaf food and drink and told him where we had gone and when we had left. He went down the street to Auntie Aminah's old house. He walked past the old citrons and down the escarpment, over the culvert. He pushed back the henna bush, which had grown as big as a baby elephant, and ducked to enter the cave. When he saw my drawings, he let out a little sound, like an *ah* crossed with a moan. The chalk boy and girl on the wall heard his cry, and then told him their secrets, as if in a dream. With the back of his fingers, he caressed the cheek of the girl on the wall, and then bent and kissed her hennaed hands, which he later swore to me were warm, and not cold as stone should be.

He started for Aden that very day. His journey south took him just two weeks—much quicker than ours—because he wasn't traveling with children or women. According to scripture, Noah's flood ended in the Jewish month of Kislev. It was Kislev when Asaf reached Aden; in the secular calendar it was November of 1934. There were heavy rains in Aden that month, but the day Asaf's donkey cart passed the grave of Cain, the sky was as cloudless and clear as it must have been when the dove brought Noah an olive branch. I know because I felt the sun on my face as Asaf stood before me and once again claimed me as his own.

Chapter 30

Asaf himself insisted that our wedding date be set as soon as possible.
I didn't protest, and that is how my nuptials came to be planned for
six weeks after he arrived. A few days before our wedding, Asaf and I—
chaperoned by Sultana—rode a lorry to Steamer Point. In the center
of Steamer Point was a crescent of shops. Behind the shops was a park,
and in the center of the park stood a statue of Queen Victoria. The
statue had been donated by Adeni merchants who had raised money
for the purpose of building a hospital for women. Alas, they hadn't been
able to raise enough, so the British officials prevailed on the leaders
of the community to spend the money on a statue of the queen after
her death. Since then, Victoria had reigned over Steamer Point, and all
visiting dignitaries came to pay homage. I too liked to visit the statue,
but for a different reason. The very first time I laid eyes on that statue,
it reminded me of my mother, that monarch of joyless spite who had
reigned over the country of my childhood. On a whim, I had asked Asaf
to come with me to the statue, and I confessed to him that the statue
reminded me of my mother.

When we reached the statue, a little yellow bird was dancing on Queen
Victoria's lap. Another came. Sultana stood with us for a moment, but
then went to a bench far enough away to leave us alone. Asaf picked up
some pebbles and shooed the birds away. He gave a little bow and made
a waving gesture. It looked to me as if he were preparing to perform
some sort of foreign blessing. I opened my mouth and almost spoke,
but couldn't. I had planned on saying, "Mother, here is Asaf; he came
back for me after all." I felt suddenly shy, speechless. I turned to Asaf.
Who did my statue-mother see? A tall, handsome young man. Skin the
color of fertile earth. Curly dark hair with long earlocks that fell below
his chin and gleamed in the sun. Under his coat he wore black leggings

and on his head he had a dark, boxy felt cap wrapped around with a checkered black and gray cloth. His beard was already full enough for stroking.

Asaf broke our silence. "Adela, your mother was always slipping me candied nuts and extra legs of chicken, trying to fatten me up or keep me alive until we could marry, I suppose. And before I left with my father, she corralled me one night when the men were praying the Sanctification of the New Moon and I was hanging around your yard, shirking prayers. She grabbed my elbow, dug her fingers into my skin, and told me that I would come back for you. She said, 'It is not a prophecy, but a fact that you are not a boy but a husband.'"

"And are you?"

"Am I what?"

"Are you a husband?"

"I will be yours before the week is out."

Then Asaf told me that before he died, Uncle Zecharia made him promise that he would return for me. He said, "Son, your marriage to Adela is a sacred stitch on the hem of eternity. Swear to me that you will go back for her."

"Is that why you came back—to fulfill your father's wishes?"

He didn't answer me. Instead Asaf offered up a brittle little smile that seemed to have a smirk tucked in the center. Just then I thought that I heard the sound of a flute, and I looked around in shock and fear, scanning the crowd. Binyamin? What if he were there? How would I face him? No, it was just a child with a toy instrument. But my heart had already missed a few beats. I didn't even know I was crying until Asaf reached out and wiped my tears with the corner of his sleeve.

"Don't cry, Adela, all is as it should be."

The tears ran freely from my eyes, and I sobbed in spite of my embarrassment.

We married just a few days later. We had been engaged when he was a scruffy imp with an amulet of mercury, baby teeth, dried rue, durra, and sesame around his neck, and the autumn rains of the north washed mud and silt down from the mountains, polluting our spirits with the mud of old creation. When it came time for my bridal henna, I thought about asking each of my cousins to do the task. Edna's designs were perfect, and yet they somehow lacked vibrancy. Nogema's hand was the least steady, but she invented marvelous thickets and vines that seemed to wrap around a girl's heart. Hamama had become a good friend to me, and her designs were pretty, but she tended to make extraneous flourishes whose esoteric meanings seemed only to blur the end result. In the end, I knew that I would ask Hani, just as Auntie Rahel had said when we were together in Sana'a. And I also knew that I would ask her for a special favor, something far beyond the ordinary.

At my henna ceremony, Nogema beat the tabl drum and Hamama and Sultana played the shinshilla cymbals. Edna mixed together the resin, myrrh, frankincense, and iron sulfate and then heated it until it was a molten waxy paste. Because my own mother wasn't there to marry me off, Aunt Rahel did the dance of the candles. With a tray on her head she swayed her hips as the flickering flames on her head mesmerized me, coming close, closer. "*Kululululululu!*" she sang, "*kululululululu!*" The henna pot was in the middle of the candles on the tray. When she was in front of me she said, "May you be the mother of multitudes," and then inaugurated the ceremony by taking a token smear of henna and inscribing a triangle of protection on the center of my palms. She took a seat of honor on my right. Edna and Hamama unwrapped the mehani cloths from my arms and feet. Yerushalmit and Sultana sat on either side of me whispering little stories, telling me jokes. Hani began to apply the waxy mixture to the undersides of my feet, and then worked her way to the tops of them, my shins, my calves. Next she did my hands, my wrists. She had me put my arm on her shoulder and completed cufflets and golden diadems like snakes that I could almost feel moving up and down my biceps. Her stylus tickled and prodded, scratched and caressed. "Don't you dare move!" she hissed when I tried to scratch an itch in the crook of my arm. "Well, then, scratch it for me!" I hissed back. Hamama knelt by my side and scratched where I showed her. Hani wrinkled up her nose.

"Oh, Adela," she said, "don't you know, a bride must be still as a statue on her Night of Henna."

"But not in bed," Nogema added with a whisper.

Hamama joined in, "And remember, Adela, Anath slays Mot."

Hani continued, "And Baal rises to be her consort."

I gave a little annoyed snort. "What does that have to do with me and Asaf?"

"Silly little Adela." Nogema rolled her eyes in mock exasperation. "You'll see, every bride slays her husband on her wedding night. No matter how much he thinks he's your master, it is you who will wade knee deep in the blood of his desires."

They teased me. "Asaf is dessert," Edna said, "sweet lahuhua bread with honey."

"No, he is the savory stew," said Nogema, "succulent lamb with potatoes, a sumptuous meal that fills you for days."

"You are both wrong," said Hani. "He is neither sweet nor savory. He is the hilbeh, the pepper relish that our little Adela must eat sparingly, for it sets the mouth on fire."

I blushed and pretended to be shocked, but really I was dizzy with the spin of my life. I felt empty inside, blank of all feeling. But I was already a bride, so I forced myself to remember when Asaf Damari had been only a boy, beautiful even then, when he first came to us as a dirt-smeared imp and I was a little girl who thought that relish was just relish, and not a metaphor for scorching desire.

Next Hani applied the shaddar, and when she finished, I sat still while it set, feeling it drying and tightening on my skin as the guests in the henna house ate pastries, gossiped, sang songs, and told lewd stories of brides who took more than their fair share of pleasure and of grooms endowed like horses, mythical centaurs, and lowly goats. There was much laughter. I was given arak to drink. It numbed my tongue and burned my throat. When the paste had set, my cousins rubbed it off my arms and legs, revealing a design that startled us all in its genuine nature, as if it had always been there, as if it were part of my skin and I had worn it since birth. Hani had combined the most vivid elements of various traditions and created a design ornate and intimate, ethereal and seductive.

"Breathtaking!" Sultana gasped. "Hani, you have outdone yourself." Edna smiled at her little sister and bent down to kiss her lips. They all stood in front of me, my cousins, sisters-in-law, my aunt, and seemed too stunned to speak. Finally, Aunt Rahel reached out a hand and stroked my flushed cheek.

"You are astonishing, Adela. You stand before us a perfect spark of the spirits of our Mothers Sarah, Miriam, Rebecca, Leah, Rachel."

I looked in the mirrors they held up for me and saw blooms and vines. I saw birds of paradise, snakes, butterflies, shooting stars, and tiny Eyes of God inscribed on the pistils and stamens of flowers. When I moved about I could smell the mossy humus scent of earth and fecundity coming from my body. I knew that the scent was the perfume mixed with the henna, but it was also the green essence of the design itself.

Aunt Rahel fit the bridal crown on my head. I bowed toward her and lifted my head when she told me to. She shifted it a bit to the right, and then to the left. "It is too big for you," she said. "We will need extra pins to hold it in place." She told Hamama to get her more pins, and then went about fastening it to my hair. We had borrowed the towering *tishbuk lu'lu'* from a Sana'an wedding dresser, who, like us, had come from the North. The helmet was made of layered coins, beads, pearls, and amulets, the front was hung with coal, agate, and cowrie shells. Woolen tassels hung off the coins and brushed my shoulders. The pins dug into my scalp. The tishbuk lu'lu' was heavy on my head and made me feel more like a soldier going into battle than a woman about to be wed. When I turned my head, I got a crick in my neck. When I moved the slightest bit, the coins tinkled.

My wedding night?

The first thing I did when Asaf and I were alone was to reach into my sleeve pocket. I held out my palm. It took him a few moments, but then his face lit up with recognition.

"Are you returning this to me?"

"No, but it is all I have from then, and I want you to know that I have kept it safe."

He put his hand in mine so that the amulet was between both our palms. It was still just a round wooden disk affixed to a square wooden backing, with one of the many names for Elohim written inside, but for a flicker of a moment, it was also more than that. It was the *Mishkan*, the tabernacle in the desert, the ark that contained the written law of our lives. I wondered what name of Elohim was written there, but I knew I would never open it to find out. One didn't open an amulet box any more than one touched the Torah with bare hands.

I undid the buttons on my wedding tunic slowly, and let it fall from my shoulders like a sheet of silvery water. Then I unbuttoned my shift and slipped out of it. I murmured a blessing, for I felt as if I had stepped out of the ritual bath, and that I was emerging into the darkness cleansed of impurity. Asaf stared, just as Hani had said he would. His eyes took in the elaborate pictures rising from my legs to my sex, to my belly and above. She had decorated more than my hands and feet. Much more.

"You want something special? I will give you an elaborate love charm," she had said, "an inscription that turns the body into an illuminated manuscript."

My husband's eyes took in the florets on my hips, the whirlpool of triplet dots and linking swirls around my navel, but his eyes lingered the longest on my breasts, which Hani had decorated with a series of concentric flowers, the petals overlapping, growing smaller as they lapped in little paisley rivulets at the edges of my nipples. I held my hand up to beckon him forward. He didn't hesitate. Asaf wrapped me in his arms, kissed my lips, suckled my tongue, and made love to me not like the boy he had been when I first knew him, but like the man he had become in my absence.

We fell into a dreamy stupor and in my satiety, I imagined that I loved the boy I had married, and that my feelings for Binyamin were the false ones, totems of the little demon who tempts lovers to betray their own hearts.

Just before sunrise we both awoke, and Asaf took me again. But this time he climbed upon me like a bull rutting out of some sloppy ancestral habit, and when he was finished he rolled over, wiped himself on the dirty shamle that had fallen to the floor, and when he next spoke, it wasn't words of love but business.

"Sometime this week," he said, "I hope to do business with a fellow my father used to know in Uttar Pradesh."

I gathered the sheets around my body, suddenly feeling ashamed of my gaudy nakedness.

"Oh? You are sure he is in Aden?"

"I got word that he arrived yesterday."

"And what sort of business, my husband?"

"Why . . . I must fill up my inventory."

"So you can open a shop in Crater?"

His face twisted into a mocking sneer. "A shop? No, I am no shopkeeper, Adela. Shopkeeping won't get you rich. I am leaving Aden late summer, before the New Year."

"I don't understand."

"I have clients. They are waiting for me. For my deliveries. I'll travel via Alexandria to Istanbul. My father's old clients are all expecting me. I have already taken orders, and have entered into professional obligations. Of course you will stay here. It will take only four or five months; I'll be back in time for Passover."

How could he leave me, when he just got here? After all these years, how could he so flippantly plan to leave me behind?

"I don't understand. Why didn't you say something before?"

He rolled off our pallet and began to dress. He faced away from me when he said, "What does it matter?"

"It matters because I am your wife."

He shrugged, and now there was a hard edge to his voice. "Well, I am telling you now."

I measured my words carefully. "If you leave Aden, I will go with you."

"That's ridiculous."

"Say what you will, but I am your wife; I will travel with you, wherever you go. You left me once, Asaf; you will not leave me again."

"And if I do?"

"You won't. You were promised to me with nails and teeth around your neck. The teeth will bite you if you forsake me. The nails will pound themselves into your heart, if you are a false husband."

"Ach! Do you believe such things, Adela?" He looked at me incredulously, and for a moment, I wasn't sure if it was my own voice coming out of my mouth. I sounded like a stranger to myself.

I shrugged. "I am not a prophetess, and I cannot tell the future, but I can tell the past, and I know that in the past we were friends. The past is thick, and it has bearing, it gives us sustenance. And because of our past, you will be a friend to me now, and take me with you when you leave Aden."

Several expressions flashed over his face. He was falling from a great height, and the wind was crushing his spirit. Then he was standing on a mountaintop, with hands hard enough to touch the sun. Finally, he painted a blankness on his face and forced a smile. I did too. And soon we reached for each other a third time, coupling in the dawn light, each of us pretending to take a wild and unruly pleasure in the parched desert of our marriage bed.

He left me lying there. I looked down over my naked body that Hani had turned into a brocade more ornate than her mother's precious

Indian tapestries. My petaled curves, my paisley dark nipples, my
secret bouquets of blossoming henna. I saw that next to me was the
indentation on the sheets from where his body had lain. I moved over,
and put myself in the outline that he had left behind. Something pricked
my memory, and I remembered that when he was a boy he had left a
sand-angel in the dunes and I had fit myself into it. Now, here I was
his bride, his wife. I lay in his spot with the realization that I had not
married an angel, and that the form of him was empty of anything but
ambition.

Why had Asaf returned? As I lay there, I began to understand
everything. He had married me for profit. It wasn't because his father
had begged him on his deathbed. That was just ribbon-talk, pretty new
words he unspooled to tie up the old box of our engagement. He must
have heard that Uncle Barhun was prosperous. He came back for me
in order to finance this business trip. Aden was an entrepôt—little
merchants from India and Africa came there to sell their goods duty
free to traveling merchants like Asaf, who would then resell them at a
profit.

I got out of bed. My cousins and sisters-in-law greeted me with a
bath and a festive breakfast, but I had no stomach for their suggestive
conspiratorial glances. By lunchtime I had learned that before the day
of my wedding, Asaf had accepted a generous investment from Uncle
Barhun, who, along with Mr. Haza, purchased a share in the proceeds
from Asaf's journey. None of the women of our family had been
apprised. Not even Aunt Rahel, who looked stricken by the news, and
by the same realization that I had had—that I had broken off a true love
connection, in favor of one that held no such promise.

"What will you do, Adela?" My aunt sat me down, made me drink a
cup of strong tea.

"I will go with him."

"Is that wise?"

I shrugged. "I am tired of waiting for my fate."

"And will he take you with him?"

"He has agreed to."

Her voice softened to a whisper. "And if he abandons you along the
way?"

I remembered the spinster dye mistress, and what she said to me
long ago about a woman learning a profession, earning her own keep.

I thought of the skills I knew. I was as good a cook as any woman, I could sew linens and clothes, and I could do serviceable henna—my skill did not match that of my cousins, but I could decorate a palm pretty enough for payment. And of course, I could make a pair of shoes so perfect that the Confiscator's wife never knew they were stitched with curses, not ordinary thread.

"I can earn my own bread wherever I am. Whether I am with Asaf Damari or not, I will see the world and return to Aden with sister-stories to your marvelous tales of far-off India."

Asaf moved into Aunt Rahel and Uncle Barhun's house with me. Not a week after our wedding, he sold his patrimony—the deerskin Torah.

David had showed Asaf where he had added panels, where he had been able to fix the flaked gall, where he had executed repairs by ingeniously sewing little parchment screens behind words. Asaf signed an agency contract with the seller of rare books who lived next door to us. Almost immediately after our wedding, the Torah was sold to a wealthy Australian Jew of Iraqi origin. The sale of the Torah left Asaf with generous capital, which, in addition to my uncle's investment, would allow him to avoid an arduous journey east and leave him at leisure to enjoy the journey west. Asaf spent his days shopping and bargaining for Eastern ingredients—choya nakh and nag champa— which he was able to purchase only in very small quantities. Cypriol and vetiver were easier to obtain, and he had quickly amassed a generous store of each.

A few weeks after Asaf sold the Torah, Edna told me she had heard that Binyamin Bashari had left for Palestine. She said that he had left the major's employ and had won petition to enter the country.

"I hope he will be happy there." I forced a smile, but I didn't feel like smiling at the news.

"You are filled with regrets?"

"Mostly I regret that I treated him poorly. And I regret that I never said farewell. It is the second time in our lives that I did not bid him a proper farewell, though this time I am much to blame. The truth is that I don't feel like I acted like myself with him."

"Then who were you?"

An image flashed into my head—of the almost-finished Muslim bride dolly that Auntie Aminah had been sewing for Suri, one of Masudah's children, when she died. After Aminah's death, I completed the dress hem and gave the doll blushing rosettes for cheeks. When I presented her to little Suri, she jumped up and down with excitement and then pressed the dolly to her breast and hugged it as hard as she could. Suri had died with Masudah. I wondered what had happened to the doll.

"I think I wasn't quite finished then," I said to Edna.

"Whatever do you mean?"

"I mean not completed, as if I were a doll with incomplete stitching. Poor Binyamin got an Adela with a hem missing, or maybe a bit of my soul wasn't fully adorned with stitches. When he courted me, I was pinned but not sewn properly. I hope that in Palestine he finds a girl whom a better seamstress has seen fit to finish. I wish him well, really I do."

"Do you?"

Edna tenderly touched my hand. "It's okay, Adela, tears can water a marriage. What do I mean? We make choices and choices make us. You and Asaf are cousins, friends, and now husband and wife. You have loved him since you were a little girl. All is as it should be."

"He said the same thing."

"Who?"

"Asaf. He said, 'All is how it should be.'"

"Well, then it must be so."

That night I had a horrible dream. It took place in Qaraah, in my cave. The chalk boy and girl came to life. They slayed brothers. Ruined sisters. Set the world on fire. Then they turned on each other. The girl was quicker. She reached out and smudged the boy—erasing him. Then she erased herself. And somewhere in the darkness someone was chanting scripture from the deerskin Torah. It began, "All was wild and waste" and ended, "They knew not their own names, nor their own faces." When I woke up, I was surprised to see the Aden sunshine streaming through my window—that bone-white glare—and Asaf sleeping next to me. I hadn't erased him after all.

Chapter 31

After my marriage, we women hennaed every three or four weeks. All the women in my life silently conspired to pretend that my marriage was a happy one. It was the easiest for everyone. After all, since I was planning to travel with Asaf, everyone wanted to believe that we were well suited and that our marriage would sustain us on the journey. Asaf played along too. He was as affectionate as any husband, which meant that he was not that affectionate at all, for other than Aunt Rahel and Uncle Barhun, it was not the custom for men and women to display their true feelings for the eyes of the world. During those days I usually wore a design that Hani had learned from an Eritrean woman in Crater market—a trail of canna flowers blooming up my wrists and on the tops of my feet. My cousins and sisters-in-law joked with me about it. Sultana said, "Adela, we all suspect that you chose this design because your husband is insatiable."

Sultana added, "She must need the female fortitude imparted by the vulvic flowers in order to match his ardor in bed." They cackled together at my expense.

I didn't correct them. I didn't tell them that when Asaf did climb on top of me at night, it was with no ardor at all, only a mechanical thrusting. I didn't tell anyone that I chose the Eritrean henna not for its blooms but for its linking curlicue chains that trailed up and down my fingers and swirled around my wrists. Hamama had told me that the chains signified the entwining of souls, the linking of fates. I chose the pattern because I didn't know how to speak to Asaf about these things—love and fate—and so I hoped to let the henna speak for me. When I lay awake at night, Asaf asleep next to me, I often thought back to our childhood and tried to remember how we spoke to each other or touched each other in my cave. It had seemed so easy then, so natural.

Sometimes I wondered if everything I remembered about Qaraah was really just the pattern on some other girl's skin, an application of lies, dreams, and shadows.

During these same months, Hani wore a henna with a Persian Eye of God on both palms and pomegranate fruits on the backs of her hands. She also insisted on dots, slashes, waves, and swirls in strictly numbered patterns. We all mistook this to mean that she and David were engaged in kabbalistic nighttime acrobatics—surely the numbers corresponded to scriptural verses and holy words? We teased her, saying, "Hani and David are tasting forbidden knowledge." She smiled knowingly and looked away, her color rising in a coy blush. Unknown to all of us, she and David hadn't lain together in many months. Their love had faded, and she was casting her spells on someone else.

Every day I cleaned up after our morning meal, tidied up the house, and did my marketing. Sometimes when I had a spare moment, I was drawn to the harbor, even though I was no longer waiting for Asaf. I didn't wonder about the ships coming in; instead, it was the ones sailing away that my eyes followed. I wondered about Binyamin, and if his ship had safely landed in Jaffa. I tried not to question whether he hated me. Sometimes I imagined him walking through a city of golden stones, and sometimes I saw myself there with him. Usually I returned from the harbor in a dark mood, but Asaf never seemed to notice.

Often in the evenings we visited family. At Yerushalmit and Sultana's house, Asaf played sheshbesh with my brother Mordechai and taught him how to play placoto, a game from Greece. Sometimes he sat with Sultana's husband, my brother Menachem, and listened to him rail against the British for putting quotas on the refugee Jews who wanted to enter Palestine. Asaf liked to bait my brother. He would argue that the refugees should look to the West, not only to Palestine. He would say, "What does it matter if they can't go to Palestine? As Jews in Aden we can travel anywhere in the Empire and be treated as citizens. It is a new day, a modern age. We Jews must learn to be more at home in the wider world."

Menachem snorted, "The wider world? We are not wanted there either, cousin. Only a dreamer or a fool would think otherwise. Which are you? You don't strike me as a dreamer, and my poor father, may his memory be a blessing, is crying in the World to Come at the thought that my sister has married a fool."

Asaf laughed. "It's all gloom and doom with you, Menachem, but a seasoned traveler like myself knows better than to believe that the doors of the world would shut in the face of a man with something to sell, and I will always have something to sell."

Whenever we went to Hani and David's, Mara climbed on "Uncle Asaf's" lap. He tickled her, and told her stories from Africa. "Have I told you about the rhinoceros who stole my hat? No? Well, I was sleeping under stars in Abyssinia when I heard a noise. It was like a purr, but also like a frog's croak. Like a croaking purr. Really, I am not lying. Like this, it sounds like this—" And he let out a sound that made Mara dissolve in laughter. Then he tickled her, and she clamored for more—"Again, Uncle Asaf, again!"

Every so often, I went with Asaf down to the docks. Everyone seemed to know him there, even though he had been in Aden only three months. When I remarked on it he said, "I was here before, remember. Many times, with my father." But it still didn't make sense to me. He hadn't been back to Aden since he was a boy. And these were transient people. The dhow captain from Eritrea, the customs agent with the long mustache newly arrived in Aden, the coffee traders from Taiz, the bring-'em-in boys who waded out into the water to catch the junks or rafts. When they saw him they all yelled, "Asaf! Asaf!" and he flashed a big smile and waved with a strong flip of the hand. How could they all know him so well?

When I remarked upon this to my cousins, they rolled their eyes. Edna said, "Don't you know whom you married, Adela?"

Taken aback, I huffed, "What are you talking about?"

Nogema laid a hand on mine. "Your husband is the sort everyone wants to know, and so they feign familiarity, they learn his name from one another so as to appear important."

"What are you saying? He is just, well, he's just a boy. Not even a boy with his own shop."

Hani retorted, "He was never a *boy* to you, Adela. And once you became a woman, you prayed to Elohim that he would come back and be your husband. He was always a man to you, the man you would marry. So why should he be a boy to anyone else?"

I felt my face go red. I flashed her the darkest eyes I could muster. I opened my mouth but was too furious to form any words. All I could think was, *How dare she spill my old secret?* Hani saw that she had crossed a line, and quickly she placated me. "Don't get mad, Adela, I only meant to say that whatever you have always seen in him, others see too. My father already treats him like a favored son. Mr. Haza took him along that time when he had that meeting with Mr. Messa. And what about the horse? Asaf was the only one who could catch the creature. And now Commissioner Reilly wants him to ride in the Othman races. He would be the only Jewish jockey. For that alone Asaf deserves praise and notice."

She was referring to something that had happened a week before our wedding. A prized chestnut thoroughbred filly had been brought in by caravan from Lahaj, a gift from one of the little sultans to Commissioner Reilly in Aden, but before she could be corralled, she slipped her halter and disappeared into the hills above the cisterns. A reward was offered, but for weeks, no one had so much as caught sight of her. And when they finally did see her, she was too fast, disappearing into the dunes before anyone could fit a bridle over her head. Asaf heard of the plight of the filly. Quietly he hired a Bedouin boy to take him to the environs where she had last been sighted. Two days after the Sabbath of Tazria, when our men read the portion concerning the affliction of leprosy, Asaf rode the filly bareback into town. The commissioner paid him a generous purse of rupees and had told him to come to the stables to ride one of his mares whenever he wanted.

"The Muslims in the market call him Zafir—'Victorious,'" Hani said. "It is a good thing, Adela. Don't begrudge your husband his popularity. This match that your mother made when you were children, she must hear all the dock boys calling his name from heaven, and smile."

On the Sabbath we gathered together as a family, usually at Uncle Barhun and Aunt Rahel's, for their house was the largest. On Friday eve, the men of the family came home from synagogue. We women served the jachnun, the men ate their fill and then relaxed at the table, singing pious songs. One Sabbath, as I was rinsing dishes, Aunt Rahel took me by the shoulders. "Don't worry. Your belly is still flat? You were only just married. But if you are still bleeding by summer, I will give you something to put in your tea. No worries, my love. No worries."

"No, Aunt Rahel, I don't want a baby just yet."

She looked shocked, but I explained that I had been using a pessary.

That Asaf sometimes used a sheath when we lay together, and that I didn't want to conceive until after our travels. I didn't tell her that this had been Asaf's idea. He had suggested it—"as a matter of convenience. After all," he had said, "traveling with an infant is dangerous. There will be plenty of time for babies when we return."

Aunt Rahel shook her head and said, "It is not wise for a girl to play with her menses before she has had a child. Better you delay your trip than waste the blood that Elohim gives you for sowing."

"But I am not playing with my menses. I bleed as usual."

"No"—she shook her head—"you bleed for naught."

That night, Asaf tossed and turned in his sleep. I lay awake a long time, watching him. In the morning, I brushed the curls out of his eyes. His forehead was damp and he looked tired.

"You didn't sleep well?"

"As well as can be expected in this heat."

I nodded sleepily and murmured, "Aden has fire for air. It's like the volcano is still erupting, no?"

At least once a week, I joined Hani in a lorry and we went together to Sheik Othman. With the aid of funds from the Jewish Agency, the British had built a camp there for the refugee Jews from all over Yemen—the hostel was no longer big enough to contain them. Aunt Rahel also went to the camp to help the nurses. Hani went to do henna, taking with her a full complement of supplies in a big red basket that she swung over her shoulder. They told us stories as we did their henna. They said things like, "I am from the crocodile swamps" or "I was born of a heron" or "I gave birth to my daughter through a wound in my thigh." From their stories, we knew what designs to give them. We knew if it was a henna of solace or of sympathy that they needed. Or a henna of hope, of happiness, or forbearance. Every so often, Hani was called upon to do a bridal application. "Even refugees get married," she said to me as we rounded the last bend of the lorry ride. "I skip the shaddar, of course. There is no time. But I do an elaborate cuff and anklet. I do the grains of wheat and sprigs or rue. For what bride can be married without the rue?"

I helped Hani with the henna. But usually I helped the teachers. The Jewish Agency wanted the girls as well as the boys in the camp to learn to read, "to prepare them for their lives in Palestine." The classes were held in an open tent next to the tent where a doctor from New Zealand gave eye exams. I drew the letters in the earth and the children put their hands on my hand—א, ב, ג, ד. "*Aleph, bet, gimel, dalet . . .*" One day I worked for hours with a girl with snarling lips and smiling eyes. I drew her name and she copied it ten times, each time worse than the one before. Her hand was shaky, her letters bloated. But still she persevered. My, how she tried. Looking up at me for approval. I clapped my hands. "Yes, yes, just like that." I put my hand over hers, and helped her make the shapes that held meaning tucked up inside them, like Hani's henna basket, full of scent, spice, and color.

Chapter 32

Tales of betrayal were always told in the henna house alongside stories of love, luck, and seduction. Ever since I received my first henna, after Aunt Rahel saved Sultana's son Moshe, I'd listened to the girls and women in my life entertain one another with accounts of domestic conspiracies and legendary romantic triangles. But I never really gave much thought to the women whose fates were dark. Those brides who were betrayed, whose most prized blessings were stolen and spun into soft garments for others to wear . . . I rarely considered them. Why would I? Years later I came to see that I should have paid better attention.

Late afternoon, four months after my marriage, I was cooking dinner. I had already made the dough for the bread and was chopping the onions for the stew. I laid the knife down and wiped the sweat off my forehead, but then I stopped, holding my hand midway between my face and the board. I had noticed a little regiment of elements on the back of my left hand. Elements that seemed to be linked to form an abstract design, a tricky pattern reminiscent of a Sudanese Eye of God but not quite as formally structured. No, I had never really seen a design like this before. Hani had given me new henna just two days earlier. Why hadn't I noticed it when she was working? I resumed chopping, and looked out the window. On the street, a lorry driver was passing by. Behind the lorry came a donkey cart laden with furniture. The cart driver was singing to his donkey in a loud comical voice. I looked back down at my hands. I was suddenly dizzy. A jolt of panic ran up my spine. Had the pessary failed? Was I expecting a baby? If I were pregnant, Asaf wouldn't take me with him. No, that couldn't be it. I had bled in accordance with my cycle. And we had barely lain together since.

Maybe it was the heat. I was so hot. The windows were open, but there was no air in the little kitchen.

I poured a glass of juice and forced myself to drink. But as I put the cup down, right before my eyes, the henna elements unbound themselves from my skin, stepped out of formation, and rolled around in my palm. There were three stacked waves, a diamond with a dot in it, a crescent moon, a sideways scroll. They played tricks in front of my eyes, sliding down onto my wrist and then climbing back up again, up and down. Then they lay back down, tidy on the perch of a perfectly executed border. I steadied myself at the cooking board. I forced myself to chop another onion. Then I put down my knife, went to my drawers, and fished underneath my undergarments for the old piece of paper. I sat down on the pallet. Unfurled my hand. Examined it. The rest of the henna faded away. Each element was a letter, the letters formed words.

A.

Let my Beloved come into his Garden and eat his pleasant fruits
Thursday midmorning,

H.

From out of the past, the alphabetical correspondences revealed themselves. It was the code. Hani's old code. *Aleph* א was a gently sloping mountain, *nun* נ was a double circle, *qof* ק was a dotted triangle, *dalet* ד three little humps . . .

I dropped the piece of paper and curled up in a little ball. I stayed like that for a long time, unable to move. When I finally tried to get up, I felt the floor tip and the walls go crooked. Like a passenger on a storm-tossed boat, I grabbed at the wall for purchase and made my way slowly back to the kitchen. My head pounded and I had to keep swallowing to keep from retching. I got myself a cup of tea and sat down again at the kitchen table. As I forced myself to drink, I stared at the henna on my arm until I saw snakes writhing in the thicket of leaves Hani had drawn on my right forearm. I shut my eyes, rubbed them, and when I opened them again, my henna lay flat, but I wasn't fooled. I felt the world dip and sway around me again, and it took all my strength to get my bearings before my husband came home expecting dinner. I said nothing to him that night. I hid my shame, and pretended that I wasn't a character in one of the sadder sagas murmured in the henna house.

The next few days passed in a blur. I barely remember them. But I do remember that my grief was all-consuming. I had been betrayed by the two people I'd thought I loved most in the world. Asaf, who had never really returned, and Hani, who had skipped into my life, taught me to read, to dance and draw and laugh like her, and had now dared to teach me a different lesson—one I would never surpass her at, because we were fashioned of different stuff entirely.

The morning of the "appointment," I took a knife and sterilized it with arak. Then, standing at the water basin, I cut the elements off my skin, by slashing straight through the line of "text." I opened up a little channel of blood that gutted the message Hani was sending to Asaf, leaving it illegible. The wound I made in my hand wasn't so deep, but deep enough to bleed until my head spun. I winced as I dabbed at my hand with peppermint liniment, and then I bound it up with straps of clean linen.

I kept the appointment too. I knew where Hani kept her extra key. I unlocked the door. *Where is Mara?* I wondered. Later I learned that she was at Edna's. Edna was not complicit, but had been duped into playing a small part—minding Mara so that Hani and Asaf could meet in secret. Mr. Haza was in his warehouse on Steamer Point, so they had the house to themselves. I stood outside the bedroom door and listened to their lovemaking, their moans, their breathy giggles and groans. I opened the door slowly. My husband's back was turned to me. My cousin's long hair hung in loose, wild curls. Her face was distorted in the ugly throes of passion.

It took them a few moments to realize that they were being watched, but when they did, they seemed to lose dimensionality and become flat like the people in Masudah's pictures. Then they grew real again, springing away from each other. Hani turned red, Asaf grew ashen. They covered their nakedness. Begged forgiveness. Flung themselves at my feet. Hani cried—big heaving sobs. Asaf couldn't look me in the eye. He got dressed awkwardly, and then approached me, touched me on the shoulder, and when I flinched, he dropped his hand and his eyes grew dark. I wondered if I had married a real boy or a clay one, a creature of mud and filth and water.

Hamama was next door tending to her husband, who was home suffering from a bad toothache. When she heard the commotion she rushed over. I suppose it was her husband who fetched David Haza at his teacher's workshop, just around the corner. When David rushed up the stairs, I ran down them. I don't remember how I spent the next few hours. I suppose I wandered through Crater. What happened next at Hani's house? In one version of the story, David stood in the middle of the room and cursed Asaf three times—twice with his voice, and then he raised his hand as if to strike him, but instead made a series of movements in the air, as if he were drawing something with his fingers, and then let his hand drop to his side. "He fought with names," Hamama said, "like a Habbani warrior. Conjuring weapons out of the letters themselves." Was Asaf stricken? Did he feel one of the many names of Elohim piercing his heart or spearing his belly? I don't know; perhaps he felt it on the inside, but he put up no resistance. In another version of the story, David entered the house enraged and went to strike Asaf, but Asaf caught his hand, and what would have been a beating ended up a queer embrace, both locked together in stasis, neither freeing himself nor wounding the other. And in yet another version of the story, Hani turned herself into a filly and Asaf rode her out of Crater, deep into the hills, before David could confront them.

We later learned that their affair had begun almost immediately after Asaf came to Aden, before we were even wed. They caught each other's eyes, flirted, and then, during a festive meal, dared to kiss in Hani's kitchen. Not a little peck of a kiss, but a "kiss of Solomon and Sheba"— the kind of kiss that lasts so long it becomes legend. They made love on the dunes behind Commissioner Reilly's stables. She brushed herself off, straightened her kerchief, and returned to David a sullied wife. And Asaf stole me from Binyamin, married me, made love to me with the stink of their coupling on his sex, though I naively mistook it for the salty tang of our own long-promised love. I was nothing but a pawn in their shameful game—an artful hide-and-seek they played not only behind my back but also on my hands and feet. At my wedding, I had let her draw on my entire body, turning me into an elaborate brocade, like one of Aunt Rahel's beautiful tapestries. Once I knew the truth, I realized that even that first night, my husband had not belonged to me. As a bride I bore the scripture of betrayal on my own body. In all my time as a wife, I was pasul, a girl-parchment inscribed with so many false words, like a Torah written by a demon or by a scribe with bad intentions.

The day after I found them together, Asaf flung himself at my feet.

"I am unworthy," he said, "but if you could forgive me, then perhaps we can all live together. I will take Hani as a second wife. She can get a divorce from David Haza. Surely he will grant it to her. We will all live together. I will be your husband still." He repeated himself several times, each time with wilting emphasis. "You will always be my first, and she will be my second wife. We can take our trip, just as we planned, and when we return we can live in our house together, the three of us, with little Mara."

I stood and stared at him. I didn't speak for a long time. I knew that he feared Uncle Barhun's wrath, and that he groveled in the hope that my forgiveness would soften the damage he had done to his prospects.

I didn't know what to say. But then I heard voices in my head, voices I recognized though I had never heard them before. Oh, how was it I didn't know they could speak? My little idols. They came to me from the past and told me the truth—and what they told me I repeated to my husband.

"Asaf Damari," I seethed, "you were *never* my true husband. I have betrayed myself and another much more than you and Hani have betrayed me."

I heard myself screaming. And I think I may have slapped him (with my good hand), raking my nails across his face. After he left, when I looked into the mirror, I saw that I had turned into a caracal, with claws as sharp as my newfound hatred and teeth in my mouth as deadly as my spite.

When we were just children and I had seen him riding Jamiya in the dunes below my cave, I had thought him a wild boy, a beautiful creature who had crossed from one side of nature to the other—a Jew on a horse, a boy who was speed and thunder and sun and light and sand. But now I was the wild one. I tore through our possessions, ruining all tokens of our life together, smashing wedding gifts, even setting fire to his clothes, which smoldered in the cooking stove and filled the kitchen with a rancid black smoke whose smell lingered long after. Remelia, Sultana, and Yerushalmit took turns sitting with me, but they were wise enough to let me unravel my marriage the way I needed to. With his pockets full of Uncle Barhun's money, Asaf had given me showy gifts—a lazem necklace, a pair of dangling rupee earrings. I flung them across the room and trampled the string of beads he had presented to me on our wedding night. When I came across the old amulet he had given me so many years before, I was more methodical. I went to the kitchen, got a knife, and pried the wooden disk from the leather backing. What name had I been expecting? El Shamayim, God of the Heavens? El Rachoom, Merciful God? Eyeh Asher Eyeh, I Am That I Am? Ein Sof, the Infinite One? Or maybe there was an angel name inside: Raziel, Keeper of Secrets? Raphael, Healer of Hearts? Cassiel, Angel of Solitude and Tears? All those years I had wondered so many times. But I had never pried it open. I let the leather backing fall to the floor, where it clattered in a tiny breathless thump. The wooden disk was cold in my hand. But the amulet was empty. No old piece of paper fluttered out. Empty. All along I had been tricked into thinking its rough magic could protect me, bind me to my beloved, shield my heart from harm.

Hani came to her father's door and begged to see me. She prostrated herself in front of me and begged my forgiveness. I would like to say that I forgave her, but about this one thing I am certain. I did not.

I didn't hesitate. I didn't for a single second waver. I said, "Hani, I know what you did. No, I am not talking about what you did with my husband; I am neither crude enough nor stupid enough to lay that shame before you. You have shamed yourself plenty. What I am talking about is this."

I held up my hand and showed her my bandages.

Her face blanched. "How . . . ?"

"Your code? I found it years ago in Qaraah in your little bag of precious things."

"You never told me."

"I never thought I would have to."

"It is not what you think."

"It is worse than what I think, Hani. It is what I believe, and believing springs from a well deeper than thought. Thought runs dry, but belief runs as deep as Noah's floodwaters."

"But Adela, I—"

"Stop. Don't say another word. It is *my* turn to speak. I know that you used your art for treachery. And that you turned me—your bosom friend—into your enemy. What do I believe? I believe that you are dead to me, and so is Asaf. Go forth from Aden without my blessing."

I slammed the door behind her, and collapsed sobbing onto the floor. I swore at her retreating shadow that I would live the rest of my life without having to shoulder the burden of her cruel charms.

For a long time afterward there was much whispered discussion. *Careless* was the word bandied about. Everyone wondered why they had made love in the morning in Hani's house. Surely they knew that they could be discovered. After all, either David or Mr. Haza could have come home unexpectedly. I overheard Yerushalmit and Sultana talking about this when they didn't know I was listening. "How could they be so careless"—Sultana finished Yerushalmit's thought—"in your own house? I would have thought they would have taken greater lengths to hide their treachery."

But their carelessness was never voiced in front of me. By discussing it, by wondering over it, it seemed as if my sisters-in-law were asking, "Why weren't they sneakier? Why didn't they do a better job of hiding their lust?" Really the carelessness wasn't in the choosing of the place, but in the simple fact they were misplacing their marriages, as if the vows they had spoken under the wedding canopy were little things to be lost, like socks or keys.

And they weren't the only ones. After all, I had misplaced Binyamin, the boy who really loved me. Careless. Yes, we all were. Very, very careless.

I had waited for Asaf for years, but our marriage was dissolved in the blink of an eye. Mr. Haza testified to the triumvirate of rabbis that Asaf had lain with Hani. Asaf himself confessed his guilt to the Bet Din. My marriage was neatly torn asunder, as was Hani's. Hani and Asaf were married soon after in a shameful ceremony with no festivity, attended only by Aunt Rahel and Uncle Barhun. And as for poor David Haza? He kept a brave face at first, but once he realized that his marriage was over, he was bereft. He moved in with his father, came down with typhus, and had to be hospitalized. When he recovered, his hands shook and he could no longer write the name of God. A scribe must write the name of Elohim in its entirety, and if he makes an error, the entire page of scripture must be buried in a sacred repository of holy books. Because of his shaky hands, David had to leave his studies, and would never again write a single word of Torah. His teacher mourned for him as if he had lost a son. When my uncle went to beg Mr. Haza's forgiveness for Hani and Asaf's treachery, Mr. Haza beat his own his chest with one of his fat hands and said, "We will be brothers forever, you and I. But my poor son has a broken heart. What is a father to do? What should I do, Barhun?" He dissolved in tears and let my uncle embrace him.

Chapter 33

Auntie Aminah once told me that I cried for the first year of my life. No one could calm me; I cried even in my sleep. I think that perhaps those tears were an early payment of water on a debt of sorrow that I owed myself, for I found I could not cry in the aftermath of my misfortune. Who was I now? Who would I be? Hereafter my arms would be forever empty. Like the dye mistress, I would have no babes to suckle and no husband to call my own. No, I didn't shed a tear. But every morning I awoke spent, bitter, and empty, with the feeling that I had cried tears that shook me to the bone.

Several weeks after my marriage was dissolved, I forced myself to go back to the camp at Sheik Othman. I went alone. As far as I knew, Hani was in seclusion. The Jews of Aden were a conservative lot, and no one respected a woman who stole another's husband. She was shunned on the streets of Crater and in our sacred spaces—the synagogue, the ritual bath, and in the market. I knew I wouldn't see her at the camp, and I suppose I was hoping to see a bit of myself there, reflected in the eyes of my students. Immediately I was rewarded. A little girl with huge gray-blue eyes put her hand over mine so that I could show her the shape of *shin*—ש—the letter that made the susurrus *ssss* sound, and also the *shhh* sound that hushes a baby. Hani had told me that *shin* originally signified an arrow's bow, but now it looked to me like a harp with too few strings, an instrument capable of playing only broken music. I must have hesitated. My hand must have shaken or hovered. But my pupil squeezed my hand, and then squeezed it again. I felt a warmth flood through my bosom, and I began to draw again. I realized that even though her hand was on my hand, this little refugee was really covering my heart, my heart that was suffering from exposure.

I rode the lorry home to Aden with my head against the cool window. The entire way, I thought about the letter *shin*. It is a magical letter, as it stands for one of the most ancient names of Elohim. *Shin* is Shaddai, שדי, God of the Breast and God of the Mountains. Shaddai was the name by which our Fathers Abraham, Isaac, and Jacob knew to call on Elohim. Shaddai, God of the Breast, was kin to Asherah, the One of the Womb. As the lorry rounded the bend that would take us through the Main Pass into Crater, my hand fell on my flat belly and I cringed, thinking that it was both a blessing and a curse that I had stoppered up my womb like the drain of a tub. What if I *had* been pregnant? Would Asaf have betrayed me even then?

A few weeks later, Hani and Asaf departed Aden on a Dutch steamer bound for Alexandria. I didn't see them go, and so their departure, like everything else that transpired since Asaf returned to Aden, seemed unreal to me, as if it had all happened to some other group of people, strangers I'd heard about but never met. They left Mara in Nogema's care. Hani claimed my place on the journey Asaf and I were supposed to take together. But they had no intention of returning to Aden, where they knew they would always receive a frosty welcome from the community. Instead they let it be known that they would make their home in Mocha, on the western coast of the Kingdom. Once there, they would send for Mara to join them.

In the beginning, relations were strained between me and my cousins. But not long after Hani and Asaf sailed, Nogema, Hamama, and Edna gave me a special henna. It was, they said, a henna of penitence, for though they could not apologize for their sister's sins, they could inscribe me with their own picture psalms of remorse, regret, shame, and sorrow for what I had suffered. When they were finished, my arms were covered from fingertip to shoulder, and my feet were covered with breathtaking designs, from soles to the tops of my shins. I looked at myself in the mirror and was reminded of what Hani looked like the first time I saw her, when she came to Qaraah embossed like a princess under her clothes. I forgave them, even though they had not sinned against me. I forgave them, and loved them like sisters once again.

* * *

In the years that followed my failed marriage, I lived a quiet life. Remelia married a teacher at the King George V School, and I moved in with them. Quickly, they filled the house with three delightful babies who distracted me with their cherub lips and chubby toes and constant need for attention. I refused any attempts by my sisters-in-law or cousins to play matchmaker. When I wasn't helping Remelia run her busy home, I volunteered as a regular teacher in the camp at Sheik Othman. I taught many little girls to read, including Mara, Hani's left-behind daughter, who sometimes came with me and eventually became my helper in the camp. Mara had her mother's quick wit and dark eyes, but she also had her father's innate goodness. I grew to love her, and to love feeling her small hand in my own. She, of course, never truly understood where I really belonged in the orbit of grown-ups that made up her universe. She felt the gravitational tug of her missing mother and it made her walk closer to the earth, and laugh less and smile less than other girls. To her, I was always "Cousin Adela" and I took comfort in the fact that in her eyes I was not a woman who had been rejected or betrayed, as I was in the eyes of others. When Mara was most sad, I told her stories of her mother and me when we were children in Qaraah. Of how Hani taught me henna, and laughter and letters, and just about everything else.

The camp at Sheik Othman was a saving place for me. Hearing those little girls say the letters and sound out words never failed to return me to myself when I was most lost. On good days, I smiled and laughed with those girls. I took pleasure in the notion that I was helping to prepare them for modern lives in Palestine. That the words they learned from me would help them author their own lives far away, under the good glare of a different sun.

At first, the family heard from Asaf and Hani sporadically. Three months after their departure, Edna received a letter from Hani and Asaf from Port Said. Five months later, my aunt and uncle opened one from Alexandria. A year later, Nogema had a letter from Cyprus. After that we didn't hear from them for over a year, and then we got word that they went to Istanbul, then back to Cyprus, and then to Corfu. Aunt

Rahel opened a final letter dated November 1940, two months after Hitler invaded Poland. By then we were regularly getting reports of the darkness that was descending on Europe. There were those who never believed a word of news from the outside world and treated the stories spread by ship captains with detachment, as if they were speaking of events occurring on a planet as distant and unlikely as Mars. After that final letter from Corfu in 1940, no one heard from Hani again.

Those dreadful years passed during which Europe cannibalized itself. We almost never spoke of Hani. Aunt Rahel wouldn't utter her name, and if someone mentioned her in her mother's presence, Rahel would withdraw into herself, often not speaking for days. Edna and Nogema held out hope that Hani and Asaf had somehow survived and would return to us. Hamama forsook her habit of prophecy and refused to weigh in on Hani's fate. As for me, at first I was glad when the letters stopped coming; I didn't want to hear of her anymore. But when I realized that the silence probably signified disaster, my feelings turned, and I would find myself lingering at the dockside, looking toward the boats on the horizon, desperately willing one of them to carry a letter from Hani, beloved friend of my girlhood, whose betrayal of me suddenly seemed a very small thing, an infinitesimal misunderstanding even, that paled in the face of Hitler's monstrous betrayal of the Jews.

I lived modestly and peacefully for nearly a decade—helping Remelia keep house, tutoring at the refugee camp at Sheik Othman, and warming myself in the embrace of my family—but then on November 29, 1947, the UN voted to partition Palestine. Four days later, the Arabs of Aden erupted in mass violence against Aden's Jews. Eighty-two Jews were murdered, among them two of our own: David's father, the wonderful Mr. Haza, and Hamama's beloved husband, Nathaniel Qafih. Scores were wounded, and almost all the Jewish shops in Crater were looted. Synagogues were burnt to the ground and more than two hundred Jewish houses were destroyed in the mayhem. The Selim School for Girls was destroyed along with the King George V Jewish School for Boys. Our houses were also destroyed. Those days were the most fearsome of my life. We were lucky to have Nogema. She and her British husband sheltered all of us. But until we reached the refuge of her home, we feared for our lives. Even now, when I think of them, those hours hurt and haunt. And when I tumble back into the chaos of the riots, I am reminded of the fear that blazed up in my head when the Confiscator visited my father's stall, but this time the fire was everywhere, lapping at our legs even as we fled.

After the riots, we became refugees, crowding into tents in Sheik Othman, alongside the families of the girls who had been my students. In 1948, the State of Israel was born out of bloody strife. Rumors of the miracle spread. Slowly, the remaining Jews of the Northern Kingdom and the midlands began to walk down through the mountains, cradling their Torahs like infants, making their way to Aden on footpaths trodden by herdsmen since the dawn of time. Bribes were paid to petty sheiks, and spies secured the passage of entire communities. More camps had to be opened in Aden, for the one at Sheik Othman couldn't hold everyone.

My family had been in a refugee camp for a year and I was thirty-one years old when the government of Israel arranged through secret channels to fly all the Jews of Yemen to Israel. It was unofficially called Operation Magic Carpet, and officially called Operation On Wings of Eagles. When our people refused to enter the airplanes out of fear— for especially our brethren from the North had no experience with modernity—our rabbis reminded them of divine passages. "This is the fulfillment of ancient prophecy," they said. "The eagles that fly us to the Promised Land may be made of metal, but their wings are buoyed aloft by the breath of God."

Between June 1949 and September 1950 almost fifty thousand Yemenite Jews boarded transport planes and made some 380 flights from Aden to Israel in this secret operation. The pilots who came for us removed the regular seats and put benches in the planes, so that more of us could fit. Each flight was a perilous undertaking, as the Arab League was at war with the infant state, and the planes had to fly over battlefields to reach Israel.

"Ouch!" I put my thumb in my mouth and sucked on the blood.

"What did you do to yourself?" Remelia wrapped my thumb with a strip of linen. That night, we were to leave Aden forever. The transports had been flying for a month, and we had just received word that we were next on the list. We were all nervous and excited. It's no wonder I cut myself while slicing onions. My hands shook and everyone's voices were shrill with nerves. I left the land of my birth and flew for the very first time, with a finger that throbbed through scraps of torn linen.

When we were on the plane, Sultana chided me. "What are you crying about? Don't you know we are flying to heaven?" I gulped back my tears and shoved my throbbing thumb into my fist. I stared out the window into the black firmament, and tried to block out the sounds of the journey—but who can *not* hear all that? The engines whirred, sputtered, and hummed; children cried and parents comforted them; and the old and the young, the sick and the well all said psalms, voices wavering like those of discombobulated angels, unsure of their own claim on the World to Come.

Next to me on the plane sat Sultana, Elihoo, and Moshe, who was now a tall and serious young man of twenty. Behind us sat my brother Mordechai, Yerushalmit, and her big brood of Masudah's children, the eldest of whom had already married and now traveled to Israel with his wife and babes of their own on their laps. Some of my other brothers had already flown on earlier flights. My brother Efrim and his wife and their seven children and fifteen grandchildren left two weeks before we did. My brother Pinny and his family had left one week earlier. My poor brother Dov also traveled with us. He had walked down through the mountains with the other refugees, and joined us in Aden. Though he had lost his wits years ago when Masudah died, he was sane enough to know that if he were to ever find them again, it would be in the Holy Land, not in Yemen.

The other Damaris—Aunt Rahel, Uncle Barhun, Hamama and Edna and Mara—were on a flight that left the day after ours. Nogema did not fly with us to Israel, but to England with her British husband. Remelia and her husband, Calev, came last, a few weeks after us, with their nine living children. We women were a sorry sight on those planes. Naked of finery, we had all left our gargushim and our heavy jewelry in sad little heaps on the tarmac, because we feared that the plane wouldn't hold our weight under the carapace of our tribal adornments. Throughout the flight I kept reaching up and patting my head—with my unhurt hand— feeling so strange without the weight of those tinkling coins. None of us had ever been in a plane before. We were equal parts entranced and horrified by this stranger magic that elevated our bodies as efficiently as prayer had elevated our souls for millennia. Sultana fainted on takeoff.

My brother Elihoo was sick for the whole flight, retching into his lap. My brother Hassan was a brave and helpful presence on our flight, soothing and comforting any man, woman, or child who needed to be comforted.

Out the window, I saw the images of my life. I saw my father in his stall, cutting a scrap of leather for a pair of shoes. I saw Asaf, the boy he was, making angels in the sand. I saw myself as a girl, tripping through the dye mistress's colorful pots. I saw Hani wearing a coat of many colors, none of them of this earth. I even saw Binyamin. He was sitting on a distant star, swinging his legs while holding out his hands to me. He seemed to be beckoning, gesturing for me to come close. I pressed my face against the window. Would I meet him again in Israel? I heard that it was a country so tiny you could fit it in your shoe like a pebble. Such a small land, surely we would bump into each other one day. I assumed he was married by now, that he had a wife who loved him as I should have loved him. I wondered how many children called him Father? With this thought, my heart began to throb. I tore my eyes away from the window and told one of Masudah's daughters to give me the toddler on her lap. Her name was Ella and she was clutching a little wooden nubbin of a doll. I dandled the child and made the doll dance while humming an old song and burying my face in her hair.

We landed on a dusty tarmac in the middle of a hot afternoon. Many of the people on the plane crumpled to the ground and kissed the earth. Others held their hands up to the heavens and loudly praised Elohim. It must have looked as if we Yemenites were giddy with our redemption, but no one really knew what was more astonishing—that we were in Zion, or that we had survived the flight in the metal bird. I stumbled out into the blazing sun along with the rest. I still had Masudah's granddaughter in my arms. I walked a few steps when I felt a tug on my shoulder. I turned around, and found myself face-to-face with a girl soldier; she had skin the color of raw dough, red hair, and freckles on an upturned nose. "Ema," she said. "Mother, you dropped the baby's doll." She handed me back the little nubbin doll. I opened my mouth to tell her that the child wasn't mine, that I wasn't a mother. The soldier kept talking, but her beautiful Hebrew words must have shed the quality of sound, because I couldn't hear them anymore. I watched the soldier's lips move, while all around us the plane disgorged more passengers, and my heart was racing, my head spinning. I clutched at the little girl in my arms, using her as ballast to keep from tipping backward into the past or forward into the unknown. The soldier was still talking. What was she saying? I tried to thank her, and to tell her who I was, who I wasn't, who I had never yet been, but she was already long gone when I finally found the words.

Quickly, we Yemenite Jews grew accustomed to questions. Self-important reporters asked us what it felt like to be "rescued from the clutches of the corrupt imams and sheiks." Sociologists asked us how the new Israeli government could have treated us better or better prepared us for life in a modern land. Ashkenazi mothers put their pale hands on our brown arms in the market and shyly asked us for advice on how to properly use certain spices. But my favorite question belonged to the native-born sabra schoolchildren, especially the little girls. They would always ask what we carried in our meager bags. *What did you bring with?* they shyly chirped. *What did you carry with you to Israel?*

I played along. I smiled and confessed that when I stumbled dizzily off the plane, I had with me underwear and socks, two dresses, two pairs of pants, one pair of shoes. I answered boringly and predictably as I felt I should. But I never told the truth—of course I didn't—that the only true possession I brought with me from Yemen was this story, even though I didn't yet have the words to fold the images into the bag shoved between my knees on the plane. I brought it all with me: the Confiscator, my cave, my Auntie Aminah, Asaf, Jamiya, Sheik Ibn Messer, Asaf's sister and her doomed babe, my Uncle Zecharia, my beloved sister-in-law Masudah. I brought my one trip to Sana'a and the laughing Muslim bride, I brought Hani as I'd first seen her, and as I'd last known her, I brought Pishtish the donkey, I brought the Habbani girls, I brought the grave of Cain, and the bone-white Adeni sun.

Part Four

Chapter 34

From the plane, we were taken north, to a refugee camp outside the city of Hadera. We lived in tents, rows and rows of them. Had she lived to make that journey with us, Auntie Aminah would have told the story like this: she would have said, "In Israel, we slid willy-nilly, as if our feet were greased with clarified butter." What she would have meant was that in Israel we had no purchase on the earth; we slid this way and that, whenever we tried to simply walk forward. The conditions in the camp were difficult. Sickness was rampant. Two of Masudah's infant grandchildren died within months of our arrival. Israelis came to gawk at us; sometimes they were charitable, and other times they were disdainful, as if we had somehow disappointed them. And we had. They were expecting us to have walked straight off the pages of scripture, when really we sweated and farted and stank worse than they did, because we had no decent place to wash, and our bellies were sick from unfamiliar food and water. Once, a tall gentleman in a white suit came from the government. He was leaning on a cane, and I could see that he had a damaged leg, as he walked with a limp. I was in a big open tent, conducting a class for the youngest children, teaching them their letters. He stood on the outskirts of the tent, and I felt his eyes on me. I lifted my eyes and stared at him, and then he took off his hat, and apologized. "Keep teaching, sister," he said, in beautiful mellifluous Hebrew.

That night, I dreamed that the man in the white suit was the Confiscator, and that the cane in his hand was the serpent of the Confiscator's jambia. I awoke with sweat on my brow, and had to blink twice to convince myself that the dream was nonsense. "What is bothering you?" a fellow teacher asked me later that day. "Nothing," I lied. I couldn't tell her the truth—that the unfamiliar sun of this new land had addled my brain, that the thread of my life had bunched up and I feared it would take a great effort to smooth it out again.

One month later, I was still living and teaching in the refugee camp when one of my fellow teachers directed my attention to a man entering our school tent.

"Adela, who is that?"

"Who?"

"That gentleman over there. He is looking at you. Do you know him?"

I looked up and shaded my eyes. At first he was a hazy blur, a shadow framed by the sunlight streaming into the tent. But then he was Binyamin Bashari, my wolf-muzzle boy who had grown into his distinctive looks and become as handsome as the new country itself, with a swagger to his walk and a gleam in his eye that was rugged and civilized at the same time. He was coming through the children, who were craning their necks to see the stranger. When he reached me, my legs almost buckled. "Don't cry, my love," he said over and over, "don't cry." But how could I not cry? In front of my students and fellow teachers, I sobbed and gasped and shook. No one rebuked me, and the children seemed to understand that mine were tears of joy and that today's lesson was about much more than ordinary letters. I had been right, on the plane, looking out the window—it was Binyamin sitting on a star; he had been out there, beckoning for me to come to him.

"Oh, my love, my dear, everything is going to be fine, I am here," he whispered into my ear. "I am here, and I have found you and we will never again be parted."

That very evening, Binyamin took me to Tel Aviv and made me ride a Ferris wheel that was as high as a ten-story building at a fair on the banks of the Yarkon River. I begged his forgiveness up there in the lofty darkness. But he shushed me and told me that I had nothing to answer for. He kissed my lips, and then pressed his lips to my crying eyes.

As we strolled together through the fair, he explained how he had heard the news of the miraculous rescue of the Yemenite Jews and had gone to the Jewish Agency offices and searched for my name among the lists of the refugees. The list also had information about where to find me in Hadera. How did he know I wasn't married anymore?

He later told me that after he was wounded, when he was lying in bed recovering, an angel came to him in a vision and told him so. He was not a religious man but a freethinker and a rationalist. "Yet I believed the angel," he said, "and never doubted for a moment that what it said was not only true, but was a radiant truth, a truth that would shine light on darkness and illuminate my life in ways I couldn't fathom."

Two months after he walked into the tent, he played the khallool at our nuptials, adorning charms of melody into the fabric of the wedding canopy.

I was unearthed by his discovery of me, dug out like a fossil from another life, and given new meaning in the context of his enduring love. I quickly learned all that had happened to him since he left Aden. Binyamin had arrived in Israel in the winter of 1935 and become a soldier. He fought with the British against the Arabs; then he left British service and worked for the Haganah, helping Jews subvert British immigration quotas. During the war, he volunteered for the Jewish Brigade, and went to Italy as a British soldier. After the armistice, Binyamin returned and fought in the War of Independence. He was wounded in the effort to break the siege of Jerusalem and recovered under the tender care of friends in Tel Aviv. In the years after the war, he opened a school to teach the music and indigenous instruments of Arabia. He worked with schoolchildren and orchestra members alike, training musicians from Warsaw, Berlin, and Kiev to play the khallool and the tunes of our homeland. I often asked Binyamin to tell me stories of those years. I wanted to know everything that had happened to him. I made him describe his fellow soldiers, the landscape of Italy, and most of all, I made him tell me over and over again the improbable tales of illegal immigration. These stories had such colorful casts of characters and involved subterfuge, danger. There were whores who slept with British soldiers and got them too drunk to do their jobs. There were knives pressed into backs and whispered threats, signal fires on beaches, yeshiva boys from Europe who sank in the water off the coast of Natanya and had to be carried like sacks of potatoes through the nighttime surf. I loved Binyamin's stories, but most of all I loved learning the contours of his life, the nooks and crannies I'd missed out on.

We settled in Tel Aviv. His school for indigenous Eastern instruments attracted students from all over the world and ultimately became part of the internationally renowned Rimon School of Music. Binyamin was never again an active-duty soldier; instead he served in a reserve regiment of the IDF that performed at ceremonial military occasions. I bore him six children. All of them lived. And when they were born, I marked all of their palms and navels with henna, for even though I didn't decorate my own hands anymore, I couldn't deprive my children of this. After they were in school, I decided to become a real teacher. I received a scholarship to study at a teachers' college in Ashkelon. My first job in Israel was teaching Hebrew to Eritrean immigrants. From the late 1940s through the early '60s, the Arab world had disgorged its Jews. Just as it had rescued us Yemenites, Israel rescued whole communities, flying myriad secret and perilous missions into the heart of Arabia. In time, I taught Jews from all over the Arab world. And even though I had hundreds of students, every time I took a piece of chalk and drew a Hebrew letter, some part of my soul was back on the banks of the Khoreiba River. Every child was a little Habbani girl, and every letter was etched in the soil of my history, the scorched volcanic earth of Yemen.

Binyamin and I made a good life together. We became Israelis not only in name but also in spirit. I was thirty-two years old when we had our first child. We raised our family; our children grew tall, beautiful, and strong. One day, a month or so after the birth of our fourth child, I dreamed that I was a little girl again, and that I had stumbled through the darkness into the tent of the great Sheik Ibn Messer. When I woke from my dream, Binyamin was by my bedside. "You spoke in your sleep," he said tenderly, in a quiet voice so as not to wake our babe.

"What did I say?"

"You said, 'Impossible, I came alone.'"

I smiled.

"What were you dreaming?"

"I was dreaming of when we were children, and of how you followed me to Sheik Ibn Messer, of how you saved me when I went stupidly stumbling through the darkness."

My husband smiled. "I never saved you, Adela. Following you was my way of saving myself."

"From what?"

He shrugged. "From a life without you." He bent down and kissed our baby, and then kissed me. When I fell asleep again, I dreamed that I was in my cave. I was holding a piece of chalk, drawing on the wall. I worked for a long time, and when I was done, I stood back and surveyed my work. I saw that I had erased the chalk picture of Asaf and drawn Binyamin instead. I had erased Jamiya the horse and in her place, I gave the new chalk boy a khallool. I was there too, a chalk girl, adorned with henna, untouched by fate or time, the minerals of my soul mingled with the minerals of stone and darkness. Just before I woke, I saw the chalk girl reach out and grasp the chalk boy's hand.

That night, I put down the babe and kissed my husband on every inch of his body. I kissed him for every step he ever took in my wake, I kissed him for every second we were apart, I kissed him for the future and for our children, tucked safely abed.

When I married Binyamin, I wasn't a Yemenite bride. I wore no towering tishbuk lu'lu' on my head, no henna on my hands. I wore a regular Western dress and a little doily of a veil in my hair. This is because we refugees tried our best to become real Israelis. We women shed our antaris and leggings and wore Western clothes. The women among us who stayed religious put away their black and red lafeh cloths and replaced them with ordinary kerchiefs. We who had left our heavy silver-bedecked gargushim on the tarmac in Aden never replaced them. Those who had brought them put them away in the bottom of drawers, to be taken out only on the most festive occasions, and ultimately half forgotten, shown to grandchildren as exotic tokens of a frayed and misty past. We left our henna behind too, for it marked us as savage, foreign, primitive. We didn't want to be biblical Jews but modern ones. We forgot our ancient matriarchal patterns and our amuletic inscriptions, and walked the freshly paved sidewalks of Israel wearing nothing but slacks and blouses, our hands and feet as blank as the yet unwritten future, our heads as bare as heathens' without our gargushim and lafeh cloths.

There were some who adhered to the old ways, but not many. Even Aunt Rahel gave up her henna. I remember when I first noticed. She was at my house helping me with dishes following a Sabbath lunch. I saw the water running over her hands and was stricken by the bareness of her skin. For a moment I remembered her as I had first seen her, standing shyly behind Uncle Barhun—how she had stepped forth into my life with hands and feet so densely inscribed I lost myself in the patterns, staring into her skin as if it were a puzzle to be deciphered. Now her skin looked like the page of a book that had lost its letters, as if the story had somehow fallen off, leaving behind a blankness that no one could read anymore. She noticed me staring. "I know," she said, self-consciously burying her hands in a dishcloth. "I feel naked without it. Sometimes I dream that I am giving myself an application, and when I wake up I am surprised that the pattern isn't there. I tell myself that I am on a journey, as when we traveled from Qaraah to Aden. And that once we arrive I will mix the paste as always. Only this journey seems to have no end." She turned away, and continued with the dishes. After that we never spoke of henna again.

Uncle Barhun died three months after my wedding, after only one year in Israel. He fell ill on the Sabbath of Ki Tavo, when our men read the portion concerning how our Father Moses instructed the Israelites on the laws and rituals of harvests in the Promised Land. My aunt was already a tired, almost-old woman when Uncle Barhun died, and she had never been beautiful, except in the henna house. But upon her husband's death, she became young again, a blazing beauty, as she buried my uncle. I realized—while she cast the first handful of earth—that at her husband's graveside Rahel became the woman he had always seen in her. It was the essence of her soul coming forth to bid her husband, her love, farewell forever. I cried for my uncle, and my cousins sobbed. My brothers and sisters-in-law did too. We all mourned as one, lamenting that Barhun Damari had not lived long enough to sow his own fruits in the land of Israel.

Aunt Rahel fell ill in the spring of 1965. When she was dying, she became once again a woman of henna and asked her daughters to anoint her. When the rest of us fled Aden, Nogema had gone with her husband to England. Now she came back to join her sisters in service of their mother. They did exactly as she had taught them. Grinding the leaves, mixing them with lemon and sugar water, adding cloves and coffee grounds and orange essence and then drawing on her body the esoteric combinations of elements that a woman wears under her shroud and under her lulwi dress with its big sleeves, fish symbols, and pearly embroidery. The pattern becomes one with the soil, inscribing her secret autobiography into the earth. Once Aunt Rahel was gone, I felt my connection to my past grow tenuous. Sometimes I dreamed of Aden or of Qaraah, but when I woke in the morning it was as if I had visited a fictional country, not the land of my birth.

The years passed. Nogema returned to England and rarely visited, though one of her granddaughters came back to Israel on her own, and settled in Haifa. Too early I buried Edna, and then Yerushalmit. Each time I fulfilled the rites of henna, a last token of who we had been when we were young together. And so it would have all ended, and I would have gone to my grave without having to write any of this story. But then one day in 1979, I received a strange phone call.

"Hello, is this Mrs. Adela Bashari?"

"Yes, and you are?"

"My name is Mr. Yoel Shaham. I am calling from Yad Vashem. I work in the archives here. I tracked you down through your brother Mr. Hassan Damari."

Yad Vashem—the Holocaust museum and memorial in Jerusalem. My heart stuttered; I had to sit down.

"Was your born name Adela Damari?"

"It was."

"And did you have a cousin named Hani?"

"I did."

I heard myself repeat "Yes, I am Adela Damari, and yes, I did once have a cousin named Hani."

Mr. Shaham said a few words, explaining something that was at its core inexplicable, and when I hung up the phone, I had promised to travel to Jerusalem the very next week.

We never knew what had happened to Hani and Asaf. After the war, and after we had been resettled in Israel, we tried to find them. Or rather, Nogema tried to find them. She sent letter after letter to the Jewish Agency's refugee offices and scanned the names from the lists in the displaced-persons camps. As the years passed, and the names of the dead from the concentration camps were published, she always looked, but they were never there. They had simply disappeared. The last place they had written from was Corfu. In 1943, Greece fell to Germany. Late in the war, the Jews of Corfu were rounded up and sent to Auschwitz. We knew that the Jews of Corfu had mostly perished. Had Hani and Asaf been among them? Or had they escaped? Were they living elsewhere? We knew it was unlikely that they had survived, for if they had, they surely would have surfaced. Hani's daughter, Mara, had been raised by all of us—I had mothered that dear girl, along with Nogema, Edna, and Hamama. No, it was impossible to think that they could have survived and not come back for her daughter. Over time we grew reconciled to the thought that she and Asaf had perished, though without proof, their deaths remained insubstantial, like the ghost of a ghost, something you could never quite believe in.

Chapter 35

I went to Jerusalem on a beautiful day in early May. On the road, the bus passed Latrun, where Binyamin had been injured in the war and where, in scripture, Joshua asked Elohim to make the sun and moon stand still so that he could finish the battle against the Amorite kings in daylight. As I ascended the mountains, I looked out the window and tried to discern the color of the sun. It wasn't the ruby-red haze of Qaraah or the buttery yellow of Sana'a or the bone white of Aden: the sun of Jerusalem was a more nuanced color, a shade from a blazing spectrum I didn't yet have all the names for. Binyamin had wanted to come with me, but I told him I wanted to go alone. I said, "I used to run out alone into the dunes around Qaraah. I have never been afraid of being alone." He reminded me that he often followed me to my cave, saying, "So you weren't as alone as you thought."

I took his hand, pressed his knuckles to my lips. "I will pretend that you are following me today, Binyamin, only you will stay home, and I will come back to you and report what I have found. Please, my love, it's just a feeling I have. I want to go by myself."

Mr. Shaham was a thin man with a kind smile. Feathered lines came out from his eyes and animated his face with a topography that bespoke an overfamiliarity with great sorrow. He wore a blue and white knitted *kippah* and offered me a cup of tea. When he called he had reported that "a new cache of papers and artifacts had been recovered from Auschwitz." He said that they were taken by an American GI at liberation and that the soldier had recently donated them to Yad Vashem. Among the artifacts was a small, handmade book. "Every page

is covered with writing," he said, "but the writing seems to be in code.
It is illegible, at least to us. The only words we can read are on the last
page. Your name, and your cousin's name, a date, and the name of a
village, Qaraah."

It is very strange to be given back an object that you have known in a
different lifetime. When Mr. Shaham handed it to me, I felt as if he were
returning to me a parcel of time, a precious quantity of lost moments
bound in leather, held fast with glue. The leather binding smelled of
my father's workshop, a nutty woody scent that made me dizzy with
memory. Masudah's paper had yellowed but was not at all brittle. I
stroked the soft leather cover. I remembered handing Hani the parcel.
The look of delight on her face. Our conversation . . .

*"What is this?" Her face brightened. She turned the little package over.
"What is this for?"*

"It's for you. My way of thanking you for what you did for me."

"I didn't do anything you wouldn't have done for me."

"But I won't ever have the chance."

"What do you mean?"

"I won't have to save you, the way you saved me."

"Now you sound like my sister Hamama."

"What do you mean?"

"Hamama can see the future. Can you?"

*"Of course not. But there is only one cave, and my idols are broken.
If I ever save you, it won't be for what was hidden, and what was holy."*

"If your mother could hear you, she would beat you all over again."

*"What was most holy to me about the cave was gone long ago. My
mother was angry about the wrong idols."*

*Hani screwed up her face, and then covered my hand with her own
and pulled it down from my heart. "You have nothing to atone for, Adela.
Hope is not a sin, and neither is fidelity."*

"Are you okay, Mrs. Bashari? Do you need a drink of water?"

I shook my head. "No, thank you, Mr. Shaham, I will be fine."

I opened the cover. Hani's elements were arranged linearly, grouped
in clusters like words in a book. The "words" were then grouped
in sentences, and the sentences formed paragraphs. I would have
recognized her "writing" anywhere. Every henna artist has her own

style, and Hani's here was as it always had been—improvised yet expert, elegant but with a haphazard approach to symmetry and flourishes.

I shut the book. Mr. Shaham and I exchanged pleasantries, and then I left, taking the book with me. I promised that I would return it once I had translated its contents.

"You don't have to, my dear, it is yours to keep."

"I understand, Mr. Shaham. And I don't know what I will find on its pages, but if the contents are relevant to history, I will donate it to Yad Vashem, as a memorial to my cousin."

The code was always with me. Even when Hani betrayed me, I hadn't destroyed it. When we traveled to Israel, I took it with me, buried in my small bundle of possessions. Over the years, the paper had become brittle and the ink had faded, but it was still legible. I almost never looked at it, but once or twice over the years, I had taken it out and run my fingers over the elements, remembering the day I found it in Hani's little bag along with her cowrie-shell dolls, and how I had copied the code and kept my discovery secret.

I spent many hours translating what Hani had written. I worked in a little sunny porch off our living room. Binyamin checked in with me every half hour or so. He brought me tea. He made me take breaks. But most important, he listened when I shared with him what I was learning. Hani had written the diary in Auschwitz. She described how she and Asaf had arrived on the island of Corfu in 1940 and that they had lived there until 1944, when they were rounded up and deported. They were separated when they entered the concentration camp. She was taken to a brothel that serviced the SS officers, and was regularly "visited" by a Nazi she referred to as Karl, who was the adjutant to the Kommandant. The adjutant insisted that Hani wear henna, and that she teach the other girls in the brothel to apply it, so that they could help her give herself a fresh application whenever the old one faded. He even procured ground henna leaves for her and brought them to her, along with the stylus, sugar water, and lemon juice she would need to apply it.

She described how she begged the adjutant for news of Asaf, and how, because she had named him, the adjutant reported to her that he had personally had Asaf killed in a particularly gruesome way. It was winter, and he ordered Asaf outside of his barracks. He had him stripped naked and tied to a scaffold. He turned a hose on him. Asaf died of exposure. But then the adjutant ordered guards to continue to spray the withered corpse with water until Asaf turned into a block of ice that didn't thaw until springtime. The adjutant mocked Hani's despair and called Asaf Ice Boy. He tortured her by saying that Asaf was alive inside the ice, begging for rescue. Hani detailed Asaf's cruel, torturous death, and her own misery—rape, humiliation, and subjugation at the hands of her many tormenters—for the adjutant wasn't the only sadist who visited the brothel and abused her body and her soul for his own pleasure. Hani's story ended three pages before the end of the book.

It took me hours to complete the translation. I read the entire account to Binyamin and then called Mr. Shaham, and read it to him over the phone. When I finished, he identified Karl-Friedrich Hocker as the Kommandant's adjutant.

Then he asked, "The young man she refers to?"

"He was also my cousin."

"His death mirrors that of others who died this way. There is an account from Mauthausen of a priest and a boy being killed this way, and made into a block of ice because the priest tried to offer the boy confession. We have eyewitnesses, prisoners who walked by the priest and boy all winter long. They describe how, when the victims thawed in springtime, they were wrapped together, the man embracing the boy."

Mr. Shaham was quiet. I could hear his slow, steady breath through the phone. When he spoke again, his voice was quieter than before. "I can tell you how your cousin Hani died."

"How is that possible?"

"We have learned many things about the monstrosities committed during the war. We continue to learn more and more. I think I can tell you what happened to your cousin. That is, if you want to hear it. The great Tolstoy wrote of families. He said that every unhappy family is unhappy in its own way. What I have learned in my years here as curator is that every Holocaust death is a harrowing death, yet each is harrowing in its own way. And each time I speak with families of the holy martyrs, I ask the same thing. 'Are you prepared to hear the details? Are you prepared to have questions answered?'"

"No, I am not. Who could possibly be prepared for such things? And yet if you have answers, I must listen to them. What choice do I have?"

"You are right, Mrs. Bashari. Forgive me. Hitler breached the castle walls of civilization. Now we all wander the prehistoric plains together, hiding from shaggy beasts and foraging for new forms of sustenance. I will speak, but stop me if it is too much to bear."

A pause, and then he began. "Here at Yad Vashem, we have archives from each of the concentration camps. In our Auschwitz archive we have a testament letter written by a woman named Perla Zandman. She is still alive, and is a survivor who was also a prisoner in the officers' brothel there. In her letter, Mrs. Zandman details the harsh facts of life in the brothel. A litany of atrocities committed by the officers. One concerns a woman she refers to as 'the Yemenite whore.' Forgive me for impugning your cousin's name. Mrs. Zandman refers to all the prisoners in the brothel, including herself, as 'whores for the Nazis.' I think, in light of the recovery of your cousin's diary, that we can safely assume that the Yemenite Jewess in the brothel at the end of the war was your cousin. Mrs. Zandman describes how your cousin was brutalized and then killed two weeks before the liberation of Auschwitz. It is a gruesome account. Do you want me to continue? Yes?

"Mrs. Zandman writes that the adjutant tied the woman to a bed and then took a blade and cut her on the lines of her elaborate henna—on her hands and on her feet. He traced the entire henna pattern with a knife, then he left her to bleed to death from her wounds. The other prisoners heard her suffering, heard her crying out during the ordeal, but were forbidden to go to her, even when the adjutant had left, abandoning her to die alone in the bed."

When I was a child I heard a story of a groom who saved a Torah from a fire. The flames shot out of his back, spelling sacred words. As Mr. Shaham spoke, I saw them in front of me—both of my cousins, Hani and Asaf, lying dead on an altar. The deerskin Torah was their shroud. The shroud was on fire. The letters that burned through their bodies spelled out passages of apocrypha, and the deer that gave its flesh for scripture was there too—a ghostly animal effigy crying and howling with the knowledge that his sacrifice was in vain, as more flesh was needed.

I felt weak; I trembled from head to toe. Even my teeth shook. Binyamin reached out a gentle hand and laid it over my own. There was no sun; I saw only a dim blaze of ash and sorrow.

"Mrs. Bashari?"

"Yes."

"If you'll permit, I have a question."

"Ask it."

"Why do you think . . . why do you think your cousin wrote her diary in code when Hebrew would have been just as untranslatable to a Nazi?"

I didn't hesitate to answer. "Mr. Shaham, Hani wrote in henna because henna was her *sefat em*, her mother tongue. She was in Gehinom, in hell. She knew that Asaf was dead, and that she was going to die. How could she tell such a story in anything but her original language?"

He considered my words for a moment. "She was writing to you, to her cousin."

"No," I lied, "she didn't know that I knew the code. I saw it only by accident, when we were girls. And I never told her that I saw it."

"My dear, it was no accident. The accident is that the diary was ever lost. The miracle is that her suffering and her death—as well as the suffering and death of your boy cousin—received its due translation."

I let these words pass. I didn't tell him that Asaf had been my husband, and that Hani had taken him from me. I didn't tell him that in a different lifetime, Hani had used her code to inscribe my own hands and feet with psalms of treachery, which had become psalms of redemption. I didn't tell him that I knew now that she had saved me twice—once from my mother, and once from Hitler.

In the days and weeks after I translated Hani's diary, I fell into a sadness that consumed me. I had terrible nightmares. I dreamed of their ordeals. Of Hani in the brothel raped by Nazi officers, then cut and left to die. Of Asaf frozen to death in a jet of ice water. Of Asaf trapped in a block of ice—but in my dreams he wasn't dead at all. He stared out at me, beseeching me for rescue. Then my dreams changed. I dreamed of Qaraah. Of Asaf riding Jamiya on the dunes below my cave. Of Hani tumbling off the donkey carriage and running to me. How she had embraced me. Her silvery voice. The first time I saw her henna. I dreamed of us young together. I would wake in the middle of one of these dreams and feel lost in my own life, as if time had reversed itself and I had wandered back through the dye mistress's yard again, past the frankincense tree and down the escarpment, and then never found my way back home. Sometimes I couldn't sleep at all, and lay staring at the ceiling through the small hours of the night. During the day, I dragged myself around, barely able to function.

It was then that Binyamin suggested I write this story. He said, "You must turn the tables on fate and take up the pen."

"What do you mean?"

"You are afflicted by emptiness, my love. Emptiness where Asaf and Hani once were. But if you write about them, you will fill in the empty space with their beating hearts. You will be together again. Souls live on in stories. And the story—why, it can be as big or as little as you wish."

I considered what he said, and then I asked Binyamin if he minded that if I were to write what he was suggesting, it would be a love story.

"Despite everything that happened," I whispered, with red cheeks and shame in my heart, "I never really stopped loving either of them."

He lifted my chin and kissed my lips, and then he said, "Of course you didn't. And you have nothing to be ashamed of. The love you still bear them? Those are your minor-key notes, the ones that give the melody its power to haunt."

I began to write, and I didn't stop until I had loved them all over again. I bowed down to the story I had to tell, prostrating myself at the altar of narrative. I was in my cave again. A girl alone in the dark belly of the earth.

Acknowledgments

Every book needs a first reader. This book was read first by my dear friend Sharon Rhodes. Her warm enthusiasm cheered and encouraged me through many pages. I am so grateful.

I want to thank Roz Lippel, Alexis Gargagliano, Whitney Frick, Amanda Urban, and Amelia (Molly) Atlas, all of whom had important roles to play in the coming to fruition of *Henna House*. I am especially grateful to Molly for reading and rereading many drafts and for working tirelessly to support my efforts. I also want to thank Tal Goretsky and Shasti O'Leary-Soudant for the gorgeous cover art, as well as the Scribner copyediting and publicity teams for all of their hard work on this book.

Every day when my kids go to school they know that their mother stays home and makes things up. I want to thank Lev, Atara, and Eden for being patient with me when I am distracted by all of the characters in my head. And I want to thank Aleister Saunders for being the most loving and supportive husband in the entire world—and that is not hyperbole. I also want to thank my researchers and cheerleaders extraordinaire—my parents and in-laws—Rita, Herb, Josh, Debbie, Howard, and Pam. Robin Warsaw, my dear friend, is a brilliant web designer; I am thankful to Robin for building *Henna House* a beautiful Web site. And thank you to all of my wonderful family in various corners of the world for supplying me with love, conversation, and history, the raw materials of fiction.

A Note on History

This is a work of historical *fiction*, not a work of history. While I have paid careful attention to history, I have done the work of a fiction writer, fashioning my own imagined world out of the clay of reality. There are countless instances in this book where I have added details that are *not* based on research but come *entirely* from my own imagination. And there are instances in this book where I changed historical facts in order to suit my narrative. For example, there was no little pogrom in Aden in 1935. There was a small riot in 1932, and isolated attacks against Jews in 1933, but no significant mass violence there until the pogrom of 1947, when eighty-two Jews were killed and the Jewish community of shops, homes, and synagogues set ablaze. In other words, when Selah Bir Ami, apprentice scribe, threw stones at gulls in Crater Harbor, he did so at my behest.

For readers interested in learning more about the history of this fascinating place and time, I recommend several of the books that were so helpful to me in my research: *The Jews of the British Crown Colony of Aden* by Reuben Ahroni; *A Winter in Arabia: A Journey through Yemen* by Freya Stark; and *A Journey Through the Yemen and Some General Remarks Upon That Country* by Walter Harris. My primary source for information on the elaborate clothing of Yemenite Jews was *The Jews of Yemen: Highlights of the Israel Museum Collection* by Ester Muchawsky-Schnapper. And for a wonderful, if somewhat dated, account of Operation On Wings of Eagles, I recommend *The Magic Carpet* by Shlomo Barer. There is also a remarkable body of scholarship on the complexity of the Yemenite experience in Israel, but that subject is mostly out of the range of this book, so I must invite readers to delve into it on their own.

A Note on Henna

I am grateful to Rachel Sharaby for her in-depth exploration of Yemenite bridal henna rituals. Her essay, "The Bride's Henna Ritual: Symbols, Meanings, and Changes," in *Nashim: A Journal of Jewish Women's Studies & Gender Issues* 11 (Spring 2006), was an essential companion to my work. Additionally, I relied upon the extensive research of Noam Sienna. His Web site, hennabysienna.com, and his blog, *Eshkol HaKofer: A Research Blog About the History, Culture, and Religious Significance of Henna Art*, were my go-to sources for the step-by-step instructions for the elaborate henna scenes in my book. Another valuable source was *Henna's Secret History* by Marie Anakee Miczak. I also gleaned important information from *Anath, the Virgin Warrior Goddess: Victory, Henna and Grain* by Catherine Cartwright-Jones.

Henna has been used since ancient times by women for medicinal purposes and for adornment. The Yemenite Jewish community mostly stopped using henna after being brought to Israel in Operation On Wings of Eagles. But since the 1990s, the tradition has enjoyed a revival. Now it is once again common for a Yemenite Jewish bride to have a Night of Henna before her wedding, and to wear the towering tishbuk lu'lu' crown as her foremothers did. But one no longer needs to be a Yemenite Jew to partake in henna. In Israel, non-Yemenite brides now occasionally choose to enjoy the henna ritual as a way of connecting to the sacred past, and infusing the present with the magic and mystery of the rites.

HENNA HOUSE

NOMI EVE

Introduction

Adela Damari's parents desperately seek a husband for their young daughter to protect her from the Orphans Decree, which mandates that any unbetrothed Jewish orphan be adopted by a Muslim family. With her father's health failing and no marriage prospects in sight, Adela's situation looks dire until two cousins enter her life: Asaf, to whom she quickly becomes promised, and Hani, who introduces Adela to the mysterious and powerful ritual of henna. Suddenly, Adela's eyes are opened to the world: she begins to understand what it means to love. But when her parents die and a drought threatens their city, Adela and her extended family flee to Aden, where Adela falls in love, discovers her true calling, and is ultimately betrayed by the people and traditions closest to her.

Questions for Discussion

1. An epigraph from the Song of Songs opens the book. Read the entire passage in context (http://biblehub.com/niv/songs/1.htm). How is it an appropriate opening to the novel?

2. The characters in this story are Jews who live, for most of the book, in a predominantly Muslim area. How does this affect their lives both practically and in the ways they think about themselves and their roles in society? What do you make of the ways both cultures borrow from each other's rituals? Are these groups truly as separate as they seem to be?

3. In the early part of the story, young Adela is said to be cursed, because every groom her parents line up for her passes away. When, if ever, is she freed from this curse?

4. "You must act the part," the dye mistress tells Adela before her scheduled wedding to Mr. Musa. "I often take no joy in my spinsterhood; I have no babes to fill my arms, and yet by acting the part of it, I convince myself that I am not lonely. And sometimes it works" (pp. 107–8). Do you believe that you can make yourself happy by acting the part? Do you think Adela believes it?

5. What really happened to Mr. Musa? Did Hani have anything to do with his death? Does Adela believe so?

6. Henna serves many roles: as a wedding ritual, a charm, and a way for women to bond. Discuss what happens in the henna house when the women adorn one another and how it changes Adela's relationships with them once she is allowed to join in. Why do you think her mother wanted to keep her away for so long?

7. In many places in the story—the death of Hani's twin sisters (p. 112), Asaf's return (p. 245), and the discovery of Hani and Asaf's affair (p. 269)—there is no definitive recounting of what actually happened, only a series of alternate versions of events. Does this

make them seem more or less true? Should the reader question the events presented throughout the rest of the novel?

8. When Adela journeys from Qaraah to Aden, she is confronted for the first time with modernity, and in the end her life butts up against the well-known historical events of World War II. How does this juxtaposition enhance the story? Does it feel jarring? Think about the parts of the culture and traditions of the old way of life Adela leaves behind as she moves on, and what she takes with her. How do these changes mirror those that are happening in Adela's perception of her place in the world?

9. Consider the role of books and writing in this story, from Uncle Zecharia's Torah to Hani's henna book to the lessons Adela gives the Habbani women on the road to Aden. In what ways is Adela's life transformed when she learns to read and write? How is the written word viewed as its own sort of magic in this story?

10. At times, there is a great tension between Elohim, the traditional Jewish deity, and other gods and personal beliefs. Think about Adela's childhood idols and the Muslim beads Jewish women put on their children for protection (p. 94), and about when Binyamin is confronted by Adela's brother about not going to synagogue and Adela admits that she doesn't mind, as she and Binyamin both believe that Elohim is everywhere (pp. 239–40); how does this tension express itself in the things characters believe throughout the story, and in what ways does it reflect their development? Is the tension between organized religion and personal belief ultimately resolved?

11. "Do stories submit to authors?" Adela wonders. "Or do authors submit to the tales that tangle up their guts?" (p. 2) Which do you believe is true? In what ways is a story shaped by its writer? Consider the many tales and stories told throughout this book, and especially the fact that the entire narrative is presented as Adela's story, written—figuratively, if not literally—in henna (p. 2). How much do we shape the stories of our lives, and how much are we shaped by them?

12. Adela and her family are refugees in Israel in the last part of the story, and the situation Adela describes in the refugee camp, rife with disease and deplorable living conditions, is terrible. Were you aware of Operation On Wings of Eagles and the repatriation of Jews from Yemen and Ethiopia before reading the book? Do you know of similar situations today?

Enhance Your Book Club

1. The historical note at the end of the book lists several resources the author used in her research about the lives of Yemeni Jews, including *The Jews of the British Crown Colony of Aden, A Winter in Arabia*, and *The Jews of Yemen*. Pick one of these books and read it, and then discuss the ways *Henna House* veered from history and how it was faithful to actual events. Alternatively, find a copy of *The Magic Carpet*, which tells more about Operation On Wings of Eagles, and discuss the importance of this true but little-known piece of history.

2. The beauty and artistry of henna is lavishly described in this story. To see pictures of henna application and to learn more about the history and modern applications of henna, visit the Web site www .hennabysienna.com and its accompanying blog, *Eshkol HaKofer: A Research Blog About the History, Culture, and Religious Significance of Henna Art*. Discuss the techniques and rituals you read about in light of the story.